PASSION'S CHALLENGE

"There is nothing you could ever do that would make me seek your touch."

"So that's the game you play . . ."

Startling her, the captain jerked her flush against him, then lowered his mouth to hers. This time his kiss was shatteringly sweet. The gentle persuasion lingered, mounting to passion as his kiss deepened gradually. He sought out the honeyed hollows of her mouth, caressing them so sensually with his kiss that she could only remain unresponsive through sheer strength of will.

Gabrielle withheld a gasp as he wound his hands in her hair, tilting her head so that he might nuzzle the curve of her chin, the smooth column of her neck. Just when she thought she could resist him no longer, he released her with a suddenness that left her staggering.

"I accept your challenge, Gabrielle . . . and I promise you that the day will come—much sooner than you think—when you will beg me to love you."

MIDNIGHT ROGUE

ELAINE BARBIERI

ZEBRA BOOKS
KENSINGTON PUBLISHING CORP.

ZEBRA BOOKS are published by

Kensington Publishing Corp.
850 Third Avenue
New York, NY 10022

Zebra and the Z logo Reg. U.S. Pat. & TM Off.

First Printing: August, 1995

Printed in the United States of America

Prologue

A fire burned in the central, open pit of the vaulted prison chamber, casting flickering shadows against stone walls where companion torches glowed. Black smoke tunneled upward from the flames, thickening air already rank with the fetid odors of dampness and filth, as a moan from the winding corridor beyond raised the head of the powerfully built prisoner.

Stripped naked to the waist, his arms and legs bound by chains and stretched between two poles, Captain Rogan Whitney struggled to draw himself upright as his bearded, meticulously dressed inquisitor repeated the question. The captain's hoarse response was met with another merciless blow.

The questioning continued.

"I warn you, Captain Whitney, my patience grows thin. You delivered your ship and its cargo over to pirates. Further denial is useless."

His pain-filled eyed an eerie gold, his face swollen and bloodied almost beyond recognition, Whitney strained to focus, repeating, "I did not. A trap . . . they were waiting for us . . . we had no chance."

"I don't believe you, Captain. Nor do Governor Claiborne or the shipowners. You can understand our skepticism, since so many American ships have disappeared without a trace in the Gulf and Caribbean of late. We consider it too great a co-incidence that you and your first mate, the only known survivors of this strange phenomenon, were discovered alive and well on a tropical island known to be a popular haunt of pirates."

"We were picked up at sea ... left there to find our way back."

"We also feel it too great a coincidence that you were in a position to know confidential information about the cargo, route, and sailing dates of three of the five ships that disappeared in the past year."

"Friends ... the captains of those ships were friends ..."

"No, I think not. Since I sustained business losses that match those of the shipowners in the mysterious disappearances of those ships, and because Governor Claiborne knows Gerard Pointreau is an honorable man, and he respects my personal and legal counsel, I was able to convince him to allow me to question you, so I might *reason* with you and *persuade* you to tell the truth. I intend to accomplish that task, Captain—at *any* cost."

"I told you ... it was Gambi."

"Liar!" Pointreau's face flushed with anger. "Vincent Gambi is a privateer with a valid letter of marque! He and Lafitte's other captains raid only Spanish ships!"

"It was Gambi ..."

"It will do you no good to persist in these lies!"

"Gambi ..."

Enraged, Pointreau signaled an iron to be drawn from the fire and held up so Captain Whitney might view it more clearly. The metal glowed red-gold as Pointreau's voice dropped to an insidious whisper.

"An impressive implement of persuasion, is it not, Captain? Both it and this chamber are remnants of Spanish rule which have seen little use in recent years. However, the faint strain of Spanish blood in my ancestry has found me favorably inclined toward this . . . effective . . . means of coaxing the truth to light. And since I am a strong believer in the axiom 'the end justifies the means,' I felt no need to inform Governor Claiborne of my intentions to temporarily reinstitute this means of coercion. So, now that you understand the situation clearly, I ask you again, Captain, with whom did you work to betray your ship?"

"A trap . . . It was Gambi."

Pointreau's expression stiffened with suppressed fury. The flickering flames reflected demonically in his dark eyes as he signaled the iron closer, hissing, "As you can see, this iron carries the brand of the letter *P*. You may believe that it will forever mark you a pirate for all the world to see, but I tell you now that the letter more accurately represents the name *Pointreau*, that of the man who will break you!"

Turning to the guard, Pointreau gave a sharp command.

"Apply the iron."

A gasp escaped Captain Whitney's throat as the glowing iron was pressed to his chest.

A groan.

A rasp.

The smell of burning flesh.

Silence.

"Captain Whitney? Damn!"

Frowning his annoyance, Pointreau turned again to the guard. "He's unconscious. Take him back to his cell. He'll talk. It's only a matter of time."

A sound of pain penetrated the swirling shadows. Forcing his eyes open, Captain Rogan Whitney faced again the reality of the filthy cot on which he lay, and the dank cell he had inhabited since Gerard Pointreau had begun his questioning days earlier.

His senses clearing, Whitney recognized the ragged moans of his first mate as they echoed down the corridor from the chamber where he had been questioned earlier. Staggering to his feet, he clung to the bars with a strength borne of hatred as Pointreau's voice droned on.

"Tell me the truth, Monsieur Dugan."

Another moan.

"The truth, I said."

An agonized groan.

"The truth!"

A sudden, strangled cry . . .

Silence.

Rogan gripped the bars tighter at Pointreau's short exclamation of disgust.

"He's dead. Get rid of him!"

The shuffle of footsteps . . . the closing of an outer door . . .

He's dead.

Staggering backward, Rogan collapsed against his bunk.

He's dead.

Unconsciousness claimed him.

Leaving the balmy warmth of the New Orleans night behind him, Gerard Pointreau stepped in from the street and turned down the passageway leading to the malodorous prison corridor he had left a few hours earlier. His slender, athletic frame erect, his bearded chin high, he bit back a smile as he congratulated himself on the conversation he had concluded with Governor Claiborne a short time previously.

It had been surprisingly easy to manipulate the man.

The secret was in knowing that William Claiborne was an American first and foremost, and a patriot dedicated to ridding New Orleans of its vices.

Claiborne's contempt for the pirates who raided in the Caribbean, seemingly above the law, was overwhelming. His frustration with Lafitte and the privateers stationed at the stronghold on Grande-Terre, pirates who raided *within* the law and who were considered a fact of life by the majority of

New Orleans residents, was legendary. The disappearances of several American ships and their entire crews in the past year, the vessels vanishing without a trace in tranquil seas, had raised the governor's agitation to a new level. He was determined to find the perpetrators and halt the attacks, once and for all.

And then Captain Rogan Whitney and his first mate had been discovered on Cuba . . .

Gerard Pointreau took a short breath, his step momentarily faltering as Captain Whitney's insistent response returned to mind.

Gambi . . . it was Gambi.

Yes, it *was* Gambi.

No one knew that better than he.

Steadiness returned to Pointreau's step as he raised his bearded chin a notch higher. He had experienced a moment of panic when Captain Whitney had spoken those words to the governor upon being returned to New Orleans, but he had handled the situation well, with Lafitte's unwitting help.

Lafitte had quickly learned about Captain Whitney's claims. His strict orders against assaults on American shipping were well known, and he had been incensed that his loyalty to his host country was being questioned. He had even made a special trip to New Orleans to impress his many, important friends with his innocence.

Lafitte's fearless appearance in the face of Captain Whitney's accusations against one of his captains had confirmed his innocence in the minds of most. Somehow, it had not occurred to the populace *or* to Governor Claiborne, that although Lafitte might be innocent of culpability in the attacks, Gambi might not.

Gambi, who was as guilty as sin.

Gambi, who was capable of any act that returned a profit.

Gambi, who had left no living witnesses to the work he had done so well . . . until now.

Gambi, now deeply in his debt for the risk he'd taken in covering up Gambi's deeds.

Pointreau unconsciously nodded. Governor Claiborne did, indeed, value his counsel. Of course, why would he not? Was he not one of the wealthiest and most successful merchants in New Orleans? Did he not have a strong legal background as well? Did his family's arrival in the New Orleans area not date back almost eighty years? Was he not known to have a great devotion to the city and to have so comfortable a fortune as to eliminate any conceivable reason to lean toward corruption?

A smile twitched again at Gerard Pointreau's lips. But so few, including Governor Claiborne, knew the true perversity of his nature, that he found the risks of his illegal and immoral endeavors so . . . *enjoyable*.

The governor trusted him completely.

So much for that fool.

Yes, he had accomplished his purpose in volunteering to pursue the matter further with Captain Whitney and the first mate. And he had established his belief in Gambi's innocence in the eyes of the governor and the citizenry. More importantly, he had also established to his own satisfaction that Captain Whitney knew nothing about his extremely profitable partnership with Vincent Gambi.

Pointreau smiled. He had just returned from reporting the first mate's death to the governor, with great sadness, of course. So regrettable . . . The corrupt young seaman's defective heart had been unable to withstand the stress of confinement.

As for the captain, he had arranged that the fellow would "escape" unexpectedly, while Gerard Pointreau attended a local ball in full view of Governor Claiborne and his peers the following night.

Of course, neither the captain nor his remains would ever be found.

Pushing open the door of the central prison chamber,

Pointreau came to an abrupt halt, his contentment draining as the guards turned toward him, their agitation obvious.

He knew that look.

His voice rang sharply against the stone walls.

"What happened, Barnes?"

"The prisoner, Monsieur Pointreau . . ." The short, perspiring guard took a spontaneous step backward. "He has . . . disappeared!"

"Disappeared!"

"Gone! When we went to check on him, the cell was empty!"

Pointreau strode down the corridor toward Captain Whitney's cell, inwardly raging. Moments later he stood over the empty cot on which the captain's unconscious form had been dumped hours earlier.

Pointreau's well-manicured hands clasped into angry fists. He was certain that he had not heard the last of Whitney.

"Put him down here . . . quickly!"

The two burly men supporting Captain Whitney responded silently to the whispered command. Lying on the soft surface of a bed, his cloudy mind gradually clearing, Rogan glanced around him.

There could be no doubt. The bedroom his rescuers had carried him into was heavily scented, softly lit, and decorated in bright satin and lace. The sounds emanating from the many doorways they had passed in the hall were unmistakable. He was in a bordello.

Captain Whitney stared at the slender fellow who counted coin into the hands of the two men who had carried him. The rescue had been conducted quickly and efficiently, without opposition. He knew he would not have expected less of this man's endeavor.

Waiting until the door closed behind the two hirelings, Rogan rasped, "I'm indebted to you, Bertrand."

Justin Bertrand's fair hair glinted in the limited light. His youthful, scarred face was sober. "Debts owed and debts repaid have no bearing on this night. Only justice is concerned."

"You're a good seaman . . . a good friend."

Bertrand's sober expression did not change. "And one who realizes that had not the fever kept me ashore when the *Venture* sailed this last time—"

"—you might have been blamed for the disappearance of the ship, as with the other ships that went down under you."

Rogan's cloudy mind drifted, his thoughts turning to the stigma that followed Bertrand, inherited from a French mother cursed by one of the most powerful voodoo women in New Orleans—a curse supposedly carried in the blood to all future generations. That nonsense had almost brought an end to Bertrand's life before he'd met up with Rogan.

His mind clearing, Rogan continued, "The crew of the *Venture* . . . all dead. Only Dugan and I escaped. Now he's dead, too."

Bertrand nodded. "I know."

"Pointreau . . . responsible . . . would've killed me as well."

"Why?"

His breathing growing ragged as consciousness gradually faded, Rogan could not respond to Bertrand's query.

Why?

The question lingered as darkness closed around him.

"Nothing? Nothing has been reported by your sources regarding Captain Whitney's whereabouts? It has been a week since his escape!"

Gerard Pointreau stiffened under Governor Claiborne's verbal assault. The governor's dark eyes reflected immediate regret at his outburst as he faced his valued friend and advisor in the privacy of his office. Claiborne took a conciliatory step forward.

"My apologies, Gerard. Captain Whitney's escape is no reflection on you. Nor are you responsible for his recapture. Those responsibilities fall squarely on my shoulders. I simply had hoped that you might be successful in obtaining a clue to his whereabouts—through unofficial channels—since I have been unsuccessful in my official endeavors. I am disappointed. There was so much I had hoped to learn from that man."

Gerard Pointreau's handsome face drew into lines of concern. "I apologize, William. I have failed you."

"Failed me?" William Claiborne shook his head, appearing suddenly older than his thirty-four years as he continued softly, "If anyone has failed in his mission, it is I. New Orleans is in great peril, Gerard. The state of affairs between Great Britain and the United States grows more difficult each day. Flagrant disregard for American maritime rights . . . the impressment of American seamen . . . I have no doubt war is in the offing. Strategically situated as this city is, on the mouth of the Mississippi, it will doubtless be attacked sooner or later, and we are all but defenseless, especially since it is rumored that nearby Indian tribes have already aligned themselves with the British in the event of conflict. In the meantime, our ships in the gulf are beset by pirates who are effectively destroying our commerce even while it is supposedly held safe from threat by Lafitte's given word. Our lifeline is in mortal danger at a time when our liberty suffers a threat as well!"

"Surely you do not believe Lafitte is to blame for these attacks. The letters of marque his men carry—"

"Damn the letters of marque! The letters of marque do not stop Lafitte from feeding the contraband from his murderous endeavors into the city at prices that bankrupt honest businessmen and indirectly make our citizens his slaves!"

"Yes, my own businesses have suffered as a result of the illegal trade."

"And now, when we finally had in our hands a man who might have been able to give us necessary information, one who might even have been convinced to testify against Lafitte so we might bring legal action against him—"

"My regrets, William." Gerard Pointreau drew his tightly muscled frame up to formal attention. "If you wish, I will make public apology for—"

"No, Gerard. No apology is necessary." Governor Claiborne smiled briefly. "It was not my intention to infer that you share blame for this situation. It would not do to vilify honest citizens when the true villains are apparent. No."

Suddenly slapping his hand down on the desk, his narrow face tightening, Governor Claiborne declared, "I have no recourse. Although I dislike offering financial remuneration as an inducement for citizens to do their civic duty, a reward is the only answer. We will offer a tempting sum for Captain Rogan Whitney's capture, one that will leave him with few friends. He will soon be back in our custody—and will tell us the truth about the sinking of his honest American vessel then, so we may take our first step toward the righting of this intolerable situation."

Closing the office door behind him minutes later, Gerard Pointreau walked quickly down the staircase toward the street.

A reward . . .

He stepped out into the sidewalk, the bright sunlight of afternoon warming his shoulders as he smiled and tipped his hat to a passing matron. He continued on, inwardly amused that the governor could be such a fool.

A reward for Captain Whitney's capture? It would be of no avail. His own report to the governor had not recounted the extreme pressure he had applied on his less savory contacts in the city . . . those who were frequenters of that part of his life of which few were aware. Yet, a full week of such pressure had allotted him no information. The reason was obvious. Captain Rogan Whitney was no longer in New Orleans.

Pointreau mentally nodded. Whitney had simply taken refuge on the first vessel to leave port . . . or had taken a flatboat up the river . . . *or* had died as a result of his weakened condition.

Whatever the man's fate, of one thing Pointreau was certain. Whitney was no longer in the city and was no longer a threat.

It was just as well, for he had already arranged that the captain would not survive recapture if it occurred. The man knew enough to be dangerous, and Gerard Pointreau would brook no danger to himself . . .

. . . or to the one person he held dear.

His step steady and sure as he moved along the cobbled street, Pointreau unconsciously reaffirmed that last thought.

Yes, most especially to the one person he held dear . . .

Captain Rogan Whitney paced the limited confines of the satin-draped room in which he had spent a long week of recovery. His powerful frame thinned but erect, the swelling that had distorted his strong features reduced, the dark bruises fading, he was restored almost to full strength. Inner wounds, however, drained his life's blood.

His first mate's tortured moans echoed in his mind, as they had throughout the long days and nights past. The sounds of the *Venture*'s last hours returned—cannons firing, guns barking, the slashing and crashing of swords, the cries of the wounded and dying. He heard the sickening crack of the *Venture*'s hull as it was rammed, the proud vessel's creaking groans as it listed under his feet, the fierce crackle of flames flaring up against the darkness of the night sea as the ship was engulfed. He felt again the final, explosive blast that carried his first mate and him into the sea, sending the *Venture* and the remainder of her crew to watery graves.

The malignity within him expanding, Rogan recalled the infamous Vincent Gambi's shouted orders to the godless men under his command as they manned their boats and searched the dark waters for signs of survivors, then systematically slew each and every one. He remembered the torment of hours spent clinging to a floating timber after the night grew too dark for Gambi's men to continue their search ... remembered that the pain he had suffered at those merciless killings by far surpassed the agony from his wounds.

And he remembered Gambi's face ...

Lit by a lantern held high beside him as he leaned over the rail of his ship to direct his men's murderous work, Gambi could be clearly seen. The man's sun-blackened skin and coarse features, accented by a heavy mustache, the kerchief tied around his head, and the gold earring in one ear, had been a mask of true evil, a match for the visage of the devil himself. It was an image Rogan would never forget.

Rogan now took a shuddering breath. He knew he would not rest until that massacre was avenged.

Halting abruptly as he glimpsed his reflection in the ornately carved mirror nearby, Rogan saw gold eyes burning with zeal for the repayment of that debt. He had believed that debt would be legally executed when he reached New Orleans and informed the authorities of the fate of his ship, but his report had been discredited.

Gerard Pointreau had taken over from there.

Why?

The question played in his mind.

Why had Gerard Pointreau so adamantly insisted that Gambi was innocent of his charges?

Why had Pointreau pressed Dugan for information—to the point of death?

Why was he so certain that had Bertrand not rescued him in time, Pointreau would have killed him, too?

His hand slipping beneath the cotton shirt he wore, Rogan traced the raw outline of the letter branded into his chest.

And *why* was he so certain that despite the part Gambi had played in the murderous affair, in the end, the man he would seek for true vengeance would be Gerard Pointreau?

Turning at the sound of a step at the bedroom door,

Rogan reached for the pistol on the stand nearby. The weapon was leveled and aimed when the door opened to reveal Bertrand and the slender, blond woman beside him.

Lowering his gun, Rogan waited until they entered and closed the door behind them before asking, "What did you learn?"

Bertrand handed him a printed sheet, his gaze narrowing as Rogan studied it and then looked back up at him.

"A *wanted poster*—offering a reward of a thousand dollars for my recapture?" Rogan's expression tightened. "It appears that I am soon to become the most hunted man in New Orleans. Pointreau has doubtlessly convinced the governor of my guilt."

The young woman responded in Bertrand's stead, in the softly accented voice that had become familiar to Rogan as she'd tended his wounds so selflessly during the week past.

"Whoever is behind the reward poster, you must understand that you are no longer safe here because of it, *mon ami*. My position here as one of Madame Renée's most valued employees—and the fact that I do not use my true name—has held you safe until now from the search being conducted for you. Nothing could convince *me* to betray you—you who have been so good a friend to my brother . . ." Clarice Bouchard glanced at Bertrand before continuing. ". . . But some of Madame's employees would not be able to resist so great a sum in return for a few words whispered in the right ear."

Rogan searched the face of the woman whose gentleness and compassion had sustained him through the tortured, pain-filled hours of the past week, and whose protection had saved his life. Dissimilar to her brother in appearance, as well as in the mannerisms and speech which so strongly reflected her mother's French heritage, she was small and delicate, with hair the color of honey and eyes of a clear blue. She was also one of the most highly esteemed prostitutes in New Orleans. But to him, she was an angel of mercy he would never forget.

"Clarice . . ."—Rogan's voice grew husky—"how can I ever repay you?"

"*Mon ami.*" Clarice's eyes filled. "I wish only to see you safely out of New Orleans."

Rogan's massive frame stiffened. "No, I cannot leave . . . not until I have settled accounts."

"Rogan . . . *mon cher* . . ." Clarice drew closer. Resting her hand lightly on his arm, she whispered, "There are times when one must choose compromise, however briefly. My protection wanes even as we speak. You are not well enough, or in a position, to wage the battle you wish at this time. You must leave now and return when you may seek justice from a position of strength, rather than weakness."

"No."

Clarice's dainty hand tightened on Rogan's arm. "You asked what you could do to repay me for my efforts in your behalf. I tell you that you may do so by leaving New Orleans now, with my brother. The *Voyager* sails within the hour. I have convinced a friend to allow you to slip aboard the ship so you may leave the city unobserved."

"Clarice . . ."

"The first port of call is in the Indies. You may go ashore there, and then make your way."

"No, I—"

"If you will not leave the city now, for your own protection, then I ask you to leave for Bertrand's sake, for the truth is, *mon cher,* he will remain at your side, and your fate will become his. He is my only brother. I would not have his life wasted when, with the brief exercise of patience, his time might be better spent in the future, in obtaining the justice you both seek."

"You ask a great sacrifice of me, Clarice. The voices of my crew cry out for vengeance."

"I ask no more than I would give."

Rogan paused, assessing the concern reflected on her beautiful face, the face that had hovered over him day and night while his mind had been locked in fever and despair. Beautiful and selfless . . . risking all for the sake of her brother's friend . . .

He spoke softly in response. "I correct you, *ma chérie*—no more than you have given." His assessment lingering moments longer, Rogan turned abruptly to Bertrand who stood silently nearby.

"Are you agreed with your sister's plan?" Rogan turned back to the woman beside him at Bertrand's nod. His bruised face twitched into a brief smile. "*Merci*, Clarice. I will not forget all you have done."

Her tear-filled eyes reflected the emotion that precluded verbal response as Clarice raised herself onto her toes to press her lips lightly to Rogan's bruised mouth.

Standing in the doorway of the satin-draped room minutes later, Rogan scanned the hall. In a moment, he and Bertrand were gone.

Music . . . laughter . . . the soft clinking of glasses . . . the glow of candlelight reflected in the endless facets of crystal chandeliers as dancing couples circled the ballroom floor . . .

Gerard Pointreau wound his way along the edge of the crowded room, smiling. In the streets beyond the magnificent ballroom, the search for Captain Whitney continued, but he no longer felt the need for concern. The threat against him and his was over.

Glancing across the floor, Pointreau caught the eye of Governor Claiborne who stood beside his young, chattering wife. He nodded, with a smile, then resumed his step. Claiborne doted on the woman, the fool. No female would ever assume so important a role in *his* life, for the simple reason that he had yet to meet a one of them who lingered long in his thoughts after his intimate use of her.

The small, heart-shaped face that flashed briefly before his mind's eye brought a true, rare warmth to Pointreau's smile.

Not a one lingered in his mind ... save one, who had touched him in a very singular way.

Another image suddenly intruded, erasing Pointreau's smile—intense gold eyes staring at him from within a battered and bloody face, promising him ...

Pointreau suddenly laughed aloud. Promising him ... ? Forever branded by his mark, Captain Rogan Whitney, if yet alive, would never bother him again.

Gerard Pointreau—victor!

As he always would be.

Turning with a graceful bow to the beauteous Creole nearby as the music surged anew, Pointreau led her out onto the floor.

The black of the night sea enclosed the deck as Rogan Whitney slid from his hiding place beneath the canvas shroud that shielded Bertrand and him from sight. Glancing back to see Bertrand asleep, he drew himself erect and slipped into the shadows. The bitterness that had denied him a similar rest surged once more.

Closing his eyes briefly against echoing cries of the dying which allowed him no peace, against remembered booms of cannon, and the final creaking groans that had preceded his ship's descent to the bottom of the sea, Rogan felt his bitterness soar into rage.

New Orleans was now far behind him, but the past was not. Memories of the men who had put their lives in his hands and of the gallant ship entrusted to his care, images of widows and orphaned children left behind, the realization that the country he had served so faithfully now marked him its enemy—all assaulted him.

Gerard Pointreau's face flashed before his mind and Rogan's pain became acute.

. . . the letter that stands for the name of the man who will break you . . .

Rogan's hand moved to his chest to trace the brand there. How wrong Pointreau had been. Rather than being the mark of the man who would break him, that scarred patch of skin was an intimate reminder of an infamy that must be avenged.

His heart pounding, his jaw set as he stared into the darkness toward a shore that had long since slipped from sight, Rogan drew himself up stiffly. He spoke in a hushed whisper to the omnipotent presence in the sea breeze that bathed his face, to the all-seeing eye that had borne witness to the bloody massacre of his crew and to the death of his friend.

"This night . . . this hour . . . this moment, I vow to avenge the slaughter of my crew, the murder of a friend, and the loss of a gallant ship. I vow to bring to justice, in any way open to me, the men responsible for those atrocities. And I vow to give that pursuit priority over all others, to follow wherever it leads me . . .

This I vow . . .

. . . on my honor,

. . . on my life,

. . . *on my soul.*"

The battering of the night wind grew stronger as the words of Rogan's solemn oath echoed in his mind and heart, as he accepted the full weight of that mortal debt he swore to repay . . .

. . . unknowing, uncaring, where it would take him.

Chapter 1

"Gabrielle . . ."

Sister Madeleine's voice bore a sting that snapped Gabrielle Dubay's gaze from the ship on the horizon, visible through the window of the convent schoolroom. Turning to the black-clad nun and preparing herself for the reprimand sure to come, Gabrielle assumed a deliberate smile.

"Yes, sister?"

"You may continue with the translation of the poem where Celeste left off."

Gabrielle's response did not falter. "I don't know where Celeste left off, sister. I wasn't listening. I was looking out the window."

Her candid reply brought gasps from the other students in the austere schoolroom, and did little to alter Sister Madeleine's stern expression.

"I see." The portly nun studied the open challenge in Gabrielle's gaze, her extended pause more revealing than words. She continued, "How long have you been with us now, Gabrielle?"

Gabrielle groaned inwardly, despite herself. Sister Madeleine's voice had deepened in a way that revealed she was in no mood to have her mettle tested that morning. The lines between the nun's almost nonexistent brows, and the pinched expression around her mouth as she had walked into the classroom, should have been fair warning. They were immediate betrayals of her state of mind—as were the twitching of Sister Marguerite's small, slightly-crossed eyes when the day was not going well for her, Sister Marisa's nervous sniffing when her patience was ebbing, Sister Juliana's twitching shoulder when she felt at a loss with her responsibilities, and Sister Juana's subtle scratching when—

Oh, what was the use of it? She could read the nun's moods as well as she could read her own! She could write a book about them if she so chose, but, somehow, all caution fell by the wayside when her own mood conflicted. She would be tempted to claim that the nuns simply did not like her if it were not for the innate honesty that forced her to admit she often willfully provoked them.

"Gabrielle . . ."

At Sister Madeleine's stiff prompting, Gabrielle replied, "I have been a student at the Ursuline Convent for six years, sister."

. . . six long years . . .

"Six years . . . and you still are unable to adjust to the schedule the other students maintain without a problem . . . to differentiate between the hours to be devoted to the education your father brought you here to receive and the hours set aside for personal diversion."

"The problem is not the hours set aside for diversion, sister, but the scarcity of them."

"Gabrielle—"

"Which grows worse as students grow older."

"That is enough, Gabrielle! You may go back to your room."

Gabrielle's mood brightened. *To that small, private room with its large window overlooking a river that flows into the sea . . .*

"And when you do, you will pull down the blind so you may not waste time staring at ships on the horizon as you are often wont to do. Instead, you will use the time you would otherwise have spent in this classroom, on your knees in prayer, asking for the perseverance to pursue your studies, a perseverance which seems to have deserted you."

Another inner groan . . .

"And during the free time that you have so little of this evening . . ."

Oh, no!

". . . when the other girls are entertaining themselves as they see fit, you will work in the convent garden."

With the mosquitos . . .

"With the mosquitos."

A soft tittering ensued from the seats around Gabrielle as she stood up. The other girls were amused. She supposed she would be, too, if she were not slated to be the evening meal of the bloodthirsty, minuscule flying demons who descended on the garden at twilight.

"You are dismissed, Gabrielle."

"Yes, sister." Gabrielle paused, adding with another deliberate smile, "Good afternoon, sister."

Gabrielle stepped out into the hall and closed the classroom door behind her, drawing herself slowly erect. Perhaps it was not so bad after all. She was out of the schoolroom that had become so much of a bore of late, even if she had only exchanged one confinement for another.

Gabrielle scanned the corridor with a fleeting glance before taking off at a run toward the broad, cypress staircase at the end of it. Reaching the stairs, she lifted the dark skirt of her uniform to her knees and started up them two at a time. She had spent enough time staring at vessels on the horizon in the past six years to be able to identify a ship with a reasonable degree of accuracy. If she was not mistaken, the one entering port was the *Noble Explorer*, the very same merchant ship that should be carrying the gown with which she would make her debut at the governor's ball after her eighteenth birthday a few months hence.

Arriving breathless at the top of the staircase, Gabrielle pushed back a heavy strand of auburn hair that had worked loose from its formal confinement and raced to her room. Years of relentless instruction and a personal sense of honor coming to the fore, she walked to the window as directed, pulled down the blind, and slipped to her knees. She crossed herself and clasped her hands together in a formal attitude of prayer. Leaning forward as she did so, she affixed the gaze of her clear, gray eyes on the ship visible on the horizon through the generous gap in the blind as she recited softly:

"Hail Mary, full of grace . . ."

She's the Noble Explorer, *all right.*

"The Lord is with thee . . ."

She should dock within the hour.

"Blessed are thou amongst women . . ."

Father will doubtless pick up the gown he has ordered for me.

"And blessed is the fruit of thy womb, Jesus . . ."

He knows how anxiously it is awaited.

"Holy Mary, mother of God . . ."

He will bring it to me immediately.

"Pray for us sinners . . ."

I shall have to work hard in the garden tonight to regain Sister Madeleine's favor.

"Now, and at the hour of our death."

I will have to be a model student tomorrow.

"Amen."

But it will be worth it.

"Our Father, who art in heaven . . ."

I will be leaving the convent shortly after my eighteenth birthday, anyway.

"Hallowed be thy name . . ."

If there is anything left of me after those mosquitos are finished with me tonight . . .

"Thy kingdom come . . ."

"Damn! . . ."

* * *

A misty azure haze hung over the "trembling prairie." The landscape of green, blue, and gold, comprised of tall grasses as high as a man's eye, cast into uncertainty the delineation between water and land with its maze of narrow, curving streams of occasionally brackish water overhung with lush foliage. The bayous widened abruptly into cypress-lined lakes, only to narrow again into small passages that appeared to lead nowhere, but the tall, powerfully built man at the helm of the flat-bottomed boat winding its way along the twisting waterway in the moisture-laden heat of late afternoon did not falter.

Paying little mind to the sleepy-eyed reptiles lining the shores or to the small slaps of sound as they slithered into the streams to float close-by, he guided the craft with the ease of long practice—his features taut, his eyes of piercing gold under black, arched brows sharp with caution.

Rogan Whitney paused abruptly, jamming his pole down into the soft bayou bottom to halt his craft as he attempted to identify a sound. Black, roughly cut hair brushed tensed and heavily muscled shoulders as lines of concentration deepened in the sun-darkened contours of his face. Motionless, the full strength of his powerful form primed, he glanced around him. The "ghost forests" of cypress hung with the eerie gray of Spanish moss had given him refuge many times in the three years since he had left New Orleans a fugitive. During that time, he had become as familiar with the hidden pathways through the Baratarian waterways as those who called the small villages scattered within them their home.

"Captain . . ."

Rogan looked back at the two men behind him. Guns drawn, they tensely awaited his command. They turned with a simultaneous snap toward two swamp deer who appeared abruptly at the water's edge, only to dart back into the tall grass with the same cracking rush of sound that had alerted all three men minutes earlier.

Rogan noted the lack of emotion on the slender, blond seaman's scarred face. Always dauntless in the face of adversity, Bertrand had proved his worth in countless ways during the years since their escape from New Orleans on the *Voyager*, not the least of which were his unquestionable loyalty and his ability as first mate. Porter, the taller, more wiry of the two, was a seaman with specialized talents that would be invaluable in the task they would undertake once ashore that night.

Turning back to the winding waterway ahead of him without speaking, Rogan poled the boat forward, recalling the many times previously that he and Bertrand had made similar journeys.

Rogan's strong jaw locked, his gaze glowing eerily in remembrance.

The Indies . . .

Rogan did not choose to recall the voyage that had delivered Bertrand and him to those islands after their being discovered as stowaways on the foul *Voyager*. The physical injuries inflicted upon him in prison had caused him pain, but his true torment had lain in the relentless echoes of his dying men's cries—sounds that still rebounded in his mind. The funds Clarice had so generously forced upon her brother before his departing had been confiscated by the captain of the ship, a man who used his authority brutally upon discovering them. As a result, Bertrand and he had arrived on the islands defenseless against the threat still hanging over their heads and penniless as well.

Difficult months had then followed, months during which Rogan's strength returned and his frustration soared. He remembered clearly his relief when he and Bertrand finally shipped out as common seamen on the swift and able merchant ship, the *Island Pearl*.

But his relief had been short-lived. The *Island Pearl* had not been to sea more than a few weeks when a ship flying the dreaded skull and crossbones of Spanish pirates appeared on the horizon. The first blast of the pirate cannon killed the captain and first mate upon impact. In the confusion and panic that followed, Rogan assumed spontaneous command, finally directing a charge that rendered the pirate ship temporarily helpless.

The *Island Pearl* limped away from that encounter to make her escape in a fog-enshrouded sea. In the gray dawn that followed, the survivors of the attack stood solemnly on the bloodied, battered deck. Before the sun rose, Rogan emerged as captain of a vessel renamed and a crew reborn in the bloody wash of terror that had assaulted it.

He recalled the promise he'd made to those men that day, that under him they would never again serve as victims.

He had kept it.

The *Island Pearl* had not been seen since that day.

In its place, the *Raptor*, was born.

It had not been difficult to obtain the letter of marque from Cartagena that legalized the *Raptor*'s forays against Spanish ships. His ability to direct his ship to appear as if out of nowhere, to swoop down on Spanish vessels like a bird of prey, earned him the name Raptor as well—Rapace, as he came to be known by the mainly French-speaking inhabitants of the gulf. He disliked the name, but it served well in concealing his true identity from all but the men who served under him, intensely loyal men who had proved they would keep his secret even at the expense of their lives.

Rogan was aware that the sobriquet Rapace also afforded him a peculiar mystique among the superstitious Creoles so influenced by voodoo and black magic.

This mystique granted Rogan a respect he had not anticipated the first time he'd sailed boldly into the harbor at Grande-Terre and stepped onto the beach of Lafitte's stronghold as a fellow privateer. He had come to know the surprisingly youthful, educated Frenchman well since then, and had

satisfied himself that Lafitte had no part in the attacks still
continuing on American ships.

Rogan remembered clearly the first time he'd come face to
face with Vincent Gambi on Grande-Terre. Freezing in his
step when the small, evil-looking fellow approached to halt a
few feet away, he soon realized Gambi had failed to identify
him as the captain of a ship he had sunk with all hands
aboard. The true potential of his position clear in that moment, and knowing that his vengeance would not be complete
until all involved in the sinking of the *Venture* and other American ships had paid the price for their actions, he decided to
play a waiting game.

The setting sun cast elongated shadows against the shore as
Rogan and his men stepped aground at last, then secured
their pirogue in the tall reeds.

Within minutes they were walking silently toward the city.

Rogan moved through the dense foliage, a brief, hard smile
touching his lips at the realization that the waiting would
soon be over ...

Gabrielle slapped and scratched, waving her hand in an effort to keep at bay the hungry, tortuous horde of mosquitos
surrounding her as she moved along the stone path of the
convent garden. The conspicuous massing and mingling of
pine, cypress, and live oak that distinguished the New Orleans landscape from any other was less obvious in the city,
but here the magnolia was in evidence. The graceful trees
lined the walk, their large, fragrant blossoms scenting the air
and drawing insects of every type as she dragged the pail she
had emptied for the second time toward weeds growing
against the brick courtyard wall.

It had been a difficult evening. Released from her prayerful
penance at the commencement of her next class earlier that
afternoon, she had returned to the schoolroom, determined to
hold her tongue and keep her eyes trained on Sister Juliana's

pale, narrow face as the earnest nun began reviewing the day's literary assignment. But the damage had been done. There had been no avoiding the punishment that had driven her straight from the evening meal to the shed in the rear of the convent courtyard, where the garden tools were kept.

Contrary to the general consensus, Gabrielle had a true respect for her teachers, the dedicated, selfless nuns who worked every day of their lives for the enlightenment of young women's minds and the betterment of their souls. It was the years of convent residence that she found so difficult to accept. She missed her father and the indulgences with which she had been raised in his household. She knew he missed her as well, and that he would not finally have acceded to the need for her residence at the convent were he not so contemptuous of the general illiteracy of New Orleans' Creole women.

Her father had never expressed that contempt in her presence. To the contrary. He was courteous to a fault and so charming that the sultry belles all but fell at his feet. But she had been aware of his underlying disdain since she was a child. She had seen it behind the smiles he bestowed on the beauties so often on his arm. She was certain he had never married for that reason, although he was considered one of the most eligible bachelors in the city.

She had sensed that hidden contempt for women . . . and an indefinable something that went even deeper as she grew older . . . but she had never doubted his paternal love for a moment. Nonetheless, that disdain of which he did not know she was aware was the reason she had accepted her convent residence as a necessity in a city so devoid of educational facilities that the young were traditionally sent to Europe for their educations.

But the monotony of the convent stifled her. The ships on the horizon that she watched incessantly had become symbols of the freedom that would be hers shortly after her eighteenth birthday. While observing each graceful vessel, she could feel the deck dip and roll under her feet, could smell the salt in the sea breeze that enveloped it. She could sense life waiting, just around the corner . . .

. . . as tedium prevailed.

Gabrielle frowned. The color of her hair, leaning heavily toward a fiery red, was indicative of a temperament that handled impatience and frustration poorly. The cool gray of her eyes, which some said could occasionally bite with frost, was indicative of a part of her personality that came to the fore when challenged. But the delicate, clefted chin on a jaw that often locked with rigid determination somehow belied the unyielding strength of will that Gabrielle candidly claimed was her best—and worst—trait.

She was restless, wanting to get on with her life! She had followed her steady physical maturing over the years in the small mirror Father had ordered installed in her room against Mother Superior's objections. Despite the nuns' admonitions against vanity, she had stood naked before the silvered glass at regular intervals in order to follow the gradual budding of her female form into womanhood. First had come her height, taller than was generally considered pleasing for women, although it pleased *her*. Then had come the gentle curving of flat, youthful hips, and the growing swell of firm, rounded breasts on her childish chest—none of which was at all apparent under the dark, shapeless uniforms she was still forced to wear!

Ah, yes, frustration! She was anxious to wear the silks and satins and the graceful fashions imported directly from France that most women in New Orleans society favored. She was impatient to attend the balls and soirées that were talked about in glowing terms . . . and in whispers. She had made herself a pledge, however, that she would not allow such pursuits to consume her as they did her empty-headed peers.

No, there were far too many things happening in the city of New Orleans, a place where male horizons were all but unlimited, for her to be content with the narrowed spectrum afforded women!

Gabrielle's soaring frustration ballooned. No one understood! No one realized that the education she had received had done more than inform her. It had stimulated a curiosity that would not be denied. She wanted to know more than was presently considered within her realm of interest as a female. She wanted to understand the conflict between England and this budding country that hinted war was again in the offing. She wanted to comprehend why the pirate scourge that pillaged their shipping and threatened their commerce was allowed to continue, wanted to know why privateers were allowed to ply their trade unchallenged when they were truly no more than pirates themselves. And she wanted to know why the criminal behavior of Lafitte and his men went mainly uncensured and unpunished while the majority of New Orleans citizenry considered themselves a civilized and humane people!

Gabrielle sighed. She had other curiosities as well, not stimulated by current events or the books available to her in the convent. In the silence of her room, she had acknowledged an embarrassing ignorance about the interactions and relationships between a man and a woman, a situation that other young women of her age, less "educated" than she, would find laughable. She did not enjoy her ignorance.

She wanted . . .

She needed . . .

Unwilling or unable to complete those thoughts, Gabrielle sighed. Contrary to a common perception, there had been times in the middle of dark, lonely nights during the years past that she had wished she could be like some other students at the convent, that she could be content to accept what she was told without question or curiosity. At those times, she had almost envied those inclined toward a sober, untormented religious life whose paths were clearly dictated and defined.

But she would never make a good nun. She was too "strong minded."

Which was the reason she was again consigned to ...

... the hoe.

Gabrielle pushed an auburn strand of hair back from her face. Drat those endless green sprouts growing in neat little rows! They were as endless as the weeds that seemed to appear from every possible crack and crevice even as she worked—even as the blood was sucked from her veins by the stinging pests that would give her no rest!

Gabrielle slapped at her arm, realizing belatedly that the thirsty villain who had made its quick escape had actually penetrated the cloth of her sleeve to do its nasty work. Was there no protection at all from these odious winged felons of the night?

Pausing as she neared the wall, Gabrielle dropped the hoe unceremoniously and stretched her aching back before tucking the same errant wisp back into her tightly bound tresses. She consoled herself that her waiting was almost over. In a few more months, after Mother Superior had satisfied herself that she had met all the requirements of the convent curriculum, she would be graduated from her classes and Father would come to bring her home.

Eighteen ... of a marriageable age ...

Gabrielle thrust away that unwelcome thought. She would not trade one domination for another! She would enjoy the gay life of the city as did her father, the man who loved her as dearly as she loved him. And, if she were lucky, she would convince him that a sea voyage would be the very thing to complete her education.

A sudden rustle of sound breaking into her thoughts, Gabrielle turned to glance around her. She frowned at the sensation of being watched that plagued her as the shadows of the courtyard deepened. Unable to see clearly in the limited light of the wall lanterns, she hastily adjusted the hand lantern so the light shone more directly on the rows of "green things" she need tend, then picked up the hoe.

She knew whose gaze followed her. Sister Madeleine was doubtless lurking in the shadows, watching to see that she was behaving honorably in accepting the punishment due.

Sister Madeleine, who felt the soul of her wayward charge would benefit from the painful experience of being consumed by insects while the other girls entertained themselves at their leisure . . .

Sister Madeleine who would certainly miss her when she was gone, if only for the challenge she had presented over the years . . .

Sister Madeleine, whom she need impress if she were not to find herself tending the hoe tomorrow night, as well.

Garbrielle chopped harder at the dark ground.

Do you see how hard I'm working, Sister Madeleine?

"Gabrielle . . ."

Her head snapping up from the task at the sound of her name, Gabrielle saw Sister Juliana standing a few feet away. The nun's pale, narrow face appeared even more pale and narrow than it had an hour earlier, and her shoulder twitched revealingly. "You will come with me right away, *s'il vous plaît.* You have a visitor."

A spontaneous smile lit dancing flecks in Gabrielle's silver eyes as she straightened.

"A visitor?"

"Oui."

Gabrielle picked up her pail, tucked the hoe under her arm, and started dutifully toward the shed at the opposite end of the yard.

"Non, you may do that later."

Gabrielle's smile faltered as Sister Juliana's shoulder twitched again.

Turning obediently, she followed the quaking nun.

The garden slipped into the distance behind her as Gabrielle walked briskly . . .

... so briskly that she was unaware of the covert gaze that lingered on her retreating back, continuing its silent, intense scrutiny until she disappeared from sight.

The empty convent reception room echoed with the sound of an angry, pacing. The slender, athletically built man paused impatiently, his handsome, bearded face twitching with anger as he drew himself stiffly erect.

Gerard Pointreau tensely adjusted the lapels on his well-tailored coat before turning toward the door, his lips tight. He had impressed Mother Superior with his outrage ... enough to have her send the pasty-faced Sister Juliana scurrying like a frightened mouse on her errand!

He had voiced no appreciation for the relaxing of convent rules which allowed his late-night visit. Those rules had never applied to him, and for good reason. His family had used its influence to support the Ursuline institution since the first six nuns had arrived from France more than eighty years earlier. With the aid of a family fortune he had multiplied many times over since the deaths of his parents, he was presently the largest private contributor to the convent school.

Gerard gave a harsh laugh. It was not that he admired the religious. In actuality, he abhorred the hypocrisy of the church they served! He had never fooled himself that there was any truth to the superstitions it perpetuated. The hereafter ... heaven ... a superior being who watched over all—the entire premise was nothing more than a clever, well-organized effort successfully conducted over a period of centuries by power-hungry churchmen who had developed an efficient means of controlling the masses!

Only one person controlled Gerard Pointreau.

A smile flashed briefly on Gerard's bearded face. Although he made no pretense at saving men's souls, he had used his superior intelligence and cunning to sculpt others to his needs, while preserving a benevolent facade that had kept him much admired and functioning at the highest level of New Orleans society. His personal friendship with Governor Claiborne was an important facet of the charade he maintained. His only true stimulation in New Orleans' intellectually deficient society, however, came from the duplicity he practiced. Without the challenge of the fine line he walked between his dual lives and the danger that added true spice to his life, he knew he might not have been able to endure the vapid minds of those around him.

But, Gerard consoled himself, there was one mind that was not vapid, one heart that had touched his. Contrarily, he had chosen to entrust that mind to the Ursuline Convent, regretfully the only educational bastion in the city. Weakness was the reason he had made that concession, his inability to suffer the enforced distance that a proper education in Europe demanded.

But he had not consigned his precious charge to the convent without provisions. He had made it clear at the outset that she was to be granted separate quarters from the rest of the boarding students, and that she was to receive specialized instruction in every field available so she might advance in her studies at her own accelerated rate, without being held back by the inferior mentality of the others. Indeed, he had stipulated that she was to be recognized as special in every way, a student apart from the others.

Gerard recalled Mother Superior's expression had been carefully controlled when he had enumerated those provisions, for she had not dared refuse him.

Yet she had presumed to allow—

Turning abruptly as the reception room door swung open to reveal Sister Juliana's insipid expression, Gerard was about to speak when a slender, uniformed young woman brushed past the nun and started toward him. His heart leaping with a pleasure unlike any other, he held out his arms as she rushed into his embrace.

"Gabrielle . . ."

After holding Gabrielle tightly for long moments, Gerard separated himself from her, scrutinizing her for any sign of abuse as he questioned, "Are you all right?"

Trailing his gaze over tightly bound auburn tresses slightly askew, surveying the bright spots of color on her flawless cheeks, noting the silver flecks of uncertainty that appeared at his question in gray eyes so similar to her mother's, he was struck momentarily helpless against the pain of loss revisited. He whispered, "You will never again suffer the humiliation of being forced to work in the dirt like a common slave! I have made my displeasure known to Mother Superior."

He saw Gabrielle's hesitation before she replied, "I wish you had not, Father."

"You wish I had not?"

Gerard was momentarily taken aback as Gabrielle shrugged, then offered, "Had you not discovered the disciplinary measure taken against me, I wouldn't have felt it important enough to mention." She flashed a small smile. "It was my fault, you know . . . it usually is."

Gabrielle's smile was all the more beautiful for its brevity as she continued, "I was daydreaming in class, and I was of a mood to test Sister Madeleine's patience when I should not have. As difficult as it is for me to admit it, I am sometimes exceedingly arrogant, and I occasionally outsmart myself in my cleverness."

"I will not listen to your self-censure, Gabrielle!" Gerard was silently furious. He had left his beautiful Gabrielle too long in the care of the self-searching, guilt-seeking, virginal hags who taught her! He continued tightly, "Any arrogance you display to others is nothing more than an honest perception of your superior intellect and beauty."

"Oh, Father, you are prejudiced!"

"I will not listen to the senseless denials you speak, Gabrielle!"

"Father, please . . ." Gabrielle's momentary amusement faded. "I didn't mean to upset you."

Struggling for control, Gerard continued more softly. "I have not found it necessary to punish you since the day you came into my care those many years ago, and I will allow no one—*no one*—else to punish you!"

Gabrielle's pale eyes grew suddenly sober. She raised a hand to brush his cheek with a fleeting caress, then whispered, "I'm sorry, Father. Sometimes I forget . . ." She paused. "I apologize for causing you distress simply because you love me."

Gerard went momentarily still, struck to the heart by the similarity of Gabrielle's words to others uttered in heartfelt earnest so many years earlier.

. . . I am sorry to have caused you distress, Gerard, simply because you love me . . .

He remembered . . .

. . . his dear Chantelle Obréon of the wild auburn hair and bright silver eyes who had enchanted him from childhood. How he had loved her! Chantelle—so good and so honest, yet so fiery and strong willed! The two of them, born of wealthy plantation families just a few miles and a few years apart, had been so alike . . . and so different.

Too clever to be controlled by him as were his other peers, his dear Chantelle had met him as an equal. From childhood, she had been aware and disapproving of his excesses. She had despised the subtle cruelties she had seen him employ, and had harangued him when he'd abused the moral codes his father had hoped to instill in him. Voicing her fear of the sinister side of him she had glimpsed emerging, she had decried his heartless manipulations.

But she had been unable to abandon him . . . because she had loved him.

And because she had known that he loved her, *only* her, she had believed that love was his sole chance for salvation.

Chantelle had loved him . . .

. . . but she had not loved him enough.

The dark side of you frightens me, Gerard. It's not physical injury to myself I fear. Rather, what ultimately frightens me is being held exempt from your machinations, being forced to witness them, even while I am impotent against them. My darling Gerard, can you not understand? I could not endure such torment.

I love you, Chantelle.

As I love you.

You don't love Philippe Dubay!

I do. I love him, too.

You won't marry him!

I will.

You cannot!

I must.

Chantelle's wedding day . . . an agony he aptly concealed from all but Chantelle . . .

The tormented night Chantelle gave Philippe Dubay a child, the beautiful daughter who should have been his . . .

The anguish of friendship where there should have been passion . . .

His self-deception in pretending that secret vices, increasing wealth, and social stature *negated* the pain of losing Chantelle . . .

Then . . . *fire!*

The Dubay plantation suddenly engulfed as he made his way home from a dinner party there . . .

A frantic race back, arriving to see Chantelle dash into the flaming structure her husband had entered minutes earlier in search of their child.

His anguish at rescuing Chantelle when her life was already ebbing . . .

His subsequent dash into another portion of the house not yet overwhelmed, where he found the child . . .

Chantelle's final, faltering words . . .

Gabrielle will soon have no one but you.

No!

Care for her, Gerard . . . Keep her safe.

Chantelle, my darling.

She loves you . . . as I have always loved you. Don't let her see the dark side . . . Gerard . . .

"Father . . ."

Snapping back to the present, Gerard swallowed tightly. He *was* Gabrielle's father—the only one she clearly remembered—and she was the only person he would ever love. He would protect her as her mother wished, from everyone and everything.

Gerard's thoughts came to an abrupt halt as he became aware of raised welts on Gabrielle's arm, large, angry bites that marred the smooth skin there. His fury again surged.

"I will have another word with Mother Superior."

Gabrielle followed his gaze, dismissing his concern. "They're just a few bites. I hardly feel them."

"You were deliberately exposed to a humiliating discomfort!"

"Father, the punishment was deserved."

"No!"

"Oh, Father," A patient smile touched Gabrielle's delicate lips. "You would call the devil an angel if he wore my face."

"You *are* an angel."

"You mustn't say that!" Gabrielle grew genuinely perplexed. "I am incapable of living up to that standard!"

"Don't you see? You already do."

Chantelle's gaze shone through the startling silver of her daughter's eyes, and Gerard's throat grew tight as he continued, "Your education is all but complete, and I have had enough of this place. You will come home with me now."

Gabrielle abruptly stilled. He saw the conflict that warred behind her gaze as she hesitated, then responded, "Strangely, only minutes ago I thought there were no words I would rather hear you say, but—"

"No further response is necessary. Get your things."

"No, Father. Please try to understand. Minutes ago I was as angry as you to be consigned to the garden, but I've suddenly realized that Sister Madeleine taught me far more than was her original intention when she decided to force me to contemplate my actions. She made me realize in viewing your distress now that responsibility accompanies the privilege of being loved, that along with the happiness one can give with love, one can also give pain."

"Gabrielle . . ."

"I somehow think that lesson is far more valuable than many of those I've learned in the past. As for leaving now . . . to do so at this negative point would be tantamount to defeat. I abhor defeat, Father."

"Gabrielle—"

"I prefer to prove that I am strong, rather than weak, and possessed of enough character to finish what I have begun here. Only a few more months . . ." Gabrielle paused, her eyes growing suddenly moist. "Somehow I think my mother would have wanted it that way."

A great upsurging of warmth again tightened Gerard's throat. Gabrielle, a kindred spirit of the mother she barely remembered . . .

Unable to refuse her, he whispered, "If that's what you want."

He drew back from Gabrielle's impulsive kiss, forcing a smile.

"As for the reason I came—"

"Yes!" The old Gabrielle returned. "Did you bring what I think you brought?"

Silent as she dug into the oversize box he retrieved from the corner, as she squealed with delight at the glory of luxurious silk and satin draped and sewn into an exquisite French gown, Gerard watched as she held the garment up against her, speaking excitedly about the evening when she would wear it for the first time some months hence.

He stood in the convent hallway after Gabrielle bid him *adieu*, waiting until she slipped out of sight on the staircase. He then barked a short command that sent his waiting driver scrambling to retrieve the gown left behind in the reception room.

Slowly stiffening, Pointreau turned toward the convent office. Entering at the soft response to his knock, he regarded the solemn, lined face of the nun awaiting him.

"What may I help you with now, Monsieur Pointreau?"

"The question is not what you may do for *me*. The question is what I may do for *you*." His expression sharpening into a vicious mask, Gerard rasped, "It occurs to me that had I not come here unexpectedly to see my daughter tonight, your treatment of her might have passed unknown to me. I do not care to think how many other times Gabrielle may have been so treated before tonight, since I now realize that she has kept certain aspects of her stay here secret from me."

Gerard paused in an attempt to maintain his waning control, continuing, "Gabrielle has actually convinced herself that the indignity imposed upon her this evening was deserved. I do not believe that! Nor will I suffer a repetition of such treatment if the convent is to continue to expect assistance from me, or from any of the sources I have availed to it!"

"*Monsieur,* I believe Gabrielle knows far better than either of us if the punishment was deserved."

"She is *my* daughter and only I will make that judgment! I brought her here for an education, not to be abused!"

"Monsieur Pointreau, we who are responsible for Gabrielle's welfare while in our care, might more truly be considered guilty of abuse if we refused her the discipline she needs to reach true maturity."

"Gabrielle will not be treated like a common slave!"

"We must all work toward our salvation."

"Not Gabrielle!"

"*Monsieur,* I beg you to understand that the sisters and I love Gabrielle far too much to corrupt her with lax guardianship."

His dark eyes taking on a maniacal glow, Gerard rasped, "I

will speak no more of this! Suffice it to say, you have been warned."

Allowing a few silent moments for the import of his words to register in the nun's somber expression, Gerard Pointreau turned with a snap, departing to leave only the echoes of his fury behind him.

"She was workin' in the convent garden alone, Captain."

Silence met seaman Dustin Porter's opening comment as he faced his captain across the confines of the satin-hung, softly scented bedchamber that was the man's only harbor of relative safety within the city. The thin, wiry sailor awaited a response, noting the sharpening of Captain Whitney's gaze. He had seen that look before, the feral glow that intensified the deep gold of the captain's eyes, likening them to the gaze of a powerful bird of prey. It sent chills down his spine, despite himself.

Rapace, the raptor . . .

Aye, the captain was more deserving of the name by which he had come to be known than he realized. Few of his crew were comfortable when pinned by that stare, including himself, despite their respect for the man.

Dustin Porter's thin face twitched as the *Island Pearl* returned to mind. That respect had been well earned. The captain had come aboard as a common seaman. In the panic that had accompanied the Spanish pirates' attack on the ship and the deaths of the captain and first mate, the captain had seized command and directed the cannon blast that allowed their escape.

Aye, he remembered . . . the fear that had set the men into near frenzy as the *Island Pearl* limped away and the fog closed in around them. The men had known that no ship or crew had ever survived an attack by Spanish pirates, and that should the fog lift, they were doomed. But the captain had stripped the fear from them. He had washed the blood from the decks and the fright from their minds with the power of his own courage. He had promised them a justice under his command that they would never receive from prevailing the maritime law. He had asked for their commitment to him and had made a commitment in return.

The men had known from the first that a need for vengeance, deeper and far more intimate than theirs, drove the captain, but they had trusted him. In the time since, he had proved to them that their trust was well placed. There was not a one of them who would now hesitate to follow his command, even if it took them into the bowels of hell.

Aye, Captain Whitney was Rapace, all right . . . a noble predator who stalked a totally unexpected prey.

"She was working alone in the garden so late at night?"

Startled from his thoughts by the captain's abrupt question, Porter hastened to respond. "The young mistress has difficulty conformin' to the rules of the convent, or so my friend in the kitchen relates."

Porter did not add that his "friend" was called by the name of Jeanette Louise Sinclair, a pretty name for a homely young woman with short legs and a thick waist who worked in the convent kitchen at menial tasks that freed the nuns for more important duties. Nor did he feel it necessary to add that Jeanette was also crazy for him and so eager to impress that all he need do was slant a simple word of encouragement in the right direction and she would tell him all she knew.

As it turned out, Gabrielle Dubay proved to be one of Jeanette's favorite subjects.

"My friend says the Dubay girl receives special privileges, that it's been that way since she came to the convent years ago. She doesn't even sleep in the dormitory with the rest of the girls because her father thinks she's too good for the other students. He insisted on a private room for her."

"The nuns allow that?"

"Aye, one of the nuns gave up her room—the one next to the linen room on the second floor, at the corner of the convent. My friend says the girl acts as if all the special privileges are her due. She says Monsieur Pointreau is feared more than he is respected in the convent, and no one dares say a word against him or his 'daughter' for fear of the consequences."

"The consequences?"

"He's rabid about the girl, I'm told. She's 'strong minded,' which is all anyone's allowed to say against her, though it's common knowledge she's hard to handle and takes risks other girls won't, almost as if she's testin' the nuns. My friend says she'll be glad when the girl leaves the convent in a few months because she's never liked her."

"The girl is leaving the convent?"

"Aye, she's to be eighteen soon, and her schoolin' will be over. She says most of the nuns will be glad to be rid of her, even though they admit it's to the girl's credit that she hasn't told her father about the many times she's labored in the garden at punishment chores. My friend says she doesn't think the girl was bein' noble or anythin' like that. It's just a game the young mistress plays—although no one is exactly certain what she's about."

The captain nodded.

"I did what you said, Captain. I got a good look at her. It was gettin' dark, but there'd be no mistakin' her, her bein' taller than most of the others, and havin' all that reddish hair and them light eyes. She's a smart one, though. It was almost as if she felt me watchin' her."

"You're sure she didn't see you?"

"Oh, I'm sure, all right, the way she was mumblin' to herself, searchin' the shadows like she expected somebody to jump out at any minute, all the while swattin' at them mosquitos. She never even thought to look up into the tree overhangin' the courtyard where I was."

The captain's gold eyes narrowed, and chills coursed down Porter's spine again. He remembered the last time he'd seen the captain looking like that, his expression so tight, the towering height and breadth of him, those powerful shoulders tensed for an explosion of power not short of deadly. It was the time the captain first saw that Gambi fella on Grande-Terre. Porter unconsciously shuddered. He'd had the feelin' then, just as he did now, that when the captain looked like that, nothing in the world could stop the man from accomplishing what he set out to do.

And he had been damned glad then, as he was now, that it wasn't him the captain was lookin' at with them eyes . . .

A sound in the hallway turned both men in the direction of the door the moment before it opened. Bertrand and the beautiful Clarice entered and Porter inwardly gasped. He didn't suppose he'd ever seen a woman more beautiful than Clarice Bouchard. With all that blond hair and white skin, she looked like an angel, despite her profession. It occurred to him as he glanced at Bertrand standing silently beside her, that there might have been a resemblance between brother and sister before Bertrand's accident, but now none remained beyond the light hair color they shared.

Clarice Bouchard smiled briefly in his direction, and Porter's heart began a heavy pounding. A whore she might be, but she was special. Word had it that there were only three men allowed in her bed, three prominent New Orleans figures who paid to keep her exclusively theirs.

Clarice turned toward the captain, her smile brightening, and Porter gulped. Nobody had to tell him that all the captain had to do was snap his fingers and she was his without any money being exchanged.

"Porter . . ."

No, he'd never seen a woman as beautiful as Clarice Bouchard. He didn't suppose he'd ever—

"Porter!"

Porter started. "Aye, Captain!"

"You did a good job tonight. I won't be needing you again until tomorrow morning."

"Aye, Captain."

Turning on his heel, Porter left the silk and satin room and drew the door closed behind him, wondering what it would be like to lie down on that bed in them satin sheets.

He'd bet the captain could find out, if he tried . . .

Clarice kissed Rogan's cheek lightly, leaning briefly against him as the door closed behind Porter.

"A kiss to cheer you, *mon cher*." The brilliant blue of her eyes caressed his face, and Rogan felt a familiar warmth soar. It occurred to him at that moment that had Clarice's situation been different, had not her mother's stigma started the lives of her two children into a downward spiral that destroyed any choice in their future, Clarice might now be at the pinnacle of New Orleans society. Her beauty was unmatched, her intelligence superior, and the warmth of her smile was dazzling. She had saved his life. He would be forever in her debt for that and for the years between when her friendship had never failed.

Clarice's gaze held his. "You seem very much in need of cheering tonight, *mon ami.*"

Rogan considered Clarice's statement. "I'm preoccupied, perhaps, but I'm pleased . . . beyond all measure. It appears our visit to New Orleans tonight was more successful than I allowed myself to believe it would be. Porter was successful enough in observing his quarry and learning about her situation in the convent to give me the perfect solution to the last obstacle in my path."

Clarice's smile stiffened. She took a step backward. "Rogan, *mon cher, pardon, s'il vous plaît.* I think Madame is calling me."

Rogan frowned, uncertain. He had not heard anyone call. He offered tentatively, "There is nothing Bertrand and I have to discuss here that I would keep secret from you, Clarice."

"*Oui*, I know, but a wise woman realizes when men feel a need for privacy. And Clarice Bouchard is very wise in the needs of men."

Watching as she moved gracefully through the room and drew the door closed behind her, Rogan considered the caustic tinge to Clarice's final comment. It was unlike her, as was her abrupt departure. Pausing a moment longer before dismissing his concern in favor of more pressing matters, he turned toward Bertrand.

Rogan's jaw ticked tensely as he spoke.

"Porter saw her tonight. He said she's easy to distinguish from the other girls in appearance, but I don't want to take a chance on his identification alone. I'm going to arrange for you and Porter to make a delivery to the convent tomorrow. A donation of linens from an anonymous source, boxes that will be too heavy for the nuns, so you'll be forced to carry them to a room on the second floor next to Gabrielle Dubay's 'private' room . . ."

Rogan saw Bertrand's light eyes flicker as he added, "It will not be much longer."

Suddenly aware that she was trembling, Clarice came to an abrupt halt in the hallway of the house in which her illicit business was carried on. Disturbed by her waning control, she forced her hand to steady with a sheer power of will belied by her fragile appearance as she smoothed the upward sweep of her hair. Her slight bone structure, small features, and the combination of honey blond hair and brilliant blue eyes had made her one of the most illustrious of Madame Renée's women, but it was the determination within that had maintained her position there for the past four years, during which so many of her peers had passed into obscurity.

Briefly closing her eyes, Clarice continued on down the hallway. The sounds emanating from the doorways she passed, sounds to which she had become inured during her extended exposure to them, took on a new significance as she forced her steps forward. Three years . . . She had loved her dear Rogan for three years, since Bertrand had brought him to her door, battered and bloodied, but still so much a man. She had recognized the bitterness in him, the craving for vengeance, but she had also felt the virility and power temporarily subdued by his weakened state.

She had nursed Rogan back to health, had become as familiar with the man within as the man without; and all choice had been taken from her. She had grown to love him, keeping her feelings secret, hoping desperately that he would one day see past her profession to the love she felt for him. In the years since, she had accepted affection in love's stead, but hope had remained.

Clarice slowly stiffened. But that was before . . .

Her jealousy soared. Another woman now claimed Rogan's thoughts, a *convent schoolgirl* who would make all his dreams—albeit dreams of vengeance—come true!

Tears of frustration glittered briefly in Clarice's eyes. She wanted no woman but herself to fill Rogan's mind! She wanted no other to represent to him the fulfillment of his dreams!

She wanted . . . no man but Rogan.

Clarice took a stabilizing breath.

Madame would advise her what course to take.

Clarice turned toward the office of the aging proprietress who had taken her in despite the curse that had turned all others away from her. Madame had given her a new identity that had saved both her sanity and her life during times that had become so deep and dark it pained her even now to recall them. Madame had been kinder to her than anyone she had ever known.

It was because of Madame's careful guidance that she had never been generally available to the patrons of the house, but had been held in favor of special clients who valued her enough to reserve her services especially for them.

It was Madame whose generosity had allowed her to open her room to Rogan when Bertrand had delivered him there in his weakened state years earlier, and it was Madame who had allowed her to offer Rogan refuge when he visited New Orleans in the years between.

And so it was with Madame alone that she had shared the secret of her love for Rogan.

Approaching Madame's office, Clarice took another strengthening breath, then knocked lightly. When bid to enter from within, Clarice pushed the door open, only to freeze into motionless as Madame smiled from her position behind the desk where she sat. Madame's carefully rouged cheeks creased into the lines of a smile that betrayed none of the warning behind her words as she offered, "Come in, Clarice. I am sure Monsieur Pointreau is well known to you. He and I were just discussing you."

"Monsieur Pointreau . . ." Clarice entered and closed the door gently behind her, her heart thundering. Rogan and Justin were so close, believing themselves safe . . .

A shudder moved down Clarice's spine as Pointreau approached to take her hand and raise it to his lips.

"Clarice, *ma petite beauté* . . ."

Pointreau's dark eyes met hers, and Clarice went momentarily weak. Dark hair and beard lightly touched with gray and meticulously cut, classic features marked by lines that lent distinction rather than a patina of age, his erect, athletic frame fastidiously and fashionably clothed, Gerard Pointreau was a man handsome beyond the norm, but she knew what lay behind the appealing visage this man presented. Aside from his outrages against Rogan and his first mate, she had heard the whispers from the women he occasionally visited while on respite from the mistress he maintained on Royal Street. She knew that a demon lay behind those dark eyes, a devil who enjoyed aberrations that humiliated even the most jaded. She knew that inflicting pain on others, both with his body and his mind, gave him pleasure, and although all in the profession were aware of his perversities, none *dared* refuse him.

Clarice looked back at Madame, smiling as Pointreau drew

her to a chair to seat her courteously. Madame's fleshy form appeared to overflow the chair on which she sat as she shifted her abundant weight and continued in her characteristically cultured voice, "Monsieur Pointreau is very interested in you, *ma chérie*. He tells me he has admired you from afar for years." She gave a delicate laugh. "I know that to be true, because he has approached me about you before. It is to my deep regret that I was unable to allow him the opportunity he sought to visit with you. Your patrons . . . they are so very proprietary."

Clarice raised her pale brows. Turning toward the man who devoured her with his lascivious gaze, she offered softly, "I am flattered that a man of your stature had noticed me, Monsieur Pointreau."

"Surely you are not." Pointreau moved closer. He slid a hand onto the clear flesh of her shoulder to caress it gently. The skin of his palms, softer than a woman's, sent Clarice's flesh crawling as he purred, "Your clients are among the most distinguished men in New Orleans, are they not?"

"Monsieur," Clarice drew back with a guise of mock consternation. "Surely you would not expect me to respond to that question. To do so would be *indiscrète?*"

"Non, ma chérie, I would never want you to be indiscreet."

Pointreau's gaze moved hotly over Clarice's face, lingering for long moments on her lips, sending wave after wave of revulsion coursing through her before he turned abruptly, all pretense abandoned as he offered coarsely, "What is your asking price for her? Whatever it is, I will pay it!"

"Monsieur . . ." Madame drew her great bulk from the chair, the signal Clarice awaited to draw herself to her feet as well as the older woman approached, still smiling, "My position is extremely difficult. Although I am not at liberty to reveal the names of Clarice's patrons, I believe you know as well as I that they are very well connected, and that they are adamant that her clientele list not be increased."

Appearing to swell with fury, Pointreau slapped his hand

down on the desk with a crack of sound that startled both women as he hissed, "Are you aware of the chance you take in refusing me, Madame? Do you realize that I have but to speak the right word in the right ear, and your establishment will be closed forever?"

"You would find many angry friends on your doorstep the following day, if you did, *monsieur.*" Her composure regained, Madame gave another short laugh. "Come now, surely you do not believe Clarice is the only desirable woman in this establishment?"

"Do not attempt to charm me, Madame!"

"Clarice," Madame's gaze met hers with a flicker of warning. "Can you do nothing to reassure Monsieur Pointreau that you are desolate at being forced to refuse his offer?"

Swallowing against the taste of bile rising, Clarice turned toward the furious man beside her. Gone was the charming courtier of a few minutes earlier. In his place was a man whose violent nature was reflected in the fist that twitched at his side as she determinedly closed the gap between them.

The angry rise and fall of his chest brushed her breasts as Clarice offered softly, "Gerard . . . you see before you a woman who has lost her freedom of choice in intimate encounters because of verbal contracts into which she has entered. I have given my word not to violate the terms of those contracts. Madame has assured her clients that she will oversee that I do not. The integrity of her establishment, as well as the livelihoods of all within, are dependent upon the strength of that given word."

Determined to follow through, Clarice inched closer to Pointreau's rigid form as she rasped, "But I tell you now, that I, too, have shared the frustration of admiring from afar that which I can not have since I first became aware of your patronage of this house. It is my deepest regret that I may not take you back to my room with me right now, so I may prove the sincerity of what I say. Instead, I will make you a promise with Madame as my witness. Gerard . . . *mon cher,*"—the words choked up Clarice—"should you still desire me when I am freed from the contract which is soon to lapse, I will offer myself to you humbly . . . with a supplication that will dismiss forever the frustration you now feel."

Holding her breath, Clarice saw the myriad emotions that worked across Pointreau face. She caught her breath as he spat out, "Bitch!"

Thrust suddenly backward, Clarice struggled to regain her footing, striking her thigh against the corner of the desk as Pointreau advanced to tower over her. His color apoplectic, he rasped, "You will regret this day." His gaze jerking back to Madame, he continued, "Both of you!"

Trembling in the horror of his wake as Pointreau slammed the office door shut behind him, Clarice glanced at Madam. Unaware of the ghostly white of her complexion, she rasped, "Rogan . . . If he should step into the hall . . ."

Flying down the hallway toward her room moments later, Clarice was about to thrust the door open when she heard the steady drone of conversation from within. Recognizing Rogan's deep tones, then Bertrand's clipped response, she felt tears begin to fall. They were safe and had no idea how very deep had been their peril. For their own sakes, she must not tell them—not now—what had happened this night.

Raising her gaze upward, Clarice whispered, *"Merci, mon Dieu . . . merci."*

Her head snapping toward the sound of a step in the direction from which she had come, Clarice turned to see Madame standing at the curve of the hallway. The older woman spoke softly, for the obvious benefit of one out of sight beyond the curve, in a tone that did not betray the compassion visible on her full face.

"Clarice, Monsieur Delise is here to see you. I have informed him that you will be delighted to entertain him, but that you will need a few moments. He has agreed to wait for you in the blue room. Do not keep him waiting too long, *ma chérie.*"

"*Oui, Madame*"

In control a moment later, Clarice knocked lightly on the door of her room, then pushed it open. The two men within looked at her as she offered briefly, "I must bid you *adieu* for the evening, for I have duties to attend." And then, her heart tugging as gold eyes appeared to study her closely, "I will not be needing this room, so you may use it as long as you wish." She hesitated. "Take care. The streets are alive with the governor's men tonight."

Drawing the door closed behind her before they could respond, she walked solemnly down the hall.

The blue room tonight . . . Pierre Delise . . . *oui* . . .

Rogan surveyed the dark street as he hesitated in the alleyway to the side of the Madame Renée's house of pleasure. Beside him, Bertrand paused with his hand on the gun at his waist.

. . . *The streets are alive with the governor's men tonight* . . .

Clarice's words ran again through Rogan's mind. How strange she had sounded when she had spoken them. Beautiful Clarice, who had made a compromise with life, who would not allow it to defeat her . . . More honest and noble than those who would condemn her . . .

Forcing her from his mind, Rogan scrutinized the surrounding area more closely. He could not risk a confrontation with the governor's men now—not when he was so close.

Motioning Bertrand forward, he slipped out onto the street. In a moment, the shadows consumed him.

"A donation from a source who wishes to remain anonymous . . ."

The morning sun shone on the stone-faced nun standing in

the convent entrance as Bertrand repeated the statement he had given the pale, smaller, sister standing behind her, the nun who had gone running for reenforcements at the first sight of him minutes earlier.

Bertrand concealed the animosity rising in him. The first nun's reaction was not uncommon, but repetition did little to ease his discomfort at the reaction some had to the ragged scars from eye to chin that twisted the flesh of his cheek so grotesquely. He supposed he would never forget the moment when the slight young whore slipped up beside him as he sat in a public house, and with a few quick swipes of her blade, removed all trace of normalcy from his visage forever. She had screamed that it was *his* fault, that he had tainted her with his curse when he had lain with her, that the voodoo woman had said she must cut herself free of it by drawing his blood, or she would be doomed.

That moment had changed his life. Clearly identifiable as the "cursed" one after that, he had been unable to escape the whispers that had followed him, disallowing honest employment, leaving him helpless against the relentless emotional assault that had also driven Clarice to the point of taking her own life before Madame Renée found her.

A prostitute . . . He recalled a time when he had associated that word with shame and with a vision of lewd, ignorant, foul-smelling women who were easily forgotten once a man had completed his business with them. Not so, Clarice. She had reclaimed her life with her new profession, and she now commanded respect not only from her patrons but from him as well.

As for himself, he had regained his self-respect and drawn himself up from the gutter into which he'd sunk after he was so cruelly marked—all because of the faith one man had placed in him. Captain Whitney had saved his life. The *Venture* had become his home, and the seamen on it, who accepted him without exception, had become his friends. The deaths of each had been a personal loss to him, as had been the destruction of the noble vessel.

Bertrand was well aware, however, that his sense of loss, though intense, did not compare with the torment Captain Whitney endured in knowing that it had been his responsibility to bring the *Venture* through.

There had never been a moment's doubt as to what course Bertrand would follow when he learned of the arrests of Captain Whitney and First Mate Dugan. In the years since, he had never faltered from it.

Aware that the second nun, a larger, broader, older version of the first, continued her perusal, Bertrand noted that to her credit, she demonstrated little of the first nun's aversion to looking at him as she quizzed, "A donation?" Lifting the loosened lid of the crate, she peeked at the linens within. "They are lovely, but I am uncertain . . ."

Bertrand's agitation was rapidly expanding when a softer voice interjected unexpectedly from the hallway behind, "May I help you, *monsieur?*"

The air of authority in the third nun's tone left no doubt as to her status in the convent community. Bertrand was about to reply when the second nun responded in his stead.

"These men claim to be delivering a donation of linens, Reverend Mother, but this man either doesn't know or won't say who our benefactor is."

Mother Superior glanced at the crate Bertrand balanced on the doorstep, then at the similar one Porter held nearby, questioning, "Both are filled with linens?"

Bertrand shrugged. "So I was told by the fellow who paid my friend and me to deliver these boxes here . . . but if you don't want them . . ."

Refusing to allow him to hurry her, Mother Superior scrutinized Bertrand with her watery blue eyes.

"This man who paid you . . . he was a merchant?"

"It appeared he was."

The nun paused, then proceeded bluntly, "You are certain this donation was legally obtained?"

"We were hired to deliver these crates in full view of all."

"In that case, we will accept them."

Bertrand breathed a silent sigh of relief as he picked up the crate. He smiled inwardly as the Mother Superior spoke again after a moment's pause.

"If you would deliver them to the second-floor linen room, I would be most grateful."

Bertrand nodded again.

Hoisting the crate onto his shoulder, he motioned Porter to follow as they were led down the main corridor to the rear of the building by the fluttering, pale-faced nun. His casual expression belied the acute attention he paid to his surroundings as he mentally committed the floor plan to memory.

Arriving on the second floor, feigning confusion as the nun motioned him on behind her, Bertrand turned left and started down the hallway.

"*Non, monsieur!* Follow me!"

About to reply, Bertrand turned instead toward the sound of a door opening at the end of the hall. Triumph flashed through his mind as a slender, uniformed figure emerged.

It could be no other. The young woman's hair was of a fiery shade, and the eyes casually appraising him as she passed were a wide, clear gray. Porter's short intake of breath as she drew by them was confirmation.

"*Monsieur* . . ."

Bertrand scanned the hallway again, fixing more clearly in his mind the locations of the rooms . . .

"*Monsieur* . . ."

He was turning back toward the pale-faced nun when the young woman paused and addressed him with distinct hauteur, "Sister Juliana is addressing you, *monsieur!*"

Yes, she could be no other.

Bertrand faced Gabrielle Dubay with a vacant glance, then turned to the nun's bidding.

* * *

The silence of night enveloped all as Rogan crept through the shadows of the convent grounds. Grateful for the brick wall that shielded his men and him from prying eyes as they drew their ladder up from the levee, he directed Bertrand and Porter silently, his mind intently focused on the task before them.

One chance was all they would get.

The ladder was barely up against the side of the convent when Rogan began climbing. Aware that Bertrand was close behind as Porter remained on watch below, Rogan did not hesitate as he moved through the open window. Finding the hallway exactly as Bertrand had described it, Rogan turned to give Bertrand a signal that left him on guard there.

In the hallway Rogan paused at the first doorway on the left.

His heart pounding, he slowly turned the knob. He opened the door only far enough to allow himself entrance before slipping inside and pushing it closed behind him. The soft rasp of slow, even breathing was the only sound in the darkness that encompassed him.

Dressed in black, he was all but invisible in the shadows, but the young woman in the bed was not. A shaft of silver moonlight pierced a broad gap in the blind, illuminating her face.

Porter was right, Captain. The girl is unmistakable.

Bertrand's words upon his return from the convent that morning resounded in Rogan's mind. That fiery hair stretched across the pillow . . . that pale skin . . . those small features . . .

Gray eyes . . . ?

He need be sure.

Rogan crept closer.

Kneeling beside the bed, he touched the young woman's shoulder lightly. She stirred, then settled back to sleep. He touched her again. He heard her mumbled protest . . . saw her eyelids flutter, then lift.

Gray eyes snapped open wide!

Gray eyes . . .

Clamping his hand across Gabrielle Dubay's mouth, Rogan muffled her shriek, grating, "Be quiet and you won't get hurt!"

The young woman fought to dislodge his hand from her mouth, kicking and pounding against him as he warned again, "Be still!" Then, in frustration, "All right!"

A quick, snapping crack to the jaw and the young woman went limp.

Wasting no time, Rogan rolled her into a blanket and thrust his human bundle over his shoulder.

On the convent grounds minutes later, all disappeared into the night.

Gold eyes in the dark . . .

Cat's eyes. No . . . something else!

A harsh voice . . . a heavy hand restraining her . . .

Fear.

Panic.

A crack of pain!

Oblivion.

A sense of motion prevailing, Gabrielle floated in a strange nether world . . .

. . . somehow uncertain she would awaken . . .

Chapter 2

She was no longer floating. The world had stabilized beneath her, but pain had replaced the sense of motion.

Her jaw ached.

Unaware of the groan that escaped her lips, Gabrielle opened her eyes slowly. It was dark . . . too dark. Where was the comforting, silver shaft of moonlight that had shone across her bed from the first night she had occupied her lonely, convent room? The scent of lavender that pervaded her quarters had changed to a strange odor of mildew and she—

Starting as a shadow moved above her, Gabrielle snapped her eyes closed. She was dreaming. She had to be. She was not lying on a hard pallet in a strange place that smelled of the swamp, and a man's shadow was not hovering over her. When she opened her eyes again, she would be back in her room at the convent and all would be well.

A light appeared against Gabrielle's closed eyelids, raising a swell of relief. The sun was rising. It was morning. This frightening episode would soon be over. All she need do was open her eyes and her nightmare would be dispelled.

Gathering her courage, she peeked through slitted eyelids, only to gasp with dismay. It wasn't morning and she *wasn't* in her room! The light she had seen was the faint glow of a lantern, and the shadow leaning over her . . .

The strange gold of cat's eyes came again into view. No, they weren't cat's eyes, despite their glowing, feral quality.

They were *human*.

The phantom figure drew the lantern closer and Gabrielle caught her breath. She had never seen shoulders so broad or a stature so powerful. The light further alleviated the darkness, and the shadowy face grew clearer. Strong, sharply planed features, a resolute jaw, heavy hair as black as a raven's wing, and dark arched brows over eyes that were the intense gold of a predator . . .

Ignoring the pain that throbbed anew as she opened her mouth to speak, Garbrielle rasped, "Who are you? Where am I? I *demand* to know what is happening!"

"You *demand?*" The face above hers set in a hard smile as the man continued, "You aren't in a position to demand anything."

"Am I not!" Gabrielle attempted to rise, but the flat of the man's hand snapped to her chest, pressing her back against the pallet. Attempting to free herself, she gasped, "How dare you lay your hand on me!"

"Don't be a fool!" The heavy hand remained. "You are incapable of thwarting me, even had I any intimate intentions toward you. But you may set your mind at rest. I have plans of an entirely different nature for you."

"I asked who you are!"

"And you'll wait for that answer until I'm ready to give it!"

"Oh, will I?" The heat of anger momentarily dispelled Gabrielle's fear. Damn the man! How dare he attempt to demean her! She was no match for his physical strength, but she would neither submit to nor endure his attempts to intimidate her!

Countering with an attempt at intimidation of her own, Gabrielle took a steadying breath. "Are you aware of who I am?"

"Gabrielle Dubay . . ."

"*Mademoiselle* Dubay will do!"

The man's deep voice took on a quality that sent little shivers down Gabrielle's spine, "Do you really believe that I would go to the trouble of removing your person from the convent in the dark of night if I *didn't* know who you are?"

Gabrielle's blood ran slowly cold. "I don't understand."

Withdrawing his hand, the man pinned her with his gaze as he began unbuttoning his shirt. Refusing to reveal her fear, Gabrielle raised her chin as he drew his shirt open to reveal a ragged letter branded into his chest.

"This mark is a remembrance from your father . . . and I never accept a gift without responding appropriately in kind."

Refusing to wince at the sight of the cruel scar, Gabrielle responded coldly, "You're telling me that my father did that to you?" And when a cold stare was her only response, "I don't believe you!"

"It's of no consequence to me if you believe me or not."

The man drew his shirt closed and began buttoning it as another figure appeared in the doorway of the crude hut. She gasped aloud as she recognized the man as the same one who had delivered the linens to the convent that morning.

"I see you recognize Bertrand."

"How could I not?"

The younger man's face hardened, and Gabrielle regretted her thoughtless response as he offered, "Porter's on guard outside as you instructed, Captain. I'll take the second watch."

Gabrielle glanced back at her captor as he drew himself to his extended height, acknowledging the younger man's words with a nod, adding, "We'll leave at the first light of dawn."

"Leave? To go where?" Gabrielle sat up abruptly. "I demand to know—"

"Lie down."

"What?" Suddenly furious at the yet unidentified captain's command, Gabrielle rasped, "You aren't speaking to one of your seamen, *Captain!*"

"Lie back as I told you, or you'll force me to take stronger measures."

"I don't take orders, *Captain!* And even if I did, I would most certainly not take yours!"

The two men exchanged glances, and a slow trembling began within Gabrielle despite her bravado. The younger man disappeared back through the doorway, only to reappear again with a coarse rope in hand. She stiffened.

"Surely you don't intend—"

"Lie down."

"I told you that I—"

Beside her in a moment, rope in hand, the captain grated, "You can have it either way. You can sleep bound hand and foot, travel hanging over my shoulder like a trussed pig—or you can do what I say."

"You wouldn't!"

No response.

He would.

Clamping her teeth tightly shut, Gabrielle lay back against the pallet and closed her eyes. She had had all she could stomach of the sight of him anyway!

She neither moved nor opened her eyes at the sound of the younger man's retreating steps, at the rustle of movement before she felt the brush of air as a blanket was laid on the floor of the hut beside her. She refused to open her eyes— she merely peeked—as the grim-faced captain lay down on the blanket beside her, reached over to lower the flame on the lantern, and closed his eyes.

In a moment, the sound of his steady, even breathing was all that could be heard.

Asleep! How could he!

Gabrielle glanced around her. The hut was small, with a dirt floor and a thatched roof. It was barren of anything other than the two of them ... but possibly ... if she could reach the lantern and—

"Don't try it."

"W-What?"

No response.

She didn't need any.

Gabrielle closed her eyes.

The little witch had closed her eyes.

Rogan withheld a responsive snort. It was hot and close within the hut, with little air circulating. The subtle, feminine scent of the young woman lying beside him teased his nostrils, increasing his annoyance. Somehow, during the months in which he had formulated his plan, he had not anticipated this moment.

He should have.

A young woman raised by Gerard Pointreau, whether truly of that man's blood or not, could not possibly be other than an arrogant, haughty shrew, despite her youth.

Her youth . . .

Turning on his side, Rogan faced Gabrielle Dubay. He studied her clear, faultless features in the limited light, the memory of the warm, rounded breasts beneath the delicate cotton nightrail she wore returning. No, Gabrielle Dubay was not a child. Neither was she an innocent, self-effacing young woman inclined toward the religious life. He doubted if anything could be further from the truth. If he did not miss his guess, Mademoiselle Dubay had strained at the constraints of the convent from the day she entered, making the lives of the nuns there a perpetual misery. What was it Porter had said . . . that she was due to leave the convent shortly before her eighteenth birthday a few months hence? He had no doubt that her departure would have been to the relief of many.

He also had no doubt that although she would be eighteen in actual years, in sapient years the lovely Gabrielle had passed that mark ages earlier.

And now she was his . . .

Rogan perused Gabrielle Dubay more closely. Oh, yes, this

young woman would have learned to use her beauty to great advantage upon entering the dissolute New Orleans society that was her father's haunt. The heavy, lustrous hair that now lay in disarray, framing her face as she slept—she would doubtless have driven young swains wild with the thought of running their fingers through its gleaming strands. They would probably have strained to taste the smooth perfection of her skin, to wander the classic planes of her face with their lips. As for the womanly swells underneath his palm as he had sought to restrain her . . .

Rogan took a slow breath. He was grateful he was beyond those youthful torments. With maturity and the advent of the singular, driven purpose that had become the focal point of his life, he had learned to satisfy his baser needs without personal involvement that might prove distracting. The many houses Lafitte maintained on Grande-Terre for that purpose had served him well, for there were few within whom he gave more than a moment's thought after leaving.

And that was the way he wanted it. There was an honesty about that kind of interaction between a man and woman . . . unlike, he was sure, what would follow an interaction between this haughty, young witch and any young man with whom she became involved. He knew her type—one who would not be satisfied with less than possessing a man body and soul, in the same way it was rumored her "father" conducted his intimate affairs.

A hard smile flicked across Rogan's lips. Yet, he had much to thank this young woman for.

Rogan's hand unconsciously slipped up to trace the brand that marked his chest. He had determined years earlier that Gerard Pointreau's crimes were such that simple revenge would not suffice, that he need find a way to make Pointreau *confess* his association with Gambi in the attack on American merchant ships. The reasons were many. In declaring his culpability and clearing the name of Captain Rogan Whitney from all charges, Pointreau would then be forced to use his fortune to pay recompense to those who had suffered because of his duplicity. But Pointreau's confession would have an even greater, more far-reaching effect. Lafitte's violent temper would doubtless come into play once Gambi's association with Pointreau revealed the man's continued violation of Lafitte's strict order against attacking American ships. Lafitte would expel Gambi from Grande-Terre, eliminating the protection that had made Gambi invulnerable.

Upon meeting Gambi on equal terms at last, Rogan had no doubt who would emerge victorious—and retribution would be fully achieved at last.

The difficulty, however, had been in ascertaining a point of weakness that would leave Pointreau vulnerable to the pressure he would exert. Years of scrutiny had revealed only one.

And now Gabrielle Dubay was his.

Rogan surveyed the still young woman more closely.

He should've been prepared for this fiery, haughty little witch, but somehow he was not. He recalled the pounding of her heart beneath his palm—a fluttering that betrayed a fear she had otherwise concealed so well. She would be difficult to control.

But he *would* control her.

He might even learn to enjoy it.

That thought lingering despite himself, Rogan closed his eyes and prepared for a watchful sleep.

"Get up."

"Uh . . ."

Gabrielle opened her eyes at the rude nudging, only to go rigid at first sight of the big man leaning over her. She closed her eyes again, inwardly groaning. It wasn't a dream . . .

"Get up, I said!"

She sat up unsteadily and glanced around the hut. She grimaced. It was even more primitive than she had imagined.

"Get on your feet!" The "captain" gripped her arm and

stood her up abruptly, startling her with the ease with which he lifted her. The reason for that, however, was apparent. The man was even bigger and broader, more intimidating than he had appeared in darkness.

If she were the type to be intimidated . . .

It occurred to her that there was only one way she could possibly escape this man.

"Don't waste your time trying to trick me. It won't work." Seeming to read her mind, the captain continued, "You can't get away. There's nowhere to run and no place in the bayou for a woman alone and unprotected to hide—no place that's safe from alligators and water moccasins on the water, and bear and wild cats on land, not to mention—"

"Do you really believe me a fool, Captain?" Gabrielle could not withhold a sneer. "Do you really think to frighten me with stories of dangers lurking behind every bush and around every corner? I have lived in New Orleans all my life!"

"Yes, pampered and protected in your father's mansion or on his plantation where you were doubtless indulged to a fault and granted your every whim. It appears even the good nuns of the convent were not immune to your "father's" influence. A private room apart from the other students . . ." He laughed harshly. "Your doting father didn't realize how convenient that would prove to be." His laughter faded. "You will find it's a far different world here. Let's go."

Pushed outside ahead of the man, Gabrielle halted abruptly. Where were they? There was no sign of civilization, just the little hut from which they had emerged, standing alone amidst dense vegetation and overhung with vines and trailing flowers. The moist air, scented with a strange mixture of exotic flora and decay, hung heavily on her shoulders as she realized she could see no farther than a few feet ahead of her!

Refusing to reveal her dismay, Gabrielle straightened her back and turned abruptly toward the towering captain.

"If you will indicate the way to the convenience . . ."

The captain waved his hand in an expansive gesture encompassing the surrounding foliage as he replied, "You may take your choice . . ."

Damn the man! He had actually smirked!

Gabrielle glanced at the two seamen standing nearby. The first, the scarred young fellow, returned her glance with the same impassive stare he had given her in the convent hallway. She remembered she had thought him stupid. She knew now that he was not.

The second fellow . . . yes, she remembered him too. He had carried the other case into the linen room, and she had inwardly laughed at his awkwardness. Now the laugh was on her.

Raising her chin, Gabrielle turned toward the nearest bank of bushes even as the captain's voice rang out with a soft warning.

"If you have any sense, you won't stray too far."

She did not deign to reply. She was not a fool. Although she had sought to deny it, she had heard tales from early childhood of those who had wandered too far into the swamps and were never seen again.

Gabrielle emerged from the foliage minutes later. She winced as she struck her bare foot on a sharp stone. Looking up, she caught the captain's assessing gaze, a slow heat transfusing her as she realized the full extent of her dishabille for the first time. The delicate batiste and lace-trimmed nightrail she wore was a far cry from the coarse cotton nightwear more commonly worn in the convent, but her father had insisted that she not be forced to surrender the luxuries to which she had been accustomed when she'd entered. The sizable supplement her father paid in addition to the tuition asked of the other students, had granted her the special considerations he demanded, both scholastically and for her physical comfort, which had included in addition to the reading, writing, ciphering, and history taught the other students, extensive instruction in literature, languages, and music—and an improvement over the common meals, including delicacies which were sometimes embarrassing when compared to the modest fare others were offered.

But, damn him, the odious captain was right! Father's insistence on specialized treatment for her had directly contributed to the situation she now faced—finding herself at the mercy of the relentless predator whose eyes seemed to bore right through her.

Damn, damn, damn the man! What was he looking at?

Gabrielle Dubay emerged from the foliage, and knots somewhere in the vicinity of Rogan's stomach clenched tight. He did not have to look at the two men standing to his rear to know they were staring as well.

Damn the little witch! She knew exactly what she was doing, standing there like that in the shaft of morning sunlight filtering through a break in the heavy foliage overhead. The brilliant rays glinted on the heavy auburn tresses streaming down her back, catching on the golden tips of the luxurious sweep of lashes framing her incredibly light, clear eyes, and illuminating the creamy texture of her skin. Even more silently daunting, however, was the slim, feminine form outlined so clearly through the fine lawn of her nightrail . . . the long, slender limbs, the smooth curves, the firm, rounded swells above her slim rib cage, and—

Rogan abruptly halted the quick progression of his thoughts as the bold she-devil advanced toward him, her chin high and proud, only to stumble, wincing, as she took a short, hopping step. Rogan glanced down at the bare feet peeking from beneath the hem of her gown and frowned. He need take care of that necessity immediately.

He turned toward Bertrand. Anticipating him, his silent first mate held out a pair of worn leather sandals. Suddenly irritated by the realization that both Bertrand and Porter had followed the progression of his thoughts, Rogan took the san-

dals from Bertrand's hand and threw them at Gabrielle's feet
with a snapping command.

"Put them on!"

Color flared briefly in her creamy cheeks. *"Pardon!* You are
speaking to me?"

"I said, put them on."

Rogan's jaw jerked with spasmodic tension as Gabrielle's
delicate nostrils flared. "I think not! I have never worn the
sandals of a slave, and I never will."

"We have a long journey ahead of us before nightfall. You
will make that journey with these sandals on your feet, or you
will walk barefooted. The choice is yours!"

The beauteous witch's stiff face twitched as she remained
rigidly and silently adamant.

So be it.

Rogan turned toward the men behind him. "All right, let's
go." Bending to pick up the bundles beside him, Porter took
up the lead as Rogan jerked his arrogant hostage into line
ahead of him.

"W-What are you doing?"

Rogan glared down into the light eyes looking up at him.
"I don't have time to waste on foolish questions."

The young woman glared in return. "We haven't yet broken our morning fast."

Disgusted with her protest, Rogan attempted to move her
forward only to have Gabrielle jerk her arm free to declare
imperiously, "I'm hungry!"

His lip lifting in an expression dangerously close to a snarl,
Rogan gripped Gabrielle Dubay's slender arm and pulled her
again into line ahead of him.

Another imperious glare.

Rogan's face turned to stone as he spoke a succinct command.

"Walk!"

Perversely tempted to laugh at the young woman's sudden
step forward, Rogan frowned instead as Gabrielle stumbled

on yet another sharp stone, then continued on in the direction he indicated.

Stubborn little witch. She'd learn.

He gritted his teeth as he trained his gaze on the long auburn tresses bobbing against Gabrielle Dubay's narrow back, tresses that rested just short of the firm buttocks faintly outlined against the delicate cloth covering them.

She was *hungry*.

Rogan's jaw locked tight.

He was beginning to discover, to his chagrin, that his *appetite* had been stimulated, too . . .

Gabrielle stumbled again, her feet already sore although they had not been walking along the heavily foliated trail for more than five minutes.

She slapped at a buzzing insect and wiped the mist of perspiration from her brow, aware that she had been a fool in allowing pride to stand in the way of accepting the sandals offered her.

Somehow, however, she sensed the discomfort she now suffered would not be the last.

This mark is a remembrance from your father . . . and I never accept a gift without responding appropriately in kind.

A chill ran down Gabrielle's spine despite the moist heat of morning. Who truly were these men who held her life in their hands? The captain—whatever his true name—was he merely mistaken in his assessment of Father, or was he . . . insane?

And what price would she be asked to pay in order to facilitate his supposed revenge?

Her life? Or worse . . . ?

Gabrielle gulped back her rising panic as she glanced around her.

"Keep walking!"

She turned a heated glare at the big man behind her, but those peculiar gold eyes allowed her little satisfaction.

Where were they going?

What did he intend to do with her?

She had to get away . . . for her own sake, and for father's.

She'd get her chance. Somewhere . . . somehow . . .

But in the meantime . . .

Gabrielle continued walking.

Rogan's annoyance swelled. The haughty Gabrielle Dubay did not fool him with her halting pace. She was deliberately trying to delay them.

He scanned the trail with a narrowed gaze despite his certainty that they were not yet being pursued. Her absence was probably at that moment being discovered in the convent, at the same time the letter was being delivered to Pointreau's door. By the time Pointreau was truly certain of what had happened, they would be deep into the bayou . . . and well on their way to reaching their coastal rendezvous point by dark.

Rogan's lips moved into a tight smile. Yes, just about now, Pointreau would be opening up the letter and he would read . . .

Monsieur Pointreau,

Although your recollection of our last meeting may have dimmed in your mind, my memory of you is very clear. For that reason, I have taken certain steps that will doubtless coax you to search your memory.

Gabrielle Dubay is a lovely young woman. You may be assured that I will take good care of her while she is under my personal protection. How long she will remain so, however, is a matter that you will ultimately decide with your response to my demands.

I will allow you some time to dwell on that thought before outlining those demands. I ask you to keep in mind that I will expect immediate response to my next contact. I advise you not to try my patience in that regard, for it is the lovely Gabrielle who will suffer my displeasure.

Captain Rogan Whitney
Of the noble ship,
Venture

A short, choking sound escaped Gerard Pointreau's throat as he stared at the missive in his hand. His body rigid, he struggled to catch his breath as he glanced around the spacious foyer of his mansion. Morning sunlight streamed through the stained-glass window above the heavy oak door, casting glorious shades of red and amber gold against the silk-covered walls and the heavily polished floor, but he saw none of it as his eyes bulged and his voice emerged in a hoarse shout.

"Boyer, come here immediately!"

An aging, meticulously uniformed negro, stumbling in his haste to respond, appeared in the entrance to the foyer. Pointreau took a sharp step toward him.

"Where did this letter come from?"

"Under the door, massa. I found it there this mornin' and I put it in the tray so's you'd see it when you come down."

"Fool!" Striking the slave a powerful blow to the face that knocked him a few staggering steps backward, Pointreau demanded, "How long has it been lying here?"

"A few minutes, massa! A few minutes, is all!"

A few minutes . . .

Pointreau turned sharply toward the door, then paused in an attempt to regain control of his emotions. No, he mustn't get upset. He need visit the convent first. This could all be a hoax—or a cruel joke of some kind.

A tremor ran down Pointreau's stiff spine. Captain Rogan Whitney . . . yes, he remembered the man. How could he for-

get the silent promise he had last glimpsed in that man's
gaze?

Pointreau took a shuddering breath. If the letter was indeed
authentic . . . if the man had indeed abducted Gabrielle . . .

His dear Gabrielle . . .

Suddenly panicked, Pointreau jerked open the door and
stepped out onto the street.

"She's gone, Reverend Mother! Her bed is empty and she
has disappeared! She did not even take her shoes!"

Mother Hélène Marie's pale face whitened as Sister Madeleine's tear-filled eyes met hers with true fear. She needed no
one to tell her that Gabrielle had not run away. The time for
such behavior was long past. Gabrielle Dubay, the indulged
child who had come to the convent years earlier, had become
Gabrielle Dubay, a determined young woman whose occasional rebellion was nothing more than a reflection of her
keen, inquiring mind and a zest for life which she had not yet
been free to indulge. But Gabrielle's distinct sense of right
and wrong would not allow her to be the cause of true consternation in the convent.

Mother Hélène Marie briefly closed her eyes, recalling the
evening past when Gabrielle had appeared at her door, sober
and disturbed, after her father had left the convent. She did
not suppose she would ever forget the sincerity in Gabrielle's
eyes when the young woman had apologized for stirring her
father's animosity toward the convent, or the forgiveness
sought for a man whom Mother Hélène Marie knew felt no
remorse for his actions.

When she accepted Gabrielle's apology without acknowledging the need for it to have been tendered, Gabrielle had
been visibly relieved. The thought occurred in that moment,
as it had many times over the past years, that it was not Monsieur Pointreau who guided his young charge to responsible
and compassionate maturity as the situation was generally

perceived. Instead, it was Gabrielle who instinctively attempted to tender such guidance, and it was only through his adopted daughter that Gerard Pointreau stood a chance of developing the portion of his personality that was so pitifully deficient.

And, in that moment, Reverend Mother had prayed for forgiveness for the uncharitable thought that Gabrielle was Monsieur Pointreau's only hope for salvation.

Gabrielle, a true jewel . . . the only true jewel the powerful Monsieur Pointreau possessed . . .

And now she was gone . . .

"Reverend Mother . . ."

Mother Hélène Marie opened her eyes, struggling against the myriad, escalating fears suddenly abounding as she instructed, "Search the convent—every room on every floor. Check the outbuildings and the grounds, and when you are done—"

"Reverend Mother!" Appearing suddenly beside Sister Madeleine in the doorway, Sister Juliana was deathly pale. "A ladder . . ." She lost her voice on a sob, then continued. "A ladder was found lying on the ground underneath the window to the upstairs hallway. There are marks underneath the window . . . the scrapings of muddy boots. Oh, Reverend Mother, someone has taken Gabrielle away!"

Someone has taken Gabrielle away.

Mother Superior's solemn words echoed again in Gerard Pointreau's mind, the shock as sharp in retrospect as when he had first heard them uttered early that morning.

Night was falling outside the window of the lavishly appointed study of Pointreau's Royal Street mansion. Pacing, his jacket discarded, his spotless white shirt carelessly unbuttoned midway down his chest, his hair ruffled from the nervous raking of his hand, and his face pale and lined with strain, Pointreau struggled to regain his composure. It had been a long day fraught with incredible anguish.

He glanced toward the window, agitation tightening his jaw at the realization that the day was indeed ending. No, it could not be true! Gabrielle's fate could not still be uncertain! He could not have failed to discover even the faintest clue to her whereabouts during the frantic hours past! If he lived to be one hundred, Pointreau knew he would never forget the moment when he'd stormed through the convent door and into the Mother Superior's office that morning. He had known at a glance that it was true, that Gabrielle was gone.

Someone has taken Gabrielle away.

The words echoed painfully once more. The urge to strike out, to wipe those words from the pale nun's wretched lips with the weight of a blow had never been stronger.

He had raced up the staircase toward Gabrielle's room without making a response, coming to an abrupt halt as he stood in the doorway and saw her bed with the coverlet thrown back and her clothes, carefully arranged for morning, lying on the chair nearby. He had turned with a snarl at the simpering voice of Sister Juliana when she had drawn his attention to the open window in the hallway and the ladder lying on the ground below it. He recalled that had he not held himself in the strictest of control at that moment, he would have struck that simpering nun from his path, as well as the others who gathered helplessly by, rosaries in hand.

He had gone directly from the convent to the office of Governor Claiborne. The shock and horror on that man's face at the news of Gabrielle's abduction had done little to calm his agitation. Even as the governor had ordered immediate patrols of the city perimeter, a search of all ships presently in port, and the reinstatement of the reward for Captain Rogan Whitney's capture, he had somehow known that the effort was to no avail. Captain Whitney had waited years for the moment to strike. He would not have abducted Gabrielle had he not had a safe place within the city to keep her or a plan that would get him out of the city *before* any patrols could be instituted.

The thought came to him that it was already too late for legal measures.

Pointreau took a shaky breath. Shortly after his interview with the governor, he had dispatched a letter to Vincent Gambi on the isle of Grande-Terre, asking him to arrange a meeting with Jean Lafitte.

Pointreau's dark eyes narrowed as his bearded cheek twitched nervously. It was not uncommon for the respected and respectable of New Orleans to visit Grande-Terre for the slave auctions held there. Many of them knew Jean Lafitte personally, did business with him, and held him in high esteem. Pointreau's close association with the governor had forced him to maintain his distance in the past, but Gabrielle's abduction had thrust those considerations aside in the realization that Lafitte's aid was essential if he were to find her.

How would he expect to enlist Lafitte's aid?

Pointreau's jaw locked as he reviewed his plan in his mind. Everyone, including Lafitte, knew that Governor Claiborne was determined to run Lafitte and his band from Grande-Terre despite the legality of the letters of marque Lafitte's men possessed. Indeed, the governor's attitude was a constant thorn in the side of the amiable but sometimes hotheaded Lafitte. And everyone knew that Governor Claiborne depended heavily upon Gerard Pointreau for advice because of his family's long-standing influence in the city.

Influence . . . the perfect bartering tool . . .

When he met with Lafitte, he would promise to use his influence with Governor Claiborne in Lafitte's favor. In exchange, he would ask only a few words as to Captain Whitney's location if the man was hiding in the vicinity of Grande-Terre. He would also promise that if he were successful in finding Gabrielle as a result of Lafitte's advice, he would *guarantee* Claiborne's acceptance of Lafitte.

His fists clenching with frustration, Pointreau paused to consider the timing once more.

Two days for his message to reach Grande-Terre, and two days to receive one in return . . .

Four days at the minimum while Gabrielle remained alone and unprotected from the man who sought to use her to wreak his revenge.

Beautiful Gabrielle . . .

Pointreau's heart wrenched painfully as he glanced at the darkening sky.

Where was she now?

What was she doing?

Was she saying . . . ?

"I'm tired, damn you! I refuse to walk any farther!"

Halting, Gabrielle turned suddenly toward the big man behind her, bringing him up short. She fought tears as anger fueled her waning strength.

Damn him . . . damn him! The soles of her bare feet were cut to ribbons from the rough trail they had traveled throughout the day and she could barely walk, but the bastard captain forced her relentlessly onward. She had been bitten by every manner of flying insect alive, her skin felt burned to a crisp by the heat of the sun filtering through the leafy swamp cover, and she had been ruthlessly pushed to the limit of her endurance while being given only enough food and water to keep her on her feet.

But she had been pushed as far as she would go.

She'd show him!

Gabrielle sat down abruptly in the middle of the overgrown trail, aware of the startled glances of the two seamen who paused, awaiting their captain's reaction. It was not long in coming.

"What do you think you're doing?"

Looming over her, the yet unnamed captain scowled down into her face as Gabrielle sat her ground.

"What do you think I'm doing?" Gabrielle defiantly closed her eyes. "I'm resting."

Silence.

The silence became so profound and extended that Gabrielle was tempted to peek.

"Get up."

"No."

"I'll tell you one last time. Get up."

Gabrielle's heart leaped with a fear that was not reflected in the adamancy of her response as she forced her eyes to remain closed.

"*No!*"

Silence again.

Then a step.

Her eyes snapping open as she was suddenly swept from her seated position into the air, Gabrielle gave forth a loud, unladylike whuff of sound as she was tossed over the captain's broad shoulder. Their furtive procession resumed once more.

Humiliated, chagrined, and possessed of the urge to strike her captor dead as she pounded and beat upon his broad back with her fists, Gabrielle shouted, "Let me go! Put me down! I *demand* you put me down!"

Stunned when she was abruptly released to flop onto the ground in an unladylike heap, Gabrielle looked up with a gasp into the narrowed gold eyes suddenly so close to her face that she could feel their singeing heat.

The captain spoke in a tight hiss. "Are you ready to walk?"

A sound suspiciously like a chortle of laughter came from the seaman who had led their party most of the day, further fueling her sense of indignation as Gabrielle snapped in return, "I can't! My feet . . ."

Her humiliation reaching new heights when a sob inadvertently escaped her, Gabrielle strained for control. Forcing a normalcy of tone, she concluded, "My feet hurt."

Wincing as the captain grasped her foot unexpectedly and turned it to inspect the underside, she did not see the twitch of his strong jaw the moment before he dropped her foot, then growled back at her, "Too proud to wear a slave's sandals ... but not too proud to wail for help when your pampered hide suffers."

"Wail for help?" Fury rose to tint Gabrielle's gaze with a blood-red mist. "Did you say, *Wail?*" Springing to her feet, ignoring the pain and exhaustion that surged in her once more, Gabrielle raised her chin high. "You may rest assured that I will never wail for *your* help, captain!"

Turning, Gabrielle barked at the skinny seaman ahead of her. "Well, what are you waiting for?"

Continuing on, each step a torment beyond her wildest imaginings, Gabrielle pushed determinedly forward as twilight faded into night.

"Will you need me anymore today, *madame?*"

Manon Matier turned absent-mindedly toward the short, silver-haired woman who stood in the doorway of her small drawing room. Unconsciously frowning despite the positive effort she usually exerted to keep her face free of such lines, so aware was she that her skin was no longer truly young, Manon shook her head.

"*Non,* you may leave if you wish, Marie."

Manon watched as Marie nodded and limped out of sight. She waited for the sound of the door closing behind her aging servant before releasing a shuddering breath. She was relieved, desperately relieved to be free of Marie's assessing glances, even though she realized that true affection was the cause of the older woman's concern. Marie had known her from childhood, too long not to realize when she was upset; and Marie was too wise not to be aware that she had true reason to be disturbed.

Where was he?

Manon walked toward the sideboard and looked squarely into the mirror there. She scrutinized the reflection she saw, hoping she did so with true honesty when she noted the image of a woman no longer in the first blush of youth but still beautiful.

What was it her dear Alexandre had always said . . . that he was the most fortunate of men to have a wife who was as lovely without as she was within? But then, he had had the heart of a poet, which was probably the reason he had died so young and so deeply in debt years earlier. Overcome with grief at his passing, she had not realized that loneliness would prove to be the least of the evils she would soon face when alone.

Frantic when she'd learned that Alexandre had left her all but destitute, Manon had sought a way to support herself while besieged with creditors and hounded to the point of desperation. Slowly selling off all of her possessions, including the small house Alexandre had purchased for her shortly after their marriage, she was gradually realizing that she was facing a life on the streets in order to survive when she had met Gerard outside a local marketplace.

Gerard, so handsome and charming, and so considerate of her in her desperate circumstances . . . She remembered feeling his gaze upon her as she had stood hungrily awaiting the opportunity to snatch some particularly appealing fruit and stuff it into her oversize bag. She recalled that he had met her humiliation with generosity, and that because of him, she had eaten well that evening for the first time in many weeks.

Gerard had courted her patiently afterward, appearing at her door with small gifts that he never allowed her to believe he knew were essential to her survival. It seemed a natural progression of events when he began paying off her debts as well. It had also seemed natural when she had finally allowed Gerard to assume Alexandre's place in her bed as well as her heart.

Because she loved him.

Manon considered the sober image staring back at her from the silvered glass. Blond hair that was still bright and full, pale skin still stretched smoothly over the graceful planes of her face, azure eyes that Gerard had said rivaled the blue of the summer sky, and lips that curved easily into a smile . . .

But she was not smiling now.

She had been Gerard's mistress for almost six months when she had first noticed a change in him. She had sensed a growing resentment that she could neither understand nor thwart. He began coming to her more often when frustrated or in a temper, and she had, at first, been flattered by the realization that she was able to soothe his distress as no one else could. She had soon come to comprehend, however, that it was her unique ability in that regard that Gerard contrarily began to resent as much as he valued it.

Manon paused at that thought. During the course of long, sleepless nights, she had finally discerned the cause of his perverse behavior. The reality was that he was new to the potency of real love. His previous alliances had been entirely of the flesh. They had left him unprepared for the power that love exerted by its very nature, a power over one's thoughts and actions *because* one loved and was loved in return. She had told herself, however, that although truly loving someone demanded sacrificing a part of oneself, Gerard would come to realize much more was eventually gained than was lost . . . so very much more.

Manon continued her silent assessment, following the smooth curve of shoulders bared in a pale blue batiste gown, a color Gerard favored. Yes, her flesh was still taut, her breasts firm, and her waist small. Beneath the full skirt of her gown, she knew her stomach was flat, her hips gently rounded. As for her legs—long legs that Gerard so admired—she was justly proud of them.

But Gerard had complimented her less often in the months past. Continuing his financial generosity, he'd become increasingly parsimonious with his affection . . . on occasions exhibiting a subtle cruelty that was more painful than physical abuse.

Why did she endure such treatment? She had asked herself that question over and again during the past months when his visits to her had grown fewer and whispers of his forays to houses of pleasure that specialized in sexual aberrations reached her ears.

Her answer had nothing to do with financial considerations. The response was simple. Gerard needed her. She was able to give him relief from agitation, a relief that he could find nowhere else. For that reason, although he had never spoken the words, she knew *Gerard loved her.*

But a disquieting pattern had begun developing, against which she remained powerless. The more Gerard grew to depend upon the relationship between them, the more he resented her. The more indispensable she became to him, the less she saw of him.

Only during the increasingly lonely nights most recently past had she had grown to suspect the pattern Gerard had established was calculated to inflict pain.

But she was ineffective even against that suspicion.

Because she loved him.

Personal concerns were not the cause of Manon's present distress, however, as she again contemplated the shocking news about which all New Orleans was now talking. Gabrielle Dubay, Gerard's adopted daughter—on whom he doted—abducted from her convent room! Gerard would be beside himself with grief. He would need her consolation more desperately than ever before!

Manon glanced up at the clock on the mantel, her expression tightening. It was already past nine ... so late. Where was he?

A sound at the outer doorway at that same moment set Manon's heart to pounding. She reached the foyer as a key turned in the lock and the door opened.

She gasped aloud. Gerard, disheveled and unkempt as she

had never before seen him, his coat badly wrinkled, his shirt unbuttoned, his cravat undone, stood in the doorway. His hair was uncombed, his face was pale, and his eyes . . .

Tears threatened Manon. Gerard's eyes were red-rimmed almost as if . . .

In a moment she was in his arms. She heard the door snap closed behind him as he buried his face in her neck . . .

. . . and she heard him sob.

The shadows of the bayou trail grew deeper as Rogan inwardly raged. The haughty Mademoiselle Dubay walked unsteadily ahead of him, and it galled him to realize that despite appearances to the contrary, the little witch had established her own brand of control over the situation.

Oh, yes, how well she had . . .

The warmth of female flesh pressed against him as he had hoisted her up onto his shoulder had not left his mind despite the tension that grew stronger with each mile they moved closer to the coast. The female scent of her still filled his nostrils, and he remembered with a clarity that was too vivid for comfort, the sensation of her female curves sliding down against his hard flesh as he had dumped her unceremoniously onto the ground.

Rogan grunted in unconscious acknowledgment. The sight of her lacerated feet had twisted his stomach into knots, and the thought that she was enduring the pain solely to spite him did little to relieve those tormenting constrictions.

But it was her own fault, damn it! He had offered her sandals, and she had declined them because she considered them slave sandals.

Rogan's full lips twitched. At least slaves had the sense to wear them!

The determined *mademoiselle* stumbled again. Rogan reached out a steadying hand just as she righted herself, and he inwardly groaned at her unsteadiness. Porter had increased his pace over the last hour with the realization that darkness would soon fall. Rogan dared not tell the man to slow his step, for the hour of rendezvous was almost upon them and they—

Gabrielle Dubay swayed again, her weakness more evident than before. Rogan reached toward her at the exact moment Bertrand prompted from behind, "Captain, she's going to fall."

Grasping her arms supportively, Rogan turned the wobbly *mademoiselle* toward him to see hatred flash in her fading gaze the moment before unconsciousness claimed her.

Beside him in a moment, Bertrand took only a minute to assess her condition before speaking in his characteristically unemotional tone.

"She's all right. She fainted."

Fainted.

Bertrand's tone was flat. "I'll carry her."

"No. I'll do it."

Lifting the limp Gabrielle Dubay over his shoulder, silently cursing every step of the way, Rogan continued on toward the coast.

The lamp flickered, sending uneven shadows dancing against the familiar bedchamber wall as Gerard plunged himself deeply into the moist warmth of the woman beneath him. He felt the intimate satin of her flesh envelop him, heard her gasp. As she opened fully to accommodate his burgeoning member, his passion soared.

Plunging again and again, aware of the delicate hands that clutched him close, of the slender legs that wrapped around him to facilitate his intimate assault, of the sound of his name whispered with loving ardor, he felt the heat within him pulsing, growing, until—

Gerard's guttural groan sounded on the silence of the

room, mingling with Manon's joyful whisper as he throbbed to culmination.

Raising himself from her damp, female softness moments later, his breathing still ragged, his heart still pounding, Gerard stared down at Manon. Her eyes were closed and her lips were parted as she, too, sought to bring her breathing under control.

Gabrielle's beautiful, youthful face flashed before him unexpectedly. Aware that the plight of his darling Gabrielle had been dismissed totally from his mind during the moments past, Gerard's resentment burgeoned.

Manon, who believed herself so wise ... How had she managed to insinuate herself into his life as no other woman ever had? How did she so accurately manage to pinpoint his inner needs? She had practiced her skill on him again that night, drawing all from him slowly, coaxing him to voice his innermost fears, his torments, even getting him to express his convoluted sense of guilt at Gabrielle's abduction.

She had stripped his soul naked!

Her control of him at that moment supreme, she had then rewarded him with the consolation of her body, fostering in yet another way his unique dependence upon her.

Harlot! He knew her game! She sought to reach a part of him he would allow to no other but his dear Chantelle—a part that had died along with her never to be revived! She sought to replace Chantelle in his heart, a heart that remained alive only for his dear Gabrielle!

But Manon had outsmarted herself! She was good at what she did, so good that he was yet unwilling to give her up. He had already determined, however, that if she would have him play her game, he would play it according to *his* rules ...

Gerard's handsome face shifted into a hard smile. Manon had consoled him and made him forget Gabrielle for a little while. She had proved her control over him once more. But the day would come when he would no longer feel the desire to indulge the need she fostered.

For the truth was, whatever *she* believed, the ultimate control was his.

Silently proving that point to himself, Gerard lowered himself against Manon again, then turned with a rolling motion that delivered her atop him. Her startled gasp excited him, as did the flush that suffused her face as he slid himself within her to resume a passion so recently spent.

Rapture rose once more, a deliberate rapture that climaxed in a burst of ecstatic abandon that left Manon limp against him.

Slipping her to the bed beside him, Gerard saw her heavy lids flutter slowly open, the feigned glow of love in her azure eyes as he moved wordlessly to his feet.

He heard her speak his name as he reached for his clothes and walked from the room. He heard her call his name one last time as, fully dressed, his passions satisfied and a sense of control his once more, he pulled the front door closed behind him.

Gerard paused briefly on the doorstep as lamplight glowed against the silent, cobbled streets. Manon had served her purpose. He was indeed a man renewed. He was able to speak with new confidence to Gabrielle's image as it flashed again before him, and he whispered, "Gabrielle, my darling girl, I will find you and bring you home. Do not despair. Do you hear me, Gabrielle? Do you hear me?"

Gabrielle groaned softly.

The steady, bobbing rhythm that had been a part of the darkness encompassing her had changed to a smooth, gliding motion that was almost soothing. She was floating, her body less tortured, almost at rest.

Slowly opening her eyes to the vast darkness of a night sky lit with countless stars, she took a moment to clear her mind. No, she wasn't in her convent bed. Nor was she in the midst of a frightening dream. She was . . . she was . . .

Gabrielle gasped as her immediate surroundings became abruptly clear. She was in a rowboat on the open sea. Her abductors were rowing steadily toward . . .

Gabrielle raised herself slightly, then gasped again.

. . . toward a great ship lying at anchor in a darkened lagoon!

She swallowed, restraining a groan as she attempted to move. Every bone in her body ached, but her feet . . . they were on fire.

A tear slipped from the corner of her eye, and Gabrielle wiped it roughly away. She had no time for tears, not now when she might be leaving the coast of Louisiana behind her forever.

"Ahoy, Captain!"

A shout from the ship's deck a short distance away caught Gabrielle's ear and she sat up. She saw the captain glance toward her the moment before he responded, *"Ahoy, Barker. Make ready to take us aboard."*

The synchronized motions of the two seamen revealed their expertise as they drew their small boat up alongside the graceful ship that dipped and rocked with the current.

The light of several lanterns held over the side of the ship gradually illuminated the darkness with the light of day. The men staring down at her—Gabrielle swallowed tightly—were a disreputable-looking lot. Ragged hair and beards appeared to be the norm. Gold earrings glinted in the ears of some, while others wore brightly colored bandannas tied around their heads, and one particularly unsavory-looking individual wore an evil-looking black patch over one eye. Gabrielle glanced back at the captain as he called out a series of commands.

Then another lantern, held high against the hull of the ship, illuminated the name painted below the carved masthead depicting a fierce bird of prey with claws bared. The name of the ship—

Oh, God, no!

Gabrielle caught her breath, her gaze darting back toward the captain who towered over her before reaching down to draw her to her feet. He couldn't be . . .

"Are you ready to board, Captain?"

"Aye!"

The captain's response froze Gabrielle's mind with terror. Her abductor was one of the most feared of Lafitte's captains, a man spoken of in whispers by the voodoo women of New Orleans who claimed that he had absorbed the soul of a captured bird of prey, thereby giving himself the ability to sweep down on the ships that were his quarry with the deadly accuracy of a winged predator! Rumored to be more pirate than privateer, a man whose past was shrouded in mystery, he was known only by the name his ship bore . . . the name that had become his own.

He was Rapace . . . the raptor!

Gabrielle swayed unsteadily as the dark world around her briefly faded. She felt a rush of night air as she was swept up from her seat to find herself again hoisted on the captain's broad shoulder.

Her involuntary whoof of sound and brief struggle elicited a succinct warning.

"Be still!"

The inky glitter of the night sea gradually retreated from view as the captain climbed up the rope ladder that had been tossed over the side of his ship. Despising the weakness that left her subservient to his command, Gabrielle drifted in a gray world of semiconsciousness.

Rapace . . .

She should have known it the moment those gold eyes had pinned her.

Yes, she should have known.

Chapter 3

Drums . . . she heard drums . . .

The pounding echoed in Gabrielle's head, steady, relentless, as she slowly opened her eyes to the bright light of morning.

She groaned aloud. Oh, no, not again . . .

It seemed destined that each time she closed her eyes, she would awaken in an unfamiliar place! This time she had wakened in what was obviously a ship's cabin. She was lying on a wide bunk over which was a single porthole. The deck between the bunk and door was mainly occupied by the broad desk in the far corner, a potbellied stove in the center of the cabin, and a small table with two chairs, between which there was barely room to move.

Those drums . . .

Gabrielle drew herself to a seated position, uncertain if the sound was inside her aching head. No . . . And it wasn't drums. It was the sound of feet stamping . . . in unison on the deck above her head.

Dancing? No, that would be insane . . .

Gabrielle's disorientation deepened. She ached dreadfully. Her skin seemed afire, her bones felt as if they had aged fifty years in the space of a day, and her feet . . .

A stinging pain pierced their soles as she attempted to move them, and Gabrielle caught her breath. Oh, yes, she remembered. She had refused the slave sandals. She had been a fool.

Her head jerking up at a rustle of sound, she stiffened as the door opened without her bidding anyone to enter.

She bit back a gasp.

It was he.

Rapace.

He seemed even larger as he entered the limited confines of the small cabin. His shoulders filled the doorway, his head grazed the opening . . . and those eyes . . .

No, she would not allow him to intimidate her, would not behave as if she truly were his prey!

Ignoring her fear as well as her pain, Gabrielle snapped, "I did not bid you to enter my cabin!"

"Your cabin?" The big man sneered. "I beg to differ with you, *mademoiselle*. This is *my* cabin, and I allow no one to keep me out of it."

Gabrielle did not immediately respond. Instead, her gaze snapped to the broad bunk on which she sat and the pillow beside hers which bore a deep indentation.

The captain's gaze did not flicker. "Do you have a question to ask, *mademoiselle*, for if you do, I will be most happy to answer it."

The loathsome man . . .

Stepping aside abruptly, the captain revealed the familiar scarred young man standing behind him with a basin in his hand. He ordered gruffly, "Get it over with, Bertrand."

The seaman approached Gabrielle. He assessed her silently as he placed the basin on the table beside the bunk. She drew back, blurting, "Stay away from me!"

"You disappoint me, *mademoiselle*." The captain's voice dripped with saracasm. "You act like a frightened child."

"A frightened child?" Gabrielle's loathing soared. "You are wrong on both counts, Captain. I am neither frightened nor a child. Rather, I am repulsed to be in such disreputable company!"

"I suggest you guard your tongue! Bertrand has agreed to treat your discomforts. I would not offend him if I were you."

"I don't need Bertrand or his treatment!"

"Listen to me, *mademoiselle!*" The captain advanced to stand towering over her, forcing Gabrielle's stubborn chin even higher as his voice deepened with warning, "Your feet are badly cut—a situation for which you bear full responsibility! I was forced to carry you for the final portion of our journey to the coast, and I have no intention of seeing that circumstance repeated. I will have you understand now that you are on *my* ship and under *my* authority. You will act accordingly!"

Gabrielle's response was a silent sneer that brought the big man's face down to her level so he might glare into her eyes.

"You *will* be on your feet again and able to travel within the next few days, for if you are not, and a situation should occur where you are again unable to keep up . . ."

The captain paused, his voice dropping to a hiss, "You may . . . not . . . survive. Do you understand?"

"How dare you threaten me!"

"I would not waste my time threatening you, *mademoiselle*. I am merely stating a fact."

"You would not dare harm me! My father would—"

"Your father!" The captain's handsome face twisted in a snarl of true menace. "I have rendered him helpless. He is the one who will not dare act against me while there is any possibility that you are still in my hands!"

"You are a fool if you think my father will sit back and allow you to dictate his actions. He will speak to the governor!"

"Neither the governor nor his men frighten me."

"My father is a man of great influence!"

"The ocean is wide and free. If I so choose, I need never set foot on Louisiana soil again."

True fear gripped Gabrielle for the first time. She struggled to conceal it.

"That was not your aim when you abducted me. You hoped to use me to further your vengeance."

The captain straightened to his full height, his features suddenly as emotionless as stone.

"Understand me, *mademoiselle*. Were I to order my men to throw you overboard, to end this affair here and now, my vengeance would be served. It is up to you to decide whether it will be worth the trouble to keep you alive so I might force your father to pay in full for his crimes."

"*My father's* crimes? You are insane! You are the criminal, not he!"

The feral gold of his eyes boring into hers, the captain so aptly named Rapace, stared down at Gabrielle, then turned abruptly toward the door. The deep rumble of his voice trailed behind him.

"If she gives you any trouble, Bertrand, leave her to her own devices!"

The echo of the door latch rebounded as Gabrielle looked up at the scarred man who stood mutely in his captain's wake. She scrutinized him silently. Slight, blond, and of medium height . . . were it not for the scar that twisted his one cheek so grotesquely, one might almost find him patrician in appearance, almost typical of the young Frenchmen of her father's social set.

Gabrielle assessed this man more closely. No, he was not like any gallant, fun-loving Frenchman she had ever known. There was a coldness about him, one she adjudged that came from deep within. She spoke abruptly.

"What do you expect to do with that basin?"

Bertrand's expression did not alter. "The captain asked me to tend to your injuries."

Were I to order my men to throw you overboard . . . here and now, my vengeance would be served . . .

Gabrielle's thin lips twitched. She scoffed, "He would never order me thrown overboard!"

No response.

"Well, would he?"

Bertrand's continued silence spoke for itself.

"All right!" Gabrielle dropped her feet over the side of the bunk. "Do whatever you must, but as soon as I'm able to walk again . . . to run . . ."

Gabrielle snapped her lips closed. She had said enough. She waited as the young seaman kneeled beside her and took her foot into his hand. His touch was surprisingly gentle as he examined the cuts. Continuing his silence, he then bathed the wounds carefully, removing all trace of soil before applying a thin salve.

The enigmatic Bertrand still had not spoken a word when he stood up and turned toward the door. Somehow ashamed of her conduct in the face of the relief from her discomforts he had afforded her, Gabrielle waited until he had drawn the door open before she spoke again.

"Thank you."

No response.

What had she expected?

Yes . . . what?

A brisk morning breeze had come up during the short time spent below. Standing on the quarterdeck, Rogan reacted instinctively as he shouted to the men awaiting his command.

"Man the topsail sheets and halyards!"

The men on deck raced to the sheets. Waiting until another group grasped the halyards, he shouted, *"Throw off the buntlines, ease the clewlines!"*

The men aloft reacted swiftly, slackening the lines which kept the sails furled.

"Sheet home!"

The men manning the sheets hauled down and Rogan called out, *"Away with the topsail halyards!"*

The ship lurched forward as the sails filled firm and taut overhead, and Rogan felt a familiar satisfaction briefly soar. He had called out those commands countless times before. He had watched topmen scamper up the shrouds out onto the

footropes hanging below the topsail yards, had seen the bending of sail that took place amidst a bedlam of shouted orders
and mumbled curses, had heard the crack of sails in the wind,
and the stamping of feet. He had felt the wind freshen, the
ship heel over underneath him, and had then started all over
again, setting the courses, topgallants, royals and spanker,
through it all never quite losing the thrill of canvas filled to
billowing on a sea of whitecaps.

The sense of freedom evoked was matchless.

Rogan recalled that he had once wanted nothing more
from life but to experience that freedom as captain of his own
merchant ship. But Gerard Pointreau had robbed him of that
satisfaction and had instilled in him another, driving sense of
purpose that would not be denied.

Turning at the sound of a familiar step behind him, Rogan
faced Bertrand's sober expression with a raised brow.

"I see you escaped alive."

Bertrand did not smile. "Mademoiselle Dubay's feet are
badly cut, but I have no doubt they'll heal quickly." He
paused, adding deliberately, "She's determined they will."

Rogan searched his first mate's pale eyes. "I take it she's
formed a plan?"

"I don't know. If she hasn't yet, I think she soon will."

Rogan nodded. Bertrand's instinct seldom failed. He was so
good at reading people, and sensing danger, that Rogan
sometimes wondered how he could have been taken unaware
by the whore who had marked him.

Bertrand, a friend who had never failed him . . . but Rogan
sensed that his friend was ill at ease with this latest venture.
He offered quietly, "A few weeks and this will all be over.
We'll return Mademoiselle Dubay to her father and what is
left of his life, and all debts will be finally paid."

A shout from the main deck turned Bertrand toward
Turner as the cook called his attention to another daily disaster below decks. In a moment Bertrand was gone, and Rogan
returned to survey the sea—the brilliance of morning sunlight

reflecting against its shimmering surface, the graceful flight of gulls swooping into the churning waves, the unexpected darkening of the water as a great school of fish passed below them . . .

. . . the image of a small, haughty face, glaring . . .

The glaring image snapping him rudely back to the present, Rogan gave a low snort. It had been a difficult night after he'd finally arrived at his ship. He had carried the exhausted, semiconscious Mademoiselle Dubay to his cabin where he might monitor her condition.

Why?

He was still uncertain.

Through the long night the only excuse he had formulated for his sudden decision to play nursemaid to the arrogant witch was the fact that he was responsible for her good health, and that, contrary to his statement to her a short time earlier, her health might yet be necessary to the full success of his plan.

What rot!

It had not been concern for his plan that had tugged sharply at his gut when he had settled the beauteous Gabrielle on his bunk and had stood over her as she immediately fell asleep. During those silent moments as his gaze had trailed the tangled reddish brown hair spread across his pillow, had lingered on the spots of color dusted by the sun on the ridges of her cheeks and the bridge of her elegant, haughty nose, as he had allowed it to settle for several moments too long on her full, slightly parted lips, he had had little thought for the plan that would come into play at daybreak.

The hours of the night to come and the intimacy of the small quarters they would share had been the sole thoughts that filled his mind.

He was still uncertain if the witch had been feigning sleep at that moment and had deliberately taunted him by turning in a way that wrapped her sheer nightrail around her to outline the smooth turn of her hip and the delicate curves of her buttocks. His hand had been an inch from those tempting curves when he had finally found the strength to snatch it back, just in time.

Totally disgusted with himself, he had stamped to the table nearby and settled himself as comfortably as possible between two chairs. It had not taken him long to realize how much he missed the comfort of his wide, comfortable bunk ...

... now filled with a warm, inviting young woman.

He had shaken his head in negative response to that thought.

The young woman had *not* invited him.

Nor would he have accepted her invitation if she had.

Would he?

He had debated that response.

Well, *would* he?

He was still debating it.

He had slept fitfully, treated each time he opened his eyes to the sight of the beauteous waif who slept like a child on his bunk ... listening to the soft groans that escaped the little witch's lips each time she turned in her sleep ...

... as he imagined hearing her groaning softly in another way.

I'm hungry ...

The lovely Gabrielle Dubay's words before they began their trek to the coast.

Rather than face the meaning his mind instinctively sought to put to them, he had closed his eyes in desperate search of sleep.

Discomfort finally victorious, he had lain down on the bunk beside Gabrielle Dubay's sleeping form for a few hours' sleep before dawn.

And the true torment had begun.

Seeking to cast the memory from his mind, Rogan locked his jaw tight, breathing deeply, filling his lungs with the sweet sea air as he drew his powerful frame up to its full proportions and reviewed the progress of plans the young woman's abduction had put into play.

Gabrielle Dubay was his hostage. His first missive to Gerard Pointreau had been delivered. Another would follow within a few days. They had reached their rendezvous with his ship on schedule and were now sailing toward the only true point of safety for a privateer in the Caribbean—the Baratarian Isle of Grande-Terre.

Jean Lafitte . . .

In truth, Rogan admired Lafitte, if not for his motives, for his absolute genius. He could not think of another man who would have been successful in organizing the cutthroats and villains who had gathered at Grande-Terre, rallying pirates and privateers of the caliber of René Beluche and Dominque You, into the formidable force that it was. No other man could have enlisted a man such as Nez Coupé, the infamous Cut Nose disfigured in a saber attack, as his first lieutenant. No other could have been successful in insisting that every Baratarian ship have a letter of marque from a country at war with Spain, and that only Spanish vessels were to be attacked. And no other man wielded the cool, ruthless hand of command so unhesitantly when defied as to demand the respect of those who respected very few, and to guarantee his own, unique form of justice would prevail.

Jean Lafitte had united warring factions that had previously ruled Grande-Terre and had introduced a sound business strategy so strong that, with the exception of Gambi's covert activities, the captains of Grande-Terre cruised when and where Lafitte indicated, turning the spoils of their ventures over into his hands for disposal.

Lafitte had a thousand men under his command when Rogan first sailed the *Raptor* into Barataria Bay, in addition to several hundred women who found the living and the men there to their liking.

Amidst the countless ships at anchor at Grande-Terre, the *Raptor* found safe harbor, and among the thugs and villains who walked the beaches, Rogan found anonymity. Satisfied to address him simply as Rapace, those who had become friends did not care what his true name was, and those who were not his friends dared not press him.

Now that he had Mademoiselle Dubay in his custody, the remainder of his plan was simple. He would remain at anchor in the Bay of Barataria while Pointreau stewed in his helplessness. Allowing Pointreau enough time to become desperate, Rogan would then set forth his demands in another letter which Porter would return to New Orleans to deliver covertly.

Porter would remain in the city to await the first three of Pointreau's capitulations. The first would be a formal confession to Governor Claiborne of his involvement with Gambi, with copies to be posted around the city so the general populace might become informed of his villainy. The second would be a public notice from the governor, dismissing all charges against Captain Rogan Whitney and his "accomplices." The third would be the transfer of all funds in Pointreau's bank accounts to an account in the name of the survivors of the *Venture* and their heirs, with Captain Rogan Whitney named as administrator—the transfer to be certified by Governor Claiborne and published in the newspaper so all with the right to benefit might immediately begin to make petition.

If Pointreau met these demands, Rogan would sail back to the city and return Mademoiselle Dubay to her father. If Pointreau refused, or if he delayed in responding—Rogan stiffened, a scowl darkening his face—then an alternate letter carried by Porter would be delivered. It would contain the simple statement that Pointreau would never see his dear "daughter" again.

Rogan scrutinized the sea once more, the clear blue sky above the ship and the trace of white clouds on the horizon. The wind was brisk, and they were moving quickly through the sea. They would arrive at Grande-Terre by nightfall. He would go ashore on the island the following morning, as was his custom upon returning, leaving only a carefully chosen skeleton crew aboard to guard his valuable hostage. He would visit with Lafitte as was also his custom, maintaining an appearance of normalcy until the situation was resolved.

It occurred to Rogan that the revelation of his covert activities against Pointreau might not sit well with Lafitte, that the wily Frenchman might consider the entire affair somehow threatening to his empire on Grande-Terre. Rogan suspected, however, that Lafitte would instantly realize Gambi's covert activities against American ships were by far the greater threat. He did not doubt that Lafitte would act quickly and without mercy to remove that threat.

Rogan's stiff lips flickered in a semblance of a smile. He would leave a penniless and disgraced Pointreau to the disposition of the courts and to the mercy of those public officials whom he had humiliated. The man would be destroyed.

Rogan's brief smile faded. As for the haughty *mademoiselle* below, she would not be his concern once she was returned to her father.

The image of a small, haughty face appeared once more, and Rogan's strong jaw twitched.

I'm hungry . . .

Rogan's unanticipated appetite nagged, and he made an abrupt decision that the nights to come would not be spent under the same intimate circumstances as the last one . . .

. . . for the sake of the plan under way . . .

. . . for the sake of the young woman below who was too arrogant for her own good . . .

. . . and, for his own.

The sun streamed through Clarice's bedroom window casting golden shafts of light across her bed as she moved restlessly, her naked flesh warm beneath the silken bedlinens. She had been up late the previous night. Pierre Delise had again visited her. He was the most consistent of her three clients, often taking up so much of her time that she need delicately remind him of her need to entertain her other patrons. She also knew that were it possible, were her other two patrons not adamant about retaining their rights to her exclusivity, he would have reserved her time for himself alone, and paid the price gladly.

Dear Pierre . . . He was a handsome young man with boyish good looks that did not reflect his age of thirty-two years. She supposed that he would probably retain his youthful appearance well into middle age, for surely the thick, curly brown hair in which she had so often curled her fingers as they had lain flesh against flesh, would resist strains of gray. The crinkles around his warm brown eyes were indicative that good spirits would forever shine in those depths and that his ready smile would keep him forever young.

Pierre was such a dear man. She remembered the first time she'd seen him. He had come to Madame's house on a lark with a few of his friends. She had been at loose ends for the evening when Henri LeMieux has canceled his intended visit, and she had wandered to the top of the staircase, where she had been standing when Pierre had entered. Pierre's eyes had met hers and he had walked directly up the stairs and taken her into his arms.

Clarice was still uncertain as to how Pierre had persuaded Madame to allow her to entertain him that night without the permission of her other two clients. It occurred to her that since Pierre was a lawyer, there was the possibility these two were his clients as well, and that he had somehow convinced Madame that he would handle the arrangements with them. Whatever the case, Pierre had been her most active caller since that time, and she had not regretted a moment of their exchange.

Oui, Pierre was a delight. He was intelligent and entertaining as well as gentle and passionate. And she knew he had a true affection for her—perhaps a little too true.

Clarice paused, somehow uncomfortable with that thought. Pierre had noticed her distraction the previous night although she had taken great pains to hide the myriad feelings churning inside her at her knowledge that the entire city of New Orleans was talking about the abduction of Gabrielle Dubay, and that Rogan and her dear brother were at that moment attempting to rendezvous with their ship so they might sail to safety.

An uncharacteristic frown had touched Pierre's countenance as he had drawn back from his lovemaking to peruse her expression. The huskiness in his voice had been all too revealing as he had stroked her cheek, then whispered, "Tell me that you are not growing tired of me, *ma chérie.*" Swallowing with obvious discomfort, he had continued, "I could not bear it if you were. You have grown dearer to me with each passing day, you see, until the thought of holding you intimately close in my arms consumes my thoughts when we are apart."

Pierre had touched her heart with those words in a way no other man ever had. She had been truly pained to distress him, and she had reassured him and dismissed his fears with an ardent response that was not entirely feigned, clutching him close long after the heated climax of their intimacy, for her affection for him was also true . . .

. . . as was the reality that there was only one man she would ever truly love.

Rogan's handsome, sun-darkened face returned to her mind, and Clarice's agitation increased. Had Rogan and her dear brother reached the ship as planned? Were they now sailing free and clear on the sea toward the safe haven of Grande-Terre? Were they unharmed?

Whatever the case, Clarice knew that the two most important men in her life shared a common goal, that their lives would not be their own until they avenged the sinking of the *Venture* and the slaughter of all aboard.

She told herself that dear Bertrand would be free to smile again then . . .

. . . and that Rogan would be free to love.

Clarice's heart gave an anxious leap at the thought, knowing that when he was, she would make him understand that although forced to accept the difficult circumstances fate had dealt her, her heart had always been his.

Rogan had suffered a similar blow from fate.

He would understand.

And, once free, he would love her.

If . . .

Clarice attempted to thrust thoughts of Gabrielle Dubay, ever encroaching, to the back of her mind. But she could not. It was rumored that the indulged and pampered Mademoiselle Dubay was quite lovely—or so Gerard Pointreau led all to believe. Sequestered as the young woman had been during her schooling at the convent, Clarice could not know for sure. She could only hope, with all her heart, that the spoiled witch who had never known a day's discomfort or want in her life was a homely wretch of little appeal who was easily dismissed from the mind, one distinguished by the self-pity Rogan so despised. She also hoped that—

Suddenly aware of the futility of such thoughts, Clarice threw back the coverlet and stepped down onto the lush carpet beside her bed. Her naked form reflecting back at her from the full-length mirror to the side of the room, she paused, indulging in a reflection of her own.

Oui, she was beautiful . . . She was of her dear *maman*'s size, daintily although womanly formed, with well-rounded breasts, a narrow waist, and a curved *derrière*. She resembled her *maman* also in coloring and facial characteristics, in the heavy blond hair that so many men admired and the thickly lashed blue eyes that seemed to fascinate them, the main distinction between *maman* and her being the delicate arch of her brows that reflected her *papa*'s side of the family.

But there was no family left now, other than dear Bertrand and herself, and as she grew older—not so much in age, but in a strange weariness that had become draining of late—she had begun to feel the need for a family of her own.

Clarice's gaze remained sober as she dismissed her reflection and reached for the pale silk wrapper lying at the foot of the bed. She was twenty-three years old. She had lived the torments and tribulations of many lifetimes during this time, and had had a full range of experiences. She had emerged victorious over the battles waged, discovering a self-respect that was not determined or deterred by the occupation with which she supported herself.

But it was now time for love.

Rogan . . .

Clarice swallowed against the emotion again rising. Rogan had filled her dreams since the first moment she had seen him, and she would soon attempt to discover if those dreams would become reality.

How long had he said it would take for the entire affair with Pointreau to be brought to conclusion. Two weeks?

Two weeks, with a lifetime of uncertainty to be lived during that fortnight.

A knock at her door drew Clarice from her thoughts. It was so early . . .

Another knock.

Too early . . .

A tremor of fear suddenly striking her, Clarice rasped, "*Entrez, s'il vous plaît.*"

The door opened and she went still at seeing the man standing there.

Gabrielle glanced around the captain's cabin, her sense of confinement growing as the buck and roll of the ship signified steady progress through the morning sea. An inner uneasiness tugged at her stomach as she glanced at the blue patch of sky visible through the small porthole behind her.

What time was it?

What was Father doing now?

Had he taken steps to find her?

What steps . . . ?

Several silent hours having passed since she had awakened earlier that morning, and since the silent seaman called Bertrand had treated the cuts on her feet, Gabrielle had assessed her situation unemotionally and without interruption. She had arrived at several conclusions.

The first was that Father would doubtless be at a loss. He would not know what the piratical madman who had captured her was talking about with his accusations of such heinous activities.

Father—a criminal? Ridiculous! Father—a sadist who would indulge in torturing a man, *any* man, going so far as branding him for some perverse, unknown reason? That was insanity!

The second conclusion was that Father, as well as she, were at Rapace's mercy.

How the thought galled . . . !

The third conclusion was that she could not depend upon her father to rescue her, because as well executed as the madman's plan had been, her father doubtless had no idea at all of where she was.

The fourth conclusion was that she could not allow her father to be subjected to the whims of a lunatic who seemed intent on destroying him, simply to protect her. She was an intelligent, educated, and resourceful woman, not a helpless, simpering female! She must form a plan of escape . . .

. . . somehow.

But that was as far as her contemplation had progressed.

She frowned, aware that her thought processes, usually so clear and quick, had grown increasingly muddled in the last half-hour. She was uncertain of the cause.

Was the pain in her feet distracting her?

Gabrielle wiggled her toes. No, the salve Bertrand had applied, absorbed so easily into her skin, had all but eliminated

her pain. She had discovered she was already able to walk
about the cabin with little distress.

Perhaps it was the strange disturbance in her stomach that
was so unnerving.

The ship took that moment to dip deeply into a wave, almost tossing her from the bunk on which she sat. Gabrielle
groaned aloud as the disturbance within her increased.

She looked toward the porthole. There was little air circulating in the cabin, so little that her breakfast, a starchy type
of porridge with a piece of salt pork lying languidly in the
center, was lying just as languidly on her stomach.

As a matter of fact, just the thought of it made her feel . . .

Gabrielle pushed a heavy strand of hair back from her increasingly moist brow.

Air. That was what she needed.

Gabrielle glanced up at the porthole again, then slipped to
her knees in an attempt to force it open. Unsuccessful, she
peered down through it at the whitecapped water rapidly
rushing by. The sight somehow dizzied her, and she sat back
abruptly.

Oh, dear . . .

A sudden lurch and the ship dipped sharply, only to rise
and fall again as waves thudded against the hull.

Oh, no . . .

That heavy porridge . . .

Another dip and roll.

That greasy pork . . .

Another merciless plunge.

Gabrielle slapped her hand to her mouth as her stomach
gave a violent lurch.

She needed air—fresh air!

Jerking open the cabin door, the urgency within her soaring, Gabrielle spotted a ladder at the end of the passageway.
She rushed toward it, all thought of her sore feet forgotten as
she emerged on deck seconds later.

She stood unsteadily, gulping in the sea breeze that battered her, whipping her hair about her face, flaying her with the brilliant strands of reddish brown as it plastered her nightrail against her. She was hardly aware of the rough-looking crewmen who turned toward her to stare with a mixture of surprise and amusement, then with deepening intensity.

The fresh air wasn't working.

The lurching of the ship, the dipping of the hull against the horizon . . . up and down, up and down . . .

Ohhh . . .

She had never felt so dreadful.

She felt it then—a sudden upsurging in her throat.

Thrusting the burly bodies in her path aside with superhuman strength in her race toward the rail, Gabrielle leaned over the balustrade, shocked by the horrible noises that emerged from her throat as her stomach emptied with a violence that was astounding.

She was clinging limply to the moist wooden railing that held her back from the sea, her stomach still seeking to purge that which was no longer within, the world whirling dizzyingly around her, when she heard *his* voice.

"Who gave you permission to come up on deck?"

Gabrielle turned slowly, a feeling of increasing menace slowly building, despite her weakness. Her captor towered over her, negating her usually impressive height as she gritted her teeth against another weakening swell.

"I asked you a question, *mademoiselle!*"

Gabrielle's whispered response was filled with true venom. "Need I really respond to your idiotic question?"

Rapace's expression grew thunderous, but Gabrielle did not react as the weakening swell became a lurching spasm.

Oh, no . . . not again . . .

Turning abruptly back to the rail, she viewed, as if from a distance, the wretched creature inhabiting her who hung over the rail as her stomach revolted with a new violence. She was still attempting to catch her breath when she was suddenly snatched up into the arms of her captor, the deck and the faces of the men nearby passing in a blur of motion as she was carried back to the staircase she had ascended minutes earlier.

Hardly aware of their quick passage down the corridor, so disabling were the spasms within, Gabrielle became conscious of her location as the captain kicked open the door of his cabin, entered, and kicked it closed behind them. The surface of the bunk against her back moments later, Gabrielle opened her eyes to see the captain's face only inches from hers as he grated, "You will *not* leave this cabin again without my permission, is that understood?"

Unreasonable cur . . .

"Is that understood?"

Damn him . . . !

"Mademoiselle, I warn you—"

"Yes, it's understood!"

Her eyes dropped closed, too soon to see the captain frown as he scrutinized her moist pallor. Drifting in a strange limbo, the threat of nausea ever near, she sought instead to clear her mind of thoughts that might jar the precarious balance of a stomach that had betrayed her. It vaguely occurred to her that her escape plan would have to wait until she was again in control.

If ever . . .

She had spent countless days dreaming of a sea voyage . . .

. . . never suspecting it could become a nightmare . . .

. . . in so many ways.

The ship plunged again.

Oh, no . . .

Gabrielle clenched her teeth as the misery prevailed.

Pierre DeLise strengthened himself against the moments to come as the door of the silk and satin-draped room he knew so well opened. Struck momentarily speechless by the beauty of the woman standing before him, he let a few moments pass, aware that surprise—or perhaps another, a hidden emotion—had stricken Clarice similarly mute. Then he spoke at last.

"Bonjour, mon amour."

Suddenly realizing he still held the bouquet of flowers he had so carefully selected from the street vendor's wares, he presented them to the tousled beauty regarding him silently.

"These blossoms pale in comparison with your beauty, *ma chérie,* but their brilliant colors seemed somehow to represent the joy you give me, and I could not resist bringing them to you."

"Merci, Pierre . . ." Color gradually returned to Clarice's pale cheeks as she smiled and accepted the flowers. She hesitated a revealing moment before stepping back to allow him entrance. A knot tensed in Pierre's stomach as she placed the bouquet on a table nearby and turned back to him, her hand moving with the only self-conscious gesture he had ever seen her make, to push back heavy golden strands from her cheek. "I was not expecting you so early . . . especially since you left only a few hours ago. I regret that you find me in a state of dishabille when you return so well kempt to visit."

Pierre pushed the bedroom door closed behind him, his smile fading as he reached for Clarice with words that came from the heart.

"Do you not realize, *mon amour,* that I feel privileged to have you greet me in a state of dishabille? It extends a feeling of continuity that gives me the comfort of knowing you have not already put the loving hours of the night we spent together behind you. It pleasures me to know they still linger."

"They linger, Pierre . . ." The heavenly blue of Clarice's eyes met his, the hesitation there dismissed as she spoke with a warmth that Pierre chose to believe was true. "I have no desire to sweep the time we spend together from my mind."

"Clarice . . ." Pierre slipped his arms around her and drew her close. His hand slipping between them, he undid the tie on her wrapper, sensing the tremor that ran down Clarice's spine as he pushed the garment aside. Her soft, white flesh was warm beneath his palm as he cupped a rounded breast briefly, as he slid his hand down the curve of her waist and hip to rest it at her thigh . . . at the site of a dark bruise there. That bruise haunted him. He had asked how she'd come to receive such a mark, taking her unawares, and he remembered only too clearly the moment's hesitation before she'd responded that she had stumbled.

Pierre's expression tightened. Clarice was a practiced courtesan, but she was not a practiced liar. Someone had *caused* her to stumble—someone whose identity she wished to conceal from him.

Rage briefly swelled once more, and Pierre clutched Clarice almost painfully close.

Her light brows knitted in a frown.

"Does the bruise on my leg still concern you, Pierre? It is nothing. I have almost forgotten it."

"Unfortunately, I cannot."

Separating himself from her, Pierre drew Clarice's wrapper closed around her slender form and tied it tight. In response to her surprise, he smiled briefly. "I would not be distracted from what I have to say by your sweet flesh."

Grasping her resolutely by the shoulders, he moved Clarice backward to seat her on the bed. Sitting beside her, he leaned forward, unable to resist her warm, slightly parted lips as he covered them with his own. He drank deeply of her mouth, reveling in the joys surging to life anew, before drawing back abruptly to place deliberate distance between them.

Clarice's obvious concern deepened. "Something is wrong, Pierre?"

"*Non*, but there is something of great importance I wish to address." He paused, then began slowly. "*Ma chérie* . . . it has been many months since I first lay with you in my arms, but I remember the first time so very clearly. It was the realization of a dream that I had long cherished in my mind, as you were the personification of the woman I had long envisioned."

"*Non*, Pierre, certainly not I!"

"*Oui* . . . you, *mon amour*. It is true that dream was filled with lust, and my feelings for you then were based upon desire, but it is also true that I knew from the beginning ours would never be a casual exchange. Myriad emotions that I can not now begin to enumerate assailed me when I entered this house and saw you standing atop the staircase. In truth, however, I did not realize then the extent to which those emotions would deepen."

Clarice opened her mouth to speak, but Pierre hushed her, continuing, "*Non*, not yet. Now that I've begun, I must express all that is in my heart, for my feelings for you are too deep and strong for me to deny them any longer. Or for me to tolerate any longer the realization that during the hours I am not with you, you are subject to the whims of other men in their intimate treatment of you. Clarice . . . I have approached Henre LeMieux and Maurice Ware."

Clarice swallowed revealingly as he spoke the names of her other patrons. Pierre stroked her cheek. He was far more aware of her agitation than she realized. The reason was simple. He loved her. He had purposely neglected to mention to Clarice that he had known from the first moment he'd seen her—that moment still so vivid in his mind—she was the woman he wanted forever in his life.

Oui . . . The thought was sometimes inconceivable, even to himself, considering the circumstances of their meeting and of their consequential relationship. But he had instantly seen behind Clarice's beautiful face and form to the soul that shone in her eyes. In doing so, he had also recognized that to speak of his desire then would have been disastrous.

For that reason, he had endured their relationship, telling himself she gave more to him than the other two who'd had previous claim to her—until he had seen the mark of rough handling on her flesh.

"You have approached Henri and Maurice?" Clarice gasped, "Pierre, what have you done . . . ?"

"Calm yourself, *ma chérie.* I know both men well, well enough to know they would understand if I spoke to them and explained that I was no longer willing to share you."

Pierre paused to assess the effect of his words. Clarice's breasts were heaving with a silent agitation that warned him to omit the fact that his conversations with both men had been heated, that it had taken much persuasion to convince them it would be best for all concerned for them to switch their affiliations to another woman.

Clarice shook her head, as if in denial of his words. "Madame will be incensed!"

"*Non,* she is not."

"You have already spoken to her, also?

"I have explained that Henri and Maurice will speak to her so she might arrange another situation for them, and have told her that I would adequately compensate her for any discomfiture she experienced."

"Pierre . . ."

Pierre prepared himself, drawing Clarice closer so he might not mistake her reaction as he whispered, "All this, *ma chérie,* only if you do not find distasteful the thought of centering your attentions on this one man alone . . ."

"Pierre . . ." Tears welled in Clarice's eyes. She managed a single word more. "Why?"

"Need you ask that question, *mon amour?*"

Clarice' trembling hand touched his cheek. He read the torment in her gaze as she hesitated, then responded softly, with innate honesty, "You are very dear to me, Pierre, but . . . I can make you no promises beyond the moments that I lie in your arms. I can only say that I will give you the best I have to give and give it gladly . . . for as long as I may."

Painful honesty.

Yet, knowing he could ask for no more, Pierre drew Clarice close. "*Cela suffit.* That is enough."

Pierre breathed deeply of Clarice's distinctive scent as it filled his nostrils, as he consoled himself that temporary commitment was enough until he might overcome her wariness, until he might court her so tenderly as to remove all uncertainty and distrust from her mind . . .

. . . and until he might supplant in her heart the unknown man she cherished there, whoever he proved to be.

The heated core of him expanding, Pierre drew back, his eyes locking with Clarice's tear-filled gaze.

Je t'aime, Clarice. I love you.

The words went unspoken as Pierre lowered his mouth to hers, as he sealed the loving declaration uttered only in his mind with a gentle kiss that grew in warmth, as he stripped back the fragile silk wrapper that shielded Clarice's flesh from his touch.

The kiss lingered. He pressed upon her another and another until their naked flesh met fully once more and he again possessed Clarice's body as he hoped to possess her heart.

Pierre whispered silently again . . .

. . . *Je t'aime.*

Rogan stared blindly out at the reflection of morning sun on the choppy sea. He continued to strain for control, although an hour had passed since he'd returned Gabrielle Dubay below.

Damn the little witch! He did not think he would ever forget the feelings that had surged through him as he'd turned to see her standing on the deck a few feet away, her glorious unbound hair blazing in the sun as the brisk breeze whipped it wildly, those enormous gray eyes wide, her fragile nightrail pressed so close against her slender body as to reveal every smooth, female curve to the eyes of all.

An emotion he dared not name swelled once more, and Rogan inwardly raged. He had seen the faces of his men as they stared at her. He had not needed the ability to read minds to know what they were thinking, for few of them had ever seen a woman as lovely as she before ... or one so tempting as she stood boldly before them in her revealing attire.

Oh, yes, he knew the dangerous Mademoiselle Dubay's game! She sought to incite a lust in his men that would leave them fighting between themselves ... a lust that she might use to her advantage to bend them to her will. What she did not know was that their loyalty to him had been baptized in fire and blood, that they had faced slashing sabers and cannon blasts in his service without flinching, and that they would sooner betray themselves than betray him or their ship.

That noble thought aside, Rogan paused.

He also knew that his men were human ... as human as he, who had been admittedly shaken by the sight of the beauteous *mademoiselle* standing clad in little more than her female glory.

Convent bred, was she?

Rogan laughed harshly. No innocent she, the glorious Gabrielle had undoubtedly spent her convent years well acquainted with the rear door and the liberties that exit afforded. He supposed he should be thankful for the dip and swell of the waves that had temporarily incapacitated her efforts to seduce his men, and the opportunity it had afforded him to nip the witch's plans in the bud.

Turning abruptly, Rogan snatched up the bundle lying nearby as he started for the staircase below. There had been time enough for the haughty miss to regain control of her stomach. In any case, he did not choose to wait any longer to face her, so agitated was he at the unanticipated problems she posed.

Standing at his cabin door, Rogan raised a hand to knock, then halted, startled by his own action. Knock on his own cabin door? Allow the woman behind it the victory of knowing he had surrendered that much claim to his own quarters?

Never!

His hand on the knob, Rogan twisted, the sharp click of sound registering clearly on the silence his only concession to the privacy of the woman within as he hesitated for a few, long moments, then pushed the door open. The silence continued, so complete that Rogan took a sharp step forward, only to halt abruptly at the sight of Gabrielle Dubay sleeping soundly on his bunk.

He pushed the cabin door closed behind him, then advanced toward her. She was in the deep sleep of exhaustion. One palm upflung against the pillow beside her head, her fiery hair a brilliant halo around the pale perfection of her countenance, the delicately smudged lace and batiste of her white nightrail framing an unexpected serenity of expression, she was the image of a fiery, if somewhat tarnished, angel.

An angel who, he supposed, could transport him to heaven if she so tried . . .

Rogan's heart began a slow pounding as he sat beside her. He took a burnished copper curl in his hand, smoothing the silky strand between his fingers. He had no doubt her skin was twice as soft and more luxurious than silk, for it was even more faultless upon close, extended scrutiny. He had not realized that the lashes surrounding those glorious eyes now closed, were so thick and of such a glowing color, or that those lips so delicately parted were of such a rich, warm hue. He longed to taste those appealing lips and he—

The lovely Gabrielle sighed in her sleep, sounding so lost and vulnerable that Rogan abruptly flushed at his wandering thoughts. What was wrong with him? Gabrielle Dubay was no more than a child—not yet eighteen to his twenty-nine years! She was not responsible for her father's crimes, and he—

Gabrielle stirred, halting the direction of Rogan's thoughts the moment before her eyes opened unexpectedly. The innocence on her beautiful face disappeared so completely as to turn Rogan's former thoughts to ash. Her celestial expression turned as frigid as the ice in her voice as she snapped, "Who gave you permission to enter my cabin?"

Anger replacing heat of another kind, Rogan responded, *"Whose* cabin, *mademoiselle?"*

"This cabin is mine by virtue of my installation here!"

"You err! Your use of this cabin is at my sufferance! You are my captive. The brig below is an alternative that may yet come into play."

"Despicable cad—"

"You err again, *mademoiselle.*" Rogan dismissed the former gullibility of his thoughts. This woman was not a child. Nor was she an innocent, for no innocent could possess so viperous a tongue.

He continued, his voice tinged with warning, "You would do far better to cultivate my good will than to alienate me, for I am aware of the reason for your visit to the main deck earlier."

"The reason?" Gabrielle surprised him with a sudden flush. "The reason was obvious. You display your ignorance in reminding me of my brief, uncontrollable lapse."

"Rot!"

"Pardon?"

Uncertain of his ability to control the inexplicable range of emotions the young woman was capable of evoking within him, Rogan stood up abruptly. Reaching for the bundle he had placed on the chair nearby, he threw it on the bed beside her.

"Put these on!"

"W-What?" Gabrielle glanced at the worn pants and shirt, outrage in her expression. "You expect me to wear these rags?"

"You *will* wear them, *mademoiselle.*"

"I will not!"

Rogan took a heavy step forward. "You will put them on, without hesitation, or I'll put them on you myself!"

"How dare you!"

"I dare . . ." Rogan's voice trailed away, only to return with new venom. "I dare because I will not have you torment my men with your virtual nakedness!"

"My nak—" The gray eyes snapped wide.

"I will not have you parade yourself before them in an attempt at seduction!"

"Seduction!"

Rogan's jaw locked tight. "This discussion is over."

"Get out!"

Ordering him from his own cabin! Rogan's anger was touched with a perverse amusement that soon faded.

"You have been duly warned, *mademoiselle.*"

"I said, *Get out!*"

The little witch's command rang behind him as Rogan closed the cabin door, then paused. Would she follow his orders?

The telltale tugging in his groin a silent reminder of the danger in his promise should she not, Rogan walked slowly down the passageway toward the staircase to the deck above.

The cabin door slammed closed behind the hateful captain as Gabrielle raged.

Her "virtual nakedness"?

How dare the arrogant wretch insinuate that she would attempt to *seduce* any of his grotesque seamen!

Gabrielle's rage soared to fury as she glanced down at the clothes lying on the bunk beside her. And how dare he believe—for a moment—that she would submit to his commands to don those inferior garments! No more than she would consent to wear the sandals of a slave.

Her feet taking that moment to prick her with a twinge, Gabrielle grimaced. Oh, damn cruel fate for reminding her of the error in excessive pride! She had suffered for it, and had already adjudged her decision to refuse those sandals an error.

Gabrielle touched the worn seamen's clothing tentatively. The cloth was coarse and stiff, but it appeared to have been freshly laundered.

You will put them on . . . or when I return, I'll put them on you myself!

He wouldn't!

Gabrielle paused to reconsider that thought.

Would he . . . ?

She recalled the overpowering strength of the arms that had swept her from her feet on the deck above and carried her downstairs to deposit her on the bunk, where she now sat.

A few more moments of contemplation drew her to her feet, and, with only a moment's hesitation, she pulled the stained nightrail up over her head. Intensely aware of her nakedness, she reached for the coarse shirt and slipped it on, then drew the baggy breeches up over the long lengths of her legs. She hiked the broad waist of the garment up around her own narrow girth and fastened the buttons determinedly.

All right, she was dressed.

Gabrielle dropped her hands to her sides.

Her breeches dropped to the floor.

Oh, damn!

She reached down to retrieve them only to suffer a sudden, queasy fit. No . . . not again . . .

An equally sudden spasm prompted her to abandon all other thought, other than to question what she had ever done to deserve such a wretched turn of events . . .

. . . as she raced for the basin in the corner . . .

. . . and the misery returned.

Rogan raised his spyglass to the horizon, scrutinizing the vast, rippling expanse of empty sea that he had similarly studied so many times in the past hour as to become totally disgusted with himself.

Coward . . .

His strong jaw twitched. How much time had passed since he had given the little witch below his ultimatum? One hour . . . two . . . three?

Who was it he was attempting to fool? He knew exactly how much time had elapsed! The afternoon meal had been served, and it would soon be time for another. And the little witch's tray had been returned untouched. Bertrand had informed him of that fact with a frown that was unusual, given his commonly unemotional demeanor. Rogan had not deigned to ask Bertrand if she had changed her clothing as he'd directed. Nor had he inquired as to her attitude, determined as he was that he would soon return below to determine those answers for himself.

He had decided he would accomplish that chore personally in order to instill in Gabrielle Dubay's mind the realization that it was *he* who was in control of her fate. Somehow he had not anticipated that the young woman would be so strong willed . . . or that he would find it so difficult to force himself to do what was necessary to impress her with the seriousness of her situation.

For the truth was, he could allow nothing to go wrong once in the Bay of Barataria. He need have her presence on his ship remain a secret so that no one would suspect Rapace was indeed the same Captain Rogan Whitney who was about to set all of New Orleans back on its heels with the series of notices that would follow Gerard Pointreau's capitulation to his demands.

Continued anonymity was essential to the safety of both his men and himself. It was not his desire to have the arrogant *mademoiselle* spend the entire time they lay at anchor in Barataria Bay bound and gagged, or locked up under special guard. He was only too aware, however, that the time was fast approaching when he would be forced to make the decision as to whether such extreme measures would be necessary.

They would arrive at the bay by nightfall. A few more hours . . .

A familiar torment returning unexpectedly, Rogan closed his eyes against the echoes of the cries of the dying, the booming of cannon, and the creaking groans that had preceded the *Venture*'s descent to the bottom of the sea. A familiar, bearded visage flashed before his mind.

This iron carries the brand of the letter P. *You may believe that it will mark you a pirate for all the world to see, but I tell you now that letter more accurately represents the name Pointreau, that of the man who will break you . . .*

Snapping his eyes open, Rogan turned abruptly toward the steps to the berth deck. He had spent three long, difficult years planning for the retribution that was at hand. He would not allow a tempting young woman just out of the schoolroom to distract him from his course to that end. She would cooperate, or pay the price.

"Why do you look at me like that, Marie?"

Manon raised her eyes to her maid's image, reflected beside hers in the mirror as the older woman stood in the bedroom doorway behind her. Seated at her dressing table, attired in a lace dressing gown that complimented her delicate features, Manon stiffened as Marie maintained her silence.

"Say what you're thinking. It annoys me to no end when you stare at me that way."

Limping into the room, the older woman came to stand beside her, and Manon steadied herself for what was to come. Marie knew her so well. Too well.

Marie spoke abruptly. "Have you told him?"

Manon's blood went cold. She stood up, abandoning her morning ritual, the creaming of her skin that maintained its youthful glow, the massage that kept the planes of her face taunt and firm, and the simple exercises she followed so meticulously—all so she might remain appealing to one man.

She faced Marie sharply. "You speak in riddles. You know I despise riddles.

"Have you told him about the child?"

Manon gasped.

"Manon . . ."—the older woman spoke softly—"you forget that I served your mother before I served you, that I know you almost as well as you know yourself."

"You're wrong!"

"I am not."

Manon's hand slipped to the stomach that was still flat and firm despite the child growing there . . . a child she had been unable to conceive with her dear Alexandre during the sweet years of their marriage . . . the child she had believed would forever be denied to her . . . Gerard's and hers.

"Does it show?"

"*Non,* not yet. But you know it soon will. You must tell him, Manon."

The heat that warmed Manon's eyelids emerged in a single tear that trailed down her smooth cheek. "I . . . I'm afraid, Marie."

The older woman did not respond other than to place a gnarled hand on Manon's as Manon continued, "I did not believe such a miracle was possible. I had believed myself unable to bring life into the world. I had accepted that circumstance as the will of God. When my monthly flow was interrupted, I did not believe there was a possibility of any cause other than the changes soon to come about at my age." Manon took another breath. "I am thirty-eight years old, Marie!"

"I know, my dear."

"It was only last week that I went to see Dr. Thoreau and I discovered the miracle had indeed happened, that I was going to have Gerard's child. I could not quite believe it was true, and when I finally accepted that reality, I wanted to rush out and shout my happiness to the world. But . . . but I could not."

"Manon—"

Manon glanced away, unable to bear the intensity of the older woman's gaze as she whispered, "Things have been difficult of late. The rumors of Gerard's attentions elsewhere—I would have paid as little attention to them as I have in the past had his attentions not seemed to be waning."

Manon paused to steady herself. "I was uncertain what to do. I did not want to speak to Gerard when there was the possibility that he would not be as happy as I at the miracle that has come to pass." Manon gripped Marie's hand tightly as she looked up at the older woman. "Then this terrible abduction of Gabrielle . . . Gerard was so upset."

Tears streamed down Manon's cheeks as she managed a shaky smile. "It is difficult for me to accept that such a terrible affair should have restored Gerard to me, but it has. He was tender and loving again as he has not been for many months, and I was able to give him the comfort he sought. But . . . but even as my happiness soared, I was afraid. Oh, Marie . . ." A sob escaped Manon's lips. "I could not tell him about the child when Gabrielle's safety is unknown. Gerard loves her so. I am afraid he would despise me if I did! And if Gabrielle is not returned—if Gerard should lose her—I am afraid he will resent the child even more."

Marie shook her silver head, confused. "*Non*, how could that be? Would a man not feel reassured to have another child soon to be born in such a case?"

"Not Gerard."

"But—"

"Not Gerard, Marie." Manon sobbed again. "Not Gerard."

Surrendering to the solace of Marie's frail arms as they slipped around her, Manon clutched the old woman close as she had not done since childhood. She whispered, "There is only one hope that Gerard will share my happiness, and that is if Gabrielle is restored to him."

"Manon, my child." Marie's voice wavered although her arms remained strong. "You must tell Monsieur Pointreau about the child . . . or you must leave him."

"Leave him!"

Marie's faded eyes held hers. "You must allow the instinct of one who carries new life, your voice from within, to guide you. If you do not feel safe in telling Monsieur Pointreau about the child, you must take appropriate steps to assure your own future and that of your child."

"*Non* . . . that isn't necessary. Not yet. I have prayed. I know Gabrielle will be returned to Gerard. She must. And when she is, and I am able to tell Gerard about our child, all will be well. You'll see. He will introduce me to Gabrielle at last—as an equal—and we will marry. Gerard will abandon his other pursuits then."

"Manon, you must not delude yourself that Monsieur Pointreau will—"

"Gerard will abandon his other pursuits then, I tell you!" Unaware of the shrillness that had entered her voice, Manon drew back from the old servant's arms, insisting stiffly, "Gabrielle will be returned to Gerard and everything will be well. I must be patient a little while longer, that's all. Just a little while longer."

Turning away from Marie's concerned gaze, Manon sat stiffly at her dressing table. Taking up a cloth there, she wiped away her tears, then picked up the cream she had abandoned earlier. Her expression set, her mind unshakable, she resumed her daily ritual.

Rogan stood at the door of his cabin. He waited, listening, uncertain of what he was listening for. What did he truly expect? The young woman within had had no choice but to follow his orders and don the clothing he had left for her, despite her protests.

You expect me to wear these rags?

He realized that the pampered miss had probably never worn such common cloth in her life—that her cossetted skin was probably a stranger to anything less than silk, satin, and the fine linens of the wealthy.

Her beautiful, cossetted skin . . .

Curtailing his wandering thoughts with the realization that he need maintain mental as well as physical distance from the young woman within if he were not to allow her the advantage she sought, Rogan rattled the doorknob deliberately. He waited a few calculated moments before pushing the door open.

As before, silence met his entrance.

And then a moan.

A pitiful moan.

Striding to his bunk, toward the male clothing piled atop it, he came to an abrupt halt at the realization that a slender figure lay dressed in the wrinkled heap of male clothing—a pale, wretchedly sick female who lay startlingly still.

"Mademoiselle Dubay . . ."

She did not respond. Neither did she appear to be breathing. Rogan's heart lurched.

"Mademoiselle . . ."

A flicker of heavy eyelids.

"Gabrielle . . ."

Another low moan.

Seated beside his pathetic hostage in a moment, Rogan silently cursed. He pressed his palm to her forehead to find a mild heat there. He touched her cheek, then her arms to ascertain if the same heat had begun to spread to her body. Satisfied that whatever fever had begun was still mild, Rogan spoke softly.

"What's wrong, Gabrielle? Are you ill?"

Those heavy lids again flickered, then rose to reflect the

acute misery within, and Rogan was strangely stricken. The
ship took that moment to rise on the crest of a wave, only to
fall sharply once more and Gabrielle Dubay's complexion
turned a revealing shade of green that spoke more loudly
than words.

Seasick . . . He had never seen anyone so badly afflicted.

Gabrielle raised a limp hand to wipe a bead of cold perspiration from her brow, only to have it fall weakly back to the
mattress beside her. He heard her whispered rasp.

"I'm dying . . ."

What?

Not realizing he had spoken the word aloud, Rogan saw
her weak gaze flicker, then heard her rattling growl.

"I said, I'm dying . . ."

"You are not. You haven't gotten your sea legs, yet. You
need something to eat and—"

"Eat?" Gabrielle's color worsened. "Vile beast . . ."

Rogan gritted his teeth. "Sit up, *mademoiselle.*"

The shake of her head was hardly discernible.

"I said, sit up!"

When there was no response, Rogan raised Gabrielle's limp
form to a seated position. He supported her with his arm,
noting for the first time how voluminous the seaman's attire
was on her slender frame when he almost lost her in the folds
of the shirt.

He instructed sharply, "Hold yourself up. You'll feel better
if you get some fresh air!"

"No . . ." Her eyes remained closed.

"Open your eyes." When there was no response, he insisted sharply, "Open your eyes!"

The beauteous gray eyes opened, only to cross weakly.

Rogan groaned.

"Stand up."

"No . . . can't."

"Yes, you can. Stand up."

Moving her to the edge of the bunk, Rogan slid Gabrielle
to her feet and propped her in a standing position.

Her britches slipped to her knees.

Jerking them back up to her waist with a quaking hand,
Rogan muttered a rare curse as he glanced around him, then
reached down to unfasten his own belt and wrap it around
her waist. He uttered a silent sigh of relief at the security afforded, ignoring the young woman's protests as he lifted her
up into his arms.

The heavy lids again fluttered. "Wh-What are you doing?"

"You're going up on deck for some air. You'll feel better
then."

"Won't work . . ." The arrogant *mademoiselle*'s head fell
limply against his chest. "Dying . . ."

Dying . . . ?

Rogan turned toward the door.

Moments later, stepping unsteadily into the battering of the
evening wind, Rogan met Bertrand's sober scrutiny.

"I'll help you get her to her feet."

Rogan shook his head. "No, go down and eat. If I need
you, I'll call you."

Rogan clutched his inert burden more tightly and turned
toward the rail. Propping Gabrielle up in a standing position,
her back against the wooden railing, he braced her with his
body. She trembled with weakness as he instructed, "All right,
take a deep breath."

"Can't . . ."

Her unbound hair whipped Rogan in startling streaks of fiery color that matched the brilliance of the setting sun in a
sky where dark clouds rapidly advanced in the distance. Her
head lolled against him as she turned her face into his chest
to whisper, "Please . . ."

A silent groan echoed somewhere deep within Rogan. The
warmth of her pressed so intimately close was incredibly
sweet as he spoke softly against her hair, "Listen to me,
Gabrielle. Night is coming and there are storm clouds in the

distance. The weather is going to worsen. If you don't get yourself in hand before it does, you'll be far more miserable than you are right now."

"Can't . . ."

"You can. Open your eyes, Gabrielle. Come on. Open them."

Her eyes opened slowly. Rogan waited until they focused before he whispered, "I'll make you well again."

An extended silence followed as Gabrielle held his gaze, as he willed his strength into her. A wave of hope swept him as her slender body grew gradually more erect, as she took a tentative breath.

"Another one . . . take a deeper breath."

So close was Gabrielle pressed against him that Rogan felt her breath feeding through her, sensed the temporary strength it afforded her . . . then her sudden, spontaneous spasm.

"No, don't give in to it. Your stomach is feeling better . . . stronger. You can control it and you're going to walk around the deck with me now."

"No . . . please . . . not yet."

Gabrielle leaned into him, and Rogan shuddered. Her head was pressed into the curve of his neck, her breasts against his chest, her trembling legs using his for support as she gripped his arm in a desperate attempt to delay him. Closing his arms around her, Rogan allowed her the comfort of his strength, obtaining a strange comfort of his own.

Uncertain how long they remained in that position, Rogan knew only that the desire to draw her closer was beginning to overwhelm him when he spoke at last, in a voice that emerged as an unexpectedly gruff bark of sound.

"You've rested long enough. You have to walk."

Those eyes . . . those incredible, light eyes turned up to his briefly before Gabrielle allowed him to separate from her. She attempted an unsteady step. It occurred to Rogan as he slid his arm around her, holding her erect as she took another step, then another, that her appearance was actually comical. With baggy pants and a shirt several sizes too large, a belt cinched around her middle to hold all together, and small, bare feet sticking out the bottom of britches meant to reach only to the knee, he knew he needn't worry that any man would give her a second look—any man but himself.

The sudden gust that struck the ship suddenly, rocking it with unexpected force, staggered Rogan even as his arm closed more protectively around Gabrielle.

But the damage was done.

Her panicked look the only warning, Gabrielle broke suddenly from his grip and raced to the rail. Right behind her, Rogan glanced up at a horizon that was rapidly blackening with storm clouds. He waited only until her spasms had ceased before sweeping Gabrielle up into his arms and heading for the cabin below.

The activity in the hallway beyond Clarice's bedroom door was growing more boisterous. Sounds of laughter, a few echoing grunts, footsteps coming and going ... coming and going. It occurred to Clarice as she closed her eyes and fought to sleep in her solitary room that she had not previously paid much attention to the traffic because she was usually deeply involved in affairs of her own.

This time, however, she lay alone beneath her satin sheets, clad in a revealing slip of lace that no one other than she could see, behind a door securely locked against the traffic moving past it—a situation that seemed unnatural, despite the fact that Pierre had spent the greater part of the day with her before he was forced to leave. Gabrielle remembered his frown when he'd said he must leave early because of a formal social affair he was to attend. She had wanted to tell him she understood that a woman of her occupation would not be welcome in the society where his presence was so eagerly sought, but she had sensed that would only exacerbate his disquiet.

Pierre . . . dear Pierre . . . driven to drastic measures by his anger at seeing the bruise on her thigh that Gerard Pointreau had caused when he had thrust her from him . . . Truly, she was uncertain how Pierre had sensed the truth, whether she had betrayed herself with a sideward glance or a flicker of the eye. She only knew she regretted the step Pierre had felt forced to take, simply because the situation could not possibly end well.

Clarice stroked back a pale wisp of hair from her cheek. She had spoken briefly to Madame. She did not know the actual sum Pierre had agreed to pay to keep her services exclusively his, but she knew it was formidable—so formidable that even if her plans would allow the affair full play, within a short time he would doubtless be forced to question so great a drain on his finances. He would then have no choice but to reconsider and surrender her to one additional patron, and then another. In doing so, he would feel his sense of integrity was compromised, and he would then suffer the need to surrender her completely.

Clarice considered with true sadness the thought evoked. Perhaps it would be for the best. It was time, after all, for Pierre to concentrate his time and finances on a woman who could fill his life with all the good things he deserved and who could take her place in the social circle in which he held so much prominence. It was time for him to begin thinking of providing the well-established Delise family with grandchildren to carry on their noble tradition in New Orleans.

That thought still lingering, Clarice admitted to a selfishness that declared, despite all, if she need serve the desires of any one man exclusively until she could belong solely to the man she loved, she was glad that man was Pierre.

A sudden blast of wind rattled Clarice's windowpanes, interrupting her thoughts as it pelted the glass with furious, rainy gusts. Glancing at the clock on her dresser as she had so many times since she had gone to bed, she realized it was past midnight. The fierce storm had ushered in a new day. The *Raptor* would suffer its rigors as she sailed to Barataria Bay—if indeed she had not already reached safe harbor there.

Two weeks . . . a few days more or less . . . and all matters would finally be resolved.

Uncertain of the emotion that thought evoked, of the reason for the sudden lump that rose in her throat, Clarice determinedly closed her eyes.

The cabin lamp flickered low as the *Raptor* rocked and dipped with the screeching force of the storm that battered her. Frowning as yet another blast of rain struck the porthole, as lightning streaked the dark sky beyond, and the storm's howling rage grew louder, Rogan cradled the silent woman lying on the bunk beside him in his arms.

His frown deepened as he looked down at Gabrielle, noting that her white, motionless face appeared even more pale and still in comparison to the rich color of the tangled hair streaming across her pillow. Her eyes were closed, exhaustion having claimed control—which was fortunate since the storm was at its crest.

Another lightning strike briefly lit the sea beyond the porthole and Rogan glanced up spontaneously. The giant palms of Barataria Bay were briefly outlined before darkness again prevailed. The ship was safely anchored and was presently riding out the storm as it had many times before.

Rogan recalled the haste with which he had shouted the series of orders that had brought the *Raptor* to rest in the billowing sea, and the fact that his mind had immediately returned to the cabin where he had left Gabrielle hours earlier. Leaving Bertrand behind to follow through, he had then made his way below.

Rogan's arms tightened spontaneously around Gabrielle's

still form as the ship dipped deeply once more, as he recalled the moment when he had pushed open his cabin door and glimpsed her lying on his bunk, steeped in her misery. Remorse for the deed that had brought her there had surged in him for the first time.

He had stripped off his oilskins then, pushed back his wet hair, and walked over to stand beside her. She had opened her eyes and looked up at him, too weak to speak. He had dropped to his knees to stroke her cheek, realizing the agony that held her in its grasp was only too real.

He recalled that she had muttered words too incoherent to understand when he had bathed her face and neck with a cloth, as he had moistened her dry lips, as he had stroked the damp tendrils at her hairline back from her cheek, barely resisting the temptation for his lips to follow the path his hand had cleared.

The storm had worsened, pitching and rolling the ship so wildly that Gabrielle had almost been tossed from the bunk, and he had sat beside her, leaning down to hold her secure on its surface. Then, when she had eventually fallen asleep, her body pressing spontaneously close for protection, he had lain beside her and taken her into his arms to provide her the safe harbor she had instinctively sought.

Rogan allowed his gaze to travel Gabrielle's still features. Silent, vulnerable . . . beautiful. She was his captive, his possession for as long as he cared to maintain his possession of her, and she was more . . . far more . . . than he had ever expected when he had first conceived his well-calculated plan.

Rogan stroked back another curling wisp of hair from Gabrielle's temple, then surrendered to the urge to brush the fine, white skin with his lips. It was cool. It was sweet. Too sweet to allow him to indulge in its confection without suffering an addiction he could ill afford.

Another lightning crack and the crash of another wave against the ship's hull raised a soft groan from Gabrielle's lips. Rogan drew her closer. Turning her toward him, he slid his arms around her, cradling her against him much as a mother would a child, but he felt no desire for a filial response. Instead, as Gabrielle's eyes flickered open briefly, he kissed them closed, her soft sigh touching a spot deep inside as she remained motionless under the caress of his lips.

Tempted . . . he was so tempted . . .

Gabrielle snuggled closer until the full length of her lay pressed against him, and Rogan mentally groaned.

A safe harbor . . . is that what he had thought?

No, not for the lovely Mademoiselle Dubay.

Not for the success of his plans.

And most certainly not for him.

No, not for him.

The truth of those words ringing abundantly clear, Rogan drew Gabrielle closer.

Chapter 4

It was hot. She was uncomfortable. What was that light?

Gabrielle stirred, hanging onto the edge of the oblivion that had so mercifully overwhelmed her when she had been able to bear no more of the storm's torment. Seeming unable to bring herself to complete wakefulness, she attempted to turn in her bed.

A frightening reality struck.

She could not move her legs!

Gasping with fright, she opened her eyes to see the light against her lids was the gray dawning of a new day. She stared at the shadow enclosing her . . . a shadow that weighed her down, holding her prisoner with its weight as it breathed slowly and evenly, bathing her face in its warm breath.

A shadow with warm breath?

Gabrielle gasped as full consciousness returned with shocking clarity.

She was hot because she was sharing the stuffy ship's cabin with another person!

She was uncomfortable because that person was in her bed!

She couldn't move her legs because that other person's long, heavily muscled leg was lying across hers!

And the shadow that enclosed her . . . weighed her down . . . held her prisoner with its weight as it bathed her face with its breath, it was, it was—

Gabrielle jumped up with a shriek! She was standing on the floor beside the bunk in a moment, stunned as the man in her bed sat up, his gold eyes suddenly alert as he demanded, "What's wrong?"

"What's wrong!" Gabrielle surveyed the strong features of the man who scrutinized her intently, unconsciously cursing him for his ability to shake her with his gaze as she rasped, "You know what's wrong! What are you doing in my bed?"

"*Your* bed . . ." The strong features hardened. "You seem to be confused this morning, Gabrielle."

Gabrielle . . .

She swallowed. Damn him! The man all but purred her name!

"I did not give you permission to use my given name, Captain!"

Swinging his feet to the floor, Rapace drew himself up to his full, towering height, dwarfing her in the way she so despised, but Gabrielle refused to give ground. She told herself it mattered little to her that the man's white, broadcloth shirt was unbuttoned to midchest, exposing a muscled expanse lightly peppered with dark hair in a way that drew her eyes relentlessly, or that the incredible expanse of his shoulders or the long length of his arms nudged somehow at memories that lay just beyond the range of total recall. Nor did she allow herself to be affected by her inability to keep herself from scanning the full extent of him, down to the tips of his stockinged feet, as he glared at her, passing britches that clung to his lean hips in a way she had not seemed to notice before and that outlined too clearly for comfort his long, muscular legs . . . one of which had lain so comfortably across hers.

As for the manly bulge so clearly outlined in those britches . . .

Gabrielle swallowed convulsively, then snapped her eyes back to his as he startled her with his reply.

"Oh, didn't you . . . Gabrielle?"

Didn't she what? Oh!

"No!" Humiliated as her voice emerged in a shocked squeak, Gabrielle cleared her throat, then repeated, "No, I did not give you permission to use my given name! Nor did I give you permission to use my bed, and I—"

Rapace's powerful arms snapped out unexpectedly to pull her against him. She was appalled at her inability to struggle free as he lowered his head to rasp in a voice that was half-growl, half-purr, "Are you sure of that, Gabrielle? Tell me you don't remember turning to me in your weakness. Tell me you don't remember inching nearer and drawing me close. Tell me you weren't satisfied until your body lay so flush against mine that not a breath lay between us."

"Liar!" Frustrated as she struggled to free herself to no avail, she snapped, "I was ill! I didn't know what I was doing!"

"So, you do remember . . ."

Did she? Gabrielle instinctively flinched. The pure, male scent of him, now so strong in her nostrils, prodded warm memories that still eluded her. The familiarity of those powerful arms holding her close jostled those memories more insistently. The lips that were so close . . . warm lips, gentle lips, caressing lips . . .

Oh, God!

"Let me go, you beast—you raptor! Rapace. You are well named, predator that you are, a man who forces himself on unprotected women!"

"Forces himself?" The full lips so close to hers tightened. "It seems you have a selective memory, choosing to forget that you sought my warmth, my touch, my consolation when—"

"I did not! I would not! You're a villain . . . a monster . . . a pirate! No debility could ever make me turn to you of my own accord! Nor is there anything you could do that might make me seek your touch!"

Rapace's lips were only inches from hers as he rasped, "Haven't you learned anything at all during these past two days? Have your feet healed too quickly to allow you to re-member that your own arrogance caused your pain?"

"*You* caused my pain by abducting me!"

"You didn't accuse me of causing your pain last night when you—"

"Liar, liar, liar!" Enraged as much by Rapace's words as by the strange emotions assaulting her as he continued holding her intimately against the hard, male length of him, Gabrielle rasped, "I tell you now, that despite anything you might ever say or do, I would never—*never*—seek your touch or feel any-thing for you other than revulsion!"

"Be careful what you say, Gabrielle."

"Your threats don't frighten me!"

"Perhaps they should."

"*Never.*" Hoping to negate the emotions surging in her, Gabrielle repeated with new heat, "You could never do any-thing that would make me seek your touch in any way!"

A low growl escaped Rapace as his mouth covered hers un-expectedly, stunning her into momentary motionlessness. His seeking kiss devoured her with a force that stole the breath from her lungs, consuming her in a way she had never before experienced as he separated her lips with his, then searched her mouth with a passion that left her quaking, awakening an unknown longing within her that she sought to deny.

Suddenly struggling with all her might, Gabrielle realized he was strong—too strong. There was no way she could fight him, except . . .

Her resistance halting, Gabrielle went limp in her captor's arms, causing him to draw back suddenly to search her face.

Gabrielle's small smile was cold. "I told you . . . nothing you could ever do would make me seek your touch."

"So that's the game you play."

Startling her, the captain jerked her flush against him once more, then lowered his mouth to hers. But this time his kiss was shatteringly sweet. The gentle persuasion lingered, mounting to passion as his kiss deepened gradually, as he sought out the honeyed hollows of her mouth, caressing them so sensually that she was almost beside herself when he finally tore his lips from hers to trace an erotic trail to the rise of her cheek, her temple, to the curve of her ear, pausing for long moments of exquisite torture on the lobe there. Remaining stiffly unresponsive by sheer strength of will, Gabrielle withheld a gasp as he wound his hands in her hair, tilting her head so he might follow the curve of her chin, the column of her neck. The rigidity she enforced was pain almost beyond endurance by the time Rapace released her with a suddenness that left her staggering.

His smile was cold.

"I accept your challenge, Gabrielle . . . and I promise you the day will come—much sooner than you think—when you will beg me to love you."

"Never, you odious wretch!"

"My dear Gabrielle"—the huskiness of the captain's voice sent little tremors down Gabrielle's spine—"you'll soon discover that 'never' is too small a word to come between us."

Holding her mesmerized with his gaze moments longer, the captain bent down to sweep his boots from the floor.

He then snapped the cabin door shut behind him, leaving Gabrielle silent and shaken.

Witch!

Rogan pulled the cabin door closed, then glanced around him at a corridor that was silent and empty. Suddenly aware of his appearance, he cursed.

What had gotten into him to make him leave his own cabin before he had even donned his boots?

Dropping them to the passageway deck, Rogan slipped them on with true disgust. He straightened up and ran a hand through his tousled hair, then scraped his palm against his stubbled chin.

Damn!

The response to his question was one he would have liked to deny, but could not. It could be summed up in a single word.

Retreat.

Caution . . . the better part of valor.

Yes, he need show caution, but he would be damned if he would allow that haughty little witch to back him down. What was it she had said, that he could never make her feel anything for him other than revulsion? He would see . . .

A telltale tugging in his groin signaling that he need set his mind in another direction, he turned toward the first mate's cabin just as the door opened. He met Bertrand's assessing gaze.

There was no need for explanation as Rogan barked more gruffly than intended, "I'll be up on deck shortly."

Waiting until Bertrand had disappeared up the steps onto the top deck, Rogan pushed his mate's cabin door open. In a few minutes he would be bathed and shaved and ready for the day to come. And it was an important day, one crucial to the success of his plan. He needed no distractions.

That thought firmly in mind, Rogan entered the cabin and drew the door closed behind him.

"Rapace, mon ami . . ."

Jean Lafitte extended his hand warmly and Rogan accepted it with a smile, walking forward as the Frenchman ushered him into the lavish brick and stone home on his small kingdom, the isle of Grande-Terre.

And a kingdom it was, with fifty ships under Lafitte's command, all flying the flag of Cartagena as they swept down on the shipping lanes to bring their prizes directly back to him at Barataria.

Lafitte's organizational hand had been obvious at first sight of the thatched cottages he had had erected for his men and their women, and of the gambling houses, cafes, and bordellos provided to keep his men amused. Even more impressive had been the huge warehouses built to house the plunder, and the barracoon wherein Negroes taken from captured slavers awaited purchasers at weekly slave auctions conducted at The Temple.

Rogan absent-mindedly recalled the moment he'd entered Lafitte's house for the first time. He had been silently astounded. The simple living quarters of Lafitte's men had left him unprepared for the luxury with which the Frenchman surrounded himself.

The finest of furniture from Europe, carefully arranged; crystal, linens, dinnerware, carpeting, all tastefully chosen; paintings of inestimable value; sculpture of undetermined origins—all selected with great attention to value and quality from the booty of raids too countless to mention—filled the mansion. Rogan had discovered that Lafitte, not one to suffer deprivation of any sort, had on his staff one of the finest chefs in Louisiana, as was evinced by the delicacies on which he dined daily and which he served his purportedly impressive list of guests when they visited from New Orleans.

Rogan supposed he should not have been surprised. Jean Lafitte was a legend in the city. So well known had he become that Rogan had sailed to the island fortress with a clear picture in his mind of the man referred to by his men as "Bos." The description had been impressive, for Lafitte had been rumored to be a man of considerable education and great personal charm who spoke English, French, Spanish, and Italian fluently. He was said to have become the center of any gathering of which he was a part without stirring the resentment of others, to have the ability to form friendships easily, and to instinctively inspire loyalty in the men under his command. He was said to be affable and possessed of great personal charisma.

It had not taken Rogan long to discover that all those things were true.

What had been spoken in whispers, however, were the tales

of Lafitte's sudden violent rages when thwarted, his cold ruth-
lessness that demanded respect from men who did not flinch
at the shedding of blood and who were more pirate than privateer.

Lafitte, the enigma, however, was also Lafitte the charmer.
Never was that more obvious to Rogan than at that moment
when the dark-haired, clean-shaven young Frenchman only a
few years older than he, and who stood almost eye to eye
with him, smiled broadly with welcome and signaled his servant to immediate service.

Satisfied only when his hospitality had been formalized by
the delicate crystal glasses of brandy both held in their hands,
Lafitte eyed Rogan with his particularly acute, dark-eyed
gaze.

"I have missed you, *mon ami.*" Lafitte winked companionably. "You may believe there are few on this island paradise
that we share to whom I may truthfully make that statement,
but I am surprised you have returned so soon, and with the
hold of your ship empty. Were the seas ungenerous to you
this trip?"

Too wise to lie to the man whose eyes and ears encompassed the entire Caribbean, Rogan shrugged. "I did not
leave Grande-Terre with the intention of another encounter.
My men are weary, and so am I. I had in mind a voyage that
might facilitate a visit to New Orleans . . . to a particular
woman in a house on Royal Street."

"Ah, *oui* . . ." Lafitte paused. "You must take particular
caution there for it is said that your 'particular woman' has
powerful patrons who would hold her exclusively for themselves. Should they learn you visit her regularly without their
knowledge . . ."

At the revealing narrowing of Rogan's eyes, Lafitte
laughed. "You need not concern yourself, *mon ami!* There is
only one person aside from myself who knows of your secret
dalliance with the lovely Clarice." He shrugged. "It was a
precaution I took when you first came to make application to

join our band. Rapace was well known, but the man behind that name was not, and Jean Lafitte is very cautious."

Rogan did not smile.

"Come, you must not be offended." Lafitte shrugged again. "I have not pried further into your life—as I would not have anyone pry into mine. I have satisfied myself as to your loyalty to our band, and that is enough. Now, what have you come to say to me?"

Rogan paused in response as he scrutinized the smiling Frenchman. Certainly, he should have known Lafitte would not accept him purely on his word, that inquiries would be made to determine his authenticity as a privateer in face of the governor's constant efforts to depose Lafitte from the kingdom he had established for himself. But Rogan had not considered that his connection to Clarice might be discovered. He wondered at the threat she suffered because of him.

Lafitte's smile slowly faded. He held Rogan's gaze intently as he spoke in a tone far softer than before.

"The woman holds a place of great importance in your heart."

Rogan hesitated, then nodded.

"I give you my word as a Frenchman that she never has, and never will, suffer danger as a result of my knowledge of your affiliation with her."

Rogan searched Lafitte's direct gaze, then nodded again.

"Now that we have settled that concern," Lafitte's smile returned. "What have you come to speak to me about, *mon ami?*"

Satisfied that Lafitte's promise was sincere, Rogan began slowly. "I've already stated the reason for my visit. I have sailed and returned with the hold of my ship empty for the simple reason that my men are tired. I know their temperaments well and see the need for a brief period of relaxation during which they might avail themselves of the entertainment that is offered on Grande-Terre."

Lafitte sipped his brandy. "Your concerns are well taken."

He frowned. "Gambi has again returned with his ship's hold full, having pressed his men past their endurance in the months past. I tell you now that the problems they have caused since returning to Grande-Terre are the basis for great concern to me, for I will not abide the shedding of blood between my own men."

His skin prickling at Lafitte's mention of the despicable Gambi, Rogan responded instinctively, "Nor will I tolerate the needless loss of the life of even one of my men."

Lafitte's gaze held his. "I am aware of your thoughts on the matter and know your words to be sincere. So, my response is that I hope you and your crew will find the relaxation you seek on Grande-Terre. When you are ready to sail again, we will talk. And you need not worry." He paused. "Your secret is safe with me."

A cold chill passed down Rogan's spine. "My secret?"

"*Oui,* but I caution you . . . as a friend. Clarice is an exceptional woman. The allure of such a woman, and the knowledge that she is tantalizingly yours but not *truly* yours, has caused many men to abandon good judgment in favor of passion, and has brought about downfalls too numerous to count. As Rapace, the raptor, you have caught the imagination of the people of New Orleans, which leaves you more vulnerable to identification than many of the other captains here. Caution, *mon ami* . . ."

Struck by Lafitte's intuitive perception and impressed by his obvious sincerity, Rogan drained his glass, placed it on the elaborate, decorative table in front of him, then extended his hand. His succinct expression of gratitude was reflected in the sober gold of his eyes.

"*Merci, mon ami.*"

Rogan was striding down the front steps of Lafitte's mansion, back in the direction of the boat waiting to return him to his ship, when the image of Gabrielle Dubay returned vividly before him.

. . . *The allure of such a woman, and the knowledge that she is tan-*

talizing yours but not truly yours, has caused many men to abandon good judgment in favor of passion . . .

Challenge him, would she?

Well, she would see . . .

That thought lingering, Rogan strode past the human rabble in his path on the way to the beach.

Damn, where was he?

Gabrielle paced the cabin that had become her prison at sea, glancing again toward the porthole, her only access to the world beyond.

She had spent a restless hour after consuming a breakfast of the same heavy porridge and greasy pork she had been served the previous day, restlessly awaiting Rapace's return. When she had tired as much of the waiting as she had of her own ineffectiveness, she had strode to the cabin door, determined to face the captain down once and for all, only to be startled to find a bearded, one-eyed cutthroat on guard.

There had been no arguing with the man. The harsh look in his one good, bloodshot eye, and his short, gruff command as he reached for the weapon at his waist, had turned her back into the cabin without another word.

The cabin door firmly closed behind her, Gabrielle had stood within for long moments, enraged. How dared the captain have abandoned her into the custody of the . . . the . . . degenerate outside her door?

That question had still been echoing in her mind when Gabrielle had paused, stunned at her own thinking.

How could the captain have abandoned her into the custody of the degenerate outside her door?

Had she lost touch with reality? Rapace was far more dangerous than that man for one, simple reason. That man was a lackey; Rapace was the devil himself!

Gabrielle sat abruptly on her bunk. Crossing her ankle over her opposite knee in an unladylike position that would have elicited dark frowns in the convent, she massaged her aching foot. It occurred to her that she need be grateful that her feet were presently causing her as little discomfort as they were, considering their condition the previous day and her present need to remain mobile. She also supposed she should be grateful for the calm seas that had dispatched her former stomach distress so completely as to relegate her hours of misery to little more than a disturbing memory. Somehow, however, she was incapable of experiencing even the faintest traces of gratitude.

Gabrielle groaned. She was truly in desperate straits. Physically, she had never felt more uncomfortable. The pitcher of cold water and the skimpy piece of soap provided had not allowed her to accomplish a toilette that left her feeling adequately clean after the previous day's physical agonies, despite her most stringent efforts; her hair had become so tangled and knotted due to the difficult circumstances she had suffered that simply to draw her fingers through it caused her pain; and she was still wearing the same, oversize clothing of some unknown seaman in which she had spent the last miserable day and night.

A glimpse in the small washstand mirror revealed that she looked little better than she felt, but even in that moment of total disgust, she realized that her unappealing appearance was the least of her present problems.

Turning abruptly toward the porthole behind her, Gabrielle moved to her knees to cautiously peer out through the dirty glass. She breathed an unconscious sigh of relief when the small portion of calm sea available to her view did not affect her stomach in any way, and concentrated instead on the narrow view afforded her.

It appeared that the ship was at anchor in a bay of some sort, the shore lined with huge palm trees. It also seemed that theirs was only one of several ships anchored there, for even with her restricted view, she was able to see at least four others—all flying the same flag as the *Raptor*.

Gabrielle's stomach clenched spasmodically. She did not recognize the flag, but she knew which country it represented. It was well known to all New Orleanians that the *Raptor* flew the standard of Cartagena, the unofficial banner of the privateers and the bloodthirsty, pirates of the Caribbean.

Which meant . . .

Gabrielle raised a shaky hand to her temple as reality dawned. Oh, God . . . Not only was she imprisoned on one of the most feared pirate ships in the Caribbean, but that vessel was now anchored in Barataria Bay! Which meant the island almost hidden behind the fringe of trees lining the shore could be no other than the pirate stronghold of *Grande-Terre* . . .

Gabrielle gulped. She closed her eyes against a familiar nausea welling, aware that tears were welling as well.

How could she ever hope to escape now?

Gabrielle indulged the horror of the thoughts that followed. She was still trembling in their wake when a sense of shame gradually invaded her fear. What was wrong with her? She had always prided herself on her resourcefulness, yet she had allowed herself to remain the captive of the villain, Rapace, for two days, without obtaining any information at all about his intended disposition of her.

Why?

Gabrielle stiffened. The answer to that question was clear. Despite her denials, she had allowed Rapace to intimidate her.

Also clear was the reality that she need face a number of basic truths squarely, without flinching, if she were to survive the ordeal presently under way.

The first was that as much as she disliked admitting it, she was totally under Rapace's control.

Second, although she was under his control, she was not totally without recourse.

Third, it was time to approach the problem unemotionally

and begin formulating that plan she had told herself she would originate.

Fourth, she could *not* formulate that plan without knowing what Rapace's intentions for her were.

And fifth, . . . She was right back where she had started.

Damn!

How could she possibly convince Rapace to tell her anything other than what he wanted her to know?

Rapace . . . What was his true name, anyway?

Gabrielle's stiff spine wilted.

Oh, why did Rapace have to be the kind of man he was? Why did he have to challenge her the way he did, so that she responded with such arrogance in her voice as to startle even herself? Why did he have to possess eyes that seemed to penetrate her soul? And why did he look at her the way he did, sending chill after chill coursing down her spine—chills unrelated to any emotion she had ever experienced before?

Despite the fact that she despised him for his actions, for the accusations he'd made against Father, and for the suffering both Father and she had endured because of him, she could not seem to erase from her mind the myriad feelings he stimulated within her when he crushed her to him so intimately, and when he—

A knock at the door startled Gabrielle from her thoughts, bringing her immediately to her feet beside the bunk. A second knock, and she gave the only response possible.

"Enter . . ."

The door opened to reveal the slim, scarred seaman, Bertrand. Somehow disappointed, Gabrielle raised her chin, noting the familiar container of medicinal salve he carried, even as she inquired stiffly, "What do you want?"

"I'm here at the captain's orders."

Gabrielle glanced automatically down at her feet, then back up to meet the sober seaman's pale-eyed gaze. "I'm fine. I don't need your help."

"Captain's orders, *mademoiselle*."

Captain's orders . . .

Gabrielle bit back the response that sprung to her lips. She gave it a second thought, then sat abruptly.

"All right."

It occurred to her that she had been less than gracious when Bertrand responded by kneeling beside her to repeat the procedure of the previous day. He did not speak as he turned up the soles of her feet and carefully examined the cuts there.

Gabrielle stared down at the honey blond hair on Bertrand's head, feeling more and more a shrew with each moment that passed as he tended so carefully to the cuts on her feet. Finally unable to abide the silence, she offered, "They're healing well. They hardly hurt at all, anymore. I suppose I have you to thank."

No response.

"Your name is Bertrand, isn't it?" She paused. "I heard the captain call you that."

No response.

Agitation entered Gabrielle's tone. "Did the captain order you not to speak to me?"

Pausing, the seaman looked up. She was somehow pained by her view of the ragged scar that distorted his features so savagely, drawing down the corner of one of his eyes and twisting the corner of his lips into a simulated snarl that was not reflected in his gaze. Her expression obviously betrayed her thoughts, and the seaman looked away abruptly.

"I'm sorry." Gabrielle touched his shoulder lightly in a spontaneous gesture. "I didn't mean to offend you."

No response.

"It's a cruel scar. I cannot imagine anyone inflicting such pain."

Bertrand went still. Gabrielle was uncertain of what to expect in the moment before he looked up again and then spoke in the level, emotionless tone that seemed to be characteristic of him.

"If that's true, *mademoiselle,* you are far more unacquainted with the real world than I am prepared to believe."

It occurred to Gabrielle in that moment that Bertrand was not a bloodthirsty pirate at all, but a young man who had suffered tragically. Her heart went out to him.

"I can only hope the person responsible has been made to pay for the damage done to you."

Bertrand paused. "So, you believe in retribution."

This time it was Gabrielle's turn to hesitate. She thought a moment, then shook her head. "No, not retribution. I believe in justice."

Bertrand's pale eyes searched hers a moment longer before he stood up and turned to leave.

Startled at the abruptness of his departure, Gabrielle called out, "Wait!" And when he turned back to her, "I . . . You can't . . ." She halted, her next words emerging in a rush. "I'm not even certain where we are! What is happening? Where is the captain? What does he intend to do with me?"

No response.

"Please . . ."

"The captain will return soon."

And then he was gone.

In the silence that followed, Gabrielle bit her lip to hold back tears.

Rogan stepped down onto the *Raptor*'s deck and turned toward Bertrand. He nodded in response to his first mate's inquiring expression.

"It went well, but Lafitte . . ." Rogan paused, then continued, "Lafitte knows of my connection to Clarice."

The anxiety that flashed briefly in Bertrand's expression indicated the depth of his shock and concern, both emotions Rogan attempted to allay as he continued. "His supposition, however, is false. He believes I'm romantically involved with her and warned me of the danger of an affair with a woman whose services are reserved by high-ranking city officials. He guaranteed that his knowledge of my involvement with her did not constitute any danger to her, and that it never would. I believe him."

"Lafitte means what he says now, but what will happen when he learns that you lied to him to further your own ends?"

"I'm sorry, Bertrand." Those words never more heartfelt, Rogan continued softly, "I would not put Clarice in danger for any cause."

He shook his head as if to negate the thoughts that followed, continuing, "But we cannot go back. We can only go forward. I give you my word that I will assure Clarice's safety *before* this affair is brought to an end. But if that doesn't adequately satisfy your concerns for her"—Rogan hesitated again—"I'll release you from your duties immediately so you may take steps of your own."

He awaited Bertrand's response. His relief was boundless when, after a few moments, it came.

"I have no doubt that you'll protect my sister with your life, just as she protected us both. If I'm to help you do that, the best place for me is here, where I'll be most effective."

Rogan nodded, then scrutinized the deck around him. "It appears the rest of the crew followed me ashore as planned."

"Aye, sir. Only six remain aboard—six of your most loyal men. You may rest assured they'll let no one steal aboard ship in your absence, and that they take their watches at Mademoiselle Dubay's door very seriously."

"Who took the first watch?"

"Dermott, Captain."

Dermott . . . Dermott lost his eye in the attack on the *Island Pearl*. He had bitter memories of that night and of the bloodridden hours that followed. He was unshakably loyal. In this instance, he was invaluable for another reason as well. His appearance was terrifying.

"And Mademoiselle Dubay?"

"Dermott reported that she came to the door one time, but that he dispatched her back inside."

Rogan sneered. "I have no doubt that Mademoiselle Dubay wasted no time in closing the door behind her."

"So Dermott reports." Bertrand continued, "Mademoiselle Dubay's feet are healing well."

Rogan grunted.

"But she is very anxious. She wanted to know where you were. I think she wants to talk to you."

Rogan stiffened. "Does she?"

"Yes."

"Well, she can wait. We have more important matters to discuss—such as an escape route should one become necessary." Motioning Bertrand to follow, Rogan climbed up to the quarterdeck and grasped the maps rolled in an oilcloth sheet there. He unrolled them carefully and searched the well-memorized lanes, even as his mind added with great satisfaction, Yes, she can wait.

Jean Lafitte scrutinized the messenger standing so tentatively in his parlor doorway—the bearer of Gerard Pointreau's letter. The slender, nervous fellow watched him with the wary fascination of a bird for a snake.

The analogy amused Lafitte, but he did smile, aware as he was that the agitated fellow would probably relate every detail to his wealthy and powerful employer.

Lafitte's thin face twitched revealingly. In the past, Pointreau had made it known that he was one of the few of New Orleans' wealthy gentry who chose not to deal with "the pirate, Lafitte."

Lafitte's annoyance surged. He was not a pirate. Nor had that been his intention when he and his brother, Pierre, his senior by only a few years, had left the service of Napoléon and come to New Orleans by way of the Indies. He recalled that his even-tempered brother and he had arrived in New

Orleans at the time of the Louisiana Purchase and the changes that followed, but they had learned early on that the uncertainty of supplies from the mother country during French Colonial days had rendered smuggling a necessity of existence for the city, and that smuggling was an accepted way of life. He had not found it difficult to fit in with that way of life or with the Creole gentlemen of the city after establishing a blacksmith shop on Royal Street that Pierre still operated as a blind for their smuggling activities.

He had prospered, had opened a fine store in addition to the blacksmith shop, and had entertained lavishly at his mansion on Bourbon Street. He had made many friends and had become well accepted at the nightly discussions of merchants and gentry in the cafes and coffeehouses of the city.

It had all eventually paled, however, and he had been somehow ready for something more when he'd become informed on the slipshod manner in which the pirates and privateers, those with whom he dealt in his smuggling activities, conducted their affairs. When the law prohibiting importation of slaves into the United States was passed, a new element and the possibility of astronomical profits was added to the smuggling activities at Grande-Terre that increased the discord on the island to the point of open warfare. He had clearly seen that a guiding hand was needed to prevent the collapse of the establishment at Barataria Bay. He had also seen that his time had come.

Lafitte's aristocratic face tightened. But he was not a pirate. Pirates attacked any vessel at sea, regardless of the sovereign power it represented. Not so he or his men. On taking control at Grande-Terre, he had insisted the captains under his command obtain legitimate letters of marque from Cartagena, the Colombian seaport at war with Spain, and that they adhere to the documents they signed by attacking only Spanish ships.

Spain . . . the inquisition . . . Lafitte's hatred soared. He had been at war with Spain all his life. He knew he always would be.

But he was not a pirate, and Pointreau's motives had been obvious to him from the start. Governor Claiborne was extremely appreciative of Monsieur Pointreau's financial sacrifices in refusing association with him. The governor had shown his appreciation to his good friend and advisor over the years by granting him special favors and a prestige that Pointreau obviously enjoyed more than the profits he would gain in dealing with the man he so defamed.

Prestige instead of profits?

Lafitte paused. That had never sat well with him.

Non, he did not trust Pointreau.

And if all he had heard about the man's night prowling in the seamiest of New Orleans bordellos was true, despite the mistress he maintained on Dauphine Street—a very beautiful mistress—then he trusted the man even less.

Lafitte wondered which side Pointreau would choose to present in this letter he held in his hand, delivered to his door by the nervous messenger standing in front of him.

Arriving with it was the news that all New Orleans was said to be talking about, the abduction of Pointreau's daughter from the convent where she resided.

Pointreau's very lovely and innocent daughter . . .

H'mmmm . . .

Opening the missive slowly, intensely aware of the scrutiny of Pointreau's messenger, Lafitte read:

Monsieur Lafitte,

I seek permission to visit you on Grande-Terre regarding a matter of extreme urgency.

I am aware that Governor Claiborne has been the greatest obstacle in the path of your accepted legitimacy in New Orleans. I recognize that my longstanding close association with the governor has formerly put us on opposing sides. However, I believe the time has come to put the past aside. As an inducement, I will add that a meeting between us will prove mutually and extremely beneficial.

The need for complete confidentiality is imperative. A prompt response is essential. My man has been instructed to await your reply, which he will deliver immediately to me.

I await your response with great anticipation.

Most sincerely,

Gerard Louis Pointreau

H'mmm . . .

Lafitte looked up unexpectedly to see that Pointreau's messenger was perspiring heavily although the temperature was unseasonably cool. He questioned sharply, "What instructions did your master give you regarding the disposition of my response?"

"Monsieur Pointreau instructed me to return immediately to New Orleans with your reply."

"What else did he say?"

"He said . . ."—the fellow took another anxious breath—"he said a delay could easily cost me my life."

So . . . Pointreau was desperate. Evidently the rumors of his daughter's abduction were true. Lafitte's brow arched as he considered that thought. Surely the man did not believe Lafitte had kidnapped his daughter. He had no need for such a complication in his otherwise smooth-running organization. No, Pointreau needed something from him . . . and needed it desperately.

Making a snap decision, Lafitte turned to his desk. He scribbled a quick reply on a piece of paper there, then sealed the missive and turned back to the waiting messenger.

"Take this back to your master."

Obviously grateful to be dismissed, the messenger was gone in a moment.

Lafitte contemplated the matter further.

Gerard Pointreau . . .

He didn't like the man.

He didn't trust him.

But he so looked forward to an encounter between them . . .

. . . at last.

Gabrielle pushed aside with disgust the tray delivered to her door a few minutes earlier. The sight and smell of the food repelled her. Some type of smoked meat again, as had been delivered at noon, and beans. The thick slice of bread lying beside the plate was of a coarse texture that she would never have tolerated at the convent—common fare that no one would have dared serve her there.

But this was not the convent, and the choice was simple. Eat or go hungry.

She would say she chose to go hungry, but the truth was, she had surrendered her appetite to an agitation that grew stronger by the minute.

Gabrielle raised her chin and glanced briefly at the sky visible through the porthole. It was getting dark, and the damnable Rapace still had not returned!

Gabrielle paused to correct that thought. Oh, he had returned to the ship, all right! She had heard his voice. It was impossible to miss that deep, rolling tone of authority. She had heard it over and over again—on the deck above her, in the passageway, and in deep conversation in passing the cabin door. She had waited each time, holding her breath expectantly, only to hear his step stride past . . .

. . . again . . . and again . . .

. . . and again.

Damn him! What was he trying to do? Drive her insane with waiting? Didn't he realize she was totally cut off from everybody and everything because of him—that his men had no sympathy for her situation and that she was desperate to discover what he was going to do with her?

Gabrielle's raging thoughts came to an abrupt halt. Of course, he realized ... He knew exactly what he was doing. He was in complete control of the situation, and he was making sure she realized it.

Villainous scourge that he was ... blackguard ... heartless beast.

A step at the door.

Gabrielle held her breath at the sound.

She watched the knob as it rattled, then slowly turned and the door opened.

Rapace.

Rage transfused Gabrielle at the sight of him.

Damn him for standing there so tall and powerful in the doorway, so unrelenting with his dark hair glinting in the meager light, his strong features unsmiling, his golden gaze intent, *and* with his fresh, white shirt open to midchest, casually exposing his muscles in a way that drew her gaze and stirred faint memories of the night past!

He looked so ... so ... healthy! His skin was freshly tinted with a golden hue by the sun, and he looked robust, as if the fresh sea air and the vigorous activity of the day had lent him new strength!

While all the while she had been rotting in a sweltering cabin, with hardly a whiff of fresh air. Wearing the dirty cast-offs of some unknown wretch.

Yes ... rotting!

Gabrielle took a deep breath, then demanded, "How dare you!"

Rapace took a step into the cabin and pushed the door closed behind him. His expression tightened into menace.

"How dare I? I dare easily ... anything I wish to dare."

"Oh, I have no doubt you do, Captain *Rapace!*" Gabrielle's tone was scathing. "You dare whatever you care to dare because you are a villain of the lowest degree, a man with no feeling for others, one who chooses to use the excuse of vengeance for some imagined wrong to cloak his atrocious acts!"

"Imagined wrongs?" Rapace's features sharpened. "Believe what you will. It's of little concern to me."

"I suppose that's the crux of it, isn't it?" Gabrielle took a step forward. "You have no concern for anyone or anything other than yourself and your personal gratification! You—"

"I'm not interested in your opinion of me, Gabrielle."

She gritted her teeth as his soft pronunciation of her name sent familiar quivers racing down her spine. He moved toward her, only to stop when he saw her tray lying untouched on the table nearby. She saw the twitch of his lips as he demanded, "Why haven't you eaten?"

"I'm not hungry."

"You're behaving like a child!"

"I'm not hungry!"

"You *are* hungry. You sent your afternoon tray back untouched, also."

"So your spies tell you?"

"I have no need for spies. Everything that happens on this ship is my concern, and nothing escapes me. You are no more or less important to me than any portion of this ship's rigging, but I tell you that as each piece of rigging is essential to the smooth operation of this ship, I see to its care. And for that reason, I will not allow you to abuse yourself in some misdirected attempt at vengeance on me!"

"Vengeance? I? No, you err, Captain. You are the expert on vengeance. I have no thoughts in that regard."

"Then why do you abuse yourself?"

"I do not!"

"You refuse to eat!"

"I'm not hungry!"

"You are!"

Pushed beyond the limits of her control by the agitation that had simmered within her throughout the day, Gabrielle leaped angrily forward to pound with all her might at the chest partially bared by that damned white shirt, shouting furiously as she did, "I'm not hungry, I said! I'm not hungry! I'm not hungry!"

She was still shouting when Rapace's strong arms snapped around her, containing her fury with their strength and holding her motionless as she squirmed and fought and screamed out her rage.

She was uncertain of the exact moment when her fury turned to despair, when her shouts turned to sobs, when her pounding fists began clutching and she grasped that damned white shirt that so taunted her. She was unsure of the point when the captain's restraining grip grew gentle, and when the gentleness became a caress. Instead, she heard only the softness that tempered a voice formerly hard and cold as Rapace whispered, "Don't, Gabrielle. It wasn't my intention to make you cry."

Crying? She wasn't crying.

"I'm not crying."

"Gabrielle . . ."

"I'm just angry—frustrated."

"And hungry."

"No, I'm not hun—" Gabrielle looked up sharply into Rapace's face. She whispered, somehow unable to manage the rancor intended, "For the last time, I'm . . . not . . . hungry."

"All right."

The captain's full lips twitched. She remembered those lips—the taste of them. She . . .

Oh, dear.

The captain continued, "But if you're not hungry, what's wrong?"

"What's wrong?" Gabrielle stared. How could this great, handsome, overwhelming man be such an idiot? "I want to go home!"

Rapace stiffened. "Not yet."

"When?"

The captain's eyes narrowed. "When you father meets my demands."

What do you want? Money? My father will pay you anything you want!"

"I don't want your father's money!"

"What, then?" Reacting spontaneously to the thought as it occurred to her, Gabrielle pushed aside the white shirt so close to her cheek, grimacing as the scar was revealed again to her eyes. "Surely, even if you claim my father did this to you, you aren't expecting to brand him in return?"

Rapace's gaze burned into hers. "My demands are not that primitive."

"What are they?"

The piercing, gold-eyed stare searched hers. Gabrielle saw a softening there as Rapace whispered, "You wouldn't understand." And at her protest, "Gabrielle, in truth, were I able to attain the justice I seek any other way but to keep you here—"

"You can!"

"No, I can't."

Sensing the resolution in that response, feeling the situation slipping away from her, Gabrielle pressed unconsciously closer to the strong body supporting hers, "You say you have no choice but to keep me here. Where *is* here? Where do we lie at anchor?" She swallowed convulsively, then answered her own question. "W-We're in Barataria Bay, aren't we? And that island I can see through the porthole is Grande-Terre."

"Yes."

Managing to restrain the sob that rose to her throat, Gabrielle rasped, "You *are* a pirate!"

"No."

"Yes. You are."

"Gabrielle . . ."

Drawing her the few steps to the bunk nearby, Rapace sat abruptly and pulled her down onto his knee. Slipping his arms around her, he held her seated comfortably there as she turned to scrutinize his sober face. It was so close. She felt the warm breath she remembered so well brush her cheek as the captain whispered, "I don't expect you to understand when I tell you that your father isn't the man you think him to be . . . or that I'm not the man Rapace is supposed to be. I can only tell you that this game, now begun, must be played to its conclusion if justice is to be finally served. When your father meets my demands, you will be returned to him as promised." Rapace frowned. "Whatever changes then follow will not be due to my machinations. Instead, they will be due to your father's."

Gabrielle hardly breathed. She could not move. The overwhelming aura of this great, mysterious man seemed to envelop her. His words gave her little consolation, but his voice was so gentle, and his eyes . . . The burning warmth in them lit a spot of heat within her that she—

Oh, God! What was wrong with her?

Bringing herself abruptly back from the mindlessness that had temporarily overwhelmed her, Gabrielle asked abruptly, "What will you do if Father refuses to meet your demands?"

She felt the captain slowly stiffen. Implacability returned to eyes that moments earlier had simmered with an inner glow. "He'll meet them."

"But—"

"Gabrielle, you've made it clear that you don't want to eat. Other than go home, what do you want to do?"

Uncertain why that improbable question, asked by the man who had turned her life upside down, had terrified her and infuriated her, caused an almost debilitating thickness to clog her throat, Gabrielle responded, "What do I want to do right now?"

"Yes."

"I want to go up on deck so I can breathe again."

A flicker of something akin to pain moved across Rapace's face the moment before he raised her to her feet, then stood beside her. His voice husky, he whispered in return, "All right, but I warn you if you call attention to yourself in any way, if you cause anyone on the ships nearby to become aware of your presence here, you'll suffer greater danger than you do here. Do you understand, Gabrielle?"

She nodded. Not quite believing what was happening, she saw the captain draw open the door and speak a few words to the swarthy, dangerous-looking fellow without. Taking her arm, he then ushered her into and down the passageway. They were climbing the stairs to the main deck when the captain stopped her and turned her toward him. Standing a few steps above him, she was face to face with him as he scrutinized her with his piercing stare for a long moment, then cautioned, "Remember what I said, Gabrielle."

Stepping up onto the open deck moments later, the cool sea air of dusk gently battering her, Gabrielle breathed deeply. A sense of exhilaration filling her, she started toward the rail, finding the captain's presence beside her strangely comforting. The sea was beautiful . . . the air fresh and clean. She felt so . . . so . . .

If only . . .

Her hands on the smooth, worn wood of the ship's rail at last, the gentle whitecaps of the ocean spread out for her view glittering in the last, fading light, Gabrielle turned to look up at the man standing beside her, words emerged without conscious intent.

"I don't like calling you Rapace. What is your real name?"

Hesitation.

Then a flicker moved over the strong features of the man looking down at her.

"My name is Rogan."

"Rogan . . ."

Suddenly at a loss, Gabrielle turned back to the sea.

His name softly whispered, hung on the balmy, twilight silence of the salt air as Rogan remained stunned by his response to Gabrielle's unexpected question.

How had this unpredictable young woman broken his resistance down to the point where he had actually told her his name?

Uncertain, Rogan watched as Gabrielle continued staring out across the dusky sea. Her delicate profile etched against the misty semilight was a cameo that was all the more exquisite for its contrast with the long unruly hair lifting gently from narrow shoulders enveloped in a shabby, oversized male shirt.

Gabrielle Dubay, adopted daughter of Gerard Pointreau—he must have been insane to allow her to penetrate his defenses, even for a moment.

Rogan again considered that thought.

But it had almost been worth the lapse to hear Gabrielle whisper his name in that husky tone that was all her own.

Rogan . . .

Gabrielle took that moment to flash him a smile that was unexpectedly shy, and a slow heat flushed through Rogan. He watched as she turned to survey the horizon, then the flickering lights of Grande-Terre.

"Most of the men have gone ashore, haven't they?"

Rogan nodded. Her scent, intrinsically feminine, yet hers alone, seemed to light a fire under his skin as he responded, "Just a skeleton crew of my most trusted men remains."

Gabrielle's light brows knotted. "You mean like the man who was posted outside my door most of the day."

"Dermott, yes."

Gabrielle did not immediately respond. When she did, her tone was cautious. "What would he have done if I hadn't gone back into the cabin when he told me to?"

"What do you think he would have done?"

Rogan felt the shudder that moved down Gabrielle's spine. He didn't like sensing her fear. The justice he sought had nothing to do with frightening a young, beautiful woman who was innocent of any of Pointreau's crimes. But caution nudged him, even as he offered, "You don't have to be afraid of Dermott or of any of the men guarding you. You're safe with them . . . as long as you don't try to escape."

Gabrielle turned toward him unexpectedly, her expression intently sober. "Did you tell your men not to talk to me?"

"Why do you ask?"

"Why don't you answer?"

"No, I did not."

"Bertrand is . . . is nice, isn't he?"

Rogan grew wary. "Yes."

"He was very kind."

"But he wouldn't talk to you."

"No."

"What did you want to talk about?"

Gabrielle shrugged. It was a disconsolate gesture that somehow betrayed a vulnerability he was certain she did not wish to convey. It made him want to hold her . . . console her.

The danger in those thoughts too obvious, Rogan still could not resist saying, "Bertrand isn't much of a conversationalist." He repeated, "What did you want to talk about?"

"I don't think that's important anymore."

"Because I answered your questions."

"Some of them."

"Do you have any others?"

"Are you ever going to tell me what the conditions are for my return?"

"Perhaps."

Gabrielle regarded him intently. He was uncertain as to what she was thinking when she asked abruptly, "What's it like on Grande-Terre?"

"It's no place for anyone like you."

"Like me?"

"The nuns wouldn't approve."

"The nuns wouldn't approve of your abducting me, either."

Rogan stiffened. Crafty little witch, turning his own words back on him.

"I think it's time to go below now."

"Not yet . . . please."

"Are your testing me?"

"Just a little while longer." Gabrielle's clear eyes searched his face with an almost palpable touch. "I'd like to walk a bit."

Somehow unable to refuse her, Rogan took her arm and started walking slowly. He felt her relief, but he didn't expect her smile—a beautiful smile that hit him hard for all its brevity.

It occurred to him belatedly, after an inestimable time had passed and darkness had fallen, that Gabrielle had manipulated him well with that smile. Seeking to restore his former control, he stated with no room for discussion, "It's time to go below."

Surprising him, Gabrielle did not resist.

Drawing her into the curve of his arm, Rogan guided her toward the stairs.

Yes, it was getting late. He was tired.

It was time to go to bed.

"Quickly, Marie! My combs!"

Manon turned back to the dressing table as Marie limped to the dresser to fetch the jeweled combs she had thrown there a short time earlier. She saw the agitation in her old servant's lined face as she took the combs in hand.

"I will hear none of it, Marie!"

Effectively forestalling the comment she had sensed was about to emerge from Marie's tight lips, Manon turned back to the glass and surveyed her image critically. She expected Gerard at any moment, and she was not yet prepared to receive him.

Another wave of nausea swept over her, raising a light veil of perspiration to her brow, and Manon paused for a steadying breath. Gerard had not said he would be coming by, but she knew he would. The need that Gabrielle's abduction had fostered within him had already brought him to her door earlier that day with no other excuse but to spend a few minutes talking with her.

A nagging discomfort unrelated to her physical distress nudged her briefly, and Manon frowned. She had held Gerard's hand and had whispered the reassurances he'd wished to hear as he had confided his plan to involve Jean Lafitte in the rescue of Gabrielle. She had not dared to state her true thoughts on the matter, that for Gerard to involve himself with Lafitte in any way was a mistake, for she had known instinctively that to do so would be to tamper with his tenuous control. She had hoped for an opportunity that evening to caution him, and she had been at her best an hour earlier, awaiting his arrival, when the nausea had returned.

And with it had come panic.

Manon dabbed nervously at the perspiration on her brow. Under any other circumstances, Gerard's unexpected visits would have thrilled her and filled her with new hope for the future, but she dared not allow even a hint of her condition to show. That thought had exacerbated her agitation as she had bowed to the rigors of her condition only minutes earlier, during an attack so severe that when the retching was through, she had been forced to strip off her carefully chosen gown, to refresh herself anew, and to begin all over again.

She was wearing yellow now, a batiste that Gerard had once commented was extremely flattering. But she had not yet recuperated, and her color was still ghastly. As for her hair . . .

"Marie . . ." Her hands trembling, Manon pinned the last blond curl up from her neck and inserted the delicate comb, then turned toward the silent woman behind her, pressing, "Do I appear ill in any way? Perhaps more color on my cheeks?"

"*Non. Vous êtes trés belle.*"

Tears unexpectedly filled Manon's eyes. She supposed she

would always be beautiful to Marie. Standing up abruptly, she slipped her arms around the older woman and hugged her tightly. Speaking in response to the thoughts the older woman withheld, she whispered, "All will be well, you will see."

The sound of a key at the front door halted Manon's words. Stiffening, she glanced one last time into the mirror, then turned toward the door. She met Gerard in the hallway. She sighed as his arms slipped around her, and she separated her lips to his kiss. The kiss was desperate, and Manon knew Gerard would waste no time with words that night.

Swept back through the bedroom that she had just left, Manon noted unconsciously that Marie had managed to disappear from sight in Gerard's presence, as was her usual tack. Gerard kicked the bedroom door closed behind them, then slid his hand into her hair to grip the pale strands roughly, causing the combs she had so carefully placed moments earlier to fall to the floor. His kiss savage, he crushed her close, demanding and taking what he did not wait for her to offer. She heard the delicate batiste tear as he stripped it from her shoulders, then pushed the bodice to her waist to expose her naked breasts.

Manon gasped aloud as Gerard slipped to his knees before her to cover the aching crests with his mouth, as he drew from them with increasing passion, fumbling at the closure on her dress until he had stripped it to the floor. Dragging her from her feet as his passionate attack raged, he forced her down on the carpeting, loosening his britches to thrust his burgeoning member within her painfully, without preamble.

Manon gasped, fear and passion mingling with physical discomfort as Gerard pressed his tempestuous assault. Her muttered protest was halted as Gerard pressed himself full upon her to rasp into her ear, "Make me forget, Manon! Make me forget as only you can—now . . . now . . . now!"

Accompanying his words with deep, penetrating thrusts, Gerard moved deep and full within her as Manon's fear yielded to compassion and she wrapped her arms around him, abetting his penetration. Incredulity soared. Could it be true? Was Gerard acknowledging his need for her at last? Was this terrible affair with Gabrielle really a blessing in disguise that would force Gerard into a commitment before the truth about her condition was revealed?

Abandoning herself to the heated fury of Gerard's lovemaking, Manon met his thrusts. She joined in the rhythm of his increasing fervor until all thought was erased but the furor within that erupted in a final rasping cry that echoed Gerard's own as he shuddered to climax within her.

Holding Gerard close as he lay spent and still upon her, Manon gloried in the culmination of the love they had shared as pictures of the glorious future that would soon be theirs flashed across her mind. Gerard and she would—

Manon was unprepared as Gerard withdrew from her abruptly and sat back, then drew himself to his feet without a word. She watched as he adjusted his britches and turned toward the bedroom door.

No . . . not again . . .

Lying naked on the bedroom floor, her hair askew and the clothes she had so carefully donned earlier lying in a rumpled heap beside her, Manon felt the cruel edge of humiliation cut deeply. She knew it was useless to call out when Gerard pulled the door open and stepped into the hall, then snapped the door closed behind him.

The decisive snap of the street door closing moments later was overwhelmed by the sound of Manon's tears.

A strange inner trembling beset Gabrielle as she descended the stairs to the berth deck and began walking back down the passageway toward the captain's cabin.

Rogan . . . Somehow she sensed he had not lied when he had told her his name, just as she sensed that the revelation was a concession he made to very few.

Arriving at the cabin door, Gabrielle hesitated only a moment before pushing it open. Rogan entered behind her and pushed it closed as Gabrielle looked up at the porthole, at the small portion of a night sky sparkling with stars beyond. It occurred to her that she had never truly appreciated the beauty of the night sky before the moment when she'd stood at the rail with Rogan close beside her, the sea breeze gently brushing her face and silence reigning around them.

Somehow, during the course of the time they'd spend on deck as twilight faded into night, the crew had disappeared from sight, leaving only the soft sound of their conversation between them.

They had talked quietly, each in turn. She had discovered that Rogan went to sea as a boy when his parents died in a smallpox epidemic, and that he worked his way up to the position of captain, one step at a time. Rogan appeared intensely proud of that accomplishment, as she supposed he should, but she almost fouled the moment when she asked how he became a pirate.

Gabrielle did not think she would ever forget the look that entered Rogan's gaze at that moment. He almost seemed to hate her—but she knew, somehow, that he did not.

Rogan's voice was tinged with sarcasm when he countered by asking her how she'd come to be the "daughter" of Gerard Pointreau. Refusing to respond in kind, she told him of the mother and father whom she did not remember, of the fire that had caused their deaths and left her orphaned. She also told him it was Gerard Pointreau, the only father she had ever known, who had risked his own life to rescue her from the flames that had caused her parents' death.

Rogan's response had been a question that startled her. *Why?*

She recalled the strange intensity with which he'd studied her as she had responded with a thought she had never voiced aloud before, that Gerard Pointreau had risked his life to save her when she was an infant not because he loved *her,* but because she was all he would have left of the woman he loved more than he loved his own life.

She had regretted her response a moment later, realizing that she had confirmed in Rogan's mind the full extent of the power he held over her father. She was momentarily infuriated to realize that he had tricked her into such an admission, only to see that despite Rogan's frown, there was no sign of triumph in his expression.

On the contrary, he had appeared momentarily saddened.

She had been saddened, too.

And it occurred to her that whatever the misconception that had led Rogan to believe her father a monster and had forced their present circumstances, she wished—

Gabrielle's thoughts came to an abrupt halt as Rogan walked past her and sat unexpectedly on the side of the bunk. As big and as broad as he was, he seemed to absorb the space there as he yanked off one boot, then prepared to remove the other.

Gabrielle was incredulous as he began unbuttoning his shirt. Her voice choked, she asked, "What are you doing?"

Rogan's response was level . . . surprisingly emotionless.

"I'm going to bed."

Gabrielle's throat worked convulsively as Rogan returned her stare. It occurred to him that his actions, his claiming of his bunk was totally unexpected to her. He supposed he could not blame her. Their time spent on deck easily conversing had lent an air to the situation that was contrary to harsh reality. It had lowered her defenses . . .

. . . just as it had lowered his.

He was keenly aware of the danger there. It appeared he was more keenly aware of it than she.

Rogan took a silent, strengthening breath. Gabrielle Dubay, for all her unaffected beauty and consummate appeal, was still the daughter of Gerard Pointreau . . . and his hostage. It chilled him to realize how close he still was to surrendering control to the young woman who had so aptly demonstrated that below the surface fire and anger she had formerly displayed was the promise of sweet, sweet honey.

Refusing to finish that last thought, Rogan knew there was only one way to maintain control.

Gabrielle was still staring. She blinked. Her tone flat, she asked, "Where am I supposed to sleep?"

Rogan was determined not to retreat. "You may share this bunk if you wish."

He saw the ice form in her eyes. He knew their brief truce had come to an abrupt end when Gabrielle replied with a ring of her old hauteur.

"I do *not* wish."

Mademoiselle Gabrielle Dubay had returned.

Drawing himself to his feet, Rogan stripped off his shirt. He noted that Gabrielle took a spontaneous, backward step. He shrugged.

"The choice is yours."

He was unprepared for Gabrielle's response as her face flamed with sudden color and she snapped, "You did it purposely, didn't you!"

"Did what?"

"Pretended to be kind—so you could get me off guard."

"No."

Gabrielle continued as if he had not spoken, "You were just trying to show me . . . to show me that you could prove me wrong, weren't you?"

"What are you talking about?"

" '*Never*' is too small a word to come between us . . .' "

"Gabrielle . . ."

"Don't bother to pretend!"

The sadness returned, even as Rogan lay his shirt on the nearby chair and sat back down on his bunk. He almost wished he could afford to restore the quiet intimacy of their time together on deck, if only so she might look at him now as she had then.

Instead, taking no enjoyment in his words, he stated in the same emotionless tone, "You shared the bunk with me last night. You're welcome to share it again."

Gabrielle did not reply.

"Or you may take the extra coverlet from the chest and make your bed wherever you find comfort."

Still no reply.

He repeated, "The choice is yours."

Gabrielle looked up at the door and Rogan frowned. "No, that wouldn't be wise. You would face a far greater danger beyond that door than you do in here."

Having made that statement, he added gruffly, "Do whatever you want. I'm going to sleep."

Rogan leaned over to lower the lamp, then lay back and closed his eyes. Through slitted lids, he watched as Gabrielle stood motionless and finally turned stiffly toward the chest in the corner. He followed her movements as she removed the coverlet there and glanced around the cabin, then wrapped it around her and curled up on the floor nearby.

Gabrielle closed her eyes, a deep dejection overwhelming her anger as she drew the coverlet more tightly around her and attempted to find comfort on the hard floor of the cabin.

Uncertain as to what had happened, why the man Rogan had allowed her to glimpse when they'd talked on deck had so abruptly disappeared, she suddenly realized that she was uncertain whether he had ever existed at all.

One thing, however, was abundantly clear.

Rogan was truly Rapace, after all.

But how she wished . . .

Her throat suddenly thick, Gabrielle mentally chastised herself for her childish stupidity.

Wishing did not make thing so . . . and reality was the cold floor on which she lay.

The sudden pain of that almost more than she could bear, Gabrielle determinedly emptied her mind in search of sleep.

The lantern flickered low, dimming the shadows of the cabin as Rogan opened his eyes to look, as he had countless times through the hours that had passed, toward the figure curled up asleep on the floor a distance away. He could not discern Gabrielle's expression, but he knew she slept fitfully. He had heard her restless twisting and turning.

He was experienced with the dampness of a ship's deck. He had slept on countless, similar decks too many times to forget it. The thought rose in his mind that his sleeplessness was probably due to those memories, but he knew that was not entirely true.

Gabrielle was not hardened to such travails. Her soft, white flesh was too delicate, her experience too limited.

She groaned softly in her sleep, as if confirming his thoughts, and Rogan winced. Suddenly angrier than he had ever been at his own susceptibility to the sound of Gabrielle's discomfort, as well as the circumstances that had delivered him to his own present unease, Rogan drew himself to a seated position on the bunk. Not stopping to consider his intention, he stood up, and within moments was crouched beside Gabrielle's sleeping form.

She did not struggle when he lifted her up in his arms. Instead, she leaned against him with a sigh. Nor did she open her eyes even momentarily when he lay her on the far side of his broad bunk and stretched himself out beside her.

He did not have to reach out to draw her close. Moving toward him like a magnet, she curled against him instinctively, as in the night past.

A torment greater than pain . . .

Was that what it was, the feeling he experienced as he

turned toward her, his face only inches from hers on the pillow they shared?

He touched his lips to her cheek.

The touch sizzled.

Silently cursing, Rogan closed his eyes.

Chapter 5

He hated the swamps!

Gerard Pointreau glanced around him. His aristocratic features drew into a snarl as the pirogue in which he sat glided smoothly through yet another channel that was part of the dense labyrinth of narrow, twisting bayous leading to the northern end of Barataria Bay. They had followed the same route since dawn. Night was falling. The sun that had flickered through the dense foliage overhead, glaring down to bake his brow with its full, intense heat as their pirogue moved briefly into open lakes only to feed back into the inevitable bayou once more, was setting. They would soon be forced to sleep on the rough ground for another tortuous night before reaching Grande-Terre at last.

Pointreau's foul disposition deepened. He was tired, uncomfortable, and anxious almost beyond endurance. He despised the primitive boat in which he sat, suitable only for ignorant, swamp-bred rabble, two of whom now guided it. He abhorred the coarse shirt and breeches, as well as the worn cloak lying nearby that completed his disguise and would serve as a coverlet through the long night ahead. And he loathed the moist, hot air that lay heavily on his shoulders, increasing his physical discomfort to the point of fury.

Oh, yes, Captain Rogan Whitney would pay for every moment of his present, physical distress! But he would pay even more heavily for the tormenting visions that assailed him, allowing him no rest, visions of the indignities his beautiful, innocent Gabrielle doubtless suffered at the man's coarse hands.

Sharp knots of pain tightened in Pointreau's stomach. He recalled the love that spontaneously shone in Gabrielle's clear, luminous eyes whenever she saw him—a love he returned with such paternal passion and pride that it all but consumed him. New Orleans society was not worthy of his dear Gabrielle, as it had not been worthy of his beloved Chantelle before her. Gabrielle was a gem whose worth was beyond measure. He would soon have her back with him, and when he did, he would take her far away from this place, to the great cities of Europe where he would indulge her slightest whim and strip the horror she had suffered forever from her mind.

But first things first.

Pointreau slapped at the voracious insect on his arm and muttered a curse. He recalled his excitement when he received Lafitte's reply a day earlier. His hands shaking, he had read the elaborate scrawl. The message had been concise. Lafitte would see him and would provide the means, as well as the men and the route he would take to Grande-Terre, stating that he could guarantee confidentiality only in that way. Pointreau had no doubt Lafitte was presently enjoying the thought of his discomfort, but he realized that fact was of little consequence. Once Gabrielle was returned to him, all would pay.

The image of Manon flashed unexpectedly before Pointreau, and his agitation swelled. He had not seen his mistress since the night he had left her lying amidst her discarded clothing on her bedroom floor. The image causing a familiar tightening in his groin, Pointreau cursed again. His desire for the woman haunted him. It was unnatural, and during the long night past, as the echo of voodoo drums had echoed through the darkness of the swamps, a new suspicion had formed in his mind. Having lived in the Creole society of New Orleans all his life, he had heard tales since early childhood of gris-gris and magic potions formulated by native priestesses that turned men into puppets manipulated at will by their women. He had determined that if his earnest mistress had indeed employed the black arts in achieving her strange control over him . . .

Pointreau did not bother to complete that thought. It was redundant in any case. He had had enough of Manon's mastery over his senses. When the present crisis was over and his dear Gabrielle was in his arms once more, he would have no further use for Manon's brand of consolation. He would see that she received her just reward.

Suddenly furious at having allowed Manon to occupy his thoughts when other more pressing matters were at hand, Pointreau turned his mind toward the confrontation to come. Admittedly, he was curious to meet Lafitte in person at last. He was also curious about the lavish lifestyle the man was purported to enjoy in his pirate's hideaway. Business acquaintances who traveled monthly to The Temple for the slave auctions held there, and who were elegantly entertained by Lafitte, had intrigued him with their tales. He considered it somehow fitting that The Temple was once a place of human sacrifice used by indigenous Indian tribes. Had he his way, he would see to it that Lafitte's use of that island also proved prophetic.

Deep in his malevolent thoughts, Pointreau was unprepared for the sudden gruff command issued by the seaman at the bow of their boat. Incensed as the command was repeated even more crudely by the man at his rear, Pointreau forcibly controlled his response, choosing instead to jump ashore as instructed when the men ran the pirogue aground.

Pointreau glanced around him at the place where he would spend the coming night. It was a wilderness filled with every crawling, blood-sucking, abhorrent creature known. He endured it for one person alone.

And when morning came, he would arrange to make the payment that was due the man responsible.

Yes, Captain Rogan Whitney would pay . . .

Gabrielle awakened slowly. The brightness of the new day glowed against her eyelids, but she kept them deliberately closed as her hand moved over the softness of the bedlinens beneath her palm. She turned to the side and breathed deeply of the pillow beneath her head.

She recognized the familiar, male scent and slowly opened her eyes.

He wasn't there.

Gabrielle refused to define the emotion that flushed through her. She had again awakened to find herself lying on the wide bunk in the captain's cabin, as she had each morning since she had first arrived in Barataria Bay. Four days of awakening in the captain's bed, without recalling the manner in which she got there.

Or was it that she did not choose to remember?

For vague images were there, of strong arms picking her up from the spot she determinedly chose for herself on the floor of the cabin each night, of a broad chest against which she rested before the surface of the bunk met her back. Dim memories of the hard, male warmth encircling her immediately afterward had been strangely comforting. She was yet uncertain if the light touch of lips against her cheek, her brow, her mouth was a dream.

But it was not a dream that Rogan left her to awaken alone in the bunk each morning . . . or that both of them, by tacit understanding, chose not to discuss her means of getting there.

An unspoken truce.

A sometimes uncertain, unspoken truce.

But a bearable pattern had begun to emerge from that truce. And if anxiety still hovered at the borders of her mind, if isolated moments found her restless and unconsciously searching for an unguarded opportunity that did not occur, she had also begun to discover things that lay below surface appearances on the privateering vessel of Rapace.

First, was the respect and loyalty evinced by the crew for their captain. It had become obvious that the seamen took turns in returning to Grande-Terre each morning in what appeared to be a carefully calculated effort to give the appearance that all aboard ship were enjoying an extended holiday—when all aboard were keenly aware that nothing could be farther from the truth.

Each man appeared to recognize and accept the part he played in the serious, dangerous game underway, and to be aware that one mistake could be the downfall of all. She knew that was true by the snippets of conversation she overhead in the passageway beyond her door and on deck when she walked there.

Second, it appeared that each man in the crew had his own, personal dedication to Rogan's purpose. That their mutual determination resulted in uniting them in some kind of plan for her father's downfall, confused her.

Third, she had truly begun to believe, contrary to the stories whispered in the convent about the rapacious conduct of pirates—or privateers, as Rogan wished to be called—that there was not a man aboard who had any intention of that sort toward her.

Oh, not that she felt comfortable with the variety of intimidating characters among the crew. The one-eyed fellow, Dermott, had never so much as turned a smile in her direction or spoken a friendly word. The other fellows left to guard her during the captain's absence were similarly alarming with their bestial appearances and rough tongues, and had made no effort to be amicable. Yet, although she was certain any attempts to escape would be met with the required force, she felt no sense of *personal* threat.

Fourth, she felt that all aboard waited with the same inten-

sity for Rogan's plan, whatever it was, to proceed to its conclusion.

Those thoughts, while granting her a perverse sense of personal safety, left her feeling even more isolated.

She had come to accept, however, that she would be
turned over to Bertrand's care during Rogan's morning visits
to the island. She had become comfortable with the young,
disfigured seaman, despite his limited conversation, for his silent courtesy never faltered. Behind that courtesy she
glimpsed another, harder man, who did not allow her to take
advantage of the part of his character he showed her.

Gabrielle recalled the first time she'd spoken to Bertrand,
referring to the captain as "Rogan." His head had snapped
back toward her, shock registering briefly in his otherwise
emotionless expression. She had been startled at the warmth
that had come to life within her at the realization that she
had indeed been correct, that Rogan had previously allowed
very few to know his true name.

She recognized that although caution still prevailed in the
treatment afforded her, the situation had become increasingly
tolerable. She had requested and been given a change of
clothing—another ragged set of seaman's attire, to be sure,
but the clothes were clean and comfortable. She had also
found a brush on the table upon awakening on the second
morning, and had been startled when Bertrand had appeared
at the cabin door midway through the morning to announce
that the captain had given him orders to take her up to the
main deck for some air.

And if the daytime hours dragged by, she had come to look
forward to the night strolls on the deck with Rogan. She had
come to revere the sight of twilight fading into the beauty of
the night sea. The silence and shadows seemed to facilitate
the flow of conversation between Rogan and her, although, in
truth, she had learned little more about the man who became
the infamous Rapace than she originally knew.

. . . *"Never" is too small a word to come between us* . . .

Those words had returned to her mind countless times in her solitude, but she sensed no ulterior motive when Rogan slipped his arm around her to guide her safely along the deck each night, when he leaned close to point out a particular star in the heavily populated night sky, or when those golden eyes of the predator grew warm . . .

Sudden guilt at her thoughts flushed Gabrielle with heat as she slipped from the bed and reached for the sandals she now wore without coercion. Dear Father—what was he doing now? Was he suffering? Was he tormented with fear for her . . . while her own fears somehow grew dimmer each day?

Questions without answers flooded Gabrielle's mind as she affixed her sandals securely and turned toward the porthole. Did she truly not know the answers . . . or did she choose not to face them?

Uncertainty suddenly overwhelmed Gabrielle. Longing with unexpected fervor for the security of the convent where such confusing thoughts and fears were spared her, and where the myriad feelings assaulting her had been nonexistent, she whispered into the silence of the cabin, "Oh, Father . . . where are you now?"

Jean Lafitte barely withheld a smile. Conscious of his own faultless grooming and spotless attire—the fine linen of his white shirt contrasting vividly with the midnight black of his hair, his britches tailored to his exact proportions, boots polished to a mirror shine rising to the knee—he stood in the back doorway of his Grande-Terre mansion as he prepared to meet his approaching visitor.

No one would believe the disheveled, travel-stained man emerging from the seldom-used, overgrown swampland trail with two brutish seamen was the proud, arrogant Gerard Pointreau.

The disguise was perfect . . . and a point of great satisfaction for Lafitte. He had no doubt that Pointreau had never before worn garments as coarse as those he had ordered provided for the man, or that Pointreau had ever experienced the discomforts he'd doubtless endured in the circuitous route Lafitte had instructed his men to take in order to maintain the secrecy Pointreau requested.

And he had no doubt the man was seething.

Bon.

Lafitte's inner smile faded as Pointreau neared and met his gaze directly. His assessment of the man was confirmed in that instant. He had known too many whose hearts were as black as pitch to allow one of that breed, however educated and respected, to go unrecognized.

Signaling his men's dismissal, Lafitte extended his hand, knowing he did not extend his confidence as well as he greeted Pointreau courteously.

"Bonjour, monsieur." Carefully avoiding the use of Pointreau's name, Lafitte ushered his visitor inside.

The morning noise and disorder of Grande-Terre faded from Rogan's consciousness as he stood frozen in his tracks a few steps beyond Lafitte's mansion. His sense of shock growing, he realized that the man Lafitte had just welcomed was no other than Gerard Pointreau!

Rogan took a backward step, then another, aware that had he not decided to visit that morning with Lafitte on an inconsequential matter, Gerard Pointreau's visit might have escaped his knowledge completely.

The danger in Pointreau's visit, both to himself and to his carefully laid plans, loomed vividly as Rogan turned and skirted the clearing to approach a fruit stall nearby. He pretended to consider the offerings there, his mind racing and his heart pounding.

Pointreau . . . disguised.

Pointreau in a secret meeting with Lafitte.

Had he made a mistake somewhere that had inadvertently

identified him to Pointreau as Rapace? Did Pointreau realize that his daughter was presently confined on the *Raptor* at anchor in the harbor? Was Pointreau at that moment negotiating with Lafitte to have his men storm the ship and take Gabrielle back by force?

Rogan took a steadying breath as he slipped farther into the morning shadows. The possible repercussions of a meeting between the two men were endless, and an alliance between them could prove his downfall.

Rogan reviewed his options. He had only one.

Clarice walked swiftly along the familiar hallway, the filmy, pink *négligée* Pierre had presented to her the previous evening flowing out behind her to expose the exquisite satin shift beneath as she turned the corner with haste. The usual morning sounds of the house—the opening and closing of the numerous doorways along the long, upstairs corridor, the sounds of stilted conversations in low, feminine tones as those emerging exchanged brief comments about the activities of the night past, and the occasional snickers and bursts of laughter that followed those making their way toward the dining table for their morning repast—had not yet begun.

It was for that reason that Madame's summons stimulated Clarice's anxiety as she continued toward the woman's office door. Her concern had caused her to abandon one of the cardinal rules of decorum she had adopted upon arriving at Madam's house, one that set her apart from the other women working there, when she had left her room so revealingly attired.

That thought was far from Clarice's mind, however, as she came to an abrupt halt before Madame's door and knocked softly. Entering at Madame's response, Clarice approached her desk with apprehension.

"I did not mean to frighten you, Clarice." Madame's expression did not afford the comfort her words intended as she continued quietly, "But since we are friends and I have concern for your safety, I thought you would be interested in knowing that I had occasion to send a messenger to the house of Gerard Pointreau this morning to follow up on a matter he asked me to consider at some time previous to his daughter's unfortunate abduction."

Madame continued more softly after a brief hesitation, "My messenger was told by Monsieur Pointreau's servant that his master had left New Orleans for a few days and that he was uncertain when he would return. Further inquiries revealed that Monsieur Pointreau was seen leaving his house covertly, commonly dressed, and in the company of two disreputable-looking seamen. It occurred to me that Monsieur Pointreau would not leave the city during this crisis with his daughter, most especially in the company of two such men, unless his travel had something to do with her abduction. Clarice, *ma chérie*, I felt you should know."

Almost as startled by the depth of Madame's perception as she was by Madame's words, Clarice felt the color drain from her face. The merit of Madame's concern could not be denied. Monsieur Pointreau had been turning the city upside down in an attempt to find his daughter. He would not leave New Orleans during this time of his personal crisis—except to locate Gabrielle.

Grande-Terre . . . Did he know?

Unable to respond, Clarice took a wobbling step that brought Madame to her feet with surprising agility for a woman of her size. She was beside Clarice in a moment, her hand supportively on Clarice's arm, her brow knit.

Madame's expression grew increasingly anxious. "I know how much your brother and 'his friend' mean to you, but because I have come to regard you as the daughter I will never have, I fear for you as well."

"Non, Madame." Realizing it would be senseless to deny her anxiety, Clarice shook her head. "There is little danger to me, but the others . . ."

"Can you not warn them of Monsieur Pointreau's suspicious disappearance? A message—"

"That is impossible, Madame."

"*Mon amie* . . ."—Madame took a deep breath—"I have never inquired . . ." She hesitated, then began determinedly, "Should you feel the need to reach Grande-Terre with a message, I would have no difficulty in forwarding one for you. My dealings with Lafitte for the luxuries demanded in this house, which only he is able to supply, have availed me of weekly communication with Grande-Terre that is incredibly swift."

Anxious and confused, Clarice shook her head. "I must have time to think, Madame."

"*Oui*, I know." Madame took a step back. "But do not delay too long. My runners leave today at noon. A communication sent in the usual manner will be received quickly and with little notice on Grande-Terre."

"*Merci, Madame.* But I must consider—"

Madame scrutinized Clarice a moment longer before turning back to her desk, dismissing her with the words that trailed over her shoulder. "Noon, Clarice. You must make your decision by then."

The import of Madame's words shuddering through her, Clarice pulled Madame's office door closed behind her.

Something was wrong.

The afternoon silence of the captain's cabin was broken unexpectedly by the sound of voices above. They were anxious voices, and Gabrielle was immediately alert. Bertrand had allowed her up on deck for a longer period than usual that morning due to the warmth of the day, bringing her below only when his duties were needed elsewhere.

Gabrielle had begun to suspect that Rogan had arranged to allow her personal contact with only a chosen few of the men in his crew. She berated herself for believing he had made that provision because he had sensed her feelings and knew she had grown comfortable with Bertrand, and with the man called Porter, surprisingly so, since both men had been involved in her abduction.

She had listened keenly for the familiar call that announced a boat from the island approached the ship, and that Rogan was returning. But this time the call was hard and clipped, and the exchange on deck shortly afterward harsh and concerned. Rogan's deep tones had been unmistakable, as had been Bertrand's softer response. She could not believe they were arguing, but it appeared—

Another noise above and the familiar scraping of the ladder against the ship's hull alerted Gabrielle to someone's descent into the rowboat only minutes prior to the thudding of heavy footsteps in the passageway. The warning rattle of the cabin door preceded its sudden thrust open.

Filling the opening with the height and breadth of him, Rogan stood framed in the doorway for a long silent moment. His sun-darkened skin was flushed and his gaze intense, and Gabrielle's blood ran suddenly cold.

Rapace had returned.

"What's wrong?" she questioned.

Rogan did not respond as he closed the cabin door behind him.

"Tell me."

Still no reply.

"Rogan—"

At the sound of his name, he took a sharp step forward.

"Your 'father' is on Grande-Terre."

"Impossible!"

Rogan's jaw ticked with restrained tension. "I saw him."

"Father wouldn't come to Grande-Terre for any reason. He despises Jean Lafitte for the common criminal that he is!"

"Criminal . . . yes, your father is an expert on the criminals on Grande-Terre. He has been in league with the foulest murderer of them all for years."

"You lie!" Gabrielle paused to stare at Rogan, incredulous at the change that had come over him.

Humiliated that thoughts of him only moments earlier had filled her with warmth, Gabrielle rasped, "Why are you doing this again? Why are you trying to make me believe that my father is a criminal? You're wrong, I tell you! Mistaken! If you would speak to him you would know that!"

"You forget, I *have* spoken to your father!" Advancing toward her with a few, long steps, Rogan gripped her shoulders and shook her roughly. "I bear the scar of my conversation with him still. But greater by far is the memory that accompanies it—the sound of my first mate dying as I lay helpless to save him."

Gabrielle twisted free of Rogan's grip, putting distance between them.

"You would have me believe that my father is not only responsible for the cruel brand you wear, but for the death of your first mate as well? Why would he do that?"

"To hide the guilt of his own association with Vincent Gambi in the attack on American merchant ships."

"The attack on American merchant ships . . . Vincent Gambi . . ." Gabrielle was incredulous. "Surely you cannot be serious! Gambi is one of your compatriots at Grande-Terre, is he not? He's one of Lafitte's men! If you are looking for guilt, look to Lafitte!"

"Lafitte is unaware of Gambi's pact with your father, of the information your father relays to Gambi when an American merchant ship is a particularly good prize that cannot be ignored. He would never sanction such an attack."

"This is insane! If it were true that Gambi attacked and sank American merchant ships, the survivors would be the first to proclaim his part in the assault!"

Rogan's features hardened. "There are no survivors."

"I don't understand."

"I mean that with each of Gambi's attacks, great caution is

taken to *assure* there are no survivors to tell the tale, just as it is made certain that the merchant ship is never seen again."

"You mean—"

"I mean slaughter . . . the systematic killing of every seaman left alive and the scuttling of the ship."

"No! . . ." Gabrielle shook her head. "I don't believe you! My father would have no part in such an atrocity. If there are no witnesses, what makes you believe my father—or even Gambi—is responsible?"

"There were no witnesses left alive on any of the ships . . . with the exception of my first mate and me."

Silent, Gabrielle struggled for composure. A mistake . . . that was what it was! She spoke abruptly, "My father would never betray his countrymen to pirates. What would be his reason? He is wealthy, respected, a confidant of Governor Claiborne!"

Rogan did not respond.

"Why? Why would my father do these things?"

The peculiar intensity of Rogan's gold eyes pinned her. "You know your father better than I . . ."

The momentary flicker of doubt those words caused, propelled Gabrielle furiously forward. Shuddering, she halted only an inch from Rogan's powerful form. She spoke in a hoarse whisper.

"How . . . how did I ever, even for a moment believe—" Emotion briefly stealing her voice, Gabrielle continued, "You are a liar! My father is innocent of those things you accuse him of."

"He isn't."

"He is!"

Seeing the futility of further argument, Gabrielle took a steadying breath. "It will be easy enough to prove what you say. If my father is here, let me face him with these accusations."

Silence, then a low response. "Do you really think me that much a fool?"

Gabrielle's mind racing, she spoke again. "If my father is on Grande-Terre, it isn't because he's in league with Gambi or Lafitte. He's come because he knows I'm here somewhere, and he intends to rescue me!"

No response.

"What are you going to do?"

The question lingered.

What should she do?

Clarice paced her bedroom as countless questions whirled in her mind. She glanced at the clock nearby, her heart racing. It was eleven o'clock. Madame's messenger was to leave for Grande-Terre at noon.

She raised a hand to her forehead, ignoring the dampness of agitation there as she sought to draw her thoughts under control.

No, Pointreau could not possibly have discovered that Rogan and Rapace were one and the same. Rogan had been successful for years in keeping that secret, and nothing had happened to change those circumstances.

There was, of course, the possibility that Pointreau had *not* gone to Grande-Terre as suspected. If that were true and she sent an urgent message to Rapace via Madame's messenger, she would stir unnecessary speculation.

And . . . how could she be certain Madame's messenger was trustworthy, that he would not turn her message over to Lafitte?

Tears welled in Clarice's eyes as she ran nervous fingers through her unbound hair. What should she do?

A knock on the door startled her into stillness. A second knock set her heart to frantic pounding.

"Clarice . . ."

Pierre. She closed her eyes, then wiped away the tears thereby released. She took a steadying breath.

"Pardon, Pierre. I am not feeling well this morning. If you will excuse me and perhaps return later."

A short silence was followed by Pierre's words, spoken in a tone she had never heard before.

"Open the door, Clarice."

"*Pierre, s'il vous plaît* . . ."

"Open the door."

Unwilling to call undue attention to herself as Pierre stood adamant in the hallway outside her room, Clarice dabbed at her eyes once more, then released the lock.

Standing momentarily silent in the doorway, Pierre then entered abruptly and closed the door behind him. His jaw was tight with anger when he turned back to face her. "I knew it. You are crying."

"It is nothing." Clarice forced a tenuous smile. "It is merely a womanly tension that often occurs. I will be fine in a few hours."

"Clarice . . . *mon amour* . . ." Pierre gripped her shoulders, all anger leaving his gaze as he whispered, "You need not pretend with me. I know something is wrong."

"*Non*, it is nothing!"

As Pierre smoothed a strand of hair back from her damp cheek, Clarice felt the gentleness in his touch. She saw the pain in his eyes as he whispered, "You know that whatever is wrong, you may tell me."

A slow shuddering beginning inside her, Clarice shook her head. "It is nothing, I tell you!"

"*Non* . . . *mon amour* . . . *s'il vous plaît*, do not upset yourself further." Pierre drew her into his arms and Clarice's throat choked tight at the comfort afforded as he whispered, "I will not press you further, except to ask you to promise me something." Separating himself from her so he might look directly into her eyes, Pierre continued, "That if ever you are in need, you will come to me so I may help you."

"But I—"

"A promise, Clarice."

"Pierre . . ."

"Promise me. I want to hear you say the words that you will come to me if you are ever in need."

Dear Pierre . . . Clarice's heart filled to bursting. Surely she did not deserve so kind and generous a man to care for her—for she knew he did—most especially when her heart belonged to another.

"Clarice, a promise, for the sake of my peace of mind, if not for yours."

Clarice looked up into the brown eyes scrutinizing her with such devotion. Her voice hoarse, she whispered, "I will promise if it will relieve your mind."

"And what of your mind, *ma chérie?*"

Surprising herself with the sincerity of her words, Clarice whispered, "To know I may depend on you if I am in need is a gift indeed."

"And your present anxiety?"

Clarice was momentarily unable to respond. The truth was that she could do nothing to help her beloved Rogan and her dearest Bertrand without risking endangering them even more.

Nothing . . . but pray.

Clarice opened her eyes to Pierre's obvious concern. To her surprise, she was able to smile.

"I would ask one thing of you now."

"Anything."

"If you would call a carriage while I dress, so I may go to the cathedral."

An unreadable emotion flickered across Pierre's features before he nodded and replied, "A carriage will be waiting."

Clarice waited only until the door closed behind Pierre before reaching for her clothes.

Oui, all she could do was pray . . .

* * *

Yes, what *was* he going to do?

The confines of his cabin seemed to shrink around Rogan as Gabrielle's question rang on the silence between them. Pointreau's presence on Grande-Terre had shocked all coherent thought from his mind as the danger of his situation became suddenly apparent.

Years of dedicated planning, the savage slaughter of countless, American seamen, the cries of the dying that would allow him no rest, all merged in Rogan's mind. Facing him was a moment of crisis in which the justice he sought was severely threatened . . .

. . . yet, the distress in the clear, gray-eyed gaze looking up at him tore cruelly at his innards.

Inwardly cursing himself, the young woman before him, and the fiendish fate which had introduced an unexpected torment at the time of his greatest trial, Rogan felt a new fury rise. It was reflected in his tone as he responded, "At the moment, I intend doing nothing."

"Nothing . . ."

"Bertrand has returned to Grande-Terre. He will uncover the reason for your father's visit."

"And then?"

"And then we will see."

Gabrielle's pallor deepened. "Y-You would not hurt my father—"

"Hurt him?" Rogan could not withhold a sneer.

"You would not injure him physically . . . ?"

"If that were my intention, I could have accomplished that long ago."

"Then, what *is* your intention?"

"To obtain justice, *mademoiselle!*"

"But . . ."

Realizing his emotions were fast slipping beyond control, that further hesitation might cause him to act unwisely as the beautiful young woman before him pleaded for the life of a man he had sworn to destroy, Rogan turned and jerked open the door behind him.

Gone in a moment, leaving Gabrielle stricken behind him, Rogan realized that for the first time in his life, he had fled in the face of danger.

The ruby red and cobalt blue of stained-glass windows . . . the scent of candle wax burning . . . benevolent expressions carved in stone . . . an echoing peace and silence encompassing all . . .

The cathedral was empty, the mahogany pews vacant except for two, still figures.

On her knees, her eyes closed, her head bent in prayer, Clarice was motionless except for the almost indistinguishable movement of her lips as she fervently prayed.

Seated beside her, Pierre was similarly silent, but it was not prayer that filled his mind as he observed Clarice's silent supplication. Unable to tear his eyes from her serene beauty as she maintained her prayerful posture, the lace covering the carefully bound gold of her hair accenting her delicacy of feature and recalling to his mind the supreme artistry of the great masters he had seen exhibited in the galleries of Europe, he recalled the moment when Clarice emerged onto the street in front of Madame's house, where the carriage and he waited. Soberly dressed as he had never before seen her in a dark, high-necked gown and a mantilla that somehow emphasized a true innocence of spirit shining from within, she had stirred within him a depth of emotion he had never felt before.

Clarice Bouchard . . . courtesan.

Non.

Pierre swallowed against the thickness in his throat. He had always known that the woman Clarice had been forced to present to the world was not the real Clarice, just as he had always sensed that the true, inner woman was untouched by her profession. However, he had not realized how deeply he would be affected when that woman was finally revealed to him . . .

. . . or that he would feel so privileged to meet her at last.

Hardly realizing his intention as Clarice shuddered in the midst of her prayers, Pierre slipped to his knees beside her and slipped his arm around her. She had not wanted him to accompany her to the cathedral, and a familiar jealousy had stirred within him as he had looked into her eyes and read the reason there. For some reason, she feared for the man she loved. She had not wanted him beside her when she prayed for that man.

Pierre's jealousy, however benign, had made him all the more determined. Clarice needed him, whether she realized it or not at that moment. It was his intention to bring her to full realization of that need, a need that would not impinge upon her inner strength—to the contrary—but which would compliment it and help it to grow. His love for her would not allow less. He would demonstrate that love in a way words could never convey. In so doing he could only hope that she would one day come to love him in a way she had never loved this unknown man.

Clarice looked up. Her cheeks were wet with tears.

Tears filled Pierre's throat as well, and his arm tightened around her . . .

. . . as he offered his own silent prayer.

"I do not know the man."

The short sentence spoken in Lafitte's precise, heavily accented English hung in the silence between them as Gerard Pointreau eyed the surprisingly youthful Frenchman. Seated across from him on a chair upholstered in a lavish brocade, his leg crossed as he tilted a crystal glass to his lips, Lafitte conveyed a natural, European elegance that could not be

We've got your authors!

If you seek out the latest historical romances by today's bestselling authors, our new reader's service, KENSINGTON CHOICE, is the club for you.

KENSINGTON CHOICE is the only club where you can find authors like Janelle Taylor, Shannon Drake, Rosanne Bittner, Sylvie Sommerfield, Penelope Neri and Phoebe Conn all in one place...

...and the only service that will deliver their romances direct to your home as soon as they are published—even before they reach the bookstores.

KENSINGTON CHOICE is also the only service that will give you a substantial guaranteed discount off the publisher's prices on every one of those romances.

That's right: Every month, the Editors at Zebra and Pinnacle select four of the newest novels by our bestselling authors and rush them straight to you, usually *before they reach the bookstores*. The publisher's prices for these romances range from $4.99 to $5.99—but they are always yours for the guaranteed low price of just *$4.20!*

That means you'll always save over 20% off the publisher's prices on every shipment you get from KENSINGTON CHOICE!

All books are sent on a 10-day free examination basis, and there is no minimum number of books to buy. (A postage and handling charge of $1.50 is added to each shipment.)

As your introduction to the convenience and value of this new service, we invite you to accept

4 BOOKS FREE

The 4 books, worth up to $23.96, are our welcoming gift. You pay only $1 to help cover postage and handling.

To start your subscription to KENSINGTON CHOICE and receive your introductory package of 4 FREE romances, detach and mail the card at right *today.*

We have 4 FREE BOOKS for you
as your introduction to
KENSINGTON CHOICE
To get your FREE BOOKS, worth
up to $23.96, mail the card below.

FREE BOOK CERTIFICATE

As my introduction to your new KENSINGTON CHOICE reader's service, please send me 4 FREE historical romances (worth up to $23.96), billing me just $1 to help cover postage and handling. As a KENSINGTON CHOICE subscriber, I will then receive 4 brand-new romances to preview each month for 10 days FREE. I can return any books I decide not to keep and owe nothing. The publisher's prices for the KENSINGTON CHOICE romances range from $4.99 to $5.99, but as a subscriber I will be entitled to get them for just $4.20 per book or $16.80 for all four titles. There is no minimum number of books to buy, and I can cancel my subscription at any time. A $1.50 postage and handling charge is added to each shipment.

Name _____

Address _____ Apt. _____

City _____ State _____ Zip _____

Telephone ( ) _____

Signature _____

(If under 18, parent or guardian must sign)

Subscription subject to acceptance. Terms and prices subject to change.

KC0895

We have
4
FREE
Historical
Romances
for you!

(worth up
to $23.96!)

Details inside!

KENSINGTON CHOICE
Reader's Service
120 Brighton Road
P.O.Box 5214
Clifton, NJ 07015-5214

ll..l..lll....lll.l.l.l..l.l..ll.l.l..ll.l.l..lll.ll...l

denied—an elegance that Pointreau sensed was contrived to deliberately emphasize his own dishevelment.

Pointreau's limited patience waned. Nor had Lafitte fooled him with the courteous welcome afforded—the concern of Lafitte's servants for his comforts, the glass of brandy which had already been refilled, and the tempting tray of delicacies that had been placed on the small table between them. All had been a deliberate calculation to consume time in the face of his present and obvious anxiety, so Lafitte might prolong his discomfort and firmly establish his control of the situation without the need for words. Were Gabrielle's welfare not at stake, Pointreau knew he would not have hesitated in throwing the aged brandy back in the arrogant Frenchman's face. But as things presently stood . . .

Pointreau forced a smile.

"As mentioned in my letter to you, my close affiliation with Governor Claiborne forced me to maintain a distance from your business operations in New Orleans in the past. That same association also demanded that I assume the governor's attitude with regard to all that transpires under your auspices here in Barataria Bay."

Pointreau paused, deciding on direct assault. "However, as it suited my purpose in the past to align myself with the governor's views, it now suits my purpose to present you with an offer that may be beneficial to us both."

"So you stated in your letter, *monsieur.*"

Pointreau noted that Lafitte's smile lacked warmth.

"And so I have understood from all you have said since you arrived. My response, however, is still the same. I do not know the Captain Rogan Whitney of whom you speak. To my knowledge, there is no captain of that name on Grande-Terre."

Pointreau's smile stiffened. "I have come here in good faith, *monsieur,* and with a legitimate offer."

Lafitte paused at Pointreau's words. "It is my hope that

your daughter is returned to you safely, but I can offer you no help in the search for her abductor."

Fighting to conceal the slow panic encroaching at the realization that Lafitte might actually refuse him, Pointreau paused to sip with deceiving composure at the amber liquid in his glass before responding, "It was not my intention to suggest that you might have present knowledge of my daughter's whereabouts. Nothing could be further from the truth. I do believe, however, that you are in a singularly unique position to discover the whereabouts of Captain Whitney and my daughter, and to effect her return to me—for which I am willing to make unusual payment."

"Your talk of unusual payment and legitimate offers is of little interest to me."

Sensing the approach of an unexpectedly abrupt end to their exchange, Pointreau abandoned all pretense to interject harshly, "Acceptance—that is what I offer you, Monsieur Lafitte! I am well aware that there is no monetary reward that would be tempting enough to force you to deal with one such as I, who have been among the greatest of your detractors in the city of New Orleans and who have persistently called for your arrest and conviction on the charges of piracy and murder! I know you are well aware of my activities in the past! But as I have formerly censured you publicly, I now guarantee you my complete support should you aid me in my present cause."

His hands shaking so severely with the passion of his words that he was forced to surrender his glass to the nearby table, Pointreau glanced back up at Lafitte a moment later. "Clearly stated, my proposition is this, if you lend your support to the safe return of my daughter, I will personally guarantee that the governor will drop all charges against you and your brother, and that his censure of you and your activities will also cease."

Despising the Frenchman all the more for the slow rise of his dark, arched brows and the skepticism he openly displayed, Pointreau fumed as Lafitte responded, "It is my thought that you promise that which you cannot deliver."

"I can do it."

"So you say."

"Do you doubt my word, *monsieur?*"

Lafitte's expression stiffened. "And if I do?"

Too incensed for caution, Pointreau growled, "Only a fool would doubt the word of Gerard Pointreau!"

Lafitte's cold smile returned, "And only an imbecile would intimate that Jean Lafitte might, under any circumstances, be considered a fool. However, *monsieur*, since you are my guest and are under the unmistakable stress of deep concern for a loved one, I will choose to overlook your offensive manner."

Standing abruptly, all affectation dropping away to reveal barely restrained fury, Lafitte rasped, "However, any further discussion between us is pointless. You are welcome to refresh yourself and to stay the night, after which my men will guide you back to New Orleans. Our conversation is at an end."

Enraged, Pointreau jumped to his feet as Lafitte left the room. His angry step in pursuit was brought to an abrupt halt by the appearance of a swarthy cutthroat at the doorway through which Lafitte had disappeared.

"Monsieur Pointreau . . ." A voice at his elbow turned Pointreau toward a sober-faced servant as the fellow continued, "I will show you to your room."

Pointreau strained to maintain control. Yes, he would accept the hospitality of the bastard Lafitte! He would sleep a few hours and return to New Orleans where he would reinstitute the search for Gabrielle with greater fervor! With any luck, a communication from that bastard Captain Whitney would be waiting and Gabrielle would soon be returned to him. And once she was . . .

His furious shuddering increasing, Pointreau made a solemn vow.

He would draw Lafitte's blood for the insult afforded him—and then he would see to it that the man was hanged.

That thought sustaining him, Pointreau followed the silent servant from the room.

Bertrand leaned casually against the scarred trunk of the great tree, the weary droop of his eyelids belying the acute attention he had paid to the angry discussion overheard through the window of the Lafitte's brick and stone mansion a few feet away.

Bertrand ran a hand through his heavy blond hair in a casual gesture that belied his agitation, determined to remain in his dangerous position of surveillance until he could be certain no further discussion between the men was imminent.

He was still incredulous.

Pointreau . . . on Grande-Terre.

His first thought when Rogan had said those words was that there was a mistake. Pointreau could not have discovered their plans. The years of preparation and the suffering endured could not have been for naught. ·

Then had come a surging fear for Clarice, whose association with them was no longer secret from Lafitte.

Following Rogan's command, he had returned to the island with haste. Arriving at Lafitte's mansion, he had positioned himself where he now stood as the discussion within was getting underway. The hostility simmering just below the surface between the two men had been obvious to his ear. Pointreau was an arrogant fool despite his position of disadvantage, and Lafitte was no man to endure arrogance. He had known from the moment the first words were spoken that they—

"So, you are still here, *mon ami.*"

Snapping around toward the sound of the familiar, accented voice behind him, Bertrand met Lafitte's assessing gaze. Tension slowly stiffened his spine as Lafitte continued smoothly, "As always, little is betrayed by your expression, although I know you are surprised that I was aware of your presence outside my window. Nor do I see a hint of panic in your gaze, when I also observe you are uncertain how I will react to knowing I have been spied upon. I begin to realize the reason Rapace values your services so highly."

Bertrand did not respond.

"Silence in the face of uncertainty. *Bon* . . . You would have me make the first move, and I am not adverse to it."

Lafitte took a step closer. His dark eyes glinted with a reflection of his former fury as he rasped, "You heard the insolent fool! Pointreau hopes to enlist my aid and thinks me to be idiotic enough to believe him when he makes promises he has no intention of keeping!" Lafitte cursed low in his throat, his fair complexion flushing with a new heat. "In his contempt for me, Pointreau believes me to be stupid. He does not realize that I have seen that same contempt in the eyes of too many men not to recognize it upon first glance. Nor am I fooled by the respectability he enjoys in New Orleans society. The governor is a fool to trust him, but I am not so gullible!"

Pausing, Lafitte studied Bertrand's expression more closely. "I read men well, you see. In your scarred face I see a man who has suffered, a man whose courage is unquestionable, one who faces death without a backward step, and whose loyalty is indefatigable when it is given. But I also see a man who has demons to expunge and is driven to be done with it. I have no doubt you have aligned yourself with your captain because a similarity of purpose drives you both . . . and perhaps because of a less clearly definable bond called 'friendship.' "

The scrutiny of Lafitte's dark eyes intensified. "True friendship is rare. There are few on this island whom I would so trust as your captain trusts you. So I tell you now to go back to Rapace and relate to him that he need not fear Lafitte will join forces with Pointreau against him."

Bertrand stiffened.

"*Oui*, I know who is the true Rapace—but I have shared my knowledge of that secret with no one, including your captain. Were it not for the situation that now presents itself, my knowledge of Rapace's true identity would remain secret even from him. It is essential, however, that you tell your captain to make haste in leaving Barataria. Pointreau is enraged. I have set his plans back temporarily by my refusal to cooperate, but there are those numbered among the riffraff here who would not balk at betrayal if offered the right price."

Bertrand spoke for the first time, his tone conveying none of the anxiety Lafitte's words elicited as he replied, "I fear you are in error, Monsieur Lafitte. Captain Rapace is not the man Monsieur Pointreau seeks."

"*Non*, do not cloud the air between us with untruths. If you seek a reason that justifies my warning to your captain, suffice it to say, Rapace will do me a service by dealing with Pointreau." Pausing, Lafitte added, "A word of caution, however. Pointreau is desperate to have his daughter back. It is my belief that a capacity for evil lies hidden in the heart of that man, and that the hatred now fomenting within him makes him a powerful force against your captain. Tell Rapace not to linger overlong in bringing this matter to conclusion. Pointreau will not give up. And as I discovered your captain's true identity, Pointreau may discover it was well if enough pressure is brought to bear."

Lafitte searched Bertrand's face a moment longer. "Go . . . with one last warning of a more personal nature to your captain. Tell him also to beware of women who are convent-bred, for feminine innocence, whether pretended or true, is a heady drug that has been known to alter a man's clarity of thought."

Lafitte's eyes narrowed at Bertrand's spontaneous stiffening. He nodded. "So, my words do not fall far from the mark." Sober, Lafitte extended his hand. "*Bonne chance* to you and your captain, *mon ami*. It is my feeling that much luck indeed will be needed before this exercise is through."

Walking swiftly down the trail toward the bay moments later, Bertrand glanced up at the early afternoon sky, his anxiety rising. Spotting a crewman standing outside a nearby tavern, Bertrand stopped and leaned companionably toward him to whisper in his ear. The man nodded briefly in response. With that acknowledgment, Bertrand resumed his path toward the bay.

"So, we've been granted a reprieve . . ."

Standing on the quarterdeck, facing the glittering surface of the bay, Rogan turned back abruptly toward Bertrand. He had spent a difficult hour awaiting his first mate's return. With most of his men ashore, he had been intensely aware that were an attack indeed launched against the *Raptor*, there would have been little possibility of repulsing it . . . or setting sail to avoid it.

That thought in mind, Rogan had immediately installed lookouts to watch the shoreline for any sign of organized activity, while ordering weapons primed and ready. But he had known then, as he did now, that he had only one viable weapon against such an attack.

Gabrielle.

The knot in Rogan's stomach tightened.

Gabrielle's life was precious to her father, a man who placed little true value on any other living person's. Rogan had known then that in the event of an attack, he would be forced to use her to save his ship. The conflicting emotions that thought had introduced within him had still not subsided.

"Captain . . ."

Bertrand's fair brows were drawn into a frown in an unusual betrayal of anxiety. But circumstances were unusual, as had been Bertrand's careful recitation of the discourse between Lafitte and himself. Lafitte, who had proved an unexpected ally . . .

The Frenchman's warning rang again in Rogan's mind.

Tell your captain to make haste in leaving Barataria ...

Rogan turned toward the shore where the last of his crew had gathered to return to the ship. They would soon be fully manned.

Tell Rapace not to linger overlong in bringing this matter to conclusion ...

Rogan paused at that thought. Escape from possible danger first. Then a reformulation of his plans ...

Tell him also to beware of women who are convent-bred ... *Innocence* ... *is a heady drug* ...

Clear, gray eyes looking up into his ... an inborn courage that did not recognize surrender ... an unconscious appeal that somehow touched his heart ...

Damn! How had this complication come about? How had it come to pass that he spent each night with Gabrielle's warmth filling his arms and each day aching at the memory? It had not been his intention to keep her with him that first night. He had intended only to watch over her, to make certain ...

Rogan was abruptly filled with disgust at the self-deception he'd perpetuated. The truth was, he had been reluctant to separate himself from Gabrielle Dubay from the first moment he had seen her face.

He was reluctant still ...

... and that was where the true danger lay.

But he had not endangered himself alone with his self-deception. He had increased the threat against his ship, his crew, and the justice he sought.

It was time to correct his error.

Rogan met Bertrand's level gaze with new determination.

The scraping sound ...

The stamping of feet on the deck above her ...

Gabrielle stood momentarily still as shouted commands grew louder. What was happening?"

Running to the cabin door, she jerked it open, only to face the glaring gaze of Dermott's bloodshot eye. Swallowing, she raised her chin. "What's happening?"

"The captain has not released you from the cabin."

Dermott's voice was a familiar growl that sent her flesh crawling, but she refused to retreat. "I demand to know what's happening!"

Suddenly all but lifted from her feet by Dermott's strong, callused hand as he moved her firmly backward, Gabrielle gasped aloud. Her face flaming as the door was slammed closed in her face, she fought to control her fury.

Damn Rogan for leaving her under the watch of that ignorant beast! She would see that the man was made to suffer for his unkindnesses to her! She would—

Suddenly realizing she was wasting time with senseless thoughts when more pressing matters were at hand, Gabrielle walked to the bunk behind her and climbed onto it to peer out the porthole. They were moving! The scraping sound she had heard was the raising of the anchor, and the stamping sounds above were the hoisting of the sails.

Where were they going?

Why were they leaving the bay so quickly?

Father . . . ?

A soul-shaking fear loomed suddenly in Gabrielle's mind.

If Father had indeed come to Grande-Terre, he had come for no other reason but to find her. He had walked into the lair of notorious thieves and murderers for her sake, putting his life at risk among men who despised him for his affiliation with the governor.

Because of her . . .

Because he loved her . . .

While she had spared him less thought than she had reserved for the great, predatorial beast who had abducted her and who manipulated her at will.

Oh, Father.

If something had happened to him because of her . . .

Gabrielle abruptly sat back on her heels and covered her face with her hands.

Guilt.

Humiliation.

Shame.

A nightmare, that was what all this was.

But, if she were dreaming, when—when would this nightmare end?

The setting sun slipped into the horizon, taking with it the brilliant hues that had turned the sea into shimmering gold, but the rapidly fading beauty of the sunset was far from Rogan's mind as he stood at the *Raptor*'s rail.

It had been a long and difficult day, in which he had accomplished only one, major task. Grande-Terre was far behind him.

A brisk breeze battering the ship; Rogan looked up at the sails that had filled firm and true to deliver them from Barataria Bay, sails now tightly furled until morning. The time had come when he must face an even more difficult task than his ship's swift departure from the bay.

Unconsciously squaring his shoulders, Rogan descended from the quarterdeck and walked across the main deck toward the staircase below. It had occurred to him earlier that he had not needed to tend to this matter personally, but he had known that to do otherwise was a concession to the emotions rioting within that he was not willing to make.

Signaling Dermott aside when he reached his cabin door, Rogan rattled the knob warningly, then pushed the door open.

Darkness.

Panic set his heart to pounding the moment before he saw the slender shadow sitting motionless at the edge of his bunk.

His step toward Gabrielle was halted by the coldness in her voice as she stood up abruptly and demanded, "Why did you leave Grande-Terre so quickly?"

Rogan did not reply. The clever little witch! The darkness had been a deliberate ploy to catch him off guard!

He turned to light the lamp, taking the moments afforded to bring his agitation under control.

"I asked you a question!"

However could he have forgotten that Gabrielle was still Mademoiselle Dubay after all?

She took a stiff step that brought her more clearly into the light. Startled by her unexpected pallor, Rogan reached spontaneously toward her, only to hear her hiss, "Don't touch me! I demand an answer! Why did you leave Grande-Terre with such haste? You said my father was on the island." She paused, her breast heaving beneath the voluminous shirt she wore. "There could be only one reason. You hurt him, didn't you! You went back to the island and attacked my father, then were forced to flee!" Her body rigid, she rasped, "Is . . . is he dead?"

Rogan did not respond.

"Tell me!"

"No."

"You're lying!"

"Believe what you want to believe!"

"I want the truth!"

"I told you the truth!"

Gabrielle swayed and Rogan again reached toward her, only to hear her snap, "I told you not to touch me!"

"You do not give the orders on this ship, *mademoiselle!* I would've thought you had realized that by now."

"Yes, I have been humiliatingly slow to comprehend the true nature of affairs here, haven't I?" The flickering light of the lantern caught in the burnished highlights of Gabrielle's hair, turning it to flame that matched the furious ardor burning in her eyes as she rasped, "How I must have amused you during our long talks on deck! How you must have silently laughed at my naïveté when I allowed you to manipulate me at will until I almost believed—"

Gabrielle halted suddenly. Then the heat of her hatred singed him as she spat out, "For some misguided reason, you despise my father. You knew the way to make him truly suffer was through me, and you were not above any machinations that would deliver that end. You believed you had me under your spell, but you went a step too far." Her delicate fists clenching, Gabrielle took another step toward him, "I tell you now . . . if you have hurt my father in any way—if you have drawn his blood or endangered his life—I will not rest until I watch you pay for every moment of pain inflicted and every drop of blood shed!"

"Nobly spoken."

"Bastard . . ."

"You are your father's daughter. I thank you for reminding me."

"Get out."

Witch.

"Leave me alone!"

"Gladly."

Rogan jerked the cabin door open. "Come in here, Dermott."

Turning back to face Gabrielle, Rogan saw the effort she exerted to still her furious shuddering as he addressed the seaman while staring directly into the icy gray of her eyes. "The cabin next door has been vacated for Mademoiselle Dubay's use. You will install her there, and you will see that no one—no one—is allowed admission without my express permission. Is that understood?"

Waiting only for Dermott's grunt of response, Rogan walked to his desk. He did not raise his gaze from the ship's log as Gabrielle left the cabin and Dermott followed behind.

Nor did he react as the door closed behind them.

* * *

Anguish . . . uncertainty . . .

The hours of night had been long and dark in Gabrielle's new quarters as sleep eluded her. The heated scene between Rogan and her had trailed repeatedly across her mind, but the torment remained.

Had Rogan told her the truth? Was her father unharmed?

Why did a nagging voice insist that Rogan would never do her father harm . . . when she knew, without doubt that Rapace surely would.

Rogan or Rapace . . . which man was he?

Rogan or Rapace—was there truly a difference between them?

And why, despite all the fear and fury, did she shudder at the solitude of the dark cabin in which she lay, longing for the comfort of strong arms to hold her close?

The arms of her abductor . . .

No!

Yes.

She wished . . .

Tormented, Gabrielle turned her face to the wall.

Rogan twisted uncomfortably on his bunk as the dark hours of night stretched sleeplessly onward. Familiar images assaulted his mind. Glorious hair sparkling with a fiery glow in the sun; light eyes, sober eyes, scrutinizing him as he spoke; delicate features composed in sleep—so close, so vulnerable.

But the images changed. Sober eyes flashed with fury. Tranquil features filled with hatred.

Rogan expelled the disquieting images from his mind. He had done what was necessary. He need proceed from there.

Yet . . .

Chapter 6

Manon walked slowly along the busy city street. Her expression composed, she directed her thoughts to the sights around her. She had always considered herself to be among the most fortunate of women to live in New Orleans, for surely no other city could compare.

Oui, it was often dirty. The gutters were frequently filled with stagnant water from which odors arose, the streets that were not cobbled were muddy and deeply pocked with soggy holes that were a hazard to carriage and pedestrian alike, and the buildings were flush with the sidewalk, impinging upon the privacy within. Unmatched, however, were the colors—the soft pinks and blues with which the homes were painted, the flowers and shrubs of sweet scents and brilliant hues in courtyard gardens visible through doorways opening onto the street—and the delicate iron grillwork worked by dedicated slaves that decorated the building's balconies and facades, allotting them their unique and gracious charm.

And the laughter . . . New Orleans was a city filled with laughter!

The tightness of tears choked Manon's throat, but she blinked them back. She forced a smile at a graying matron tending a nearby stall as she entered the French market. There she saw well-dressed shoppers strolling, their children running ahead of them as their slaves laughed and chatted behind; American and British sailors mingling companionably; Negroes in bright finery, some of the women carrying baskets of incredible weight on their heads; and Indians sitting wrapped in colorful blankets, selling herbs from handwoven baskets.

Betwixt and between all were the rumblings of various languages, singsong cries of merchants, excited shouts, and the inevitable laughter. The sights and sounds were of such brilliance and diversity that she was certain they could not be duplicated in any other city.

Manon's composure again faltered, but she pushed herself on. The vibrancy of the streets was a tonic for her troubled mind. She walked often when disturbed, finding the continuity of an atmosphere that saw little change despite political and personal upheavals comforting. But it was hot, and the air heavy. The pale blue cotton she wore lay damply against her skin, unusually so, for she was not one to heavily perspire. She dabbed daintily with a small, lace-trimmed handkerchief at the sparkling beads that marked her brow and upper lip, conscious of growing discomfort. She was weary, but the weariness was not solely of the body.

Manon's spirits momentarily rose. The child growing within, the precious child whose presence was not yet perceptible on her slender form and that she had believed herself unable to bear, often drained her strength. Malaise seemed to follow her through the day. Malaise . . . and a sadness that would not abate.

Malaise, a result of the babe.

Sadness, due to one man alone.

Manon's swayed weakly. Refusing a supportive hand from a woman nearby, she took a deep breath, nodded her gratitude, and moved on. She had met Gerard in this same market on a similar day. She recalled that the sky had been blue and clear . . . and that she had been hungry enough to steal.

Poverty, however, was no longer a problem. Her purse was

never empty due to Gerard's generosity, although her heart . . .

Manon slid a delicate hand to the flat surface of her stomach, in an unconscious effort to comfort the babe there. Five days had passed since she had last seen Gerard. The memory of her humiliation when he had left her lying on the floor of her room among her discarded clothing, without a word, returned to flush hot color to her face. She had been discarded just as easily as had been those pitiful garments when she had served her purpose. And she was to be pitied as well.

Manon fought the assault of tears. *Non*, she had shed far too many already.

She had cried at the realization that although she had met Gerard with love in every thought, kiss, and touch exchanged between them, and had believed that in his heart he felt the same, she had merely been deceiving herself.

She had sobbed at the admission she had forced herself to concede at last, that Gerard's need for her, a need he resented more than she had permitted herself to recognize, had changed his feelings for her to hatred.

And she had been cast into a well of despair so deep and black that she had not thought she would survive at the knowledge that the only emotion still tying Gerard to her was lust.

Lust, which when indulged without love shamed her more than she could bear.

If not for the babe . . .

Manon pressed her hand warmly against her stomach. Were she another woman, she would have vacated the house Gerard had provided the same night he had shamed her so cruelly. It would not have been difficult. She had been cautious with the sums he had given her. She had a small amount put aside, enough to support herself until the babe came. By that time, a wise investment she had made months earlier would come to fruition, and she would be financially independent, no **longer** needing to **rely on any** man.

But she was not another woman.

For that reason she had decided to remain until Gerard returned so she might face him with those things she had never allowed herself to say before bringing their relationship to an end. She knew he would come back. It was commonly known that Gabrielle had not yet been restored to him. He would ultimately submit to his need for the consolation she had never refused him.

In truth, it was not with animosity that she would end their liaison. The thought of saying goodbye pained her, just as it had distressed her to make the decision to leave without informing Gerard that she carried his child. To walk away would be the hardest thing she would ever do.

Because she loved him still.

Fool that she was.

No longer able to withstand the force of her suppressed emotions, Manon turned abruptly back in the direction she had come. She walked swiftly past the strolling matrons, the laughing children, the gregarious slaves, the curious seamen, the brightly dressed Negroes, the solemn Indians seated outside, her step growing faster and more unsteady.

"Mademoiselle . . ."

Halted by a touch on her arm, Manon turned to a young seaman's scrutiny. A sincere concern tinged with admiration was reflected in his dark eyes.

"Are you well, *mademoiselle?* Is there anything I might do for you?"

Realizing that her face was streaked with tears, Manon brushed them away and forced a smile as she slipped her arm from his grasp.

"Non, but I thank you for your kind offer."

Drawing herself erect with sheer strength of will, Manon raised her chin high. She would be strong for her child . . . stronger than she had ever been.

But the day was hot and the air heavy.

She was perspiring.

She forced herself on.

Rogan steadied himself against another strong gust of wind, glancing briefly upward as the sails flapped and cracked loudly overhead in a cloudless sky. They had traveled smoothly and quickly out to sea since leaving Barataria Bay two days earlier. Uncertain as he had been as to Pointreau's next tack, he knew his only true safety lay in the distance he could put between himself and Grande-Terre while Pointreau was concentrating his efforts there. The water and supplies they had taken aboard immediately upon reaching Barataria, as a precaution against just such an emergency, had served them well. They could remain at sea for weeks if the situation demanded.

He hoped it would not.

He supposed he should be pleased that they had escaped a potentially dangerous situation so easily.

But he was not.

For the torment continued.

Rogan glanced toward the main deck and the two figures walking there. Bertrand and Gabrielle. There was seldom conversation between them as Bertrand maintained sober guard over her during her brief outings on deck. He had been able to dispense with the need for a guard at Gabrielle's door with the use of a simple chain lock, thereby freeing his crewmen for their daily duties. He despised its use but had deemed the precaution necessary with the new animosity between Gabrielle and him since their last encounter.

Rogan continued his surreptitious scrutiny. Gabrielle was sober and pale. The fiery color of her hair as it blew about her face was in stark contrast with her pallor. She was thinner than she had appeared when they last spoke face to face two days previously, her slender proportions even more lost in the shabby male clothing she wore. He supposed he should not be surprised. It had been reported that her trays had gone back to the galley all but untouched since that night.

Rogan turned resolutely back to the horizon. She was so clever—clever enough to use his concern for her as a weapon against him—but he had no intention of falling into her trap.

And a trap was what she was, with her hair blazing in the sun, her pale skin warmed for his touch, and her perfect profile etched against the blue of the sky beyond. He remembered the taste of that taut skin on his lips, her soft sigh. He—

Rogan silently cursed, his gaze returning to Gabrielle as she progressed across the deck, despite himself. Had Pointreau not arrived on Grande-Terre and interfered with his plans, he would still be anchored in Barataria Bay and would now be waiting for the man's response to his demands in exchange for Gabrielle's return. Instead, he was at sea again, forced into endless days of waiting and watching . . .

. . . and aching.

Unprepared for Gabrielle's sudden turn in his direction, Rogan stiffened as their gazes met. Myriad emotions combining in a fleeting moment of excruciating pain, he made an abrupt decision. He had had enough! He would turn the ship back tomorrow and make for the inlet they had previously used. He would dispatch his demands to Pointreau and be done with it.

And with the tormenting *Mademoiselle* Dubay.

Damn her!

Damn him!

He looked at her with true hatred!

Unconsciously steadying herself against the ship's roll as she held the enigmatic Rapace's gaze, Gabrielle wondered if he knew she hated him as well.

Emotions held under tight restraint choked Gabrielle's throat as she brushed flying strands of hair back from her face. That same lump had refused to allow her to swallow anything more than a few bites of the food delivered to her in the past two days.

Or was it her guilt?

Gabrielle struggled to maintain her composure. She had not spoken to the captain since their last furious exchange. She needed no one to tell her that they had headed directly out to sea upon leaving Grande-Terre and that they continued on that course. Where were they going? Why were they going *away* from shore if he intended to press his demands on her father?

Gabrielle closed her eyes against a recurrent fear. He denied he had harmed her father. She wanted to believe that was true.

"Are you all right, Mademoiselle Dubay?"

Gabrielle opened her eyes. Bertrand, ever considerate. Strangely, his scars did not seem so grotesque to her now.

"I'm all right." She could feel the captain's gaze burning into her back. "I . . . I'd like to go back to my cabin now."

Escape . . . from the gaze of a predator.

Refusing to explore the emotions those thoughts raised, Gabrielle turned toward the stairs below.

He could feel the old hag watching him.

Turning abruptly toward the servant who hovered in Manon's sitting-room doorway, Gerard demanded, "Why are you standing there? I told you to go back to your work!"

The old woman frowned, and Gerard was possessed of an urge to wipe the lines of her obvious disapproval from her wrinkled face with the power of his fist. He had read her thoughts the moment he had stepped through Manon's front door and had met her standing in the foyer. She had never liked him. After his last visit to Manon, she hated him. But he would not waste physical effort on an ugly crone such as she.

He would handle her silent defiance in a far more effective way.

He would make Manon dismiss her.

Pointreau inwardly laughed. Yes, that would do. He should have insisted upon it earlier. He would tell Manon as soon as she arrived, and she would not dare refuse him.

When she arrived . . .

Where was she?

Gerard's impatience flared. Manon was his mistress. He paid well for the services she rendered. While their liaison still prevailed, he expected her to avail herself to him whenever and wherever he so desired. He disliked being kept waiting as if he were an unwanted guest in his own house! It was an outrage which he intended to settle to his satisfaction the moment Manon walked through the door.

Gerard snapped to his feet and took a few paces. He was particularly provoked to find himself visiting Manon despite his determination to the contrary . . . but the days had stretched long and the nights longer. His visits to illicit houses specializing in deviations he had hoped would purge the incessant fear for Gabrielle from his mind, if only for a little while, had been ineffective. There had been no relief from the tension caused by Gabrielle's abduction.

No word! No correspondence of any sort from that bastard Captain Whitney! Why did the man tarry in forwarding his demands? Surely the villain knew he would pay any price to have his dear Gabrielle returned to him?

In the meantime he had exhausted every possible avenue of assistance. The governor remained sympathetic to his plight and continued to keep his men on alert, but the effort had seen no results. Contacts in the New Orleanean subculture, in which he secretly indulged his more bizarre tastes, had been similarly unsuccessful.

As for Lafitte, the frustration of that meeting ate insidiously at his innards. He was still incredulous that the man had refused him. He had been so certain the privateer would snap at the chance to have him for an ally. Instead, the bitter humiliation the man had dealt him had delivered nothing but another dead end.

Alone with his fears for Gabrielle and able to find no respite from them, Pointreau had only one person to turn to.

Where was she?

A sound outside the front entrance caused Gerard to turn toward the foyer. He was standing in clear view of the door when it opened.

He paused as Manon's azure gaze met his. It occurred to him that she had never looked lovelier than at that moment, with the upswept gold of her hair curling at her hairline from the moist heat of the day, the shine to her faultless skin lending an aura of youthful dew, and the slight shadows beneath her eyes somehow emphasizing their beauty while adding a hint of fragile appeal.

And she was wearing blue. He preferred to see her in blue.

Gerard tensed. Witch! She had known somehow that he would come today! She had dressed accordingly and then left for the afternoon so she might leave him waiting! And this tantalizingly new quality about her, this aura which he could not quite identify . . .

Voodoo? Black magic?

Anger surged once more at the reality that whatever ruses Manon employed, she had all but enslaved him.

Waiting only until she had closed the door behind her, he demanded, "Where were you?"

Manon raised a hand to a brow glistening with perspiration before taking extended moments to remove her *chapeau* and place it on the foyer table. She paused, noticeably breathless as she dabbed at her forehead with a handkerchief before replying, "I went to the market."

To the market . . . yet she had returned empty-handed.

"I asked you where you were."

"I have already answered that question."

"Not to my satisfaction."

Manon's response was unexpected. "It seems to matter little what I do or say, Gerard, for the outcome is always the same."

What was this new tone to her voice? His eyes narrowed as she walked past him into the sitting room. She waited until he followed before addressing him again.

"There is something that must be settled between us, Gerard."

He nodded. "I would say there is."

Manon made no attempt to alleviate the tension between them. Instead, she rested her arm on the back of an upholstered chair as she prepared to speak. For all her cool composure, he noted that her fingers trembled against the woven fabric as she began.

"There was a time when we first met that I believed I could contribute to your life and return in a way that only I was able the generosity you had shown me. Our liaison was not a business matter for me. You are the only man I have known intimately since my husband's death."

"Yes, your loving, destitute husband who left you penniless."

"*Oui*, my husband who died without leaving me provided for . . . but then, he did not expect to die so young."

"He was a fool who squandered his money without a thought to tomorrow!"

"He cherished me."

"He cherished you enough to leave you hungry and ready to steal to survive!"

"His love was shortsighted. It did not provide for me monetarily after his death, but his love did not debase me."

So, that was it.

"You are angry."

"*Non.*"

"You are displeased with the manner of my departure the last time we were together."

A tremor moved down Gerard's spine when Manon did not reply.

"I was upset. You know how dearly I value Gabrielle. I had had no word of her. I've received no word of her still."

"It was not fear for Gabrielle which drove you to demean me."

"Demean you?" Gerard reached toward Manon, silently cursing to see his hand was trembling. He advanced a step toward her only to see her withdraw. "I was crude, but I did not mean to humiliate you."

"You did."

A gradual panic began to unfurl within Gerard. "You are determined to read premeditation in what was merely a thoughtless moment."

Manon paused in response. Her blunt question was stiffly issued. "Do you hate me, Gerard?"

"Manon"—Gerard closed the distance between them—"you are angry, but you know that I have never needed a woman in the way I need you."

"Oui." Manon stepped back from his touch, her eyes glazing with moisture. "And for that reason you hate me."

"You are wrong."

"I am not wrong. You see, Gerard, I know you well. I knew you resented me because you found in me something you had with no other woman. Strangely, I understood. I knew it threatened you to want me in that special way. But I believed that with time you would come to realize how much could be gained between a man and a woman when a common, intimate need that no one else could satisfy was shared and sated with true affection."

Manon paused, a single tear falling. She brushed it away. "You will notice that I did not use the word 'love.' I would not enter that word in our discourse now, for to use it would be a form of sacrilege."

"Sacrilege!" Gerard felt a slow incredulity encroaching. This Manon who spoke so coolly of their intimacies as if they were a thing of the past was a women he had never seen before. She was a stronger woman, one he could not manipulate as he previously had. No, he need pursue another tack ... for, in truth, he could not yet lose her.

Gerard continued, a new tone of entreaty entering his tone.

"Sacrilege is more properly applied to the thoughts you now utter. Manon, you know how highly I esteem you!"

"You do not."

"I do! But I have been tense of late and I—"

"You hope to appease me now because you don't want me to end our relationship before you are satisfied that you no longer have any use for me."

"*Non!*"

"Because to lose, even something that you intend to eventually cast aside, is against your nature."

"I value you more than you could ever know. I need you, Manon!"

"You do not!"

"I need you *especially* now. Manon, can you not understand? I am alone in my torment without you! Gabrielle is lost somewhere. She is in the hands of a man who feels he can repay a debt of vengeance against me through her. There is not a moment that passes that I am free of tortuous thoughts of how she must be suffering because of me. She is innocent, Manon, hardly more than a child, and she may never be the same again because of an experience for which I am at fault. You—you are the only one who has the capacity to truly understand how I feel, who really cares. You are the only one to whom I may turn."

Trembling, Gerard drew Manon into his arms. The slender warmth of her was a solace that dulled his pain as he whispered against her hair, "*Je t'offense, Manon.* I have offended you. But I will never treat you so cruelly again. Gabrielle is lost to me for I know not how long. I cannot lose you as well!"

"Let me go, Gerard."

Manon's words were a whispered rasp that he ignored as he pressed heated kisses against her fluttering eyelids, her forehead, her cheeks, muttering with true desperation, "I cannot lose you, Manon."

"Gerard . . ." Manon's breast was heaving heavily. He could feel the pounding of her heart echoing his own as she struggled to resist him. But she was losing the battle, a battle he dared not allow her to win as he brushed her lips with his kisses, her throat, her ear, as he pleaded, saying words he had never expected to hear himself speak.

"Forgive me, Manon. *Ma chérie, mon amour,* forgive me." He covered her lips with his, shuddering with the powerful passions his fear of losing her had evoked. He could not lose her . . . not now.

"Manon . . . je t'en prie . . ."

Je t'en prie . . .

I beg you . . .

Gerard's whispered words stunned Manon into breathlessness.

Gerard, *begging* her to forgive him!

She shuddered uncontrollably as he bathed her face with kisses and his whispered litany continued.

Loving words.

Gentle passion.

He loved her.

He did.

He loved her!

Joy abounding, Manon separated her lips under his kiss.

It was night again.

Rogan's cabin was silent, the absence of sound exaggerating each creak and groan of the ship as it rode gently at anchor in the tropical sea. He did not have to look out the porthole to know that the sky was filled with stars more brilliant than a monarch's crown and the sea was gilded with silver in reflection of the great, full moon that ruled over all.

But there was no peace or serenity in the silence. There was only the sound of his restless twisting and turning as the night wore on, along with the barely perceptible rustle of movement in the cabin next door.

Rogan recognized the sounds. Gabrielle could not sleep. Nor had she slept well the previous night, or the one before it. Their last words to each other had been harsh. He had been angry when she had feared for her father—a man who did not deserve her concern or her love. He had wanted to tell her that her father was not the man she believed him to be, that Pointreau was perverted, that he tortured at a whim and enjoyed inflicting humiliation, pain, and even death.

Rogan's thoughts came to an abrupt halt at another sound from Gabrielle's cabin. Suddenly tense, he listened more closely, then was on his feet.

The passageway was dimly lit as he unlocked her cabin door, pushed it open, and stood motionless on the threshold. He heard the sound again.

Crouched beside Gabrielle's bunk, he touched her cheek.

It was wet with tears.

A thickness rising in his own throat, Rogan succumbed to the plethora of emotions assaulting him as he drew Gabrielle into his arms. She did not resist him as he whispered against the familiar fragrance of her hair, "I never wanted to make you cry, Gabrielle. Nor did I ever—for a moment—want to cause you pain."

Rogan raised Gabrielle's face to his. The semidarkness did not conceal the dampness still glistening on her cheeks, the clear translucence of her eyes, or the trembling of her lips as she awaited his next words, the words he could no longer withhold.

"Gabrielle . . . all I truly wanted was to love you."

* * *

The sweet wonder of Rogan's familiar warmth and scent encompassed Gabrielle as his words reverberated in the silence between them.

As he'd stood tall and broad in the cabin doorway moments earlier, in dark relief against the light of the passageway behind him, she had known immediately it was he. But she had been somehow unable to move or utter a sound as he had entered and come to stand over her where she lay. His heavy, dark hair ruffled as if from an impatient hand, his expression sober, the burning gold of his eyes intense in the dim light of the lamp nearby, he had crouched beside her and touched her cheek. It had seemed only natural when he had then taken her into his arms and drawn her close.

All I truly wanted was to love you . . .

Those words, hoarsely and passionately spoken, but . . .

Uncertainty touched Gabrielle's mind.

Was it truly Rogan who was holding her now, speaking to her with such longing? Were these really his arms drawing her closer, his lips touching hers, his kiss drawing from her a yearning so strong, an ardor so deep, that she could do no more than lean into him and respond with the full fervor of her aching heart?

Or . . . was it Rapace?

Gabrielle drew back abruptly from the sweet ecstasy consuming her.

"What's wrong, Gabrielle?"

Quaking, suddenly rigid in his arms, Gabrielle rasped, "Is it truly you, Rogan? Or is it—"

"Rapace?"

The gold eyes that had moments earlier glowed with loving zeal, narrowed, but the predatorial threat did not return. Instead, dawning in them was a hesitance filled with meaning as he whispered, "I wish . . ."

Halting, he stroked back a wisp from her face with a trembling hand, then slid his fingers into her hair, clenching the heavy strands, drawing her closer as he continued earnestly,

"I can only tell you that the man who holds you now is the man you see, Gabrielle. He's the same man who abducted you from the safety of your convent room, the man who held you hostage, who threatened you and imposed his will upon you. He's the man who infuriated you, taunted you, and gave you no rest as you challenged him every step of the way."

Rogan's voice deepened. "But he's also the man who held you safe through each travail, who suffered your discomforts as if they were his own, and who cherished the conversations and simple honesty shared."

Pausing, he continued with a new depth of emotion. "And he is also the man who held you nightly in his arms—arms as empty as his heart while separated from you—and who knew from the first moment he saw you that the time would come when all else would be cast aside and he would hold you as he's holding you now."

Lowering his mouth again to hers, Rogan pressed his kiss more deeply, causing a glorious wave of color to wash across Gabrielle's mind until she floated in a sea of brilliant sensation, each crest taking her higher than before on such magnificent swells that she—

Rogan tore his mouth from hers, his chest was heaving, his features suddenly tight. She saw his difficulty in maintaining restraint as he forced himself to add, "But make no mistake, the man who holds you now is also Rapace, your father's sworn enemy, who will not desert a vow signed in blood."

Gabrielle saw his distress at her soft protest, and the difficulty with which he continued, "But the full truth is that as Rapace holds you hostage, Gabrielle, he is a hostage as well—your hostage, who will know no true triumph or joy in what he is sworn to do."

Her throat so thick she could barely speak, Gabrielle reached up a trembling hand to stroke the lines of strain in Rogan's cheek. Her response was a ragged whisper.

"There is one thing I must know for sure. My father . . . you would not harm him physically . . ."

The lines of strain tightened. "No."

"You will allow justice to be served by the law."

"No."

His unvarnished response shook her.

"Rogan . . ." Her voice caught on a sob. "Tell me something I may cling to!"

Rogan's voice deepened, reflecting her anguish. "I have only one promise to offer you, Gabrielle, that the moments we spend in each other's arms will be beautiful, because I'll make them beautiful. I'll give you all I have to give, so we may put to rest the aching need that is devouring us both. Together, Gabrielle, as it was meant to be . . ."

Oh, yes, she knew the truth of those words. They had been written in the heart that Rogan had gradually revealed to her. She heard it in the sound of his voice as he now spoke, and felt it in the emotion he struggled to restrain as he awaited her response.

No apologies.

No promises.

No tomorrows.

Just a passion that would bow to restraint . . . if she refused him.

If she *could* refuse him.

But . . .

. . . she could not.

Long moments stretching into eternity as vocal response eluded her, Gabrielle slid her arms onto Rogan's shoulders. She saw the effort he expended to hold himself immobile as she raised her lips to his, caught the revealing twitch of his jaw as her fingers slipped into his hair and she cupped his head with her palms to draw his mouth to hers. A shudder racked him the moment before his arms snapped around her to crush her close.

Rogan ... Rapace ... one and the same, the man who had stolen her heart.

The beauty of the moment supreme, Rogan clutched Gabrielle close as he lay beside her. She was an unexpected wonder, a boundless joy, a treasure he had never expected to possess. He kissed her, winding his hands in the burnished strands that had so tempted him, splaying his fingers wide.

The heavy locks were warm silk against his callused palms. Her brow clear and smooth as he traced it with his lips. Her fluttering lids warm under his kiss. He felt the life pulsing though her as he pressed his mouth to her temple, against the rise of her cheek, the curve of her ear, and then her lips again—so sweet ... so incredibly sweet.

Unable to suffer a buffer between them, Rogan tore his mouth from Gabrielle's to throw back the coverlet. He heard her gasping breath as he loosened the cotton shirt she wore. He saw the momentary fear that gripped her as he stripped the garment away, leaving her naked to his gaze and he felt her stiffen as he dispensed with his gaping shirt as well and then undid the buttons on his britches.

The tremor that shook Gabrielle as his naked masculinity was fully revealed to her raised in Rogan a tenderness unlike any he had ever known. Lowering himself slowly upon her, he withheld his own gasp of supreme pleasure as their flesh met for the first time, forcing restraint to ease her uncertainty with an instinctive assurance that came from the heart.

"This night is ours, Gabrielle. It will be ours forever."

He covered her parted lips with his then, devouring them until he could stand the torment no longer. He again tasted her cheek, her chin, the column of her throat, the curve of her shoulder. He drew back, feeling the pounding of her heart as he cupped the swells of her breasts, then slowly, deliberately covered an erect, roseate crest with his mouth. A jolt of ecstasy shooting through him as Gabrielle gasped aloud, he suckled the virgin mound, drawing deeply, his hands roaming her silken flesh.

The narrow waist, the curve of her hip, the flat expanse of Gabrielle's stomach—these were a feast he tasted with growing ardor. He felt Gabrielle stiffen as he neared the shadowed delta between her thighs and brushed it with his lips. Her mumbled protest raised him to note the shadow of fear in her eyes, and his throat tightened.

No, it was too soon . . .

Sliding himself back atop her, Rogan covered Gabrielle's lips with his once more, lingering to search the hollows of her mouth with loving indulgence. The urgency within growing gradually more than he could bear, he drew back from the kiss with an ardent whisper that reflected a last, nagging uncertainty.

"I want to hear you say you want me, Gabrielle."

Tenderness again surged as the pink tint of Gabrielle's cheeks deepened to a flush, as her eyes searched his with innocent need.

Oh, yes, she wanted him. She needed him.

He encouraged her softly. "Tell me, Gabrielle."

Rogan's hand slipped down to caress the soft nest he had abandoned moments earlier. A chill raced down his spine at the damp proof of the emotions Gabrielle could not express. A new shuddering beginning within him, he fondled the moistness, slipping within to find the bud of her passion. He stroked it gently, noting the escalating beating of her heart against his as he whispered, "Tell me how you feel, Gabrielle."

Gabrielle's eyelids fluttered as his gentle stroking grew bolder. He brushed her trembling lips with his, tracing their delicate outline with his tongue as his intimate caresses continued.

"Do you like me to touch you, Gabrielle? Tell me . . . tell me what you want."

He gnawed tenderly at her lips, at the delicate indentation

in her chin. He felt her hand in his hair as she rasped, "I like you to touch me . . . like that."

"Like what?"

"The way . . . you're touching me now."

"Like this?" He stroked her more sensuously.

She caught her breath.

"How much do you like it?"

She was breathing heavily.

"How much?"

"Very much."

"Do you want me to stop?"

"No."

"What else do you want, Gabrielle? Tell me. Darling . . . tell me."

"I want . . ."

"Gabrielle . . ."

"I . . . I want more."

Her whispered gasp raising his blood to liquid heat, Rogan kissed her with bruising passion, the fire within him expanding.

Yes, he knew what Gabrielle wanted . . . even if she did not.

Drawing back from her lips as he deepened his intimate caress, Rogan felt Gabrielle's wonder move to torment. He urged, "Do you want me to kiss you, darling?"

Her heart thundered against his. "Yes."

"Deeply?"

It pounded harder. "Yes."

"Do you want me to make you feel—"

"Yes . . . yes . . . yes."

His own crying need suddenly beyond control, Rogan slid down upon Gabrielle. His palms brushed her trembling flesh, slipping beneath her as he cupped her firm buttocks with his hands and raised her to him. He felt the shudder that racked Gabrielle as he brushed the dark, moist curls between her thighs with his lips. Her warm, female scent rose to his nostrils, inflaming him as he pressed his lips to the damp crevice below, as he slid his tongue into the moistness, seeking the tender bud he had stroked to aching life.

Gabrielle's soft cry raised his gaze to hers. He soothed the flicker of panic he read there with his throbbing whisper.

"Tonight is ours, Gabrielle. Ours alone."

Maintaining Gabrielle's gaze for long moments as her panic slowly faded, Rogan then lowered his mouth to the warm crevice awaiting him. He pressed his gentle assault there, finding the sweet bud of her passion and drawing from it with his intimate kiss. His ardor deepening, he spread her thighs wide, laving her, suckling, indulging the rioting passions within as Gabrielle's sensuous writhing grew intense, as her groaning intensified, as she quaked and quivered and—

Rogan drew back abruptly.

Her heart racing, her sense reeling from the wild range of sensation Rogan had raised within her, Gabrielle knew a moment's panic as Rogan drew back abruptly from his intimate pursuit. But the heat within her flamed hotter as he stared up at her, silently communicating the new depth of passion reflected in the burning incandescence of his eyes, as he slowly, with great deliberation, lowered his mouth to her waiting flesh once more.

She felt it rising then, a wave of inner heat and wonder that left her breathless, an excitement almost more than she could bear, a feeling of expectancy, a trembling, aching vibrancy about to burst within.

She heard Rogan rasp. "Let your feelings soar. Give to me, Gabrielle . . . now. Give to me, darling."

Somehow freed by the burning intensity of his tone, Gabrielle's body quaked with the first warning shudder, then coursed with a rapture that swelled on brilliant waves of heat and light . . . so high . . . so bright . . .

Her eyes fluttered closed as Rogan shifted atop her, the full, hard length of him flush against her, silk against steel, as she sought to catch her breath. The shaft of his passion probed her moistness, and she opened her eyes to see Rapace's predatorial gaze devouring her ... even as Rogan's passionate voice whispered, "You're mine, Gabrielle ... tonight you're mine."

With a sudden thrust that elicited both pleasure and pain, he was within her.

Gabrielle saw regret flicker on Rogan's face as she sought to catch her breath, then resolution as Rogan plunged deeply once more.

The rhythm of loving began.

Caught up in its cadence, Gabrielle was uncertain of the moment when her arms slipped around Rogan, when she began rising to his thrusts, when they became truly one in the loving union that had joined them. She knew only that his strength renewed her. His fervor heightened hers. His loving words echoed in her heart and mind until she could hear no other sound.

"Gabrielle ..."

Her name rang softly in the silence, drawing Gabrielle's eyes open to see Rogan poised above her. Passion written in the tight lines of his face, he whispered, "Tell me you want me, Gabrielle. Tell me you need me."

Hardly recognizing the husky voice that emerged from her throat as her own, Gabrielle replied from the deep well of emotion Rogan had stirred to life within her, "Oh yes, I want you, Rogan. I need you ..."

It happened then, the starting cataclysm that assumed control as Rogan's pressed his final thrust, as his powerful body shuddered with violent spasms, carrying her with him as he careened from the pinnacle of his passion in the glory of total culmination.

The light of the lamp flickered weakly as Rogan raised himself above her. Gabrielle opened her eyes to the sight of his silent anxiety as he scrutinized her with a gaze of soul-shaking tenderness.

She knew there was only one way to salve the concern she read there. She did it lovingly as she drew his mouth down to hers once more.

The passageway lights flickered as Bertrand paused outside Gabrielle's cabin door. The chain was loosened, and he had heard the sounds within. There had been no mistaking the low rumble of Rogan's voice, or Gabrielle's gasping reply.

Bertrand frowned as he turned slowly back in the direction from which he had come.

Manon was dozing.

Silent, lying beside her in the ruffled, lace and batiste bedroom that so stifled him, Gerard studied his mistress's sleeping countenance as the hours of night stretched on. He had made certain to eliminate any remaining doubts she harbored about his feelings for her with his devoted attentions throughout the day.

He had exhausted her.

Gerard's expression hardened. They had made love several times, the first being immediately after he had won her back from her intended departure. Oh, yes, he had made certain to impress her with his passion then.

He had lingered through the afternoon and shared the evening meal that the old crone had prepared, making certain that after they returned from their brief promenade, he proved his devotion to Manon again.

Manon had been ecstatic, passionate in each encounter . . . at her very best.

Gerard sneered. He had been at his best also.

He had perpetuated the lie between them for a while longer,

and he would make certain that the situation remained so, while it suited his purpose.

Gerard scrutinized Manon's fair, unlined face, a familiar emotion tugging in his groin. She appeared so innocent, but he knew the truth. He no longer had any doubt that she employed the black arts against him. Nothing else could have caused his overwhelming panic at the thought of losing her.

Je t'en prie . . .

Humiliation flushed Gerard's bearded face at the words he had uttered.

He had *begged* her to forgive him.

Gerard fought to draw his emotions under control. Whatever her power, Manon had worked her magic again. In her arms he had found a release that had cleared his mind and renewed him. He was prepared for the day that would dawn in a few hours, and somehow certain that he would soon hear from the delinquent Captain Whitney.

Yes, he was in control again, and during the hours recently past when his mind had been freed from the agitation formerly binding it, he had experienced a revelation that he was certain would eventually deliver the bastard captain into his hands. He was incredulous that he had not realized it before.

He would set a new plan into motion when the day dawned.

But in the meantime . . .

Gerard moved closer to the sleeping Manon. Rock hard and ready, he adjusted her carefully, spreading her legs as she mumbled in her sleep. He then slipped to his knees, straddling her as he arched himself above her. He was smiling as he positioned himself, then thrust full and deep within her.

Smothering Manon's pained cry with his kiss, Gerard clutched her close. Refusing to release her, he continued his painful, intimate assault, halting only when he erupted in full, throbbing ejaculation.

He whispered softly against her lips in response to her tears.

"My need for you was so great . . ."

Manon did not respond, but he did not fear.

She would choose to forgive him.

Again.

He inwardly laughed.

Oh, yes, in so many subtle ways, he would make her pay.

Gabrielle was dozing.

The cabin's lamp flickered low, casting Gabrielle's delicate features into the shadows as Rogan clutched her close. Her head was pillowed against his chest, rising and falling with his steady breaths, her fingers wound in the dark hairs. They had seemed to curl spontaneously as sleep gradually overcame her. He knew because he had not been able to tear his eyes from her.

She was beautiful. He had not fully realized how beautiful, for surely there was no hair more gloriously glowing than Gabrielle's as it spilled against his chest, no lashes were as long as those that lay against the faultless skin of her cheeks . . . no lips were so warm and so vibrantly colored.

Carefully slipping back the coverlet so he might view her in her entirety, Rogan experienced a heated rush of emotion as her naked form was fully exposed. Her breasts, so perfectly shaped with the blushing crests he had come to know so well . . . her female delta, the sweet taste of which lingered . . . He trailed his gaze down the long, slender, perfectly shaped legs that afforded her unusual height, smiling at her feet, surprisingly small for her size, their toes curling tightly as she pressed closer.

His smile gradually fading as another, more intense emotion assumed control, Rogan turned onto his side, toward Gabrielle. She frowned in her sleep, mumbling softly as he adjusted her flush against him. Face to face, chest to chest, heat to heat, he licked lightly at her lips, and they parted. He slipped his tongue between them, and her mouth met his. He cupped her head with his hand, holding her close as he kissed her fully, and her eyes fluttered open. Her arms slipped around him as their lips melded once more.

Wonder was reflected in Gabrielle's light eyes when he drew back at last. Suddenly intensely grateful that he did not see remorse, Rogan spoke softly, with a depth of meaning that went beyond his words.

"You're beautiful, Gabrielle."

"No."

"Yes."

Slipping onto his back, Rogan carried her with him to lie prone atop his naked length. Her heavy hair brushed his face, and he inhaled its scent as she raised herself to look down into his face. Supporting herself on one arm, unexpectedly sober as her heart pounded against his, she held his gaze for long moments before lowering her mouth to his for a tentative kiss.

A sudden flush set Rogan's heart to pounding, but he resisted the urge to clasp Gabrielle close to pursue the emotions she had so easily raised. Instead, sensing a need she did not herself recognize, he remained motionless, waiting as she stroked his cheek, tracing the lines there as she followed the curve of his jaw, then ran her fingertips across his lips.

Seeing the hesitation that followed, Rogan whispered huskily, "Do you want to touch me, Gabrielle?"

Gabrielle's throat worked tightly. Her lips parted as she nodded, her expression intent. Taking the hand she rested tentatively against his jaw, Rogan pressed her palm flat as he slid it down his throat, along his shoulder, then moved it slowly across his chest. Releasing her hand as it rested warmly there, he cupped her rounded breasts. She gasped as he fondled them gently, his callused fingertips working the erect nipples as he whispered, "Touch me, Gabrielle. It's all right."

Rogan held his breath, stroking her more impassionedly as she stroked him in return, as she caressed his chest with increasing fervor, as she followed the course of dark hair that dwindled gradually downward, pausing as she reached the male organ that lay hard and stiff against him. His grating whisper of her name was as much an encouragement as a plea.

"Gabrielle . . ."

Rogan caught his breath as Gabrielle touched him, then closed her hand more firmly around him. He saw that his breathlessness raised the same breathlessness within her as she caressed the stiff flesh, as she released him abruptly, then slipped up to press her mouth passionately to his.

A jolt of flame seared Rogan as Gabrielle's tongue brushed his. Her sudden moistness warmed his flesh, snapping his restraint as he rolled abruptly atop her, crushing her beneath him to press the kiss deeper, more passionately, as he laved her neck and shoulders with his tongue, then suckled her breasts with growing fervor. She did not resist when he slid again onto his back, reversing their positions as he adjusted her to straddle him, then drawing her up so he might suckle her breasts with greater ease. Abruptly carrying her to a seated position with him, raising her hands to cup the back of her head to lend him full access to the firm white mounts that so inflamed him, Rogan swallowed them with his kisses.

His emotions at a fever pitch, knowing Gabrielle was similarly aroused, Rogan then covered her mouth with his, reveling in the passion she returned to him without restraint as he lay backward, drawing her down with him.

Gabrielle was stretched out upon him, the heat of her searing him when he sensed her first inner quaking. Knowing the time was near, wanting to allow her passion full rein, Rogan raised her to a seated position upon him, then took her trembling hand and closed it around his aching member, urging, "Take me inside you, Gabrielle."

Her light eyes held his, but she remained immobile. Recognizing her inexperience, Rogan massaged the moist nest pressed tight against him, whispering, "Bring me home, darling."

His heart pounding so violently that he believed it might burst, Rogan waited as she raised herself slowly above him. He echoed Gabrielle's gasp as she gripped him with her trembling hand and lowered her body upon him to bring him to rest within her.

Wonder ... elation ... joy!

Soaring emotions ignited within Rogan! Gabrielle's ecstatic flush set the wonder to flame as he moved subtly within her. His rhythm rapidly accelerating, he felt the moment approaching as she groaned softly, then echoed his gasp to join him in the burst of shuddering ecstasy that brought the wonder of their lovemaking to fruition.

The moistness of their mutual passion binding them, Gabrielle lay motionless atop Rogan moments later. His arms refusing to surrender her, Rogan clasped her breathlessly close.

Gabrielle—spark to his match, tinder to his flame.

His, and his alone ...

... if only for a little while.

That thought sobering, Rogan clutched her with an intensity that did not lessen despite the passionate moments past.

Gabrielle—a treasure, a torment.

His passion, his love.

Yes, *his love.*

Oh, God ... what had he done?

Gabrielle came to gradual awakening as the sounds of morning reverberated beyond her cabin door. Her eyes half-closed as images of the passionate night past flashed before her, she swallowed tightly. She moved her hand on the bunk beside her, her eyes snapping fully open when she found it empty.

Disappointment tinged with uncertainty touched Gabrielle when she glanced around her. Rogan was gone. He had not awakened her to say goodbye.

Her face flamed. That wanton who had emerged in Rogan's arms . . .

Gabrielle took a steadying breath.

But the tenderness . . . the beauty . . .

The knot of emotion within her was almost painful.

She loved him.

She did.

Oh, God . . . she did.

At the sound of a footstep outside her door, Gabrielle's heart leaped.

"Mademoiselle Dubay . . ."

Bertrand.

Gabrielle clutched the coverlet around her nakedness, calling out unsteadily, "Yes?"

"Do you wish to go up on the main deck now?"

She blinked. Was it already so late?

Her flush deepened as she responded, "If you will return in a few minutes . . ."

Jumping out of the bunk at the sound of Bertrand's retreating step, Gabrielle raced to the washstand, a sense of apprehension slowly dawning.

Rogan—Rapace—which would be the man to greet her?

Her hands shaking, she reached for the washbowl.

Gerard closed the front door of Manon's small house quietly behind him and stepped out onto the street. A tight smile flickered across his lips as he adjusted his cravat, straightened his coat, and entered the morning traffic passing by.

His smile broadened at a glance from a flirtatious young maid, but he dismissed her from his mind moments later as thoughts of the woman he had left asleep filled him with a true satisfaction.

He had given Manon little peace through the night, despite her increasing groans at the fierceness of his attentions. He had allowed himself a brief, satisfying glimpse of the bruises left on her white flesh, marks he was certain she would convince herself were inadvertently inflicted in passion. He would return tonight—and every night until Gabrielle was back with him. He would allow Manon no opportunity to claim neglect.

In the meantime . . .

Pointreau's lips tightened.

Yes, in the meantime . . .

The sea was rough, the wind increasing. The darkening sky portended poorly for the day to come. A storm was in the making.

Rogan fixed his gaze on the seaman descending the shrouds after securing a loose sail. The fellow stepped onto the deck and turned toward him. Rogan nodded, signifying a job well done, his mind immediately returning to the two walking along the main deck below him.

Frowning, Rogan recalled meeting Bertrand as he'd stepped into the passageway from Gabrielle's cabin in the first light of dawn. Disapproval had been clearly written on the scarred face, and Rogan had been stunned by the intensity of his rage at Bertrand's presumption.

Then he had seen himself through Bertrand's eyes.

Despite all his previous disavowals as Gabrielle had led him from one furious encounter to another, she had been vulnerable, defenseless, and innocent of any culpability in her father's crimes. He had taken advantage of his position of power, knowing full well that nothing would change his intended plans. He had also known that in destroying her father, he would earn her hatred and destroy her future as well.

Yet he had taken her innocence, taken it with a loving passion that would leave her unprepared for what was in store.

He had succumbed to his desire without thought to the result.

And, he had made an error in judgment which he could not afford to repeat.

Gabrielle glanced toward him unexpectedly and Rogan's frown deepened. He had no choice in what he must do.

The ache within intense, he turned his back on Gabrielle to scrutinize the swelling sea.

So, it was over.

The deck dipped beneath Gabrielle's feet, rising again on another billowing crest only to dip once more as the wind surged relentlessly. But the growing turbulence of the sea was far from her mind as her gaze lingered on Rogan's broad back.

Suddenly aware of Bertrand's gaze, Gabrielle turned swiftly away, the knot in her throat tightening.

It was not as if he hadn't warned her.

No apologies.

No promises.

No tomorrows.

Rogan had fulfilled the only promise he had made. He had made it beautiful between them when she had lain in his arms. He had made the night they shared theirs forever.

"Mademoiselle Dubay . . . are you all right?"

Gabrielle looked up at Bertrand. His emotionless expression betrayed little, but she knew he was concerned. She wondered if he knew that she . . .

A slow flush transfusing her, Gabrielle glanced away, struggling against the rising heat under her eyelids.

"Yes, I'm fine. I think, perhaps, the uncertain seas have—" She halted, unable to continue her falsehood. She looked back up at Bertrand, attempting a smile. "I think, perhaps, that it's best I not make excuses that would be unbelievable at best. I-I'd like to go below now."

She turned toward the stairs to the berth deck, tears suddenly blinding her. She had been such a naïve fool. She had convinced herself, when Rogan had held her in his arms, that she heard an emotion in his voice that went beyond his

words. She had told herself that he could not have taken her
with such loving tenderness if his feelings were not deeply involved. She had made herself believe that when morning
came, he would not be able to part from her . . . just as she
knew she would not be able to part from him.

She had been wrong.

Vengeance had been Rogan's motivation in abducting her.
Nothing had happened to change that. Nothing would keep
him from it.

Her vision blurred by the tears she held so tightly in check,
Gabrielle did not see the coiled rope lying in her path. Stumbling over it, she lurched suddenly forward, gasping as the
hard surface of the deck rose up to meet her. Saved from the
impending contact by a rough grip on her arm, she turned to
thank Bertrand, only to meet angry gold eyes only inches
from hers.

"Rogan . . ."

He gripped her arm more tightly, not bothering to respond
as he turned, addressing Bertrand instead.

"You may return to your duties."

Gabrielle was not conscious of the revealing few moments
of hesitation before Bertrand followed Rogan's command. Instead, she waited until Rogan turned back toward her, noting
that the anger in his gaze did not lessen as he cupped her arm
with his, guiding her stiffly toward the far rail.

Halting a distance away, where they might not be overheard, Rogan turned toward her, his features tight, his voice
clipped.

"There are some things we must settle between us before
distraction becomes injury." He paused, then continued,
"Last night was unwise. It would be even more unwise to allow the situation to continue."

Vocal response was beyond Gabrielle.

"I have ordered the ship back toward New Orleans so I
may slip men ashore to deliver my demands to your father. If

he complies without delay, you will be home with him within a fortnight at most."

Gabrielle nodded again.

Rogan searched her face with a gaze that was almost palpable in its intensity. His voice deepened. "I felt it best to leave your cabin before dawn so you might not be compromised. It was not my intention . . ." He paused again. "I hoped to spare you."

"I understand."

Rogan's jaw tightened. "Do you? Gabrielle . . ." Rogan's gaze flickered, dropping briefly to her lips in a way that started her heart slowly pounding. "I have only one true regret about last night, however unwise it was—that it must be the last night we share. But too much stands between us."

Gabrielle swallowed. "Too much?"

"I will show your father no mercy in my demands, and he will meet them to save you from me. That eventuality appears very distant now, but the truth is, you will return to him to share all that follows. You will look back on these days differently then."

"A fortnight."

Rogan searched Gabrielle's face.

"No longer."

"No longer . . ."

The molten gold of Rogan's eyes consumed her, and Gabrielle knew. She had made her choice long before any had been offered to her. Uncertain whether there was yet any choice remaining, she whispered, "Do you want me, Rogan?"

Rogan's jaw locked tight.

"Because if you do, I am yours."

Aware of the rigid control Rogan maintained, she moved closer so her soft voice might be heard over the battering of the wind. "Last night was ours alone, because while I am on this ship, the world beyond is a distant place where difficult realities need not yet be faced. This is still the case—for a little while."

Rogan's expression did not change. "Do you know what you're saying?"

"I do."

"You're certain?"

"I need no time to reconsider." Never more sure of her feelings than at that moment as love swelled within her, Gabrielle lay the palm of her hand against Rogan's chest. She felt the tremor that shuddered through him at the contact and the responsive thundering of his heart. It gave her the courage to speak the words she had withheld. "I want you to love me."

"Gabrielle . . ."

"I want to spend each night remaining in your arms."

"Your father?"

"A fortnight, Rogan . . ."

A sudden blast of wind almost knocking her from her feet, Gabrielle welcomed Rogan's arms which snapped around her. She saw the glowing heat in his eyes as he pulled her briefly close, then turned her firmly toward the steps below.

The wind howled, hammering the hull of the *Raptor* with the raging torrent that poured from the angry night sky. Her sails tightly furled, her anchor secure, the ship pitched and rolled, rising and falling as she rode out the last hours of the summer storm.

In his cabin below, Rogan curled his arm more tightly around Gabrielle, smiling fleetingly as she burrowed closer. Her eyes flickered open, and she returned his smile. He recalled the circumstances of the previous storm they had ridden out together, grateful that Gabrielle had conquered the sea's torment without difficulty. Somehow he would not have expected less.

Her gaze lingered on his face and Rogan dipped his mouth to hers. The loving hours recently past had been more tempestuous than the storm that had raged around them. In their wake, the afterglow of love remained . . . an afterglow that would burn forever in his heart.

Rogan's lips clung to Gabrielle's. He could not get enough of the warmth that set him aflame. He could not get enough of the taste that tantalized his senses.

He could not get enough of Gabrielle.

Gabrielle pressed herself closer to Rogan. The soft litany of love that he whispered against her ear was a gentle prayer that echoed in her heart.

The exquisite moment was a precious gift, yet a torment beyond bearing, when she recalled . . .

. . . how short their time would be.

Chapter 7

Clarice maintained a deliberate pace as she walked along Royal Street, past the impressive mansions along the way. She glanced up at the blue sky above, at the small puffs of clouds floating in the otherwise clear expanse, recalling a time when Maman, she, and Bertrand lived in a great house similar to those she now passed.

Maman had been beautiful and adored by all after Papa died. It had been generally believed that although Papa's fortune had deteriorated badly in his final years, their future would not be affected, for Maman was pursued by some of the most wealthy men in New Orleans.

Clarice's pleasant memories turned abruptly bitter. But Maman was too kind. She took in a poor and broken woman who came to her door penniless and without friends because she remembered a debt owed to her. She refused to surrender the woman to the curse that followed her, incurring the wrath of that same curse herself.

Maman died badly, and the curse was passed on.

Clarice did not care to remember the times that followed and torments the she and Bertrand suffered. She knew only that during those trials she learned the value of true friendship . . . and love.

Her step unconsciously slowed as she neared the well-kept mansion at the end of the street. Her heart began a heavy pounding as she stared at the polished oak door. It occurred to her that she could not even be certain Gerard Pointreau was at home behind that door. She had found herself certain of very little during the days recently past.

She had received no word from Rogan or Bertrand.

No news of Gabrielle Dubay.

There was no hint of where Gerard Pointreau had gone when he'd left New Orleans so mysteriously, then returned.

There was not even a rumor that ransom demands had been delivered to Gerard Pointreau.

What had happened?

Why the delay?

Where were Rogan and Bertrand?

What were they doing?

Clarice attempted to settle the disquiet that fluttered in her stomach as she raised a tentative hand to the pale yellow chapeau that rested on her golden curls. She was impeccably and tastefully dressed, and outwardly composed as her position as a discriminating courtesan demanded.

But inwardly her fears raged. For that reason she had been so foolish as to find herself deliberately strolling past Gerard Pointreau's house in the hope that she would encounter the man ... perhaps engage him in conversation ... or possibly be fortunate enough to find a way to discover—

"Clarice, *ma chérie* ..."

The sound of a familiar voice caused Clarice to turn to the carriage drawing up beside her.

But within was not the man she had hoped to meet.

Pierre stepped down from the vehicle sweeping off his hat to expose the thick, brown curls he could not seem to tame as he took her hand and drew it to his lips. His eyes searched hers with uncertainty.

"I paid you an unexpected visit only to have Madame extend her regrets. Were it not for Mimi's help, I would not have known where to seek you." Pierre looked toward the doorway at which she had been staring, his gaze concerned. "I did not interrupt your plans . . . ?"

Disquiet tightened Clarice's stomach into quick knots. Mimi, the slender brunette whose room was a few doors down from hers, paid far too much attention to affairs not of her concern. Pierre's curiosity, perhaps even suspicion, had been stirred. For all the kindnesses he had shown her, she dared not allow him to consider that she had any interest in or connection to Gerard Pointreau.

Her mind raced as she dabbed her handkerchief at her forehead, managing a casual sigh.

"Pierre, I am so pleased to see you. The day was too beautiful to squander indoors. I thought to stroll through the streets where I spent my childhood." And as Pierre's brow rose in surprise, "Did you not know that my brother and I once lived well, behind great oak doors such as these?" She shrugged. "*Oui*, we did. It is strange how the path of life sometimes deviates, is it not?"

Taking a step closer to Pierre as he released her hand, Clarice slanted him a coquettish smile. "Did you come to invite me for an outing, Pierre? I am available, you see, for I have tired of my visit with memories."

"I can think of no better way to spend the day than with you."

Pierre opened the carriage door and helped her step within. He seated himself beside her and issued curt instructions to the driver before turning to cup the back of her head with his palm and draw her mouth to his. It occurred to Clarice as he separated her lips with an unexpectedly passionate kiss, that Pierre was an expert at all forms of intimate exchange, so much so that she found herself sometimes wondering—

Gabrielle was snapped from her thoughts as Pierre drew back abruptly to whisper, "You are mine, Clarice, or so our agreement claims. But will I ever claim your heart?"

"My heart? *Mon cher* . . ." Clarice smiled teasingly, "Surely you know that the heart of one such as I is not truly hers to give."

"Do not demean yourself, Clarice!" Pierre's face flushed with hot color. "I ask you to remember that in demeaning yourself you demean me as well."

Pierre's unexpected anger raised the heat of true tears under her lids as Clarice returned softly, "I apologize, Pierre. It appears I have offended you. That was never my intent."

"Clarice, can you not see." His anger fading as quickly as it had come, Pierre continued, "As you regard yourself, you regard me—as your attend yourself, you attend me . . . for you have become a part of me. You have secured yourself a place in my heart, even if I have not secured myself a place in yours."

"All this talk of hearts," Somehow unable to face the serious vein their discourse had taken, Clarice took Pierre's hand and placed it over her breast, her voice growing husky, "Do you feel how mine is pounding?"

"You do not deceive me *mon amie*." Pierre stroked the soft swell gently, "You hope to distract me from the conversation we have been pursuing. It must be obvious to you how easily you achieve your purpose, for I ever desire you. But as this moment fades, another will eventually appear, because my feelings will not pale." Pausing, Pierre added with gentle intensity, "It is my hope you recognize the sincerity of my words, *mon amie*."

"I do, Pierre."

Leaning forward, he whispered against her lips, "Shall we draw the shade?"

Clarice's heart leaped as Pierre slipped her gown from her shoulder and kissed the delicate skin there.

"Oui"

The sound of her breathless response resounded softly as he leaned across her to pull down the shade.

Thoughts of the house with the great oak door momentarily cast aside, Clarice moved into Pierre's arms.

* * *

The morning was clear, the wind brisk, the ship bobbing like a toy on the choppy sea as the Raptor's crew prepared to lower a boat. It had been a difficult few hours, with a sail badly hooked upon a spar impeding their progress, and with men forced to work aloft in the dangerous wind, increasing the tension that abounded. Rogan had known that the success of their plan depended heavily on the timing involved. He had also known they could ill afford mistakes in the dangerous task ahead.

Rogan turned to scan the gleaming surface of the sea around them. He disliked this change of plan that Pointreau had forced by his appearance on Grande-Terre. His intention to lie at anchor in Barataria Bay while his men made their way back to the city to deliver his demands to Pointreau fouled, he was forced into an alternate plan that was far more dangerous.

To drop anchor so close to New Orleans, although the inlet was relatively obscure, had been dangerous enough when he had abducted Gabrielle. Now, with the governor's men actively alerted for the appearance of any suspicious ships, it was even more precarious. The need to put his messengers ashore without detection was essential.

Rogan reviewed his revised plan in his mind. He would use two men to deliver his demands, one as guard due to the new risk involved. Enough time had passed, and enough avenues had been exhausted for Pointreau to become desperate to hear word of Gabrielle's welfare. Rogan's men would immediately deliver the communication to him. He would then allow two days for the copies of Pointreau's confession of involvement with Gambi to begin appearing around the city, another two for the dismissal of charges against Captain Rogan Whitney and his "accomplices" to be posted as well, and the final two days for the newspaper announcement that Pointreau had transferred funds to an account that might be petitioned by the heirs of the seamen who had lost their lives on the *Venture*.

Six days . . .

He would return to rendezvous with his men at the inlet on the night following the sixth day. He would send Gabrielle back to her father upon confirmation of Pointreau's compliance.

If the man did not agree to his terms, however . . .

Rogan had not yet composed the letter that would then be delivered, informing Pointreau that he would never see his daughter again.

A surfeit of painful emotion suddenly assaulting him, Rogan forced himself to face the alternative measures he would be obliged to take. Prior to meeting Gabrielle, he would have had no difficulty in finding a port where a young woman such as she could easily be placed, never to surface in her father's world again. Nor would he have had any qualms in following through on that. But now . . .

Rogan shrugged that thought away. Pointreau was certain to meet his demands and save him from considering alternative measures. The man was vain enough to believe that once Gabrielle was returned to him, he would be able to reverse the downward spiral of his life.

Rogan was determined he would not.

"Captain . . ."

Rogan turned as Bertrand appeared beside him. Porter stood waiting a few feet away. Two men whom he would trust with his life . . .

Rogan searched Bertrand's sober expression. "You are prepared?"

"Aye."

"Rendezvous on the sixth or seventh day. We will be awaiting your signal from the shore."

Bertrand nodded.

"You will convey my warm regards to Clarice and tell her that if all goes well, I will see her again soon."

"I will."

Scrutinizing his first mate a moment longer, Rogan offered, "Justice will soon be served and the years spent in preparation will be justified for us all."

Unable—or unwilling—to define the feeling with which he watched Porter follow Bertrand over the side to the boat awaiting below, Rogan was intensely aware that the clearly defined quest for justice long overdue had become a complicated morass from which he could only extricate himself by going forward.

Fixing his mind on the common purpose shared by all, he watched Bertrand and Porter's descent until they reached the boat, then signaled preparation for quick departure.

Standing silently on a secluded corner of the deck, her baggy seaman's attire blending so well with the garb of the men working around her as to leave her ignored amongst the frantic activity, Gabrielle watched Bertrand and Porter reach the waiting boat. Pervading the tense scene as it unfolded was the sense of a common purpose shared by all aboard . . .

. . . except her.

Gabrielle stared at Rogan as he turned with a few terse words that snapped his seamen to his command. She had grown familiar with the sight of him, his impressive height and powerful stretch of shoulders as he gripped the rail with tight fists, his dark, shoulder-length hair blowing in the stiff breeze, his strong features almost hawklike in their unyielding intensity as he followed the progress of the boat toward shore.

The chilling, penetrating gold of his gaze . . .

Rapace had again returned.

. . . *You will convey my warm regards to Clarice and tell her that if all goes well, I will see her again soon* . . .

She had heard him speak those words.

Clarice . . . Was this the woman to whom Rapace would return when she was back with her father?

That thought only one of the painful uncertainties assaulting her as she observed the silent vigor in the activities of all, Gabrielle felt her puzzlement grow. All this—the elaborate plans involved in her abduction, the devotion of countless seamen to Rogan's cause, the unyielding fervor she had seen evinced not only in Rogan's gaze, but in Bertrand's, and in that of each man aboard—what had Father done to deserve such hatred?

Suddenly recognizing the direction in which her thoughts were traveling, Gabrielle brought them up short. What was she imagining? Father could not have done anything so vile as to earn such fierce animosity! It was all a mistake. It could be nothing else.

Following Bertrand's and Porter's progress toward shore, Gabrielle was suddenly aware that mistake or not, the dangerous game now set into play must be followed through to the end.

She had no doubt Father would pay her ransom and meet the demands stipulated. She would be returned to him. She would then endeavor to set matters aright.

. . . tell her that I will see her again soon . . .

The aching lump in her throat suddenly more than she could bear, Gabrielle slipped down the nearby staircase and disappeared below.

"You will rue the day, I tell you."

Marie spoke, taking a spontaneous backward step as Manon turned toward her. Her hand holding the hairbrush froze in midair as Manon hissed, "Stop this, I say! I will listen to no more of your harangues! Gerard regrets the distress he caused me in the past, and I have accepted him back into my life!"

Marie did not respond as she strove to steady herself against her beloved Manon's distress.

The day had started badly. The elegant beast, Pointreau,

had left early, on an errand so secret that he had snapped fiercely at Manon when she had asked his destination. Manon had been tense throughout the day because of her lover's angry parting from her, aggravating a physical distress that she was finding more difficult to conceal each day. As she was expecting him to return any moment, her tensions now soared.

Marie's sagging chin tightened. The man was a brute who took pleasure in the tears that had welled in her dear Manon's eyes upon his departure. She knew, because he continued in so many insidious ways to cultivate those tears.

Not to be denied were the bruises, intimately placed, that marked Manon's skin; the dark circles shadowing her eyes, intimating an exhaustion that Marie knew the fiend carefully cultivated; the silent torment of uncertainty Manon silently suffered, also cultivated despite his avowals of devotion.

The danger was so clear! Why could her dear Manon not see? The man despised her, even as he desired her. He lusted for her at the same time he desired to cause her pain. He longed for a woman long dead, and hated all women who were still alive. The great and respected Monsieur Pointreau was inwardly twisted beyond redemption; his soul was as black as the midnight color of his eyes!

Marie's aging heart ached. Her poor Manon was so good. She had not deserved the careless conduct her husband had shown in his affairs, leaving her all but penniless. Nor had she deserved the cruel twist of fate that had left her only living ally, Marie, stricken with an illness that had placed an additional burden on Manon at a time when her load was already too heavy to bear.

Marie had recovered too late to help Manon. The elegant beast, Pointreau, had already insinuated himself into Manon's life.

Marie knew, with frightening certainty, that the time had come when her mistress must escape the man before it was too late for her and for the sweet babe growing within her.

But to convince Manon in the face of that foul creature's "loving" deceit seemed an impossible task.

The torment in Manon's great, moist eyes tore at Marie's heart as Manon continued, "Are you unable to see what you are doing to me, Marie?" A single tear slid down Manon's cheek, increasing Marie's pain as she viewed the beautiful woman she loved as a daughter. "Are you blind to the toll the silent conflict you maintain with Gerard, and the pressure you put upon me with your ceaseless diatribes against him, is taking?"

Manon drew herself to her feet, turning from her dressing table to face Marie squarely. Her lips trembled. "Gerard has asked me to dismiss you."

"Dismiss me!"

"To dispense with your services and send you away. He says you make him uncomfortable in his own house. It *is* Gerard's house, Marie! He says you are trying to turn me against him. And you *are*, Marie! He says ... he says that once the distraction of your negative presence is dispensed with and he is able to think and act more freely in this house, he will be able to think more clearly about a *permanent* relationship between us!"

Marie's matronly body began a slow shaking. She had not realized the man was such a complete fiend! She rasped, "Can you not see what he is trying to do, Manon? He hopes to deprive you of your only support—the only person who sees him for what he truly is and hopes to protect you from him!"

"Stop! Stop this, Marie!"

"He hopes to slowly undermine your confidence and strength of will so he may control you as he has all the other woman he has ever known!"

"No, he has changed! He loves me! We have settled our differences, and his feelings are constant?"

"So, you are now sure of him."

"*Oui.*"

"So sure that you will now tell him about the babe."

"Marie . . ." Manon took a nervous step toward her. "Please—Gerard may return at any minute."

"You do not intend to tell him."

"Not yet. After Gabrielle is back with him, I—"

"And if the young woman is never returned?"

"Do not even think such thoughts! Gerard would never recuperate from the loss. He would never . . . never—"

". . . Never accept your child then."

Manon did not respond. Instead, her body trembled, her frail, thinning body . . .

"Marie, if you have any affection for me at all, I ask you to consider the hardship your dislike of Gerard places on me. I ask you to make an attempt to accept him."

"Non."

"If you can not do that, I ask you to tolerate him, so I will not be forced to—"

"All right." Unable to allow Manon to say the words, suffering the pain of realizing how deeply she had slipped under the foul beast's control, and knowing that her dear Manon needed her more than she ever had, Marie brushed a tear from her cheek, nodding, "For you, *ma petite*—for you I will attempt to see only what you see and to know only what you would have me know. *Cela suffit?"*

Closing the distance between them, Manon hugged Marie tightly in an unusual display of affection that revealed the depth of her former despair. Drawing back a moment later, she attempted a smile.

"Oui, it is enough. *Merci, Marie."* Manon's voice caught on a sob. "It would pain me so to lose you."

Drawing the bedroom door closed behind her moments later, the significance of Manon's tearful words ringing in her ears, Marie realized the game had been set into play, and she was powerless against it.

Her poor, dear Manon . . .

* * *

"Of course, Gerard."

Governor William Claiborne stood up abruptly behind his desk and approached Pointreau. Midafternoon light streamed through the office window behind him, holding his modest frame in dark relief as he rested a hand sympathetically on Pointreau's shoulder. He continued compassionately, "You were right to come to me. I will dispatch men immediately to the task as you have outlined it, for our responsibility in the abduction of Gabrielle is clear."

His hand falling back to his side, Claiborne shook his head. "One of my greatest disappointments since I became governor is my failure in bringing the brigands on Grande-Terre to justice. I have no doubt this Captain Rogan Whitney is one of their ilk. With his abduction of Gabrielle, however, he has gone too far. The citizens of New Orleans are up in arms as never before, as am I. You may rest assured that I will do anything I can to help bring Gabrielle back to you and to bring Captain Whitney to justice as well.

Smiling, Gerard extended his hand. "William, you are my good friend."

Out on the street moments later, Gerard reviewed the conversation with his "friend" in his mind. Amusement ticked at his bearded cheek. William Claiborne continued to trust and believe in him, completely.

So much the fool, he.

So much the useful fool.

Gabrielle would soon be back with him . . . on his own terms.

"I don't believe it . . ."

Gabrielle's words trailed away as Rogan remained motionless and silent in their wake. A sense of unreality cast the shadowed captain's cabin into an eerie tableau, the setting sun beyond the porthole illuminating the semidarkness with a shaft of amber-gold that further perpetuated the dreamlike aura of the moment.

Further comment was momentarily beyond Gabrielle.

The seemingly endless day since Bertrand and Porter had been dropped at the inlet had taken a distressing turn for which she was not truly prepared. Strangely, in the time she had spent with Rogan, they had spoken little of Bertrand's and Porter's mission, the subject so carefully avoided that, as evening approached, she had been sick with the stress of it. She had broken the unspoken taboo minutes earlier by asking Rogan outright what he had demanded of her father for her return, and had been stunned by the scope of the items he had listed.

"You can't be serious!" Regaining her voice, she rasped into Rogan's narrowed gaze, "You ask too much! A formal confession to Governor Claiborne of my father's involvement with Gambi, a public dismissal of all charges against you and your men, the transfer of funds from my father's personal account to an account where it might be distributed to the heirs of the seamen lost in the sinking of your ship—all to be certified by Governor Claiborne and publicly published? You are insane! To agree to such terms would ruin my father!"

Rogan did not respond.

"Rogan . . ." Gabrielle took a tentative step toward him. "How can you do this to him?"

Hatred flashed in Rogan's gaze. "I have little difficulty in demanding justice that is long overdue."

"Justice? You are in error, I tell you! My father could not have done the things you accuse him of! He is a difficult and complex man, but he is not the villain you paint him to be."

"He is more than a villain. He is a sadistic murderer."

"No!"

"Gabrielle . . ." The heat of hatred faded, leaving only tight lines of strain as Rogan whispered, "Your father, the man you know Gerard Pointreau to be, is doubtlessly incapable of such acts of villainy, but the true Gerard Pointreau, the total man, is not."

"You are wrong!"

Beside her in a moment, Rogan wrenched aside the white cotton of his shirt, baring the brand Gabrielle had seen many times before. She gasped as he grasped her hand, forcing her to trace the letter with her fingers as he grated, " 'The letter *P* which stands for the name of the man who will break you . . .' " Her fingertips burning at the heat of Rogan's flesh, Gabrielle remained silent as he rasped, "Your father's words. Do you truly believe I could be mistaken about them?"

Gabrielle attempted to snatch back her hand, but Rogan would not allow it. Instead, he confined her palm against the lightly furred surface of his chest. She felt the heavy pounding of his heart as he pressed, "You didn't answer me, Gabrielle."

"I didn't answer you because I'm without explanation for an event you believed to have experienced."

"An event that I *believe* to have experienced?" Rogan's lips tightened. "This brand then is a figment not only of my imagination, but of yours as well!"

"Rogan, please—"

"Please what, Gabrielle?" He released her hand to grasp her shoulders. "*Please* tell you that your father did not order the iron pressed to my flesh when the previous torture he'd personally directed and witnessed had not availed him of the answers he sought? *Please* tell you that the torture he ordered inflicted did not result in my first mate's death— a death he observed without compassion? *Please* tell you that I lied when I said I know without doubt your father is in league with Gambi in the attacks against American ships and in the slaughter of innocent American seamen?" Rogan's gaze seared her. "No, I cannot. The truth remains the truth, no matter how much difficulty there is in facing it."

"You're wrong, I tell you!"

The pain of the moment suddenly more than she could bear, Gabrielle attempted to free herself from Rogan's grip.

Twisting and turning, she was breathless from a struggle that was to no avail, too mentally exhausted to protest when Rogan slowly gathered her into his arms. She was not aware of her tears until the moment when he tilted her face up to his and smoothed the dampness from her cheeks. She did not realize that Rogan was distressed as well until she saw pain mirrored so clearly in his gaze.

Nor did she realize that his anguish could so deeply intensify her own until he rasped, "Gabrielle, the man you and I know as Gerard Pointreau are not truly one and the same. I bear no animosity against the man who raised you as his daughter, with a gentleness and love that earned him your loyalty and your love. But I am sworn to bring to justice— any way I can—the man who laid so many American lives to waste without a qualm."

His captive embrace tightening when she sought to avoid him, Rogan forced up her face until their eyes again met. "This moment just now coming to fruition was put into motion long before we met. It was as inevitable as our meeting—as inevitable as the emotion with which we came together. Neither you nor I are in control of the consequences any longer. We can do nothing more than follow the instincts that guide us and wait until the game has been played out to its conclusion."

Pausing, his voice hoarse with emotion, Rogan continued, "We have no control over the course the future will take, but the present is still ours. Gabrielle . . . six days, seven at the most . . ."

The shuddering that had beset Rogan's powerful frame reverberated within Gabrielle as he devoured her with his gaze. Rogan . . . Rapace . . . one and the same, both wanting her. And she wanted him as well. But a nagging voice lingered.

"Rogan, my father will be ruined because of me."

"Whatever comes to pass will be as a result of his actions, not yours."

"B-But I love him."

No response.

"Rogan ..."

He met her mouth with his, fiercely swallowing her words with his kiss. The kiss lingered, softening, deepening, raising a yearning that gradually erased the emotional words previously spoken.

The consolation of Rogan's arms for a heart that was breaking ...

... the joy, the wonder, if only for the moment ...

... the sweet, sweet moment.

The house was active, the evening traffic outside her door constant as Clarice drew herself from her satin-draped bed and reached for her wrapper. She turned with a smile as she covered her nakedness with the silken fabric, to see Pierre standing fully dressed beside her. Her smile softened as she slid her hand up to cup his cheek and whispered, *"Vous êtes un homme très beau."*

"So, I am handsome." Pierre's smile was rueful as he slid his hand beneath her wrapper to encircle her naked waist and draw her against him. His voice dropped a notch lower. "I would much prefer to hear you speak other words at this intimate moment, but I suppose this must do for now."

He drew her closer, whispering against her unbound hair, "Clarice, *mon amie*, you do not know how deeply I regret leaving you so early in the evening, but an early meeting tomorrow ..."

Clarice drew herself slightly back to look into Pierre's boyish face. She gave a soft laugh. "We have spent the major part of the day together, first in a long carriage ride." Her eyes fluttered passionately closed as the heated memory surged. She felt the responsive tremor that shook Pierre before she met his gaze again to continue, "The long walk through the gardens that followed, the dinner at Antoine's, and then our leisurely hours here ... Our day has been full, Pierre."

"Ah, yes, but the night—"

Raucous laughter from the hallway beyond interrupted Pierre, raising his frown. Clarice sensed him tense as he continued, "I dislike leaving you here on a night such as this."

"I am accustomed to noisy nights."

"It is not the noise that bothers me."

Clarice's smile gradually faded. "Surely you do not believe that Madame would press me into service should the demand grow greater than she can meet? She is an honorable woman who keeps to the word of all agreements reached. And even if she were not, you must realize that I—"

"Clarice—stop." The lines on Pierre's face deepened. "It is not Madame's—or your—integrity that concerns me. Your safety is ever on my mind."

"Pierre ..." Clarice was astounded at his words. "I have spent countless similar nights in this room. I am well equipped to handle any eventuality, I assure you."

"I do not *want* you to 'handle' such a situation."

"Pierre ..."

Intensely sober, he drew her close. "You are mine, Clarice—only mine. I dislike having you exposed to the riffraff that walks the hallway outside your door."

She chided gently, "You seem to forget that you were once part of the riffraff in that hallway."

"Never. I had eyes only for you from the moment I walked in the door below."

Touched to the heart, Clarice brushed his lips with hers. "And now I am yours."

"*Oui,* but—"

Covering his lips with her fingertips, Clarice whispered with a sudden intensity of her own, "*Mon cher,* do not say more ... more than I am prepared to hear." Regretting the pain she saw reflected in his eyes, she continued honestly, "The moments when I lie in your arms are beautiful. I treasure them. Let us not endeavor to anticipate the future. Instead, let us enjoy what is presently ours—yours and mine."

"Clarice . . ."

"I ask that of you, *mon amie*, with true humility."

"Never humility."

"Then, with true affection that comes from the heart."

His gaze momentarily flickering, Pierre responded with a smile that was tender, however forced. "All this talk of hearts . . ."

The warmth of Pierre suddenly overwhelming, Clarice curved her hand around the back of his head, winding her fingers in the unruly curls there to draw his mouth down to hers. She felt the swell of his passion as he slid both arms inside her wrapper to draw her close. The familiarity of his smooth hands against her flesh . . . their stroking touch . . .

She sighed as Pierre withdrew from her.

His smile true, he whispered against her lips. "Do I sense regret at my early departure?"

"You do."

"May I console myself that you will miss me lying beside you when I am gone."

"You may."

"You know it is difficult for me to leave you."

"Pierre . . ." Clarice whispered sincerely, "The same sentiment resounds within me."

The pleasure her words obviously gave him, stirred a wave of loving guilt as Clarice closed her bedroom door behind him minutes later. Leaning back against it, Clarice again sighed, then walked toward the washstand and removed her robe.

Engrossed in her toilet minutes later, she was startled by a knock. She glanced toward the clock, her heart pounding at the lateness of the hour. It could only be . . .

She managed a breathless, "Who is it?"

"Open the door, Clarice."

Bertrand, at last!

Throwing on her wrapper, she ran to obey. She turned the lock with trembling hands and pulled the door open, a welcome that caught on a sob echoing in her throat as she pulled her brother inside and pushed the door closed behind him. Throwing her arms around him, she hugged him close, another sob escaping her as he enclosed her in his embrace.

"What's wrong, Clarice?"

"What's wrong?" She drew back, a smile trembling on her lips. "Did you not realize I would worry? I hadn't heard form you. There was no word of a ransom being asked for the Dubay woman. When I learned that Gerard Pointreau had left the city on a mysterious mission—"

"He came to Grande-Terre."

"I knew it!"

"The captain was forced to alter the plan."

"Rogan is all right?"

"He is." Bertrand searched her face, hesitant as he began, "Clarice, the change in plans ... you are my sister and I know you well. It is no secret to me that your feelings for the captain go deeper than those of a friend."

She remained silent.

"Unanticipated consequences have come about. The captain remains dedicated to his cause, but he—"

A sound outside the door halted Bertrand's words. He stiffened, turning the moment before the door was suddenly thrust open.

Clarice gasped aloud as Bertrand's hand sprang to the knife sheathed at his waist, his eyes cold as death.

Grasping his hand and expelling a spontaneous "Non!", she held him fast as she turned to address Pierre who he stood in the doorway. "I thought you had left."

Shuddering with rage, Pierre entered and snapped the door closed behind him. His face flushed an unnatural hue, he spoke in a voice that was hardly recognizable as his for the depth of fury in its tone.

"I did not want to believe it was true!"

Clarice shook her head. "I do not understand."

"I was at the front door when Mimi spoke in a voice calculated to reach my ears. She said that Clarice plays a clever game with her special patron, hardly allowing the bed to cool after he leaves before calling her lover up to take his place."

"My lover!"

Pierre took a threatening step toward Bertrand. "I want this man out of your room, Clarice—now!"

"But—"

"Now!"

"Bertrand is my brother!"

Pierre's virulence froze.

Catching her breath in the silence that followed, Clarice slipped between the two men who eyed each other warily. She addressed Pierre tensely.

"Mimi . . . I should have expected it. She envies my position in this house."

Pierre's expression did not change. "You have not introduced me to your brother, Clarice."

Clarice spoke hesitantly. "I spoke of him only this afternoon on the street, as you must recall. I have been awaiting his arrival. He returned to the city tonight."

She glanced at Bertrand. His expression had not changed—nor had his hand moved from the knife at his waist. She took another tense breath.

"Pierre, I would like you to meet my dear brother, Bertrand. Bertrand, my special patron, Pierre."

The moment of silence that followed was broken abruptly when Pierre stepped forward and extended his hand.

"*Pardonnez-moi, s'il vous plaît, Bertrand.* It is plain to see that Clarice is telling the truth for the resemblance between you is clear now that I have taken time for rational thought. I was a fool to have doubted Clarice's integrity even for a moment, but jealousy overwhelmed my good judgment. I hope you will not hold my lapse against me."

Clarice held her breath for the eternity it took Bertrand to accept Pierre's hand.

Relief surged as Pierre addressed her directly.

"Since I interrupted your visit with your brother so rudely, I will now take my leave." Clasping Clarice's hand in his, he drew her with him to the doorway, his expression one of sincere regret.

"Jealousy is ugly, and you were never meant for ugliness, *mon amie*. I make no excuses for my conduct. No apologies would be adequate for the affront I have afforded you. I will only say that the scene enacted today will never be repeated. I hope you can believe me."

"I can and do."

Pressing his mouth lightly to hers, Pierre whispered, *Je t'aime, Clarice."*

I love you, Clarice.

She was still breathless at the words Pierre had spoken when he drew the door closed behind him.

Tears suddenly streaming, she walked into Bertrand's arms.

The darkest hours of early morning prevailed as Bertrand and Porter moved silently through the convent grounds.

Caution.

Bertrand halted in his step, turning to signal Porter to do the same. So much depended on the success of their mission this night.

Bertrand surveyed Porter's thin, bewhiskered face. He looked tired. Porter had made good use of his time with a new woman in Madame's house while his partner had lingered to talk with Clarice.

Clarice, who cherished a silent love for the captain . . . Halted by Pierre's unexpected interruption, Bertrand had somehow been unable to resume the conversation he had initiated, to tell his sister that her dreams were now imperiled by the very woman on whom the success of the captain's plan for vengeance hinged.

As for Gabrielle Dubay . . . A spontaneous respect stirred in him. It appeared the daughter was all that the father was not. He did not doubt Pointreau recognized her value, and that once Porter and he had successfully delivered the terms of the ransom to the convent, Pointreau would comply with any demands in order to get her back. But neither did he doubt the man would do so with some sort of plan in mind. The need for caution would be greater still once the time came for Gabrielle to be returned to her father.

That thought increasing his uneasiness, Bertrand glanced briefly at Porter before scrutinizing the dark convent yard again. He then signaled Porter to follow as he moved forward.

Bertrand's hand slipped up to the missive concealed inside his shirt as they turned the corner of the building. Porter's familiarity with the routine of the convent, learned through the talkative and amorous kitchen maid, Jeanette, had revealed the perfect vehicle by which to deliver the ransom demand.

Sister Madeleine, always the first to rise, would walk to the rear convent door immediately upon emerging from her room. There she would pause for a morning prayer as was her custom while she overlooked the convent yard. She would then proceed to the kitchen. This time, however, she would discover an envelope marked with the Reverend Mother's name at the door. She would immediately deliver the envelope to her superior, and the letter inside, addressed to Monsieur Pointreau, would then be forwarded to him with great haste.

Uneasiness again tugged at Bertrand's stomach. The rear door of the convent was a few feet away when he reached inside his shirt and withdrew the envelope. His heart beginning a heavy pounding, he signaled Porter to wait where he was as he prepared to—

A sound in the darkness behind them!

A shouted command to halt!

The shuffle of footsteps as uniformed men closed in around him.

The envelope snatched from his hand.

Resistance!

Pummeling fists.

Porter's groans echoing his own.

Shadows fading to darkness.

A darkness without sound.

Oblivion.

A pounding at the door!

Pointreau awakened abruptly to the scented shadows of Manon's room. She stirred beside him as he drew himself to a seated position, then jumped to his feet, his heart pounding. Grasping the robe lying on the chair nearby, he raced into the hallway.

Thrusting Marie aside as she stepped into his path, he walked swiftly toward the front door and jerked it open.

"Monsieur Pointreau?"

Pointreau nodded to the youthful officer who addressed him, his gaze slipping to the uniformed men behind him. An official contingent. It could mean only one thing.

"I am sorry to awaken you, sir, but Governor Claiborne instructed us to inform you immediately and referred us to this address. Two men were apprehended an hour ago as they attempted to deliver the ransom note you were awaiting to the Ursuline Convent. They are presently in custody in the *calabozo*. The governor directed us to provide escort if you wish to go there."

Exaltation swept over Pointreau. He had known it! Governor Claiborne had ordered Pointreau's offices and mansion to be kept under strict surveillance in the hope of trapping the person who delivered the ransom demands. It had come to him as a revelation in the middle of the previous night in

Manon's bed that Captain Whitney was too smart to attempt delivery of the ransom demands at either place. That left only one other where Whitney's communication was certain to reach a person literate and trustworthy enough to forward it immediately.

The convent.

It was over!

He had won! Whitney's men were in his hands. The captain was soon to follow.

It was only a matter of time until Gabrielle would be returned to him.

That thought momentarily choking him with emotion, Gerard paused before responding to the officer still waiting.

"I will be ready to accompany you in a few minutes."

Turning swiftly, ignoring Manon who stood a few feet behind him, Gerard again pushed Marie out of his way as he strode toward the bedroom. He dressed swiftly.

"The ransom note has been delivered and the men captured?"

He did not respond.

"Gerard . . ."

Drawing on his coat, Pointreau did not bother with a cravat as he turned toward the door.

"Gerard!"

His step did not slow as he reached the front doorway and started down the steps, the uniformed officers falling in behind him.

Bertrand stirred on the moldy bunk on which he lay. Battered and bruised, he attempted to raise himself to a seated position, finding the effort momentarily beyond him as he surveyed the narrow cell.

The *calabozo*. He did not remember being delivered there. Succeeding in sitting up, he then drew himself to his feet with sheer strength of will. It was difficult to breathe, a stabbing pain stealing his breath.

His ribs were broken. But that was not his immediate concern.

Bertrand staggered to the barred door in time to see a small contingent marching down the hallway toward him. At his door within moments, the uniformed guards unlocked it and grasped him by the arms, all but lifting him from his feet as they ushered him back in the direction from which they had come.

A strange sense of *déjà vu* overwhelmed Bertrand as he remembered carrying the captain down a similar passageway in much the same manner years earlier, when they made their escape. But he had no doubt that now a far different reception awaited him.

Blinking as he was dragged into a well-lit room at the end of the corridor, Bertrand caught his breath with the pain as he was thrust roughly toward the man standing before him.

The heat of his captor's animosity momentarily overwhelming, Bertrand glared at the dark, bearded fellow who returned his stare in silence.

There was no mistaking Gerard Pointreau.

Nor was there any mistaking Pointreau's malevolence as he grated out, "So you are the fool who was selected to deliver the ransom note to me." Pointreau took a step closer. "Where is Gabrielle? If your captain has harmed her in any way . . ."

Bertrand allowed himself to smile.

Taking a quick step forward, Pointreau delivered a staggering blow to Bertrand's face, almost knocking him from his feet.

"Insolent fool! But I use fools like you very well. It is fortunate that you resisted when captured and are physically marked. The governor visited while you were unconscious and remarked upon your bruises. He will not notice a few more . . ."

Pointreau's smile turning evil, he motioned for the guards

to close the door. "I made certain to renew my acquaintance with these men, in anticipation of your capture. I have been kind enough to supplement their small incomes in the past. They are very receptive to my influence, and since I have convinced the governor to allow me to question you . . ."

Pointreau laughed. "You will tell me everything you know before they are finished with you."

Hatred a hot, burning heat within him, Bertrand did not have time to respond . . .

. . . before the first blow was struck.

Rogan awakened with a start. Uncertain of the cause of his sudden uneasiness, he glanced toward the porthole. No, it wasn't morning.

The disquiet prevailing, he curled his arm more tightly around Gabrielle. She was safe and secure where she lay sleeping in the curve of his body, her back against his chest, her firm, naked buttocks pressed intimately against him, yet . . .

An indeterminate anxiety prickled again up his spine, and Rogan frowned. Five more days to wait and wonder . . . He was both anxious for and filled with dread of the sixth day as he silently questioned the cruel fate that had delivered Gabrielle to him, only to snatch her away.

B-But I love him.

Yes, Gabrielle loved her father. She would never truly believe him guilty of all that of which he was accused. She would come to hate the man who would not rest until her father was destroyed. She would come to hate *him*.

Suddenly realizing that sleep was beyond him, Rogan withdrew himself from Gabrielle, carefully tucking the coverlet around her as he stood up. He dressed silently, then turned to look down at her for long moments. Strangely, even when she was closest, he could feel her slipping away from him.

The pain of that inevitability never stronger, Rogan turned

toward the door to seek escape from his thoughts in the last fringe of night still pervading.

At the ship's rail minutes later, Rogan stared into the darkness, breathing deeply of salt-laden currents of air that cleansed as they gently battered. The moon peeked out briefly in the overcast sky, its shimmering shaft of light abruptly clarifying in Rogan's mind the cause which had brought him to this point in time.

A truth that must be served, justice that must prevail—he could not abandon that now, at any cost.

"Rogan . . ."

Turning with a start, he saw Gabrielle standing behind him. Bare feet peeking out from the coverlet she clutched around her, her glorious, unbound hair fluttering on the soft night air, she looked up at him with eyes that appeared an extension of the silver moonlight as they pinned him with their translucence.

It occurred to him in that moment that Gabrielle was another truth, one that had taken root in his heart.

Slipping his arm around her, he drew her tight against his side, cushioning her against him as he turned back to the sea and the inevitability of the new day that was dawning.

Chapter 8

Two days!

Pointreau strode down the prison passageway. Fury marked his stiff, heavy tread as he recalled seaman Bertrand's silent defiance.

Bertrand. The name was the only information he'd obtained from the blond, scar-faced felon through two long days of intense questioning. In retrospect, he realized the fellow had not revealed his name in a moment of weakness as originally believed. Rather, the silent seaman with the truculent stare had revealed it deliberately, to impress it upon his mind.

Bertrand. The name was on his mind, all right. When all was over and Gabrielle was returned to him, he would make certain that everyone who had ever been close to this man was made to suffer.

In the meantime, however, he was forced into caution.

The capture of the two men had been kept from the public by Claiborne's order. The fact that no other communications had been received from Captain Whitney confirmed both Claiborne's, and his own suspicions that the captain was not in the immediate vicinity where he would be in constant contact with the two men, and that he was probably presently ignorant of their capture. How long that situation would continue, however, was uncertain.

Pointreau's bearded cheek twitched. Governor Claiborne

had ordered Bertrand and the man identified as Dustin Porter separately confined in different parts of the prison for security purposes. The governor had also made certain to visit these men personally several times for questioning since they had been captured.

It was obvious to Pointreau that the ransom note had raised questions in Claiborne's mind about him. The prisoners were so closely watched that his hirelings had been ineffective in pursuing the physical persuasion he had hoped to press on them. Pointreau worried little about Claiborne's suspicions for he had never experienced any difficulty in manipulating the man. His present impotence, however, was driving him wild.

Two days, and neither Bertrand nor Porter showed any signs of breaking. The demands in the ransom note were clear. The first, a public confession of his involvement with Gambi was due to be posted around the city. Was Whitney now waiting for those notices to appear? What would happen to Gabrielle when they did not?

Time was running out!

Pointreau neared the street door, his agitation increasing. He had slept little during the two nights past. The visits to Bertrand and Porter had convinced him that they would not break. His torment was now so extreme that he was tempted to make the confession demanded to guarantee Gabrielle's safety. He had only one chance left of avoiding that disaster.

That reality clear, Pointreau drew open the prison door and strode out onto the street.

Her spoon frozen midway to her lips, Clarice was incapable of movement as the whispered conversation between the two young courtesans seated at the table beside her continued.

"It's the truth, I tell you. Jacques is one of my most faithful clients. He is in a position to know, and he confides in me. He would not lie!"

The steady buzz of conversation continued around Madame's luncheon table. The only formal meal of the day drew the women of the house together for humorous exchanges, ribald comments, and occasional complaints that seldom missed Madame's ear. It was also the time of the day when rumors were exchanged in laughter or in whispers . . . such as the whispers that held Clarice rigid with inner terror as the young courtesans continued.

"*Impossible.*" The brunette shook her head. "Monsieur Pointreau holds the sympathy of the city since his daughter's abduction. Everyone is awaiting word of a ransom note being delivered. If it is true—what you said—the entire city would be talking about it."

"It *is* true, I tell you! Jacques said the men were apprehended in the convent yard when they attempted to deliver the ransom note to Mother Superior! They have been confined in separate cells under close guard and in complete secrecy. Had I not questioned Jacques so intently about his need to return to supervisory duty last night, he would not have allowed word to slip."

"No . . ."

"They are keeping the apprehension secret because they hope to lay a trap for the man who abducted Monsieur Pointreau's daughter."

"It would be impossible to keep such a thing secret!"

"Believe what you like then!" Exasperation flushing her face with color, the lighter-haired courtesan snapped, "It makes no difference to me. I should not have told you, in any case. Jacques warned me that if Monsieur Pointreau learned someone had leaked word—"

The slender brunette shivered. "Don't tell me anything else! I don't want to know anything that concerns *that* man!"

"Celeste, you are a fool! Monsieur Pointreau—"

"—is a monster!"

"But—"

"Tell me nothing else!"

The conversation came to an abrupt halt.

Clarice lowered her spoon to the plate in front of her. She attempted to swallow against the lump in her throat, but was unable. Her breathing suddenly short, she stood up and started toward the door.

"Clarice . . ."

Turning to see Madame looking at her intently, Clarice offered, "My stomach rebels, Madame. Excuse me, *s'il vous plaît.*"

Not waiting for a response, she climbed the staircase with rapid steps, refusing to think further until her bedroom door was closed behind her.

Her heart pounding, her breathing labored, she leaned back weakly against the door. She knew it! She'd known something was wrong when Bertrand did not contact her the day after he was to have delivered the ransom note! Her tension had grown with each hour that passed, to the point where she had even been short with Pierre the previous night. But she had told herself she was worrying for naught, that the unusual activity at the house during the past two days had demanded caution on Bertrand's part.

What was it Yvonne had said . . . the two men were being confined in separate parts of the prison and Pointreau was hoping to set a trap for Rogan? *Non*, she could not let that happen! If Rogan were taken, Bertrand and Porter would stand no chance of escape! She needed to do something.

Bertrand had told her that a rendezvous had been set up with Rogan's ship in four days, but he had not told her where! She needed to find out—and to find a way to get into the prison to talk to him.

But how . . . how?

A knock on the door startled Clarice from her thoughts the moment before she heard Madame's voice.

"May I come in?"

"I—I am unwell, Madame."

A moment's silence. "I also overheard Celeste and Yvonne speaking."

Clarice stepped away from the door and drew it open. She waited until Madame closed it behind her elegantly dressed bulk.

"I must find a way to see Bertrand, Madame. I must talk to him."

"No, you must not. It is too dangerous."

"He is my brother!"

"Too risky! There must be another way. I will look into it."

"I cannot wait! Two days have already passed, two days while he has been in Pointreau's hands!"

"Non, he is in the governor's hands, which is a different thing entirely."

"Pointreau twists the governor around his finger!"

"Not this time, he won't. The governor is not a man to disregard lessons learned from the past."

"Madame . . ." Clarice's fine features drew into an anxious mask. "Can you not see? I cannot take that chance!"

"Nor can you risk attempting to reach Bertrand on your own." Madame nodded, her jowled cheeks moving loosely. "I will make inquiries."

"Time grows short!"

"Listen to me, Clarice. You will do your brother no good if you are confined in a prison cell beside him. Should the relationship between you and Bertrand be discovered, you will only have succeeded in giving Pointreau greater power over him."

"Madame."—Clarice's heart wrenched with pain—"I must do something!"

"You must wait here. I will make inquiries."

"Madame—"

"Wait here."

Clarice sank to the bed as the door closed behind Madame, her thoughts whirling. Madame was a true friend who meant well, but Clarice could **not allow Bertrand's fate to lie** in the hands of another. She **could not risk losing Bertrand** and Rogan as well. She needed **to get into the prison as soon** as possible. There was only one way . . .

Her stomach churning at the sight of the luncheon tray Marie had meticulously prepared and delivered to her room minutes earlier, Manon pushed it away with distaste. She had had no appetite since the night two days earlier when Gerard had walked out of her room without a word.

The nightmare had returned.

"You must eat, Manon."

"I cannot!" Manon raised a shaky hand to her brow. She was not feeling well. She had seemed to grow continually weaker since that time, with the nausea increasing. In silent moments during the lonely nights recently past, she was certain she had felt the babe stir within her. That reality had given her both intense pleasure and demoralizing pain.

She did not want to believe it was happening again! She did not want to consider that Gerard had cut off all contact with her after deliberately encouraging her to believe there was a permanence—a future—to the emotion between them. She did not want to allow that he had simply used her as he had so many times before.

Je t'en prie . . .

I beg you . . .

Gerard had *begged* her to forgive him. Surely that meant he loved her, yet—

"Manon, you cannot go on this way." Marie was concerned. "You will become ill. You must think of the child."

"Gerard's child."

The lines in Marie's face deepened. "Your child. If Monsieur Pointreau does not choose to acknowledge it, you must—"

"Stop! Gerard has not done this deliberately. He is obsessed with finding Gabrielle and all else has slipped his mind."

"You must face the truth."

Manon closed her eyes, the panic within growing. She did not want to acknowledge the look she had seen in Gerard's eyes in his last, brief glance at her, did not want to believe he truly *hated* her.

"Manon . . ."

Manon forced a smile. "Two days is not so long. I will send him a note and remind him that I am worrying."

"You waste your time. He—"

"I will send him a note!" An emotion akin to hatred rising within her as Maria stood so resolutely a few feet away, forcing her to face her innermost fears, Manon repeated, "I will write the note . . . and you will deliver it to his home. You'll see. He'll come—or at least send a response saying when he will be free to visit again. You'll see!"

Deliberately turning her back on Marie, Manon walked to the desk nearby and sat down. She picked up her pen with a shaking hand.

"I tell you, it's the only way!"

William Claiborne assessed Gerard Pointreau silently after the outburst, aware that he was witnessing a side of the man that he had never seen before. This new Pointreau was a stranger.

Claiborne drew himself to his feet behind his desk, breathing slowly and deeply in a way that calmed him in times of extreme stress. And surely this was one of those. Gerard had forced his way into the office minutes earlier and had approached him without a semblance of his usual suave demeanor. There had been panic in his eyes, as well as another unidentifiable, venomous emotion that had somehow raised the hackles on Claiborne's spine.

The ransom note returned abruptly to Claiborne's mind.

He had been stunned by the terms. They did not entail personal monetary gain for Captain Rogan Whitney. Instead, they were a call for justice. Still he could not be certain whether the "justice" Whitney demanded was being honestly sought or whether the move was inspired by a thirst for vengeance.

Gerard had, of course, denied there was any truth in the confession Captain Whitney demanded in his ransom note. In searching his memory, however, Claiborne recalled Whitney's first mate had died while incarcerated, and that Whitney had maintained throughout that Vincent Gambi was the man responsible for the sinking of his ship. It did not seem unreasonable that if Whitney was indeed innocent of any involvement and Gambi was responsible for the sinking of American merchant ships as Whitney claimed, Gambi might have an ally who passed information to him about which American ships were the true prizes.

But was that man Gerard Pointreau?

Gerard . . . his close friend and advisor.

Searching his mind further, Claiborne had recalled that it was Gerard who had fueled his fury against Captain Whitney and had encouraged him in the unusual practice of offering a reward for the captain's capture, making the captain one of the city's most sought-after fugitives. At the time, he had believed Gerard merely shared his antipathy for a man who had profited on the blood of his own countrymen. Now . . .

His hesitation causing Gerard's face to flush to a more apoplectic hue, Claiborne frowned as Pointreau took a furious step forward.

"How dare you hesitate with my daughter's life at stake?"

Indeed, how dare he?

"You are risking little! Were I to urge you into this deception with the seaman, Bertrand, I would understand your hesitation. But Porter is a fool! It is obvious that the man was employed simply because his association with the convent kitchen maid availed him of intimate knowledge of the grounds and routine!"

"Seaman Porter doesn't impress me as a fool. He—"

"He is a fool, I say! And *you* are a fool if you don't see it!"

Silence.

Claiborne watched as Pointreau struggled to regain control. The change from a specter of chilling malevolence to the Gerard he had believed he knew so well was finally complete when Gerard spoke again. "William . . . forgive me, please. I am upset. I fear for Gabrielle's life." Pointreau took an unsteady step. "I beg you to consider—"

"All right, Gerard."

Gerard went so still as to appear to have stopped breathing.

"I said, all right."

Gerard's breathing resumed, deep and fast.

"Where are you going, Clarice?"

His hand tight on her arm, Pierre refused to relent as Clarice attempted to shake herself free of his grip.

Seemingly unaware of the curious glances she was attracting in the foyer of Madame's busy house, Clarice grated softly, "Let go of me, Pierre! Let me go, I say!"

"Non! Not unless you tell me where you are going."

Clarice's fine features were tight with an anxiety that did not suit the balmy temperature of the sunny, late afternoon as she hissed, "Where I am going is none of your affair! Contrary to your assumption, you do not own me!"

"Clarice . . ." Pierre mentally stepped back. He was astounded by her unexpected animosity. Clarice had forgiven him for interrupting her brother's visit two nights previously. He was certain of that because he had returned the following morning bearing flowers and a more solicitous apology, and had been met with a loving warmth that was forever impressed upon his memory. Yet, when he had returned that night, he had sensed a growing tension in her. The tension had appeared to escalate the following day, and when he had been unable to visit that same evening, he had known he must seek her out as soon as he was free.

That thought in mind, he had arrived to find Clarice on her way out the door to a destination she would not divulge.

Pierre scrutinized her more closely. She was trembling. The tension about her that had so concerned him now approached desperation. And there was something else. The way she was dressed . . .

Suddenly determined to uncover the cause of her confusing behavior, Pierre gripped her arm more firmly and dragged her into the small anteroom beside the front entrance. He snapped the door closed behind them, demanding, "Why are you dressed like that?"

Clarice raised her chin. "I don't know what you mean."

Pierre scrutinized the garish green gown she wore. The color was overly bold, the bodice excessively revealing, and the workmanship of the garment far below the standard of Clarice's usual attire. He skimmed the firm, white swells that rose above the deep neckline, raising his gaze to search familiar features that were brightly painted . . . almost in the manner of . . . of . . .

"You are dressed like a *putain!*"

Clarice's color drained beneath the heavy rouge on her cheeks. "Surely you realize, Pierre."—her chin rose instinctively—"that a whore is exactly what I am."

"You are not!"

Her chest heaving under the revealing gown, Clarice exerted a visible effort to retain control before replying, "I have no time for this conversation. Please unhand me."

"If something is wrong, you must tell me, Clarice."

"Nothing is the matter."

"I will help you!"

"Nothing is wrong!"

"Clarice—"

"Clarice!"

Both heads turned toward the rear exit of the room, where Madame stood framed in the doorway. The glances exchanged by the two women confirmed Pierre's fears as Madame spoke with quiet authority.

"Please return to your room, Clarice."

"*Non!* I must—"

"Go back to your room! I will settle matters with Monsieur Delise."

"Madame, you know I must—"

"Go upstairs now. I will speak to you later."

Silent during the exchange, Pierre felt the tremor that shook Clarice the moment before she shrugged free of his grasp and walked toward Madame, passing her without speaking as she exited the room.

Approaching him in the silence that followed, Madame addressed Pierre's obvious agitation.

"Clarice suffers personal anxieties that have affected her judgment. Contrary to my advice, she was attempting an outing that would not be advantageous to anyone. I am pleased that she has decided to forgo it." Madame paused. "However, it is plain to see that she has distressed you . . . perhaps even embarrassed or insulted you. That is unforgivable. *Monsieur*, the policy of our house does not allow our valued patrons to be treated so inhospitably. If you will follow me to my office, I will refund the payment you advanced for Clarice's services so you may consider your contract null and void."

The shock of Madame's words cut deep, and Pierre stiffened. "Is your offer for the cancellation of my contract at Clarice's request?"

"*Non.*"

He released a tense breath that he had not realized he had been holding. "It does not matter, in any case. The contract was struck in good faith. In good faith, it still stands."

"As you wish, *monsieur.*"

Madame's obvious approval left Pierre as unprepared for

the hand she clamped on his arm, halting him as he attempted to brush past her to follow Clarice, as he was for the sudden intensity of her tone as she spoke.

"Non, s'il vous plaît. Clarice needs some time alone. It is my suggestion that you do not attempt to see her until she is again herself."

"And how long would that be?"

"A few days ... a week ... perhaps longer."

Silence.

"My dear Monsieur Delise, surely you realize there is not a woman in the house who would not be happy to accommodate your needs in the interim."

"Madame"—Pierre slowly stiffened.—"surely *you* realize that my feelings for Clarice transcend the limits of the agreement struck for her services. You may trust me; whatever is troubling Clarice so severely, I only wish to help."

"Monsieur, what you do not understand is that it matters little whether or not *I* trust you ..."

The implication of Madame's words stabbing painfully, Pierre could not respond.

"If you truly care for Clarice you will allow her the time she needs."

Pierre withdrew his arm from Madame's grasp. He paused to further scrutinize her unyielding expression.

In a moment, he was gone.

His spirits high, Pointreau climbed the front steps of his city mansion. His heart was pounding. Just a few hours longer ...

He pushed open the door and entered the foyer as his servant appeared in a nearby doorway.

He snapped, "You are right to look apprehensive, Boyer. Your lazy hours are over. I have an important appointment tonight and just a few hours to refresh myself before I must again leave. I want a bath drawn immediately, fresh clothing prepared, and my dinner waiting when I am through. You'd do best to warn the others not to dally. It will be hard on them if they do. Is that understood?"

"I understands, massa."

"Then get moving!" When the aging slave did not immediately react, Pointreau demanded, "Why do you hesitate?"

Boyer took an uncertain step forward, an envelope in his hand. "A letter come for you massa."

A letter . . .

Pointreau stiffened with sudden apprehension. No . . . Captain Whitney could not have sent another communication that would endanger his plan at the last moment. Not now, when he was so close to getting his dear Gabrielle back.

Snatching the missive from his servant's hand, Pointreau ripped it open to read:

> Dearest Gerard,
>
> The manner of your abrupt departure and my fear that something has gone amiss in your effort to have Gabrielle returned to you has left me greatly disturbed. A word from you would put my fears to rest.
>
> My happiness is dependent on yours, *mon cher,* as is my peace of mind. With that thought uppermost, I hope to hear from you soon.
>
> My love to you.
>
> Manon.

Pointreau's bearded face flushed hot with sudden anger. How dare the wily witch badger him with petty concerns at a time such as this? How dare she make so open a demand of him?

Furious at the trepidation Manon had so thoughtlessly caused him, Pointreau ripped the carefully scripted letter into pieces and tossed it onto the table nearby.

"You be sendin' a response, massa?"

Pointreau turned with a look that set the aging Negro a stiff step backward, before he turned and disappeared from sight.

Gabrielle's precious image appearing unexpectedly before him as he ascended the staircase to his room, Pointreau whispered softly to her in his mind, "Just a little while longer, *ma petite,* and you will be home. Then I will never allow us to be separated again."

Another night was falling.

The third.

Gabrielle assessed her reflection in the small washstand mirror of the captain's cabin. Time was moving incredibly slowly—and incredibly fast—each moment both a torment and a joy beyond imagining.

It occurred to Gabrielle that the person she saw reflected in the silvered glass had changed in ways too numerous to count in the incredibly short period since she had first opened her eyes to the predatory, golden-eyed gaze of Rapace. Gone was the convent-uniformed figure with hair tightly confined and rebellion in her eyes. Gone was the child/woman who dreamed of experiencing life, but who was so far removed from its realities as to have no true concept of its scope. She was no longer the young woman whose goals had been circumscribed by her youth and so singularly set as to now humiliate her with their shallowness.

She had learned so many things. She now realized that true fulfillment did not lie in the gown she would someday wear, the places to which she would travel, or the people she would someday meet. Nor did it lie in the material or monetary accumulations to which so many aspired.

Instead, she had discovered that true fulfillment lay in the fragile linking of her inner self to another, a mutual blending unrelated to the act of physical joining which made her complete.

Rogan or Rapace—he was that missing part of herself that had made her whole. She accepted that truth as she had accepted the physical ecstasy . . .

. . . and the painful reality of the price of fulfillment.

For she loved Father as well.

Gabrielle did not attempt to deceive herself. Rogan would not relent in the demands of the ransom. Her father would submit to ruin rather than risk her life. She would be powerless against the distance forced between Rogan and her, and Rogan would then turn to those who had been true to him during his years of trial.

. . . tell her I will see her again soon . . .

Rogan, the man whose relentless strength of conviction she both admired and deplored, the man who had touched her soul . . . How would she be able to bear knowing he held another woman in his arms?

A sob caught in Gabrielle's throat and a tear streaked the cheek of the image staring back at her.

Suddenly disgusted with herself, she brushed away the tear. Yes, the person now reflected back at her was not the convent-bred girl she had once been. This was a woman who loved.

Three days longer.

She would make them three, glorious days.

Running down the passageway moments later, Gabrielle emerged on the main deck, breathless. Rogan frowned when she reached his side, assessing her anxiety with the gold eyes of a raptor that had once stirred such trepidation.

Words unnecessary, she slid her arms around his neck and drew his mouth down to hers.

Night had fallen beyond the barred window high on his cell wall, but Porter paid it little mind as he drew himself slowly to his feet. Wincing as his bruised parts protested with pain, he walked to the barred door and peered out into the corridor beyond. He hardly remembered the moment of capture. He recalled only that the convent yard had been silent at one moment and that in the next—before he had had time to react to Bertrand's warning—he had been overwhelmed.

He had fought spontaneously and fiercely, but had succumbed to the pounding fists and relentless boots that had battered him into unconsciousness. He had awakened in the cell where he was now confined, one in a long line of similar cells filled with criminals who, in the time since, could be heard boasting of their crimes. The most vocal of all was a loud-mouthed braggart in the cell next to his who could also be heard whispering long into the night with the fellow in a cell up the line.

The shared secrets of his fellow prisoner had slipped quickly from Porter's mind at the realization that Bertrand was confined nowhere near . . . if, indeed, he was alive.

Porter had been startled when Pointreau had been ushered into his cell shortly after his apprehension. He had pretended to be slow witted. He smirked. He had developed that defense long ago, having learned to utilize a deceptive appearance. From Pointreau's obvious disgust, Porter judged he had been successful in convincing the man that he was totally ignorant of the overall plan of ransom.

Governor Claiborne had interviewed him several times since then, but Pointreau had not returned. For that reason, Porter had come to believe that Bertrand was being confined in another part of the prison and that Pointreau had concentrated his questioning there.

Porter's narrow shoulders twitched with suppressed agitation. He could not understand how the governor's men had come to be waiting for them when they'd arrived at the convent in the middle of the night.

He wondered what the captain would do when neither Bertrand nor he arrived at the rendezvous and he then learned that they had been captured. He knew the captain would not abandon them, not willingly, but . . .

Porter paused in his troubled reflection as the hairy, malodorous guard who had been on duty for the greater portion

of the day walked down the corridor toward the metal exit
door to scrutinize the corridor beyond through its small, barred
window. Prison routine had become established firmly enough
in Porter's mind for him to know that the change of guard was
late. Their present guard was impatient to be relieved.

A scraping sound suddenly alerting him, Porter stiffened at
the same moment the exit door was thrust abruptly open
from the other side, knocking the unprepared guard down
against the stone floor, on which he struck his head with a resounding crack!

Events moved with startling rapidity then, and Porter had
not a moment for conscious thought as three men ran down
the corridor and the braggart prisoner shouted, "I knew you
was comin'! I knew you wouldn't let me rot here!"

Reaching out to grab the arm of one of the rescuers, Porter
shouted over the rising din, "Let me out, mate! I'm a dead
man in here if you don't!"

The second of hesitation before the unknown fellow unlocked the cell door an eternity, Porter took a relieved breath
and started toward the exit.

In the alleyway behind the prison before he truly realized
what had happened, Porter forced himself to cast aside the
shock of the unanticipated turn of events before disappearing
into the shadows.

Observing the escape from where he crouched in the shadows, Pointreau hissed, "He's off! They'd better not lose him!"

Beside him, Governor Claiborne nodded, his expression intent.

It would not be long now.

Called from her bed in the middle of the night, Clarice
faced Madame across the tense silence of her office. She
trembled as Madame spoke softly.

"The news has just reached me that there's been an escape from the prison ... several prisoners. One was a fellow in whom Monsieur Pointreau had a deep interest."

"Was it Bertrand?"

"A tall, wiry fellow with dark hair.'

"Porter. What about Bertrand?"

"I do not know."

In the strained moment that followed, Clarice was struck with a sudden realization. Unable to speak, she clutched the desk tightly for support.

"Clarice ..."

The response was a quaking whisper. "It's too late. The trap has been set."

Flesh against flesh.

Heat against heat.

The silver moonlight streaming through the porthole bathed them in its glow as Rogan clasped Gabrielle close.

Tongues tasting.

Hands caressing.

Bodies joined.

Rogan indulged the sweet, sweet joy that was Gabrielle ... For a little while longer.

Chapter 9

"It has been six days, Manon . . ."

Marie's voice trailed away as Manon turned from the window overlooking the darkening street, her heart wrenching. Manon's beautiful eyes were darkly ringed, her smooth cheeks hollowed. She had barely eaten during the six days that had elapsed since she had last seen Gerard Pointreau.

"You cannot go on this way."

"Marie . . . s'il vous plaît." Manon placed a trembling hand on her stomach. "I . . . I am unwell . . . nauseous. It is typical of my condition, is it not?"

Marie gathered the courage to speak the words she knew she must say. She spoke softly.

"He is not coming."

No response.

"Manon . . ."

Manon raised her chin. "I will write him another letter."

"You have already written."

"I will write again—just one more time." Manon's obvious attempt to still her quivering lips pierced Marie with pain. "If Gerard does not respond within a week, I will leave with you . . . travel up the river for a brief holiday while I search for a temporary residence."

"Manon, ma chérie . . ." Marie's weary eyes filled.

"But he will come. You'll see. Just one last letter. I will write him now."

Manon turned to her desk. She did not see Marie's tears spill.

The sixth day was fading.

Porter halted abruptly on the rocky path that led to the beach. He glanced cautiously over his shoulder to again scan the surrounding area. His narrow, unshaven face drawn into anxious lines, he then continued along the trail until a clear view of the familiar inlet met his gaze.

The uneasiness—it had been with him through the long days since he had escaped from prison and made his way to the inlet—remained.

It had been a damned, lonely wait. He had no doubt Pointreau had seen to it that the governor continued the search for him in the city. For that reason, he had ignored his first inclination to make his way to Madame's where he had found refuge so many times before, and had instead followed a circuitous path to the inlet. He had breathed a deep sigh of relief when he'd finally reached the spot previously allocated by Bertrand as a personal rendezvous point if a problem occurred.

He had waited for Bertrand to appear, hoping until there was no point in doing so any longer that somehow Bertrand had also been able to escape in the unexpected turmoil that had temporarily prevailed in the prison corridors. He had then uncovered the provisions they had buried upon arriving, secreted for just such a situation as the one in which he now found himself, and had prepared himself to wait some more.

It did not concern him that he had neither bathed nor shaved since he had stepped off the rowboat onto the beach six days earlier. Nor did it truly bother him that he had consumed nothing but hardtack, salted beef, and water that seemed to thicken more with each hour that passed, or that the sand fleas had bitten him raw. He had suffered greater hardships in the past.

Anxiety, however, had given him no relief.

Porter stared at the darkening horizon. Bertrand was a good man and a good friend. Somehow things had gone awry, and he could not help but feel that he was partially responsible. Had the young whore he had used at Madame's grown suspicious of him somehow? Would he have been more keenly attuned to the danger that had been lurking in the convent grounds if he had not indulged himself in her perfumed flesh with such abandon? And Bertrand . . . where was he now?

Using the spyglass that had been hidden with the provisions, Porter scanned the surface of the sea for the ship that would soon appear, his breathing growing agitated. It was a clear night, with a brilliant half-moon already visible in the sky. He had come to this spot the previous evening, watching the sea at the outside chance that the *Raptor* might appear a day early. It had not, but the appointed night had finally arrived.

Uneasiness again tugging sharply at him, Porter surveyed the surrounding area before returning his gaze to the horizon.

"Damn it! I'm beginning to believe the man is demented!"

Concealed in the foliage on a rise a cautious distance away, Gerard Pointreau adjusted his spyglass as the evening shadows gradually overwhelmed Porter's image. He cursed again under his breath. The seaman had followed the same procedure the previous evening, going down to the fringe of trees bordering the beach to sit and wait, his spyglass trained on the sea until the early hours of morning.

Pointreau lowered his glass to the ground on which he crouched, impatience a tight knot within that refused to unwind. He did not believe he would ever forget the excitement that had pounded through his veins at the time of Porter's carefully arranged escape. Later, when the governor's men had come to report that Porter had been followed to an obscure inlet a distance from the city, and that Porter appeared to have settled down for the duration, he had realized immediately what the bastard captain had planned.

Oh, yes, Captain Whitney was shrewd. He had dropped off two of his seamen to deliver the ransom demands, with instructions to wait until the specified time for those demands to be met had elapsed before rendezvousing again at the inlet. At sea, Whitney was relatively safe from apprehension. The captain was obviously familiar with the primitive cove where Porter awaited him and considered it a secure temporary harbor. The bastard had possibly used it the night he'd abducted dear Gabrielle.

Pointreau's shoulder twitched. However, the little inlet was safe no longer.

He allowed himself the momentary satisfaction of glancing around him. The governor's men were dispersed throughout the area, awaiting command. A heavily armed ship remained primed for action in a secluded location nearby, where it could not be seen from shore or by an approaching ship.

And it was the sixth day. The deadline for the ransom demands had finally arrived. He had no doubt Whitney's ship would make its appearance this night.

Pointreau's throat abruptly choked tight. Yes, Gabrielle would soon be safe in his arms.

Pointreau's tender emotions turning suddenly virulent, he silently vowed that once Gabrielle was returned to him, he would see to it that Captain Rogan Whitney paid more dearly than he'd ever dreamed for his crimes!

That thought a hot blade of hatred that did not abate, Pointreau turned to the uniformed officer crouched silently near him.

"Your men are ready, Lieutenant Carrier?"

The young officer met his gaze.

"*Oui*, Monsieur Pointreau. The governor made our orders very clear. You need not worry. All will be well."

Pointreau stared at the fellow's ardent expression, his lips tightening. "Your time would be better spent checking on the deployment of your men instead of patronizing me, Lieutenant!"

The flush that suffused his face visible even in the deepening dusk, the young lieutenant dipped his head.

"*Oui, monsieur.*"

Taking up his spyglass with another muttered curse as the fellow scrambled away, Pointreau raised it to the horizon.

Suddenly rigid in his place of concealment within the fringe of trees lining the beach, Porter scanned the darkening sea. His hand trembling as a dark speck appeared there, he adjusted his spyglass and looked again.

It was a ship.

It was the *Raptor*.

He would recognize her anywhere!

Porter laughed low in his throat, the muffled sound jubilant as he reached for the torch nearby.

A ship!

Pointreau snorted; the muffled sound chilling as he regarded the lieutenant who had returned to his side minutes earlier. The fellow remained motionless, his spyglass trained on the horizon.

"Do you see it?"

"*Oui, monsieur.*"

"Are you ready?"

"*Oui, monsieur.*"

Pointreau's heart began a heavy pounding.

* * *

Tension simmered below the surface calm as the *Raptor*'s seamen worked mechanically at their tasks and the shoreline of the inlet came into view.

The wind was brisk.

The ship was moving well.

Gabrielle knew the moment was near.

She glanced toward the quarterdeck where Rogan directed his men with concise orders, his sober features masked by the deepening twilight. She turned away, abruptly overwhelmed as desperation swelled in her.

Oh, yes, if two totally different men resided within the man who had held her in his arms the previous night, the man who had loved her with exquisite gentleness and passion, she need acknowledge that two women resided within her as well.

The first was this person who stood at the rail, needing the strength of Rogan's arms around her, dreading the moment when it would be confirmed that their time together was over.

The second was the woman she knew would reappear the moment her father held out his arms to her, the woman who would recognize her loyalty to the man who had saved her life, had raised her with love . . . with love he had spared for no one else.

Gabrielle breathed deeply, filling her lungs with the refreshing scent of the sea that was soon to be denied her. That second woman, however, was a stranger as they drew closer to the shore. It was the first who suffered.

It was she who wished—

Powerful arms slipped around Gabrielle from behind, fulfilling that wish as they drew her back against the muscular wall of a familiar chest.

Rogan's arms . . . Rogan's chest . . . Rogan's lips against her neck . . . Rogan's deep voice whispering—

They both saw it simultaneously—a torchlight, the signal from shore!

With a whispered word, Rogan released Gabrielle to stride toward his men while uttering short, sharp commands.

* * *

Porter waved his arm, signaling wildly. He waited, holding his breath, as the *Raptor* appeared to lunge suddenly toward shore through the darkening sea.

So intent was he that he did not hear the rustle of footsteps until the second before a blinding blow struck him from behind and the torch was snatched from his hand.

Porter's consciousness faded, leaving in its wake only a fading glimpse of Pointreau's victorious smile.

Rogan stared at the torchlight on shore. Confining his thoughts to the tense moments unfolding as a rowboat was lowered to the water, he refused to allow his mind to wander to Gabrielle, who stood clutching the ship's rail a few yards away.

Under rigid control, he watched the strong, sure strokes of his men as the rowboat traveled smoothly on the calm sea. It would not be long now. The next time he and his men entered New Orleans, they would do so unencumbered by a legal threat, as men cleared of past charges against them.

But what . . . ?

Rogan stiffened. His men had stopped rowing. They were turning the boat around, attempting to head back to the ship.

Gunshots from shore!

A warning shout came from a seaman nearby. "Captain! Look behind us!"

Turning, Rogan saw the outline of a ship fast approaching in the moment the deck beneath him rocked with the force of a cannon blast striking the sea beside their hull.

At Gabrielle's side in a trice, aware of the tears spilling down her cheeks, Rogan shielded her in the curve of his body as he shouted to his grim-faced seamen.

"Man the cannon! Fire at will!"

Another cannon blast rocked the *Raptor*, bringing the main

mast careening to the deck! One more struck the ship broad-side as his men scrambled to his command, some falling wounded as others prepared to return fire amidst the smoke and flames.

Gabrielle shuddered in his protective embrace, and Rogan glanced down, his pride surging at the silent courage in her gaze despite her trembling.

The tenacity of his men no match for the advantage of the surprise attack, Rogan sensed a bleak inevitability as his guns were disabled, the crack of splintering wood rending the ca-lamitous din over and over again until the smoke and fire be-came overwhelming.

The *Raptor* listed suddenly, and Rogan knew it was over.

His shouted command brought all defensive activity aboard to a halt. Looking down at Gabrielle once more, he saw de-spair reflected in her gaze and recognized in that moment the myriad things he wished to say, but dared not.

Refusing to relinquish her shivering form, shielding her from the fire and smoke with his body as the *Raptor* listed more heavily with each passing second, Rogan shouted to his men in final command.

"Put down your arms and prepare to surrender!"

Releasing Gabrielle as the approaching ship drew along-side, Rogan hushed her protest with a glance. Immune to the formal words directed at him as manacles were snapped around his wrists, as his men were hastily transferred to the waiting ship, as he prepared to follow behind them, Rogan turned to see Gabrielle being urged toward another boat that would take her to shore.

He had no doubt as to who awaited her there.

That thought almost more than he could bear as a growled command was snapped into his ear and he was thrust sud-denly forward, Rogan turned back in time to see Gabrielle's last, lingering glance. Meeting it for a sober moment, he then turned to follow his men.

Yes, it was over.

Chapter 10

He remembered the smell.

Rogan's nostrils twitched as he paced the damp cell, agitation tightening already taut sinews aching for release after two days of confinement in an area allowing no more than a few steps in either direction. The fetid odor of the prison was peculiar to it alone. Aside from the dampness and filth, it was rank with the scent of despair.

Rogan remembered other things as well, memories that had returned with disturbing clarity as he'd walked through the familiar corridors in chains.

. . . A fire burning in a vaulted prison chamber as he stood stripped almost naked and helplessly manacled.

. . . Black smoke tunneling upward as irons were heated to a red-hot glow.

. . . The smell of burning flesh.

. . . His own.

Sounds, equally vivid and harsh, had flooded his mind.

. . . The echoes of a friend's agony reverberating into his cell.

. . . Questions repeated over and again before each tortured cry arose.

. . . A final, rattling gasp.

Silence.

He's dead. Get rid of him.

Pointreau . . .

Rogan's anguish returned. He had vowed to avenge the heinous murder of his friend and the betrayal of his ship. He had worked diligently toward that end for three long years.

But he had failed.

Rogan's pacing step abruptly halted. Despair overwhelmed him as Gabrielle's image appeared in his mind, multiplying his anguish.

He loved her.

But she had returned to Pointreau, the father she idolized. He had never doubted that she would.

It wasn't ended yet, though. He couldn't let Pointreau escape again! He couldn't let the deaths of so many go unavenged!

Nor could he allow Gabrielle to spend her life believing a monster's lies!

There had to be a way.

Rogan scanned the bare stone walls and iron bars confining him.

There had to be a way . . .

The elegantly furnished, formal sitting room of Pointreau's city mansion was silent as Gerard faced Gabrielle, his incredulity growing. Afternoon sunlight streamed into the foyer beyond as he addressed her softly.

"You can't mean what you say, Gabrielle! Surely you see that Captain Whitney is a criminal. He is responsible for the deaths of countless American seamen and he—"

"No, Father, you're wrong!" Her glorious pale eyes, somehow more similar to his beloved Chantelle's each day, were fixed on his face as she continued, "Captain Whitney convinced me that a mistake was made, that he's innocent of the charges against him!"

"He is in prison, where he belongs!"

"No."

"He abducted you. He held you prisoner in the hope of having *me* confess to his crimes so he would be free to walk the streets of New Orleans, so he might regain his former status and begin his betrayals all over again!"

"No!"

"Gabrielle . . ." Gerard took a step closer, anxiously scrutinizing the only person dearer to him than his own life. This was the same Gabrielle who had been stolen from him a short time earlier, yet it was not. She had changed in a way he could not quite ascertain. She was still in her mother's beautiful image—her hair the color of burnished flame, her features delicately duplicating Chantelle's, even as she looked up at him with a silent intensity that was hers alone. She had rushed into his arms when the rowboat had returned to shore from Captain Whitney's burning ship, and he had held her tightly as she had sobbed her relief against his chest.

It had only been in the days since, during their difficult conversations and on the occasions when he'd turned to find her studying him covertly, that he had begun to wonder if Gabrielle's tears that night had been stimulated by relief or by . . .

Gerard shrugged that thought away. He had brought Gabrielle directly home after their reunion on the beach. He was determined she would remain there, her return to the convent school, which had failed to hold her safe, no longer considered. He had entertained great plans for the brilliant future they would savor together . . .

. . . until the questions had begun.

Haunted by uncertainty, Pointreau was driven to question Gabrielle as he had once before.

"Captain Whitney—Rapace—he did not harm you in any way . . .?"

"No, he did not, Father."

"He did not try to—"

"The captain treated me well."

Gerard felt a slow anger rise. "No, he did not! He deceived you! He attempted to win you over with kindness, to gain your confidence so he could turn you against me and affect the ultimate revenge!"

"Father, please . . ."

Her face paling beneath the foreign, sun-touched color of her cheeks, Gabrielle closed the distance between them and hugged him tightly. When she looked up at him again, her eyes were brimming.

"No one could ever turn me against you."

Beautiful words, balm to the ache inside him, even as Gerard suffered at the rise of Gabrielle's tears.

"I don't want you to cry."

"I'm not."

"I want you to be happy."

Gabrielle did not respond, and the anxiety within Gerard expanded. Incapable as she was of deceit, he knew she could not force herself to say the words he wanted to hear, that she *was* happy, simply because she was home with him again.

Captain Rogan Whitney had done that to her.

Captain Rogan Whitney had done that . . . *to him*.

Aching at Gabrielle's distress, his hatred soaring for the man who was responsible for the intangible, seemingly unbreachable distance between Gabrielle and him, Pointreau whispered, "You have not yet recuperated from your terrifying experience, *ma chérie*. It pains me to realize that I was impotent in protecting you from the final horror—the cannonade from the governor's ship. But I swear to you, that was not supposed to happen! Surely you know I would not have sanctioned any action that risked your life!" A chill ran down Pointreau's spine. "And you may rest assured that I will see the captain of that vessel severely punished for his irresponsible actions."

"No, Father. There has been enough suffering already."

"Gabrielle, you are young and inexperienced and have been subjected to mental stress. You are confused."

"No, I—"

"Say no more. You will see things more clearly when you have had more time."

"Father, please, there is one thing you must tell me." Gabrielle hesitated before continuing hoarsely, "Wh . . . What will become of Captain Whitney and his men?"

Pointreau slowly went rigid.

"Father?"

"They will suffer the punishment due them!"

"But—"

"It is time for us to conclude this conversation. You need rest, Gabrielle. I think it would be best if you went to your room."

Gabrielle's silence in response tormented Gerard anew. He realized the true extent to which she, too, suffered when she attempted to reply, only to uncharacteristically abandon the effort and turn slowly toward the staircase behind her.

Gerard watched as Gabrielle walked slowly up the stairs and slipped out of sight, a virulent fury rising in him. That bastard captain had bewitched his Gabrielle! He had made her doubt him! He had compromised her love for him!

Gerard's shuddering approached apoplexy as another nagging thought followed.

What *else* had the bastard captain done to her?

Unrelenting, feral emotions assailed Pointreau in great, overwhelming swells. Gabrielle had been at the mercy of Whitney's demands! The man had manipulated her in her innocence until she no longer knew whom to trust . . . or whom to love.

No! He would not allow that bastard the final victory of diluting Gabrielle's love for him! There was only one true way to break the grip Captain Whitney had gained over Gabrielle's senses, one way to restore his dear Gabrielle fully to him.

Pointreau's frame grew rigid. Whitney was held separate from his men, the other cells off that passage empty, a precaution the governor had personally ordered. That corridor was watched by a single guard. It would not be difficult to arrange an attempted escape that would go awry . . .

. . . or to see that a single, well-placed shot forever removed Captain Whitney's shadow from Gabrielle's future.

He would make immediate arrangements. It would be done quickly, within the next few days, before the governor had an opportunity to alter the situation that lent itself so easily to his plan.

Turning with a snarl at the sound of a step behind him, Pointreau saw Boyer standing tentatively there.

"Massa . . ."

"What is it?"

Boyer stepped back at the viciousness of his response.

"I asked you want you wanted!"

"A letter, massa . . ." The old Negro's voice shook as he offered him an envelope. "Bessie put it on the table in the library for you. She say she worry 'cause you didn't see it yet."

Gerard snatched the letter from Boyer's hand and tore it open. The malevolent heat within him steamed hotter as he read Manon's careful script:

Dearest Gerard,

Once more I write to tell you that I despair at your absence and am filled with concern. I hope to hear from you soon so I may set my mind at rest that you are well.

Your loving,
Manon.

Nagging witch!

He had had enough of her and her plaguing distractions!

He would dispense with her services before another hour passed—once and for all!

Tearing the scented sheet into little pieces, Gerard tossed them aside and strode into the foyer.

He reached for his hat, calling to the silent slave behind him, "I have instructions for you, Boyer!"

The trembling slave was beside him in a moment.

"You may tell Mademoiselle Gabrielle that I have several errands to attend to but that I will return later tonight." When Boyer made no response, he grated out, "Did you hear me, you old fool?"

"Yessa."

Gone in a moment, Pointreau did not look back.

Standing out of sight in the upstairs hallway as the door closed behind Pointreau, Gabrielle attempted to still the turbulent emotions within. She was home as she had once so longed to be, but the nightmare was not over. It had only begun.

What was she to believe?

Whom was she to believe?

The lump in Gabrielle's throat tightened. Father was so sincere when he proclaimed his innocence of Rogan's accusations. His gaze did not falter, and although she knew she hurt him with her doubts, neither did his love.

His arms had trembled when he'd embraced her after her rescue from Rogan's burning ship. His cheeks had been wet with tears when he'd whispered over and again how happy he was to have her back.

Those arms had protected her from childish fears. That voice had soothed her woes. Those eyes had always shone with love and pride in her alone, as they had moments earlier, even when she had doubted him.

But Rogan . . .

Love surged so deeply within Gabrielle that she was almost overwhelmed. She had not seen him since he had been taken away in chains. She longed for him.

She shuddered, recalling her terror when the *Raptor* was struck with cannon fire. The noise . . . the smoke . . . the crack of splintering wood—the sudden bedlam as the deck beneath them shuddered with the impact of the shells and the listing of the ship as the fire blazed higher!

But somehow, amidst it all, she would not have wanted to be anywhere else but in Rogan's arms.

Rogan had not for a moment abandoned her to the emergencies growing ever greater as the *Raptor* had been gradually overwhelmed. He had protected her from the flame with his body and had sheltered her from her fears with his dauntless courage. When no choice but surrender remained, he released her only when the ship appeared alongside. Stepping back from her then, he halted her protests with a glance.

A glance that said it was over.

Gabrielle choked back a sob, a plethora of painful emotions assaulting her. The shackles snapped around Rogan's wrists had crushed her with their weight, her pain so great that she had been beyond speech when Rogan was removed to the waiting ship and she was taken ashore to her father.

She had not seen Rogan since.

Unable to bear the uncertainties besetting her a moment longer, Gabrielle moved toward the staircase.

Stepping down onto the foyer, she called out, "Boyer!"

The old Negro appeared immediately behind her, his expression anxious. It pained her that Father was not always kind to this slave who had always been so kind to her. She attempted a smile. "Do you know where my father went?"

"Massa tell me to tell you he goin' on an errand and he be back later tonight."

Revealing her eavesdropping, she asked, "The letter you gave him, who sent it?"

Boyer avoided her eye. "I . . . I don't rightly knows."

"Boyer . . ."

Gabrielle was aware of the courage it took for the old Negro to say, "It from—from a lady friend of the massa."

"A close lady friend?"

"Yes'm."

"Was it from Madame Matier?"

Boyer blinked. His shocked expression was the only answer she needed. Father would be delayed. She would have the time she needed.

"Summon a carriage for me, quickly."

"The massa won't like you goin' out by yourself, *mam'selle*."

"Call the carriage."

"But—"

"I'll need to change. Tell the driver to wait."

Boyer hesitated.

"Please hurry."

Turning, Gabrielle raised the hem of her gown high as she ran up the stairs.

Clarice smiled coyly as she smoothed the golden curls she had swept to the top of her head in studied disarray, pressing closer to the malodorous cook who eyed her with lascivious interest. Behind him, the prison kitchen, located a distance from the main prison building, steamed with heat as perspiring workers struggled to transfer a greasy stew into great buckets in preparation for serving the evening meal.

A low undercurrent of grumbling prevailed among the workers. The late afternoon sun was hot, the air sultry, increasing the abominable heat of the poorly ventilated room and adding to the discomfort of the overworked staff. Clarice had taken great pains in the two days recently past to determine the schedule at the prison kitchen. She had timed her entrance well and knew she had no more than a few minutes to accomplish her purpose.

That thought in mind, she fought to control the spasmodic tugging in her stomach her words evoked as she lazily traced the deep neckline of her bold, green gown with her index finger. Aware that the cook followed its path with avid interest, she whispered, "Have you seen him yourself? Is it true that

Rapace looks the true monster he is—that he is seven feet tall and grotesquely ugly?"

The sweating cook laughed. "Who told you that, *ma petite pigeon?*"

Clarice shrugged her shoulder, allowing the sleeve of her gown to slip provocatively. "The other girls at the Silver Coin told me. I said I didn't believe it, but"—She unleashed the full power of her smile and moved closer, the damp heat of the man's fleshy body penetrating her tawdry dress as she whispered—"I am curious. I confess to a desire that I cannot suppress to see the great beast."

"Oh, ho . . ." The cook laughed aloud, his yellowed teeth glinting nauseatingly as his hand strayed up to caress the curve of her breast. "So you like great beasts, do you?" He leered. "I have a great beast of my own I would be happy to show you."

Clarice shrugged again. "The Silver Coin welcomes all visitors . . . as do I when I am there. But, you see, I am not working now. I have an hour to spare, and I would like to see him before he is hung."

The cook's hand slipped lower and Clarice's stomach churned. "So why do you come to me, *ma chérie?*"

"Because Rapace is allowed no visitors."

"So?"

"I would ask a favor."

"A favor . . ." The fellow's leer deepened. "Ah, but favors are costly . . ."

Clarice pressed her breasts gently against the man's bulk. "And poor I, who have no manner of barter to offer but myself . . ."

The oaf swelled hard and firm against her. "What favor do you ask of me?"

Clarice was close to retching as she motioned delicately with her chin toward the workers behind them. "Your staff is so tired. Surely they would not protest if you were to send me into the prison to lighten their burden by serving the cells

where Rapace is confined . . . so I may see him and touch
him."

The cook's breathing grew heavy. "Rapace is confined
apart from the others."

"Ah . . . so much the better."

The obese fellow frowned. "A word from me would get
you inside and allow you time to linger, perhaps until the villain has had time to . . . empty his plate." The cook laughed
suddenly, as if the choice of words amused him; then his
frown returned. "But would you remember the favor when
you were through?"

"Monsieur, you hurt me with your distrust!" Clarice slipped
her hand down to caress the bulge pressed so tight against
her. "Were time not so short, with the evening meal ready to
be served, I would express my appreciation for your favor in
advance, but"—Clarice fluttered her lashes—"you know
where to find me."

"The Silver Coin, you say." The cook squinted, considering. "Later tonight?"

"I will reserve time for you, ample time for true enjoyment—if your wife will let you out."

"My wife!" The cook snorted. "The old hag will let me out,
all right." His bulbous nose twitched. "And if she objects, I'll
lay her flat with the back of my hand!"

"So you *are* a great beast."

"I'll show you how great a beast I am, *ma petite poupée.* But
first I will show you how generous I can be."

The cook turned gruffly toward a perspiring, middle-aged
woman behind him. "Margot, you will allow—" He glanced
back toward Clarice. "What is your name, *ma favorite?*"

"Clarice."

"You will allow Clarice to accompany you in serving the
evening meal. You will send her to the cell where Rapace is
confined."

The old woman squinted at Clarice assessingly. "And if the
guard questions her presence?"

"Tell him she is a temporary worker, personally hired by me."

The woman grumbled.

"What did you say, Margot?"

Addressing Clarice in lieu of a reply, the woman pushed back an oily strand of gray hair from her face. "Take that pail over there. I'll bring you to the corridor where the fellow, Rapace, is confined." The woman grunted. "But it looks to me as if he'll have little mind for food this night."

Clarice bent down to pick up the heavy bucket. At the cook's sharp gasp, she glanced up to see his gaze fastened on the white swells bulging above her neckline. She gritted her teeth in a smile. "A favor for a favor, *mon cher* . . ."

Pail in hand, Clarice slipped into the weary kitchen procession as it made its way to the prison's rear door.

"He's here, Marie!"

Manon stepped back from the window overlooking the street, her heart pounding. It seemed to her that she had waited an eternity for Gerard to again visit, only to have him catch her at less than her best.

The stifling heat . . . her persistent nausea . . .

Manon smoothed her damp batiste, then ran toward the kitchen in a moment's panic. Grasping a cloth, she moistened it with water and patted it against her face as she turned to the cracked mirror in the corner. The truth could not be denied. She was pale, and her cheeks were sunken. Her eyes, deeply ringed, appeared to overwhelm her face.

Despairing, she pinched her cheeks vigorously, then smoothed a few, flyaway wisps at her hairline, stepping back quickly to survey herself from a distance. She was thinner, unappealingly so. She experienced little consolation in the knowledge that her figure would not remain thin much longer.

The click of the front door reverberated down the hallway and Manon jumped with a start. She heard the mumble of voices, then Marie's limping step as she approached the kitchen.

Marie's face was drawn into familiar lines of disapproval as she announced in a deliberate, formal tone, "Monsieur Pointreau is here to see you, madame." And then in a softer voice. "Beware, Manon. He is in a foul mood."

Her moment of hesitation brief at Marie's warning, Manon walked quickly up the hallway. She entered the sitting room to find Gerard standing with his back toward her. The sight of him unleashed true joy. Gerard had returned to her, and she loved him! Everything would be well.

Manon rushed to his side.

"Gerard, *mon ami,* I have missed you so."

He turned abruptly and Manon gasped at the florid heat that colored his face the moment before his hand snapped out to deliver a stunning blow to her cheek. Staggering backward, she struck her hip sharply against a nearby chair. She clung to the bulky piece to steady herself as the acrid taste of blood met her tongue. Her head was still reeling when Gerard advanced toward her to stand so close that she could feel the hatred radiating from him when he spoke.

"How dare you press me? How dare you affront me with your nagging letters? How dare you assume, even for a moment, that you have a right to expect anything more from me than I choose to give you? You are my mistress—bought and paid for—and nothing more! I installed you in this house to service my desires as I did with others before you—as I will again after you have long slipped from my mind! You missed me?" Gerard sneered. "Does it come as a shock to you to know that I have not missed you at all, ambitious witch that you are?"

Manon gasped and Gerard laughed harshly.

"So you believed me under your control! You thought to have so paralyzed my mind with desire for you that you could manipulate me to your wishes! I tell you now, I was never taken in by your wiles! You entertained me well. You amused me with your loving pretensions. You were useful to me, Manon! While Gabrielle was lost to me, you filled a void—a temporary void—but as with all greedy wretches who think to demand ever more from a man, you overreached yourself with your whining letters and calls for attention!"

A throbbing began inside Manon's head, incredulity holding her speechless. The pounding grew louder as she struggled to respond, managing, "B—But I love you!"

"Love! I never asked for or wanted your *love!*" Gerard laughed, the obvious pleasure he took in speaking so cruelly heightening Manon's pain as he continued, "You were a convenience to me! A well-used convenience that has, unfortunately, grown tiresome."

Gerard paused, sweeping her with a scathing glance. "Have you looked at yourself lately, Manon? You are rapidly aging. So tell me, why would a man who has proved his value to the governor and the City of New Orleans over and again, who is celebrated and cheered as the savior of American seamen, and who can have any woman he wants—why would such a man bother with the demands of an aging whore such as you?"

Manon closed her eyes. *"Mon Dieu . . ."*

"Ah, so now we petition God in an attempt to intimidate! But you see, Manon . . ."—Taking her roughly by the shoulders, Gerard shook her hard, forcing her to open her eyes as he glared at her venomously—"you waste your breath, for *I* am *my* own god, and I put no other god before *me!*"

Gerard released Manon with a thrust that propelled her backward. She struck the wall heavily, pain jolting her as he continued, "And when I leave you now, I go to arrange for the final conclusion of another affair in which someone thinks to have gained the final victory because he believes he has usurped that which I hold most dear! But, as always, Gerard Pointreau will have the ultimate triumph, for Gerard Pointreau does not hesitate to take the steps necessary to eliminate an enemy, once and for all!"

At Manon's incredulous silence, Gerard swept his eyes over her deprecatingly once more. "An aging whore . . . What did I ever see in you?"

Striding into the foyer, he snatched up his hat, turning to add, "I will expect you and your hag of a servant to be out of this house by the end of the week! That might allow enough time, even for an old slut like you, to find another man."

Unable to move as Gerard slammed the door behind him, as the pounding in her head escalated to a painful thunder that stole all sound, Manon did not feel the first hot gush that spurted from between her thighs. Nor did she hear Marie's frightened cry as the pain exploded inside her, leaving her in darkness as she crumpled to the floor.

Rogan halted his pacing, coming to sharp attention. He strained to verify the light footsteps echoing down the corridor between the cells, a woman's footsteps totally unlike the dragging tread of the weary dame who delivered his tasteless meals.

Rogan tensed. He dared not allow himself to hope.

Refusing to think, Rogan gripped the bars of his door in tight fists. His knuckles whitened as the light steps drew closer, as a slender figure rounded the corner and he saw—

Clarice.

She halted abruptly. The pail she carried dangled limply from her hand for the short second before Rogan managed a hoarse whisper.

"What are you doing here?" He glanced down the deserted corridor, "It's unsafe for you! If Pointreau learns of your connection to Bertrand or me—"

Clarice raised her voice loudly enough so it might be heard at the guard's station around the bend, "Rogan, *mon amour*, I have missed you so."

She moved closer, continuing in a whisper as she filled a

metal plate from the bucket and handed it to him. "Quickly, take this. If someone other than the guard comes, you must follow my lead."

Accepting the plate, Rogan slipped it onto his bunk. "It was a mistake for you to come here!"

"I had to see you." Clarice's beauty glowed through her heavily painted cheeks and tawdry dress. It was easy to see the ploy she had used to obtain admittance. Tears welled in her clear blue eyes as she rasped, "You are allowed no visitors, but I found a way to gain admittance. I had to make sure you were all right." She paused. "The whole city is talking of your capture, but"—her voice faltered—"there has been no word of Bertrand."

"He is all right, or so the guards have intimated to me. The governor has seen fit to separate me from my crew until we are brought to trial."

Clarice's eyes briefly fluttered closed with relief before she stepped closer and stretched a hand out to him. He accepted it, holding it tightly.

"You must go before you're recognized. If Pointreau discovers your link to us, you will suffer."

"*Non.*" Clarice's gaze was steady. "First you must tell me what to do so I may help you and Bertrand escape this place."

Anguish knotted tightly in Rogan's chest. Clarice, loyal, self-sacrificing, a true gem—yet there was only one jewel that glittered in his heart.

Rogan squeezed Clarice's hand tighter. "You can do nothing for Bertrand or me now, except to keep yourself free of involvement so Pointreau will not have another weapon to use against us." Remorse tightened Rogan's brow. "I'm sorry, Clarice. Were it not for me, Bertrand would not now be a prisoner here."

She responded with unexpected adamancy. "You have no reason to apologize to me, Rogan! Whatever the outcome of this encounter, your faith in Bertrand raised him up from desolation and returned him sound and whole to me when I thought he was lost. I can never fully repay you for that gift."

"I failed him."

"Your quest for justice restored my brother's dignity and gave your seamen hope. There is not a man among your crew who regrets the time he spent under your command."

"Clarice, we have no time for this now."

"You are right." Her beautiful face flushed. Her tone grew desperate. "Quickly, you must tell me what to do."

"There is nothing you can do."

"Non! I will not accept that!" Clarice glanced warily down the corridor as approaching sounds grew louder. "It appears the serving of the meals has almost been completed. I will soon have to leave, but it will not be necessary for me to use the same manner of admittance next time. I have made a friend of the guard who is stationed in this corridor."

Rogan's jaw tensed. "A friend?"

A brief smile touched Clarice's lips. "I've convinced the guard that you are my lover and my only wish is to send you to the gallows a happy man."

"That was foolish! If Pointreau—"

"Rogan, *s'il vous plaît,* we have so little time!"

Silent for a long moment, Rogan whispered, "I don't want you to come back here, Clarice."

"I will. I must."

Rogan's gaze lingered on her. "No."

"There must be something I can do!"

He hesitated, uncertain. "One thing, if you could . . ."

"Anything, *mon cher.*"

"If you could use your contacts at Madame's . . ." He paused, his voice dropping, becoming softer, "If you could inquire as to Gabrielle's welfare."

"Gabrielle . . . Dubay?"

"She is innocent of her father's crimes, Clarice. She is courageous and good, but she is confused by her father's lies. I fear her father will not accept it well if she should question him." He paused. "I'm concerned for her safety."

Clarice's clear eyes searched his face. Rogan felt their silent intensity, recognizing how much he had revealed as she whispered, "I understand."

"If you could get word to me by way of your 'friend,' the guard . . ."

"I will."

Realizing the magnitude of the debt he owed this brave, beautiful woman, Rogan raised her hand to his lips.

"*Merci*, Clarice, for all you have ever done for me."

Following her slender form, noting the tilt of her head and the jaunty step she assumed as she walked back in the direction from which she had come, Rogan swallowed tightly.

Alone once more, he glanced up at the barred window of his cell, frustration rising.

No, it couldn't end this way!

Clarice's step slowed as she rounded the curve in the corridor and Rogan's cell slipped from sight. Her smile slipped as well.

She had told Rogan that she understood when he'd asked her to inquire about Gabrielle Dubay.

She did.

She understood too well.

She could deceive herself no longer.

Forcing herself forward, her smile even brighter, Clarice paused at the guard's station. She leaned toward the fellow she had spoken to briefly upon entering. She had easily charmed him, but knowing a need to fortify her position, she reached into her pocket to withdraw the silver coins there. She pressed them into his palm.

"*Merci, mon ami.* You have made my lover and me very happy." She gave him a flirtatious glance. "If I were to return to see him again, you would not turn me away?"

The fellow glanced around, then slipped the coins into his pocket. His gaze dropped briefly toward her neckline before appreciatively going back up to her face as he whispered, "Come to the back door and ask for Jacques. I will come out for you if the corridor is clear. Then you may—"

"Are you ready to leave, Clarice?"

Turning toward the old woman behind them who assessed her with obvious suspicion, Clarice responded, *"Oui,* I am."

Falling in as the kitchen workers filed back toward the exit door, Clarice turned with a last wink to the guard. She forced a smile as he called out behind her.

"Au'revoir, Clarice . . ."

But her smile quickly faded.

Dropping her bucket in the kitchen, Clarice avoided the cook with practiced dexterity and a husky promise she had no intention of keeping as she slipped out into the shadows of the prison yard.

Her breast heaving, tears close to falling, Clarice remained unmoving in the darkness, allowing herself silent moments to acknowledge a truth she could no longer deny.

The dream she had cherished would never be.

Rogan would never love her as she loved him.

The reason was simple.

He loved Gabrielle Dubay.

Mon Dieu . . .

He did.

Gabrielle walked quickly up the prison corridor. She approached the curve of the guard's station as a male voice echoed from the area beyond.

"Au revoir, Clarice . . ."

Clarice.

Gabrielle halted, the familiar name jolting her. She had identified herself at the prison door minutes earlier and had demanded to see Rogan on the pretext of affirming to her satisfaction that he was truly no longer a danger. She had dismissed the escort assigned her at the previous guard station, with an air that left the startled fellow no choice but to remain silently submissive when she stated that she was determined to face her abductor alone. Almost beside herself with anticipation at the realization that she would soon see Rogan again, feel his touch, she had continued on until—

How had she allowed herself to forget Clarice?

Moving forward again despite the torment within, Gabrielle approached the guard station. She noted the guard's startled expression as she came into view. She did not choose to identify herself as he assessed the quality of her garments with a glance, then addressed her with obvious caution.

"I fear you turned down the wrong corridor, *mademoiselle*. This is no place for a lady like yourself. There is only one prisoner in this section—a dangerous felon."

"Oh . . ." Gabrielle's hesitation was genuine. "I—I thought to have heard a woman departing . . . a woman someone called Clarice."

The guard's oily face grew tense. He shifted uncomfortably, then shrugged. "The man will doubtless be hanged, so I saw no harm in it when his woman visited him with the excuse of serving his evening meal."

"His woman . . ."

"She thought I did not know who she was, but I did. Her name is Clarice Bouchard. She is an exclusive woman from Madame Renée's house."

"Madame Renée's?"

The guard flushed. "I—you would not be well acquainted with such a place, I am sure. Clarice said she and the prisoner are deeply in love and she needed to see him, to . . . to soothe his anxieties. I saw no harm in it."

Gabrielle was incapable of response.

"You will not report me, *mademoiselle?*"

"No."

Gabrielle took a backward step, her throat suddenly so

tight it inhibited her breathing. Clarice, the woman so special to Rogan that his last words to Bertrand before the man left the ship were for her, was a prostitute.

But love knew no common bounds. She was proof of that, was she not?

No, she could not face Rogan now, not while his lover's kiss was still fresh on his lips.

"Mademoiselle?"

Gabrielle raised a shaky hand to her brow. She attempted a smile. "You are correct. It appears I have wandered down the wrong corridor." Knowing a need she could not quite define and uncertain as to where else to turn, she continued, "I . . . I come here on a mission of mercy, seeking a man named Bertrand who was part of Rapace's crew. A relative of his is deathly ill and has sent me with a message for him."

The guard appeared relieved. "That fellow is confined in another section of the prison. If you will return almost to your starting point and turn right instead of left, then follow the corridor to the end, you will find someone to direct you further."

"Thank you."

Gabrielle turned blindly back in the direction from which she had come, her heart speaking one name alone.

The light of her bedroom appeared strangely muted as Manon struggled to fully raise her heavy eyelids.

The task beyond her, she allowed them to close once more. She had difficulty breathing.

Voices came from a distance . . . familiar voices.

"Doctor."—Marie's tone was anxious, close to panic— "Manon will be all right? She is so pale."

"She has suffered a serious mishap, but she will survive. I have managed to stop the bleeding, but . . ." A second's hesitation. "She has lost the child."

Non! She did not want it to be true!

"You must tell me"—Marie's voice broke.—"what I can do to help her."

"Come now." The voice Manon recognized as Dr. Thoreau's mumbled comfortingly, "You must be brave, Marie. Manon will need your strength when she awakens."

"When will that be? She has been unconscious so long."

"She is weak. She hemorrhaged badly, but she should awaken soon. I must leave for a few minutes, but I will return and stay a few hours longer so I may be completely certain of her condition."

"She is so pale."

Manon heard the doctor's sigh. "She will be all right, Marie, but you must be ready to console her."

Console her . . .

The sound of the door closing.

The pain of reality.

Manon sobbed.

"Manon . . ."

Manon fought to open her eyes at Marie's trembling touch. A pain unrelated to physical distress surged deeply when she saw the older woman's lined cheeks were still damp from the tears she had hastily wiped away.

"How are you feeling, Manon? Are you in pain?"

"Marie . . ." Another weak sob. "My babe . . . it will never be born."

"You must not think of that now." Marie stroked her forehead, then her cheek. "You have had a difficult time. You must think only of getting well again."

"I am so ashamed . . ."

"Ashamed?" Marie's stroking hand momentarily stilled. "You did nothing to be ashamed of, *ma chérie.*"

"It is my fault."

"You bear no fault in any of this sad affair, *ma petite.*"

"I do!" Her breath short, Manon clutched Marie's stroking hand. "You were right! I should have left Gerard—should have known he would never love me. I sought to force his love. It is my fault that my babe is gone." The sob came from the deep, inner core of her.

Increasingly anxious, Marie whispered, *"Non,* Manon, you must not blame yourself! All you did was done in the name of love! You were not responsible because Monsieur Pointreau was incapable of returning your affection. He is a master of deception and because you loved him, you wanted to believe in him. It was not your fault!"

"If I had listened to you, I would still have the babe within me!"

"You must not reproach yourself. You did not know."

"I knew . . . I knew . . ."

"Ma petite, if you must accept blame, then you must also forgive yourself, for if you erred, you erred in the name of love."

"I erred in the name of selfishness, not love!"

"Untrue!"

"Non—true! I wanted Gerard to love me because I loved him. That was my only thought! I should have been thinking of the babe!"

"You had no way of knowing what he would do."

"Oh, I did." Manon grew breathless. "Gerard's fiendish streak . . . showed in subtle ways . . . in hurting me when we made love. But I convinced myself all would be well when Gabrielle was returned to him."

Another sob.

"Manon, *je t'en prie,* do not continue."

Je t'en prie . . ." Manon gave a gasping laugh. " 'I beg you.' Gerard said that to me. I believed he loved me then."

"Monsieur Pointreau is incapable of love."

"Non. He loves."

"He loves himself!"

"He loves Gabrielle as much as himself." Manon's eyes grew feverishly bright. Her breath grew more labored as she forced herself to continue. "But he will destroy her, in his way. I heard him. He said it . . ."

"Manon, you must not upset yourself."

"He said it when he left—that he went to arrange to eliminate his enemy, the one who believed he had usurped what Gerard held most dear! Gabrielle's love—that is what Gerard holds most dear! Gerard will kill . . . kill the man she loves!"

"You are upset, Manon . . . weak. You hallucinate."

"*Non.* I know what he is going to do. You must stop him, Marie! I c—can not have the stain of another death on my soul!"

"Manon . . ." Marie looked up as she heard the front door open. Dr. Thoreau had returned. She took an anxious breath. "The doctor will give you something to relax."

"*Non. Je t'en prie* . . . I beg you with your own words—with the same words Gerard used to corrupt me. Go to Gabrielle . . . warn her . . . tell her she must stop Gerard. She must."

The door opened and Marie turned anxiously to see Dr. Thoreau entering the room. His concern was obvious as he approached the bed.

"What's happened here?"

"Marie . . . go now . . . Promise me . . ."

The doctor spoke gently. "You must rest, Manon."

"Marie, go . . . before it is to late!"

The doctor turned with obvious confusion, toward Marie. His expression forced her to respond.

"All right, Manon. I will go."

"Now . . ."

"*Oui,* if the doctor will stay."

"Marie . . ." Manon's eyes maintained their feverish glow. "Tell Gabrielle . . . tell her I am sorry to send you with such news. Tell her I share her pain because . . . because I, too, loved the Gerard whom I glimpsed so briefly . . . who revealed himself fully to her alone. Tell her I wish I wish . . ."

Manon's voice faded. She closed her eyes as tears streamed from beneath her trembling lids.

Thrust aside as the doctor leaned over Manon, Marie

backed away from the bed. Turning with a quickness of movement that belied her age, she slipped out the door.

Bertrand heard the footsteps approaching. Light steps out of place in the gloomy corridors beyond his cell. He was no longer confined in isolation as he had been after being captured in the convent yard. Instead, the cells around him were filled with his shipmates, a fact that gave him little comfort.

Bertrand's scarred face creased into a frown. He was still uncertain about the captain's fate. In an attempt to taunt him, the guards he knew to be in Pointreau's employ had told him that the captain was held apart from them at the governor's explicit order, to forestall any organized attempt at escape. They also said that the governor expected to gain information against Lafitte through the captain.

Bertrand knew he never would.

But that was not his main concern.

His primary anxiety was Pointreau and the fact that the captain was sequestered in a private area of the prison, where there would be no witnesses to any vile deeds Pointreau hoped to execute. During the time since he had been captured, it had become clear to him that there was no feasible means of escape without outside help. Porter continued to harangue himself for not realizing that truth, and for the unwitting part he had played in setting the trap that had brought the captain down.

But that was not Bertrand's only torment. Through the long nights of incarceration, he had suffered for the anguish he knew Clarice endured because of her uncertainty as to his fate. He was tormented by all the things he had never said to express his love and pride in her, and his gratitude for her loyalty.

He suffered because he knew Clarice loved the captain, and that her anguish was twofold because of it.

And he suffered for the words he had not had the courage to voice to one who had become an unexpected friend.

The mumblings in the next cell heightened, drawing Bertrand's attention back to the present. He was unprepared, however, when the light footsteps came closer, when he stepped out of the shadows of his cell to see—

"Mademoiselle Dubay!"

Spontaneous concern touched with warmth propelled Bertrand toward the bars separating him from the slender, soberly clad young woman. He questioned sharply, "Why are you here?" He glanced behind her. "You are alone? You were allowed to travel these corridors without a guard to guide you?"

The seamen confined nearby stepped to the rear of their cells to afford them as much privacy as possible as the daughter of Gerard Pointreau stood silently before Bertrand, temporarily unable to speak.

Bertrand prodded, "You have seen the captain? He is all right?"

Gabrielle's throat work convulsively. "No, I haven't seen him. I could not . . ." She left the words hanging. "But he is well."

"It is dangerous for you to wander this prison alone."

"No one would dare touch the daughter of Gerard Pointreau."

That sentence delivered flatly, without emotion, deepened Bertrand's frown. He repeated, "Why are you here?"

Gabrielle blinked back the moisture brimming in her pale eyes, hesitating again in response as she stepped closer. In the moments that followed, Bertrand recalled the silence of the captain's cabin as he'd tended to an angry young woman's lacerated feet, the gradual ease that arose between them . . . the airings on deck during which he came to a gradual sense of the young woman's true worth.

He also recalled the day when he'd realized Gabrielle no longer saw his disfigurement, but only the person beneath. It came to him with sudden clarity that Gabrielle began to effect a cure that day of a malady of which he had never expected to be free. Just as suddenly, he realized he had prejudged her as harshly as he had been prejudged, upon appearances and on the blemishes of family name.

No, Gabrielle Dubay was not molded in her father's image. Of that he had never been more sure.

His voice a notch softer, Bertrand spoke again.

"Why are you here?"

"I ... I don't really know." Gabrielle blinked. "I didn't know where else to turn to find a friend."

A friend ...

Yes, she was.

"Bertrand, I must know the truth!" Gabrielle's impassioned words came in a sudden rush. "I don't know what to believe anymore! My father says he is innocent of the crimes Rogan accuses him of. I saw his eyes. They were sincere and pained because I doubted him! Yet I remember Rogan's eyes, and I remember his voice. He—" Her words caught. "Please help me to discover the truth!"

"I can't tell you what to believe, Gabrielle." Slipping as easily into the familiarity of her given name as he'd slipped into the sudden candor between them, Bertrand whispered, "I can only tell you that the captain is innocent of the charges brought against him, those that caused him to become a fugitive, and that your father was responsible for the interrogation and torture of the captain, as well as the death of his first mate and friend."

"No ..."

"It's also true that your father is in league with Gambi in the attack against American merchant ships."

"Oh, no!"

"I'm sorry."

Silence.

"I don't know what to do, Bertrand. He is my father. I love him."

"There is nothing you *can* do."

"Nothing ..."

That thought striking her hard, Gabrielle turned abruptly away. Snapping back to face him again before she had taken a step, she managed to say, "Thank you."

And then she was gone.

The stench of stale ale and filth overwhelmed the back room of the dockside tavern, assailing Gerard Pointreau's nostrils as he emptied a pouch onto the table. Gold coins spilled out, glinting in the light of the overhead lamp. The three men opposite him eyed the glittering heap lustfully as he spoke.

"I want it done as quickly as possible. Tomorrow."

"That is impossible." Benchley, shortest of the three prison guards and the unacknowledged spokesman, shook his head. "We need more time to make certain of the men who will be on duty. There are some, one fellow in particular on watch in the captain's corridor at night, who could cause us trouble."

"Kill him, too!"

Benchley flashed an evil smile. "That would cost an additional fee, Monsieur Pointreau."

"I don't care about the cost! I want it done quickly, without raising suspicion. The story you will tell is simple. Someone smuggled Captain Whitney a gun, and he attempted an escape. He killed his guard in the process. He was loose in the prison corridor when you discovered him. You attempted to apprehend him, but he was killed in the process. It could not be easier!"

"We need more time. Three days . . ."

Pointreau shook his head.

"Two days."

"No longer!"

The spokesman nodded and reached toward the glittering coins as Pointreau spoke again.

"Do your job well and I will match this amount, with more to spare."

Benchley's sinister smile flashed again. The two behind him snickered under their breath as he replied.

"You may depend on us, Monsieur Pointreau. It will be done."

Disturbed, Governor William Claiborne stared out his office window at the cobbled square below. New Orleans, never an easy post in the time since he'd executed the formidable task of arranging the transfer of Louisiana from France to the United States eight years earlier, was a city beyond comparison with its European flavor and distinctive beauty.

He had gradually grown to understand its customs and its people who clung so obstinately to the French manner and language, but it had been a difficult process.

William Claiborne's frown darkened. That difficult process had been eased by the help of one man in particular, a man whom he depended upon as a friend and a patriot loyal to the city, to the country, and to him.

That man was Gerard Pointreau.

It had been obvious upon their first meeting that Gerard was brilliant. He was also well educated, charming, and deeply devoted to his beautiful adopted daughter whom he treasured above all else. Claiborne had considered himself fortunate to have so good a friend and advisor. He'd trusted Pointreau completely.

For that reason he had suffered the man's devastation when his daughter had been abducted. He had promised Gerard and himself that he would do anything he could to help restore Gabrielle to him and to bring the man responsible for her abduction to justice. He had followed through with that promise . . .

. . . even as the first doubts began to rise.

Governor Claiborne's disquiet deepened. Captain Whitney's demands in exchange for Gabrielle's return had startled him. A call for justice with no personal monetary gain in-

cluded, this did not fit the picture of the man he had believed
Captain Whitney to be. Gerard had been extremely proficient
in his explanations of the man's devious attempt to discredit
him with those demands. He had believed Gerard, until . . .

The memory of that startling moment when Gerard had
looked at him, revealing a venom within that had raised the
hackles on Claiborne's spine, returned to nag viciously at him.

Turning back to his desk, the governor picked up the communication he had received earlier that afternoon. He
scanned the flowery hand, then went back to the beginning to
again read:

"My dear Governor Claiborne,

We have not been allies in the past, but although
your belief runs to the contrary, I consider myself a
loyal American with the best interests of our great
country at heart. For that reason I write to you today.

It is difficult to learn one has been betrayed, especially by one considered to be a friend. So I pray that despite your desire to dismiss that which follows, you
consider my revelations carefully.

It is my belief that Captain Whitney was innocent of
the original charge of betraying his ship to pirates years
ago. I believe he was wrongfully persecuted through the
devious efforts of the man who sought to conceal his
own involvement in the crime of which Captain Whitney was accused.

That man was Gerard Pointreau.

A simple investigation, never previously instituted by
you, I am sure, because of your trust in Monsieur
Pointreau, will reveal that he is not the man you believe
him to be.

That point is proven by the visit I received from
Monsieur Pointreau after his daughter's abduction, in
which he hoped to solicit my aid by promising to deliver your favor to me in return. Rather than being

made out of desperation, that offer was made with open contempt for you—and with his claim that he had always been able to easily manipulate you to his end, a claim he doubtless believed.

I tell you now, that I, who have been defamed by so many, have never attempted to deliver a friend to one whom he considers his enemy.

I declined Monsieur Pointreau's offer because, despite our differences, I believe you to be an honorable man and would have no part in compromising your ideals.

It is my hope that you will receive this letter in the spirit with which it is sent and that justice will be served.

Your servant,
Jean Lafitte.

Governor Claiborne stared at the missive moments longer, doubt surging in him. He took pride in being honorable, and he had always considered Gerard an honorable man.

But now . . .

Suddenly disgusted with the line his thoughts were taking, Claiborne crumpled the letter up and tossed it across the room.

The truth was simple.

Lafitte was a pirate.

Gerard was a friend.

And that was the end of it!

The muted light of Manon's room faded to shadows as she struggled for breath. She strained to see.

A male figure beside her bed . . .

Dr. Thoreau.

"Doctor . . ."

Thoreau looked up. He moved closer.

"Yes, Manon?"

She tried to speak. She felt no pain, only breathlessness. She rasped, "Marie ... she has returned?"

"She left only minutes ago, Manon."

Minutes ... a lifetime.

"She must warn Gabrielle ..."

"Marie understands."

"A life ... at stake ..."

"You must remain calm, Manon."

"I was wrong."

"Manon—"

"W-Will he forgive me?"

"Will who forgive you?"

"God."

"Manon, you—"

"Pray for me."

"Manon—"

"Pray for me!"

"Manon ... ?"

Brilliant light.

Manon saw her.

Her babe ...

Her babe!

A rattling breath.

Manon held out her arms.

The red-gold of the setting sun disappeared beyond the horizon as Gabrielle pushed open the front door of her father's city mansion and stepped inside. She pushed the portal closed behind her, leaning back against it, closing her eyes. She had walked the few blocks from the prison, her mind racing.

Rogan's image rose in her mind, and the pain within Gabrielle heightened. She longed for him—to feel his arms around her, his mouth against hers; to experience again the certainty, stronger each time he had touched her, that only with him was she truly complete.

Rogan or Rapace . . .

Lover or felon . . .

Either or both . . .

She loved him.

He had loved her—she knew he had—for a little while. There had been no denying the emotion that had softened his predatorial gaze to liquid gold. There had been no denying the passion throbbing in his voice when they had lain flesh against flesh, nothing but honesty between them.

No artifice.

Only truth.

But where had the truth ended and all else begun?

Rogan and Clarice . . .

A hot knife of pain slashed deeply, but Gabrielle thrust it aside. That truth was clear. She need determine the rest. She would talk to Father when he returned. She would—

"Mam'selle Gabrielle . . ."

Gabrielle opened her eyes to see Boyer standing tentatively nearby.

"What is it, Boyer?"

"Someone here to see you."

"Where?"

"In the sittin' room."

Gabrielle glanced toward the entry to see the panel doors drawn. Boyer responded instinctively to her unspoken question.

"The massa still out."

She walked stiffly toward the sitting room and slid back the doors. She was momentarily taken aback at seeing the old woman standing there. The woman's appearance was common, almost servile, except for the peculiar light in her small eyes.

Uncertain, Gabrielle inquired, "Did you want to see me?"

"You are Gabrielle Dubay?" The woman took a limping

step forward to scrutinize her more closely. "*Oui*, I can see that you are."

"May I ask—"

"*Non*, it would be best if you did not ask anything at all but listened instead. I have lost enough time here already, and there is much to say."

"Your name?"

The old woman advanced to within a few feet of her. Gabrielle saw the resentment in the old woman's gaze as she began abruptly. "My name is Marie. I was sent here by my mistress, Madame Manon Matier."

"Oh." Gabrielle took a spontaneous backward step. First Rogan's lover . . . now her father's. She was not prepared for this. "What does Madame Matier want with me?"

Hatred flashed in the woman's eyes. "She wishes to save a life!"

"A life!"

"She begged me, and so I came! She pleaded with me to warn you of your father's plans. She did not want to be responsible for the death of the man you love!"

Aghast, Gabrielle shook her head. "What are you talking about?"

The old servant pinned the younger woman with her gaze. "Manon knows what he is going to do. She finally admits to herself that Gerard Pointreau is a monster who will stop at nothing to gain his ends!"

"My father?"

"He will allow no one to stand in the way of the future he has planned for his darling Chantelle's daughter!"

A knot of incredulity tightened in Gabrielle's throat at the woman's steadfast assault. "What do you know of my mother?"

"I know that your father loved her, and *only* her! He allowed other women only close enough to him to serve his needs while he kept her image forever enshrined in his heart and mind! You are flesh of Chantelle's flesh, and he loves you as the child that should have been his. But Manon knows . . . She knows that you will be made to suffer for loving Pointreau, as she suffers, even as your mother did before you."

"My mother loved Gerard Pointreau in an entirely different way than she loved her husband. She—"

"Your mother was wise! She knew that Gerard Pointreau's love stifles—that it kills! I warned Manon. I told her to be careful, that he was not capable of love as she knew it, but she told me I was wrong. Now she suffers. But Manon is too good. She would not have you suffer as she does. She sent me to warn you."

"Of what?"

"Your father told Manon—he said that when he left her, he went to arrange the elimination of the man who thought to usurp your love from him! Captain Whitney."

Gabrielle gasped.

"So, Manon was right."

"It can't be true."

"At this moment the exchange is being made—gold for blood. It is your father's way! He would then be free to indulge you until you neither remembered, nor cared, about the needs of others, until you became so obsessed with self that you were as corrupt as he!"

"No!"

"He has an evil in him—an evil Manon acknowledged too late." Tears suddenly streaming down her lined cheeks, the old woman rasped, *"Ma chère* Manon—she begged me to console you, to tell you that she understands the torment you are now feeling. She said to explain that she understands because she loves your father, too, the part of him she glimpsed only briefly, the part of him that is yours alone."

"Mine . . . You are saying my father loves me, but would kill one *I* love!"

"Leaving only himself in your heart."

Suddenly enraged, Gabrielle rasped, "Why are *you* here to

tell me all this? Why did Manon not come herself if she wished so desperately to console me?"

"Because the evil in your father struck Manon down and destroyed the babe growing within her—his own."

"No . . ." Shock . . . incredulity. Gabrielle was torn by the emotions assailing her. "What can I do? How can I help—"

"Save yourself! Leave him! Run away! Do not allow him to appeal to the part of you that wants to believe him, as he did with Manon!"

"But Rogan . . . how can I save him?"

"Go to the governor. Tell him!"

"You are asking me to *destroy* my father!"

"Before he destroys the man you love!"

Rigid from the daggers of pain impaling her, Gabrielle was unable to react when Marie broke contact with her gaze and brushed past her, limping toward the door.

"Where are you going?"

"To Manon. *Ma petite* needs me."

"Please . . . please tell Manon that I'm sorry." Gabrielle's voice broke. "Tell her I wish . . . I wish—"

"I will tell her."

Staring at the doorway through which the old servant disappeared, frozen into motionless by the horror of her revelations, Gabrielle took a shuddering breath.

Her father—her enemy—planning to kill the man she loved *because* she loved him.

Her father, who had already killed . . .

Because he loved her.

Oh, God, it was true! She knew it was!

But could she go to the governor and destroy her father when all he'd done was because he loved her?

She could no more sacrifice him than she could trade Rogan's life for her father's!

Because, no matter what they had done, she loved them both.

What could she do?

Nowhere to go
No place to turn.
Except . . .
Taking a moment to brush the tears from her cheeks,
Gabrielle walked determinedly toward the door.

Gasping, her limping gait growing more labored by the
moment as she climbed the front stairs and pushed open the
door of the sweet little house Manon had thought to be
home, Marie quietly entered. She struggled to draw her
ragged breathing under control as she closed the door behind
her. She did not want Manon to see her distress.

Marie smoothed back the gray strands that had adhered to
her cheek due to perspiration and straightened her back,
waiting only a few moments before starting toward the bedroom. The house was quiet. She was grateful that Manon was
finally resting.

Her mind returned unexpectedly to Gabrielle Dubay.
Strangely, she pitied her. The young woman was not at all
what she had expected her to be. There had been shock and
horror in Gabrielle's eyes when she had been informed of
Gerard Pointreau's evil misdeeds; and, strangely, Marie knew
the young woman had believed all she'd said.

Her throat choked with emotion at remembering the
young woman's words.

Please . . . please tell Manon that I'm sorry.

Sorrow expressed by one who bore no blame.

Manon would be happy to know that her warning had not
been ignored, that Gerard Pointreau would not be successful
in corrupting his daughter or in taking another life that might
be saved. Perhaps then Manon would be able to forgive herself and go on.

Marie pushed the bedroom door open, careful not to dis-
turb the silence. The room was dimly lit. Dr. Thoreau stood
beside the bed, silent and pensive as she approached. It was

not until she was beside him that she saw his face was wet
with tears.

Tears . . .

Marie took a gasping breath. Manon's beautiful face was so
still. She did not move. She did not breathe!

The sudden sob was torn from Marie's soul.

"Manon! Ma petite Manon!"

On her knees beside the bed, Marie grasped Manon's
hand. It was cold when she pressed her lips against it. She
hardly heard Dr. Thoreau when he spoke in a hoarse whisper.

"I could not save her, Marie. Another hemorrhage . . . I
did not want to lose her."

I did not want to lose her . . .

"She was smiling, Marie . . . When the angels came to take
her, she was smiling."

A smile, followed by tears . . .

. . . Marie's many, many tears.

The house was busy, the hallway outside her door active,
the tread of heavy feet punctuated by an occasional burst of
feminine laughter. The desire to escape, to find a place of solitude where she might hide her head and sleep away the torment building within her almost more than she could bear,
Clarice walked to the washstand and picked up the damp
cloth there. She blotted it against her face, closing her eyes
against the image reflected back at her.

Clarice Bouchard . . . helpless and alone.

She had never thought to again be consigned to that condition in life. She had believed, after having survived the horror following her mother's death and all it entailed, that she
could overcome any obstacle in her path through sheer determination. But she now knew that was not true. She could not
survive the loss of Bertrand and Rogan.

A perverse amusement suddenly struck Clarice. How she

flattered herself! She had not *lost* Rogan! He had never truly been hers, had never loved her, not in the way she had cherished in her mind. And he never would. He loved another. He had made that clear. The pain of that realization was so strong that she had been impotent against it in the time since she had returned from the prison and locked herself in her room.

A knock on her door startled Clarice from her thoughts. She turned sharply toward the sound.

"Who is it?"

"Madame wishes to see you in her office."

"Tell Madame I . . . I am indisposed."

"Madame said she will be waiting."

Clarice closed her eyes. She knew Madame. If she did not do as she was bade, Madame would come to her. She would not be able to face the explanations that would then be demanded. She sighed.

"All right."

Waiting to hear footsteps retreating from her door, Clarice inhaled deeply, then started forward. It occurred to her as she exited her room and walked down the familiar hallway, that in the garish green gown she still wore, she looked the part of the woman she felt herself to be, a lost and discarded whore.

That thought painfully fresh in her mind, Clarice knocked on Madame's door. She turned the knob at Madame's response and stepped within, only to halt abruptly.

"Close the door, Clarice."

Clarice did as Madame had bade her.

"As you can see, you have a visitor. I don't think I need introduce you."

"*Non.*"

"Then I will leave you two alone so you may discuss your business in private."

Madame walked past her. The door closed behind Madame's bulky figure, but Clarice's gaze remained fastened on the person standing beside Madame's desk.

The click of the door lock suddenly freeing her tongue, she demanded, "What are you doing here?"

"So, you know who I am."

Gabrielle Dubay paused. She was garbed in a simple, dark dress that emphasized her pallor even as it accented her subtle beauty. The contrast with Clarice's flamboyant costume was both startling and humiliating as Gerard Pointreau's daughter continued, "It appears I am the only one who was ignorant of the intricate web of affairs involving me. I confess that I did not know of your existence until—"

"Does it matter?"

"I suppose not." Gabrielle Dubay walked closer.

Stiffening under her intense perusal, Clarice took those moments to study her as well. It hurt to realize that the young woman was even more lovely upon close scrutiny. There was an earnestness and an innocence about her clear eyes that, along with the determination therein, could not be denied.

Gabrielle Dubay spoke again. "You are very beautiful."

"My beauty is inherited from my mother. I take no credit for it. It is a gift I have used to great advantage."

Gabrielle frowned. "I'm sorry. I seem to have offended you." She took a breath. "I have just come from the prison."

Clarice did not respond.

"You were there, too."

Clarice remained silent.

Gabrielle Dubay hesitated. "You saw Rogan."

Clarice raised her chin. "I did."

Exquisite pain flashed across the young woman's face. "I . . . I need your help. I spoke to Bertrand. He said—"

Clarice blinked. She gasped, "You saw Bertrand?" She took an anxious step forward, tears suddenly brimming. "You saw him tonight? He is all right? You must tell me how he looks!"

Silence, long and extended, as Gabrielle Dubay returned her stare with astonishment.

* * *

Gabrielle looked at the beautiful Clarice Bouchard, astounded. She had been uncertain of what to expect when she had made the bold decision to come to Madame Renée's house to seek the only other person she had felt she could trust to work selflessly toward saving Rogan's life. It had surprised her that it was not necessary to introduce herself to Madame Renée, that the woman had immediately recognized her.

Coming face-to-face with Clarice, the woman Rogan had chosen over her, had been difficult. The sumptuous beauty had been cold and untouchable upon entering, upon discussing Rogan, but at the mention of Bertrand, her emotions had come to the surface.

"Tell me! Bertrand is well? Did he send a message to me?"

"He is in good health." Her confusion abounding, Gabrielle further responded, "No, he did not speak your name."

"Of course." The beauteous whore gave a shaken laugh. "He would not."

Her puzzlement compounded, Gabrielle knew she could not afford to waste a moment when, with each that passed the threat against Rogan's life deepened. Her heart pounding, she began.

"Mademoiselle Bouchard—"

"Affectations offend me. I am known to all as Clarice."

Gabrielle nodded. "Clarice, please, I come seeking your help."

"*My* help?" Clarice's fine features grew tight. "Strange, is it not, that you should seek my aid when you travel at will in places where others are not allowed, visiting prisoners who are refused visitation or communication with those who love them!"

Gabrielle stiffened, Clarice's open declaration of her love

cutting deep. "I don't know what you mean. You admit to having seen Rogan."

"Rogan. *Oui*. But Bertrand—I knew nothing of his welfare until tonight!"

"I don't understand." Gabrielle paused, then plunged on, "Does your intimate liaison with Rogan not cause him to resent your intense interest in Bertrand?"

The beautiful courtesan went suddenly pale.

"Rogan and I are not lovers."

"But I thought—"

"Rogan and I were *never* lovers." Clarice's brilliant gaze became glazed. "It is you he loves."

Gabrielle took a gasping breath. Refusing to surrender to the elation rising within, she whispered, "But I heard him when he spoke to Bertrand. His last words when Bertrand left were a promise to you that he would see you soon. The guard in the prison said you were his woman."

"A pretext to gain admittance, no more."

"And Bertrand?"

"Bertrand is my brother."

Gabrielle took a staggering step backward. She gripped the edge of the desk, her slender fingers whitening against the dark wood as she rasped, "I thought . . ."—she brushed away the tear of elation that fell—"I thought Rogan loved you. I thought he . . . we . . ."

Gabrielle's growing joy blended with fear, forcing a new urgency to her voice. "We must save him, Clarice. Rogan's life is in danger."

"What are you talking about? How do you know this?"

Gabrielle swallowed against her mounting pain. "I know . . ."

"Who told you?"

"A . . . friend."

"Why do you come to me? Why did you not go directly to the governor?"

"Because . . ."

"Why?"

"Because the man who is planning to kill him is my father!"

Clarice's pallor deepened. "When is this to happen?"

"Soon."

"How soon?"

"I don't know." Gabrielle covered her eyes with her hand, emotion suddenly overwhelming her as Rogan's image appeared in her mind.

"Gabrielle . . ."

Gabrielle looked up at a touch on her arm. Beside her, the ice gone from her gaze, Clarice whispered, "You must tell me all—from the beginning."

After scrutinizing her intently for a silent moment, Gabrielle started to speak.

The mantel clock struck the hour, the sound reverberating in the silence of the library. Pierre Delise raised his head, glancing toward it. It occurred to him that it was a futile exercise, this checking of the time on each occasion that the hour sounded, for he remained at his desk in any case, poring over the work he had brought home from his office to fill the empty night.

The written page before Pierre blurred. It astounded him that a life he had considered so full and so vibrant—his active legal practice, his prominent position in New Orleans society, a social schedule that kept him in constant demand—had suddenly turned as cold and dry as dust.

The reason was simple.

Clarice.

Standing, Pierre turned abruptly from his desk and walked to the window overlooking the courtyard garden. His athletic frame rigid, the white shirt he wore over his well-tailored britches open to midchest in deference to the evening heat, he ran a hand through his thick, curly hair. His boyish face was tense. The courtyard was dimly lit by a single lantern, but he saw not the fragile shadows that wavered in the warm, evening breeze. Instead, his mind returned to the image of the woman who haunted him.

He did not care to count the days since he had last seen Clarice.

. . . Clarice suffers personal anxieties that have affected her judgment . . .

Madame's words had rung over and over in his mind, as had Clarice's angry tirade.

. . . Where I am going is none of your affair! Contrary to your assumption, you do not own me!

Yes, he had thought he owned her.

An agreement made, a sum exchanged, and he had convinced himself that Clarice was his and his alone—because he had wanted so desperately for it to be true. Somehow, he had overlooked the emotions of the woman within.

He had known Clarice did not love him as he loved her. But he had been so sure he could make her forget the phantom man she loved.

He knew now that he could not. The look in her eye when he had stopped her at the doorway of Madame's house—the fire and the torment he had seen there—could only have been inspired by a love that was deep and true.

He had not seen Clarice since.

His certainty that the terms of his agreement with Madame kept Clarice from the desires of other men, however briefly, allowed Pierre his only consolation as his torment deepened.

. . . It is my suggestion that you do not attempt to see her until she is again herself.

And how long would that be?

A few days . . . a week . . . perhaps longer . . .

An eternity.

Would Clarice ever be his again? The crisis—would it remove her from his grasp forever? And, aware as he was now, would he be satisfied to hold Clarice intimately close while knowing she thought of another man?

The question an endless torment, Pierre attempted to turn back to his work as a knock at the door interrupted his thoughts.

"What is it, Henri?"

"You have a visitor, Monsieur Delise."

"A visitor?"

"A Mademoiselle Clarice Bouchard."

Incredulity!

Elation!

Pierre's tormenting question was answered the moment he started toward the door.

The unfamiliar foyer of Pierre's elegant mansion was imposing as Clarice stood waiting. The crystal chandelier above her glittered with myriad colors, the silk-covered walls catching the faceted hues. The graceful mahogany furniture was a silent statement of quality that was echoed in the imported rug and in the portrait of a man so closely resembling Pierre that it negated any possibility of his being other than a revered relative as it glared down from the wall with disapproval.

However, Clarice was prepared to bear disapproval and any manner of indignity in order to save Rogan's life.

Gabrielle Dubay loved Rogan.

Clarice's eyes flickered briefly closed. The thought brought her both pleasure and pain, for if Rogan loved, she would have him loved in return. She loved him too much to want it any other way.

She had spoken to Gabrielle—a revelation—for she had discovered an innate honesty about the young woman that was somehow unaffected by her close relationship to the devious and dissolute Gerard Pointreau. Despite an inability to comprehend it, Clarice realized Gabrielle loved her father. She pitied her for that love as much as she admired her courage in coming to Madame's. All now relied on the confrontation to come.

The snap of a door . . . a rapid step . . . Pierre approaching, coming into view . . .

Clarice, her throat suddenly tight, emitted a sound caught between laughter and tears when she saw him. Dear Pierre, his boyish face so open and sincere, she had missed him dreadfully through the terrible days past.

"Clarice . . ."

Pierre's gaze was filled with anticipation—and love.

Non, she could not deceive him, at any price.

Stepping back as Pierre reached for her, she rasped, "Pierre, *mon ami,* I have come to you for help."

He halted, his sudden flush revealing the emotions he sought to restrain. His chest heaved under the fine linen of the shirt he wore. She remembered the warmth of that muscular surface beneath her cheek, the sound of his heart pounding against her ear, the scent of his flesh and the brush of the fine mat of dark hairs there. Dear Pierre . . . loving Pierre . . .

She waited, then asked, "Will you aid me?"

Pierre searched her face. She saw the realization dawn that love had brought her, but not love for him as he had hoped. She noted disappointment, then the hot anger that followed.

She waited anxiously, knowing that with each passing moment Rogan's danger grew greater.

Gerard pushed open the door and stepped into the silent foyer of his house. His spirits high, he glanced around him.

"Boyer!"

He heard a familiar, shuffling step before the old servant appeared.

"Mademoiselle Gabrielle—where is she?"

"I'm here, Father."

Startled as Gabrielle stepped out of the shadows of the sitting room, Gerard walked quickly toward her. Her face was pale. She was dressed in a sober gown that reminded him too closely of the convent for him to be comfortable with it. But she was beautiful, she was back with him, and she would soon be his alone again.

Gerard's spirits soared as he enclosed her in his embrace and held her close. The joy of her flushed through him as he whispered against her glorious hair in a voice that shook with emotion.

"Gabrielle, *ma petite chérie*. All will soon be well."

He drew back when there was no response, when Gabrielle did not return his embrace. A tremor of disquiet shook him as he whispered while looking into the clear gray of her eyes, "You believe me, don't you, Gabrielle? You know I would do anything to restore to you the serenity of the past, to make you happy again."

"Anything, Father?"

"Anything, *ma chérie*."

He saw the intensity with which her gaze searched his face. Her lips quivered with words she could not seem to make herself speak. Her pain was evident in her eyes, and he felt it within him. He did not press her. There was no need. The torment would soon be over, and they would be as before.

He noticed the tear that streaked Gabrielle's cheek the moment before her arms went around him and hugged him close.

And Gerard's heart was filled with the reassurance of her love.

Another night had fallen. Rogan continued his restless pacing, glancing as he had countless times toward the barred window of his cell as his frustration mounted to near madness.

Sitting abruptly on his cot, Rogan covered his face with his hands in an attempt to retain control. His anxiety heightened as the image of clear, gray eyes glowing with love returned once more.

No, damn it! He could not allow his emotions to distract him. He must keep in mind that Gabrielle was now unprotected against a peculiar strain of madness centered on her alone. He must remember the danger hanging over his incarcerated crew and the miscarriage of justice that had gone too long unrighted. All were the work of one man.

Pointreau.

Rogan stood up abruptly, determined all would not end here.

Chapter 11

Otis Benchley walked down the familiar prison corridor. It occurred to him that although a brilliant morning sun shone on the cobbled street outside the door, its glow never reached within the dank walls now surrounding him.

Benchley grunted. Had the situation been different, he would not have arisen in time to see that early morning sun after the previous night's debauched revelry, made possible by Pointreau's advance payment on the task he and his compatriots were to accomplish. Nor would he be in the prison at this particular hour. But, unlike the friends he had left asleep in the back room of the tavern where he'd awakened, he had been only too aware of the conditions stipulated by Pointreau to ignore them.

Benchley yawned and scratched his head, adding another layer of oily residue from his scalp to the deeply embedded grime underneath his stubbly fingernails. The line of dirt under each nail was symbolic of Benchley's character, which was so contaminated by layer after layer of iniquitous deeds that it could not be scrubbed free.

It pleased Benchley beyond measure to know that it had somehow never occurred to the prison officials to question his actions or those of his two compatriots when Pointreau questioned Captain Whitney and his first mate three years previously, despite the fact that the first mate had died so unexpectedly during the questioning. Monsieur Pointreau had been above suspicion—and so were they. He enjoyed that part of his association with Pointreau almost as much as he enjoyed the generous sums he had been paid for his services over the years.

So, it was time to attend to business.

Benchley's jowled face sobered. Two days . . . an extremely short time to arrange the details of the task Pointreau had set them to.

Important to their plan was the notice that would be posted that morning, specifying any changes in the guards' schedules. It was his hope that there were none, for changes would necessitate a delicate maneuvering that would take time to accomplish and could possibly cause suspicion.

Time was important to Pointreau. The man's anxiety to have the matter over and done was obvious, and Benchley had learned years earlier that whatever was important to Pointreau need be important to him—for the continued success of their scurrilous relationship and for his own well-being.

For he did not doubt the man was a fiend who would act accordingly should anyone fail him.

Benchley had never met a man who enjoyed the pain of others more than Pointreau.

He hoped he never would.

Turning down the corridor, Benchley came upon the main desk. He walked toward the posting and checked it with a casual glance.

He smiled.

Pointreau would be pleased.

They would do it this night.

Fully dressed, Gabrielle waited just out of sight at the head of the staircase as her father moved around in the sunny foyer below. She despised the dishonesty of her present position as she waited for him to leave so she might go out without raising his suspicions.

The encounter between Father and her in the sitting room the previous evening weighed heavily on her. The questions she had longed to ask when she had faced him, the many things she had wanted to say, had remained frozen inside her.

The truth had gone unspoken.

The reason was simple.

In a moment of sudden clarity, when she had looked into her father's eyes to see them filled with love and devoid of any sign of deception, she had realized that it would always be that way between her father and her, for her father saw only *his own* truth.

Gabrielle swallowed against the emotions rising in her. Her father's truth was not *her* truth.

Her truth had been written in Rogan's eyes and in the heart he had opened to her.

It had been revealed only too painfully in the suffering which had prevailed as a result of her father's sinister machinations, and in the deaths which need be prevented.

Her truth lay in the step she would be forced to take should Clarice have failed in obtaining help after Gabrielle left her the previous evening.

She had prayed, how sincerely she had prayed, that she would not be forced into the ultimate betrayal of her father's love, a step that would break her father's heart . . .

. . . and her own.

Voices in the foyer below growing louder, nearing the door . . . Father's curt, final words of instruction to Boyer . . .

The sound of the front door closing reverberated up the staircase. Trembling, Gabrielle forced herself to wait until the carriage could be heard pulling away from the curb before she started down the stairs.

"Boyer!"

The old Negro responded immediately to her summons.

She questioned tensely, "Did Father say where he was going this morning?"

"Massa say he have a full day. He see you in the evenin'."

Gabrielle nodded. "I'm going out ... to Madame Babette's Boutique. I have some important shopping to do. I'll be gone most of the day."

She turned toward the door, looking back at Boyer's soft warning.

"You be careful, Mam'selle Gabrielle. Massa, he ... he ..."

The concerned slave faltered and Gabrielle paused, grateful for his concern. She whispered, "I'll be careful."

Gabrielle peeked out onto the street moments later, her aching heart pounding at her subterfuge.

Father did not deserve this treatment from her.

Held at bay was the question that she had avoided through the long, sleepless night—what did her father truly deserve?

Whatever the answer, Gabrielle knew she had no choice in what *she* must do.

Out on the sidewalk, she walked quickly along the familiar street. She wound her way through the pedestrian traffic that grew rapidly heavier, arriving breathless some time later before a small, exclusive shop.

Hesitating only briefly, her agitation soaring, Gabrielle pushed open the door of Madame Babette's Boutique. She walked rapidly toward the rear, jumping with a start when a hand reached out to close firmly around her arm.

Her breath escaped in a startled rasp.

"Clarice!"

Clarice Bouchard's delicate features were sober. She spoke one word. "Tonight."

Pointreau's muscular frame grew rigid with indignation. He took a few moments to gather control before replying to the question in Governor Claiborne's eyes.

"Are you telling me you are actually considering the possibility there might be some truth in this letter from Lafitte?" Pointreau tossed the wrinkled sheet down onto governor's desk. "I tell you now, William, I am deeply offended!"

"I have no desire to insult you, Gerard. I only hope to discover the truth."

"You know the truth!" Pointreau's bearded cheek twitched. He had not appreciated being forced to forgo a busy afternoon at his office for an urgent meeting with the governor, only to be greeted by this accusation in the form of a letter received by Claiborne from Lafitte.

Lafitte, of all people! Gerard was incensed! It mattered little to him that the missive was factually correct. He resented the governor's lack of faith in him!

"Lafitte of all people!" Gerard continued tightly, speaking the words that had run so furiously across his mind moments earlier. "The man is a pirate! He is responsible for the deaths of countless seamen, yet you tell me you actually believe his warning that I have been dishonest with you in the past—I, who have guided you through so many of your successes as governor!"

"I do not discount the help you have been to me, Gerard." The governor's dark, sensitive face was sober. "Nor do I wish to offend you. I confess that my first inclination was to discard Lafitte's letter. I have decided, however, that it is my obligation as governor to investigate the accusations made. I did not make that decision lightly."

"And I confess to you, William, that I do not *take* that decision lightly!"

"So, in order that we might dispense with unpleasantries quickly, and that I might satisfy my duty, let us get quickly to the purpose of this meeting." William Claiborne's dark brows knitted in a frown. "I ask you now, Gerard, so you might make formal reply to Lafitte's charges, is there any truth to Lafitte's claim that you visited him after Gabrielle's abduction and offered to deliver him my approval if he would help you?

I must warn you before you respond that I am aware you left the city for several days during the crisis."

"There is no truth to the accusation."

"And your destination while you were absent from the city?"

"I was not absent. I was incommunicado at the home of my mistress, where I sought a brief respite from the stress of my anxieties. You may check with Madame Matier, if you wish. She will verify my extended stay there."

The governor nodded. "And the accusation that you were responsible for the crimes of which Captain Whitney was accused?"

"A lie. All lies!"

The governor nodded again. He hesitated, continuing, "I must be honest with you, Gerard. I will follow through on these accusations with an investigation. I owe it to the citizens of New Orleans not to allow my personal feelings to interfere with my responsibility to seek the truth. I also owe it to myself . . . and to you."

"You are wrong, William." Livid, Pointreau rasped, "You owe me nothing—and from this point on, neither do I owe *you* anything. You may consider that our association, as well as our friendship, has come to an end!"

"I beg you not to be hasty, Gerard."

"Au revoir, William."

"Gerard . . ."

Turning on his heel, Pointreau strode furiously from the governor's office. Out on the sidewalk, he paused in an attempt to draw his rage under control, his gaze affixed on the afternoon sun slowly descending toward the horizon.

So, William intended to pursue his investigation into the truth of Lafitte's accusations! He sneered. One could not do so with a dead man—which was what Captain Rogan Whitney would soon be.

As for Manon . . . He gave a harsh laugh. She would not dare betray him.

Pointreau's handsome face hardened. He was through with New Orleans, in any case. He had already made his decision. As soon as Captain Whitney had been disposed of and the blackguard's influence had been removed from Gabrielle's life, he would transfer the funds in his accounts, then sail for Europe with Gabrielle as he had planned.

A smile gradually softened Gerard's features. Gabrielle and he would have a glorious tour. He would sell his business interests and property in New Orleans, retaining only the family estate. He would then allow Gabrielle to pick the site of their new home—England . . . Italy . . . France . . . whichever country suited her—where he would spend the rest of his life indulging his darling daughter's slightest whim.

Pointreau's smile faded. All tribulations would be over when Benchley and his cohorts accomplished the task he had set them to.

Determined, Pointreau turned back in the direction from which he had come. He had much to accomplish in the next few days—the days before he and Gabrielle began their new life together.

"After the evening meal is served at the prison and all is settled for the night . . ." Pierre stood silent and sober in Clarice's room. He held himself stiffly apart from her as he detailed the plan for Rogan's escape.

"I have arranged to be allowed into the prison through the rear door. The guard will take me directly to Captain Whitney's cell, which a second guard will unlock. I will then make the payment promised, and the two guards will guide Captain Whitney and me back safely to the rear door. They will sound the alarm after we have drawn away in my carriage."

"Non." Clarice fought to still her trembling as she shook her head adamantly. "You must arrange another plan. I will not allow you to place yourself in danger. You must find someone else—"

"There *is* no one who can be trusted."

"B-But the guards—how can you be sure they will not turn on you after payment is made?"

"There will be no danger, either to Captain Whitney or myself, as long as I am there to personally oversee all."

Clarice felt the rise of anxious tears. Pierre had honored the promise he had given the previous night. She had known he would. Just as she had known he would not refuse her.

She had been totally honest with him, knowing that if he would, indeed, be risking his good name for her in helping the city's most notorious criminal to escape prison, he deserved the truth.

Myriad emotions had flashed across his face as she had related the tale of her long association with Rogan from beginning to end.

She knew he'd believed everything she had told him, that he'd realized she loved Rogan.

She had made it clear that Rogan did not love her, that he loved Gabrielle Dubay.

She had also made it clear that whether or not Rogan returned her love, she would always love him.

She had hurt Pierre with her truth—Pierre, who loved her so selflessly.

"I cannot thank you—"

Pierre interrupted her, frowning. "I am uncomfortable bringing the captain back here afterward. If there is a problem, you will be implicated."

"Rogan will be safe here. Madame has always been generous with her protection."

"Still—"

"Pierre . . ." Clarice took an uncertain step forward. She placed a hand on his chest. His heart pounded heavily under her palm as she whispered, "You will please take care. I would not have anything happen to you."

He did not respond.

The emotion in Clarice's throat tightened to pain. "I am sorry, Pierre. I wish ..."

Removing her hand, Pierre stepped backward abruptly. In a moment, he was gone.

His exchange with the governor earlier that afternoon still rankling, Pointreau reached his home as the sun began its final plunge toward the horizon. His disposition vile, he thrust open the front door and walked inside. He was hanging his hat when he heard a step behind him.

"Massa?"

He turned sharply. "What is it?"

"Bessie find this note slipped under the door this mornin'."

Snatching the envelope from Boyer's shaking hand, Pointreau ripped it open.

He smiled.

The concise message was faultlessly clear.

"Tonight."

"Is something wrong, Gabrielle?"

Gabrielle looked down at her plate, suddenly aware it was all but untouched. Realizing her father assessed her silently from his position at the opposite end of the dinner table, knowing that to raise his suspicion would threaten the success of Rogan's escape, she attempted to still her inner trembling.

"No ... yes." She shrugged. Struggling in the face of her father's obvious concern, she steeled herself against yet another lie, the last before she would bid her father a final farewell.

Her decision had been made during the long day of waiting for the events that would soon unfold within the prison. There had never been a discussion between Rogan and her that went beyond the moments they had spent in each other's arms. Clarice had said Rogan loved her, but Rogan had never said these words.

And if he did, would love be enough?

Even liberated from his prison cell, Rogan would never be truly free until justice was served.

Could she bear to stand beside the man who sought to destroy her father?

The answer to that question beyond her, Gabrielle only knew that she could not stand beside the father who sought to destroy the man she loved.

Whatever the outcome of this night, she was intensely aware that her last moments with her father were drawing to a close.

Her emotions near the breaking point, she stood up abruptly.

"Gabrielle . . . ?"

"I-I'm unwell, Father." She avoided her father's gaze. I think it best that I retire."

Beside her as she turned toward the door, her father tipped up her face to study it more closely. The tenderness, the concern—they shredded her heart.

Gabrielle heard the promise in her father's voice that went beyond his words as he whispered, "All will be well soon. Rest, *ma chérie*. I will see you tomorrow." He added as if in afterthought, "I have an appointment at Duvalle's Coffee House. My opinion is sought in a political discussion that has raged for several nights. You may reach me there if you need me."

"I'll be all right, Father."

"Oui, ma petite, for I will always be there when you need me."

Words sprang to Gabrielle's lips, only to remain unspoken, washed away by her unabating sadness as she raised herself to kiss her father's cheek.

She turned toward the door.

The last kiss . . .

The last hour . . .

* * *

Pointreau watched as Gabrielle climbed the staircase to the second floor. She was sad. He dared not allow himself to ponder the reason for her sadness, for he dared not indulge the rage that would follow.

Suddenly impatient almost beyond endurance for the momentous events soon to occur within the prison walls, Pointreau shouted for Boyer. In the foyer, reaching for his coat, he turned sharply toward the sound of his slave's step.

"Mademoiselle Gabrielle is unwell. You will make haste to fetch me at Duvalle's Coffee House if she needs me. I warn you now that you will suffer the consequences if you delay. Is that understood?"

"Yessa."

Dismissing Boyer curtly, Gerard stepped out onto the street and breathed deeply of the night air. A keen sense of anticipation set his heart to pounding as he raised a hand to hail a passing carriage.

One snapped forward at his short command, and Gerard settled back into the seat. All was progressing according to plan.

He would be shocked when the news of the shooting at the prison arrived at the coffee house.

He would hurry home to be with Gabrielle.

And he would console her.

Intensely aware that she would soon leave, never to return, Gabrielle crossed the foyer of her father's house and approached the front door. Her throat was tight. Father had left minutes earlier. She need leave quickly, before—

"Mam'selle . . . ?"

Boyer. Gabrielle turned toward him.

"The massa be angry if he know you goin' out."

Gabrielle did not dare respond.

"Mam'selle . . . ?"

Gabrielle turned back toward the door only to be halted by

Boyer's touch on her arm. She looked up to see his dark eyes moist.

"Boyer get you a carriage, *mam'selle*."

Gabrielle was incapable of reply.

Pierre's carriage drew to a silent halt in the dark alleyway beyond the prison. Grateful for the clouds that briefly obscured the moon, he whispered final instructions to his coachman, secure in the certainty of the man's loyalty as he stepped down onto the street. He slid his hand into his pocket for the brief reassurance of the pistol concealed there before slipping into the shadows to cross the prison yard.

Pierre hesitated only momentarily before stepping up to the guard at the rear door.

"You are Thomas?"

The man nodded.

Pierre jostled the heavy bag of coins in his other pocket. The sound unmistakable, he whispered, "I would like to visit my friend."

The guard glanced around him, then stepped back into the corridor and motioned Pierre forward.

Benchley again checked the gun he had readied a short time earlier, then turned to the two men beside him.

"Collins is guarding Whitney's cellblock tonight. The fellow's a fool. He won't suspect anything until it's too late." He paused, his small eyes drilling into the faces of his cohorts. "We must work quickly. There is no room for error. I'll distract Collins while one of you hits him from behind and the other releases the prisoner. As soon as Whitney emerges from his cell, I'll shoot him with Collins' gun. The I'll shoot Collins and put the gun near Whitney's hand. We'll hide in the shadows and slip out in the confusion that will follow."

Benchley snickered.

"An escape gone wrong. What a shame. Both the guard and the prisoner killed. I wonder who managed to slip Whitney a gun."

Benchley's smile dropped away. "No mistakes, you hear? Pointreau ain't a forgiving man."

That thought firmly impressed, the three started cautiously forward.

The night had deepened beyond Rogan's cell window. The evening meal had been served and the remains cleared away. The corridors were silent, yet a relentless air of tension prevailed within the prison.

Rogan stood up, his powerful frame tense as hackles crawled up his spine. He had had this feeling before, a sixth sense warning of danger.

Footsteps in the corridor . . .

He prepared himself, straining to see into the shadows. He heard a brief exchange . . . the footsteps resuming.

Three figures rounded the curve.

Rogan demanded, "Who are you? What are you doing here?"

The unfamiliar, curly-haired man stopped in his approach. An indefinable emotion flashed in his eyes the moment before he motioned the guards forward to unlock the door. Rogan did not move.

"I asked who you are."

"Pierre Delise."

Rogan recognized the name.

"Clarice sent me."

Clarice . . .

Rogan moved out of his cell as Delise withdrew a pouch from his pocket and placed it in the hand of the guard, then turned back to address him tightly.

"Follow me. Quickly. We have no time to waste."

They were walking rapidly back down the corridor when

they heard footsteps ahead of them. The guards muttered softly before motioning them into the shadows.

Too late!

Surprised grunts as the three approaching guards saw them!

A shouted command!

The bark of gunfire.

Another and another!

A hot burst of pain slammed into Rogan, thrusting him backward. The world wobbled around him as he struggled for breath. He felt a strong hand grasp his arm supportively even as the dim light of the corridor wavered.

He could not breathe.

He could not see.

Regrets loomed.

Things left undone . . . words gone unsaid.

Gabrielle.

Too late.

Gabrielle moved restlessly, her gaze traveling the small rear room of Madame Renée's house of pleasure. She had been ushered there immediately upon arriving, down a dark hallway that was obviously seldom used. She had found Clarice awaiting her.

Clarice, who obviously loved Rogan . . .

Clarice, obviously anxious . . .

She had sat silently on a chair beside the other woman, joining her in her vigil.

Gabrielle glanced unconsciously at the clock nearby. It was broken, yet the time ticked slowly past in her mind as she continued her silent scrutiny of her surroundings. The room's original function was obvious since the only furniture there was the huge bed that dominated its center, a nightstand on which rested a single, stained lamp, a dresser that was presently stripped clean, and the two chairs on which Clarice and Gabrielle herself sat.

Madame's house . . . filled with many similar rooms, she was sure.

"They are late."

Gabrielle started as Clarice's anxious voice broke the silence.

"They should have been here by now."

Clarice's delicate features were taut with concern. The knots within Gabrielle tightened as she responded, "You said Monsieur Delise could depend on the men he had bribed—that the guards would cooperate."

"But I did not say nothing could go wrong!" Clarice took a shuddering breath. Tears filled her brilliant blue eyes. "Pierre is an intelligent and meticulous man, but there is a limit to his control."

Fear gradually overwhelming her, Gabrielle fought to retain her composure. She forced back the tears brimming. "I . . . I don't know what to say. My father—"

"Your father is corrupt and a murderer!"

Gabrielle did not respond.

"He and his heinous deeds are responsible for this entire affair!"

Gabrielle's silence continued.

"Because of him, both Rogan and Pierre are now in mortal danger! He—"

"He is my father."

Clarice went suddenly still. Gabrielle sensed the scorching scrutiny of her brilliant gaze. It touched on the torment within her—the aching, the love for Rogan that she could not deny, and the sorrow.

Clarice blinked. She took a short breath. "So, we are both tormented by loves against which we have no defense—loves of various natures. Nonetheless, they give us more pain than joy. Gabrielle . . ." Clarice's voice softened. *"Pardonnez-moi, s'il vous plaît.* It is difficult for me to admit to myself that Rogan was correct in his assessment of you and that you are truly the person he believes you to be."

The lump within Gabrielle's throat pained her.

"Clarice, Rogan and I—"

A thump in the hallway beyond the door brought Gabrielle's words to an abrupt halt. She heard male voices speaking with urgency.

On her feet in a moment, Clarice behind her, Gabrielle yanked the door open. Her breath caught in her throat as two men rushed toward her, struggling under Rogan's weight as they supported him between them.

Rogan's shirt was stained with blood, his face was pale, his eyes were closed!

Beside the bed at the moment the two men placed Rogan on it, Gabrielle leaned over him. Unaware that her face was streaked with tears, unconscious of the words she spoke as she whispered softly into his ear, seeking a response that did not come, she knew only the overwhelming terror rising within her. Rogan's skin was cold and moist. His eyes were closed, the lids still. He barely breathed.

"A doctor—he needs a doctor!"

Standing stiffly behind her, Clarice moved immediately toward the door as the man Gabrielle knew to be Pierre Delise leaned over the opposite side of the bed to examine Rogan's wound. He shook his head as Gabrielle looked up at him.

"A chest wound . . . I do not believe the bullet punctured the lung, but I can not be sure." He glanced toward the spot where Clarice had been standing. "Clarice has already gone to summon a doctor, I am sure." He frowned. "Captain Whitney has lost considerable blood."

Pierre's frown darkened as Gabrielle looked again at Rogan. He continued speaking as she stroked Rogan's cheek, as she slipped her hand over Rogan's and held it tightly although there was no pressure in return.

"A few minutes later and it would all have been for naught. They were coming for him. We ran into three guards in the corridor upon leaving, all three known to be Pointreau's men."

. . . Pointreau's men . . .

The horror of Pierre Delise's words shuddered through Gabrielle, causing her to release a soft sob as she leaned closer to Rogan. She pressed her lips against his cold cheek as Delise continued.

"We were too late to hide. They fired on us and we fired back. Captain Whitney was hit. Two of Pointreau's men were also shot. The third threw down his gun. We managed to escape in the confusion that followed."

Gabrielle smoothed a black lock of hair back from Rogan's forehead.

"He . . . he is hardly breathing." She looked up to see Pierre Delise's concerned expression. Her voice cracked on a sob. "He mustn't die."

Footsteps sounded in the hallway the moment before the door burst open to admit a gray-haired man in shirtsleeves who was carrying a small black bag. At his rear, Clarice offered as she closed the door behind them, "Dr. Thoreau was in an upstairs room with Nicole. He has helped us with difficult situations in the past."

Rigid as the doctor examined Rogan with practiced dexterity, Gabrielle started as he turned to snap, "Get soap and water, Clarice—clean cloths and a change of bed linens so we can rid him of this blood and get him warm. Hurry up! Everybody else—out!"

The doctor's hawklike gaze met Gabrielle's when she did not move.

"I said *out!*"

"No."

"I will not—"

The doctor's voice halted abruptly as Rogan's eyelids moved, then opened into narrow slits that allowed a peek at predatory gold as he rasped, "Gabrielle . . . stay."

The doctor jerked an assessing glance toward her. "You are Gabrielle Dubay?"

She nodded.

"And he is ... Captain Whitney?"

She nodded again.

"Stay."

Distracted as Clarice arrived carrying a pitcher and bowl, Pierre following behind with clean cloths and bed linens, Dr. Thoreau turned momentarily away. He did not see the moment when Gabrielle's clear gray eyes caught and held that meager slit of glowing gold, when she leaned closer, her lips brushing the cold skin of Rogan's cheek ...

... as she whispered into his ear, "I love you."

Nor did he see Rogan strain to whisper those same words in return before his eyes closed and he went suddenly still.

Clarice went motionless as stone as Rogan's eyes closed.

Unable to breathe, to think, she waited, staring at his chest. An eternity passed before it rose with an intake of breath and his shallow breathing continued.

A soft sob escaping her, Clarice turned blindly toward the door. She glanced up as a strong arm closed around her and guided her into the hallway.

The door clicked closed behind her as Clarice looked up into Pierre's gaze to find it was filled with compassion as he whispered, "It is difficult, *ma chérie*, to love so powerfully when one is not loved the same way in return. But you must console yourself that you have been true to that love, that you have done all you can. The rest is up to Dr. Thoreau and the power above us that will ultimately assume control."

"Pierre ..." Clarice's voice broke on another sob. "Rogan loves Gabrielle as he never loved me, but ... but I desperately want him to survive and be happy. Can you understand that to see Rogan happy will give me a measure of joy that would otherwise be denied me? He must not die!"

"Clarice . . ." His brown eyes becoming moist as well, Pierre drew her close. Clarice breathed in the warmth of him—the safety, the love—as he continued, "I understand, so very well."

An aching swell arose within her, "I wish . . ."

A long moment passed before Pierre whispered in return, "I, too, wish."

Choosing to leave his words incomplete, Pierre drew Clarice gently against his side as he urged her down the hall-way.

His tense, relentless ministrations to Rogan's wound finally coming to a halt, Dr. Thoreau broke the silence of the small back room as he stepped back from the bedside and ad-dressed Gabrielle for the first time.

"Well, I have done all I can." His expression stiff, he con-tinued with obvious reluctance. "Since this man has clearly shown that he chooses you above all to be with him during this crucial period, I will reveal my professional estimation of his condition to you."

Dr. Thoreau's rheumy eyes closely assessed Gabrielle's pale face. He saw the hesitation with which she drew herself to her feet from the position she had steadfastly maintained at the captain's bedside throughout the long hour during which he had ministered to the injured man. He saw the reluctance with which she released the captain's hand to approach him.

Waiting until she reached his side, the doctor inquired bluntly, "Are you up to the truth?"

Gabrielle nodded.

"Before I go any further, I would be totally open with you." Dr. Thoreau paused, the tense lines on his face deepen-ing. "I do not hold your father in esteem as do the majority of New Orleans society. My opinion of his character has been irredeemably tarnished by the many times I have been called to treat the results of his perverted fancies in houses such as this, and by a deplorable event I recently witnessed. Nor do I feel comfortable in discussing my patient's condition with you—because of your relationship to Monsieur Pointreau and because of the circumstances of your abduction. But, since it is not my place to contradict the wishes of my patients, and because Captain Whitney has made his desire clear, I can only hope I am not making a mistake by speaking to you in absolute candor."

Gabrielle's reply was softly spoken. "You are not."

Doubt obviously remaining, the doctor began cautiously. "It is not Captain Whitney's wound that causes him the most danger now." At seeing Gabrielle's obvious confusion, adding, "Captain Whitney has lost a grave amount of blood. His transportation here from the place where he was wounded— the jostling, the delay in receiving medical care . . ." He shook his head. "The wound had all but stopped bleeding by the time I arrived—a bad sign."

"A bad sign?"

"*Mademoiselle* . . ." The doctor's sagging jaw tightened. "Captain Whitney had all but bled himself dry."

Refusing to submit to the dizzying nausea that arose at the doctor's words, Gabrielle swallowed tightly.

"And his wound . . . ?"

"By some miracle, the bullet seems to have missed all vital organs and passed through him."

"Which means?"

"Which means, *mademoiselle*, that should the captain survive the tremendous blood loss he has suffered, he may have a chance!"

Gabrielle's head snapped toward Rogan who lay so silent and still. His face was gray. A shudder shook her the moment before she turned back to the frowning doctor.

"What can I do for him?" She swallowed the sob rising in her with sheer determination. "He cannot die, Doctor."

"Oh, yes, *mademoiselle*, he can . . . and he may."

The persistent sob broke through as Gabrielle looked back at Rogan once more.

The doctor's hand closed unexpectedly on her arm, steadying her. Regret softened his gaze as he turned her back to face him.

"I apologize, Mademoiselle Dubay. I was purposely brutal." Thoreau attempted a conciliatory smile. "I had to reassure myself. I did not feel secure in leaving my patient vulnerable to the actions of Gerard Pointreau's daughter. I have finally satisfied myself, however, that this young man, for all he has suffered at your father's behest, is safe under your care."

Dr. Thoreau paused. He patted her arm, then released her, continuing, "The truth is this, *mademoiselle*. Captain Whitney is obviously a man of strong constitution. The texture of his skin, his muscle tone, the very size and breadth of him, as well as the active life he has led—all are irrefutable evidence of that, which is extremely important. For I tell you now, I have done all I can. The rest is up to him. If he survives the night, if his heart does not falter because of the blood loss he sustained, he will survive."

"But—"

"Mademoiselle Dubay—Gabrielle—I repeat, the rest is up to him. I will return in the morning."

Gabrielle stood silent and immobile, the doctor's words echoing in the deep well of pain within her as the door clicked closed behind him.

"The maritime rights of our great nation have been impinged upon! Great Britain has removed our seamen from our ships and forced them into service in the British Navy. Over eight thousand men have already been so impressed, and the number is still mounting! Our ships have been wrongfully seized in unlawful blockades! Unwarranted attacks against our peaceful merchant vessels continue! We have suf-

fered breach after breach of our sovereign rights without re-
ciprocating. How much longer must these outrages continue
before war is declared!"

Shouts of concordance echoed from within the crowded
room as youthful New Orleans firebrands rocked Duvalle's
Coffee House with their raging discontent at the current state
of affairs with the former mother country. Seated at a table a
distance from the young man presently holding the attention
of his peers, Gerard Pointreau inwardly smiled. He had been
summoned to attend by the friends surrounding him. During
the crisis of Gabrielle's abduction, he had been absent from
this familiar haunt where gentry and merchants gathered for
nightly political discussions. He had known instinctively, however, that the time had never been better for him to return.

Vigorously applauding as young Marcel Notoire stepped
down to the hearty congratulations of his friends, Pointreau
pretended an absorption in the discussion that commenced
around him.

"Young Marcel is correct! These outrages cannot be allowed to continue! We must do something. A petition perhaps, signed by the most powerful men in Louisiana . . ."

"A petition will not be effective! A delegation sent directly
to congress will receive more attention!"

"A waste of time!"

"No!"

"Yes!"

The controversy continued, growing ever louder as it was
echoed at surrounding tables . . . while Pointreau's attention
wandered and his agitation swelled. How much longer would
it be before news of the attempted escape from the prison
reached them? Why the delay? Had something gone wrong?

He shifted uncomfortably in his chair, covering his agitation by raising his cup to his mouth and draining it dry. He
signaled the waiter for another, his expression stiff. He had
made his contribution to the controversy upon arriving, cer-

tain his attention would falter as time passed. He knew no one expected him to again offer his concerns.

His thoughts coming to an abrupt halt, Pointreau noted the entrance of a young merchant. The fellow was obviously in a state of excitement as he paused at a table to impart news that abruptly halted all conversation. He lingered there, leaving as soon as the interested listeners would allow, turning to a table nearby to converse in a similar fashion.

Pointreau's heart began a slow pounding. It would not be much longer now!

"Did you hear the news, Gerard?"

Pointreau turned toward Paul Charlot as the graying banker appeared suddenly at his elbow, the man's concern evident.

"News?" Pointreau shook his head. *"Non."*

"There has been an escape at the prison."

Pointreau went suddenly cold. Aware that the attention of all at the table had turned toward him, he responded, "An *escape?*"

"Oui. I thought you would want to know immediately. Captain Whitney is free."

On his feet in a moment, Pointreau demanded, "What are you saying? Is Captain Whitney now loose in the city?"

"Oui! It happened no more than an hour ago! There was great confusion at the prison when gunfire broke out in the corridor just beyond Captain Whitney's cell. When guards responded from other areas of the prison, they found two men dead."

"What two men?"

"Two guards. No one is certain of what happened. It appears an unidentified fellow slipped into the prison and held two guards at gunpoint, forcing them to unlock Captain Whitney's cell. Whitney and his confederate were making their way to the rear door, still holding the guards at gunpoint, when guards from another area of the prison stumbled upon them. The gunfire was evidently spontaneous, and when the smoke cleared, the captain and the other man were gone! Reports say it was a bloody scene, and there is a possibility that either Whitney or his confederate was hit in the exchange of gunfire."

His rage barely controlled, Pointreau turned toward the door.

"Gerard, wait! My carriage is outside. I will summon it."

Ignoring the concerned banker's shouted offer, and aware that the coffee house had gone unusually silent, Pointreau pushed his way through the crowded room toward the door.

Shuddering with rage and rapidly mounting apprehension, Pointreau unlocked the front door of his city mansion and thrust it open. Not bothering to close the door behind him, he took the steps to the second floor two at a time, his heart pounding with exertion and excitement.

The short ride from Duvalle's to his home had stretched into an eternity, his thoughts revolving in endless torment.

Two guards dead! The stupid fools! He had no doubt the two were his men, for Whitney and his accomplice would not have escaped otherwise!

Two dead . . . When he was through, there would be *three*. But that was not his first concern.

His agitation mounting, Gerard struggled to catch his breath as he turned down the darkened hallway. He attempted to console himself with the thought that his torment would soon be over. A few steps more and he would open Gabrielle's bedroom door to find her safely asleep in her bed. He would wake her then, just as he had planned. But the news he would give her would be far different than he had expected. Instead of consoling her at the death of her abductor, he would spirit her away to where the bastard captain could not again find her. They would leave Louisiana, never—*never*—to return!

His steps coming to an abrupt halt before Gabrielle's bedroom door, Pointreau paused. All rage deserting him, he suddenly found only fear remaining as he slowly, with a shaking hand, turned the knob and pushed open the door.

A shaft of light from the corridor lamp shone into the room, and Gerard's breath caught in his throat.

No! No . . . no . . . no!

Unable to believe his eyes as his nightmare loomed starkly and horrifyingly real, Pointreau saw that his beloved Gabrielle's bed was undisturbed—and *empty!*

She was gone!

The pain within loomed so strongly that Pointreau doubled over under its stress.

Gabrielle . . . Gabrielle . . .

The pain increased, overwhelming him, because he knew Gabrielle had not been abducted.

She had left him.

The night deepened. The lamp flickered low. The silence of the room was broken only by Rogan's rasping breaths. The activity of the illicit house beyond the isolated rear quarter could not be heard as Gabrielle sat alone beside Rogan's bed.

Glancing again toward the bandage that covered his shoulder and chest, she took a shuddering breath. It was lightly stained with blood, but she gained little consolation from the realization that the stain had not widened since Dr. Thoreau had left.

. . . Captain Whitney had all but bled himself dry.

A shudder ran down Gabrielle's spine and she inched closer. Clarice and Pierre had returned briefly after Dr. Thoreau's departure, placing on the nightstand a powder that the doctor had left for her use should Rogan become fevered. They had departed shortly afterward, needing to maintain a facade of normalcy by showing themselves to the patrons of the house in order to avoid suspicion.

It had been obvious to Gabrielle that the stress upon Clarice had been inordinate. She would have preferred to maintain a vigil at Rogan's side, but had sacrificed her feelings to Rogan's wishes. It had also been obvious that Pierre Delise had been ready to sacrifice himself as well—for Clarice—and would remain constant at any cost.

A man in love . . .

Gabrielle's throat tightened to the point of pain as the beauty of the days and nights she had spent in Rogan's strong arms aboard his ship returned with soul-shaking clarity. But Rogan's arms were no longer strong! They were limp, almost lifeless! And she was at fault.

She had been a coward, too weak to take the step that would have alerted the governor to the threat Rogan suffered from her father! She had weighed Rogan's life against her father's and had fooled herself into believing she had found the perfect alternative, a way that might serve the love she felt for both.

But she had been wrong.

The lives of two good men had been endangered because of her weakness.

And Rogan's life lay in the balance.

Moving closer still, Gabrielle allowed her gaze to trail the strong planes of Rogan's face, remembering the gamut of emotions they had reflected in his contacts with her—fury, scathing contempt, uncertainty, and then . . . love. She remembered the golden heat that had shone in his eyes as they had lain heart to heart, the beauty of the emotions that had soared between them. She recalled that, as the quiet afterglow lingered, she had discovered the full scope and power of the love they shared did not lie solely in their intimate, physical exchange, but in the gradual awareness that in their coming together, two halves of a whole had been united, that separated, she would forever feel the loss.

Tears . . . sorrows . . . regrets . . .

Laying her head beside Rogan's on the pillow, so close that

her lips were only inches from his ear, Gabrielle breathed in his fragile warmth as she reached up to curve her trembling hand around his cheek. Uncertain if he could hear, but knowing a need to speak the words brimming within, she whispered haltingly.

"Rogan ..." Her voice momentarily faltering, Gabrielle began again. "My darling, I'm so sorry. I've been such a fool. I wasted so much precious time hating you after you abducted me. I convinced myself, despite the growing certainty within me, that you were the bloodthirsty pirate and murderer you were reported to be. I was appalled when other feelings for you began to rise. And even when I lay in your arms, when the beauty of the loving we shared was still so strong, when my days and nights were so filled with thoughts of you that I chose not to think past the present toward a future without you, I could not accept the truth.

Gabrielle took a shaken breath. "I accept it now, Rogan. I know that I love you. I know the emotion you raised within me, the fear I felt when I first opened my eyes to see you leaning over me in my convent room, was partially inspired by an unconscious realization that the man I was destined to love had come to me in a most difficult way, a way that would demand courage to accept—perhaps more courage than I possessed.

"I betrayed that love, Rogan. I know that now. The moment was right when the governor's boat came alongside your burning ship and you released me, allowing me my decision. But I let us be separated, as if the time we had spent in each other's arms had never existed. I have regretted that moment, Rogan. I regret it still, with all my heart."

Pausing as tears choked her up, Gabrielle touched her lips lightly to Rogan's motionless cheek. "Can you forgive me, my darling?" Her voice again failing, Gabrielle forced herself to continue, "Can you forgive me, please, because I love you, and because ... because I will never truly be able to forgive myself."

Silence her only response, Gabrielle could not restrain the low sobbing that then began, the anguish that shook her as tears squeezed past her closed eyelids to drench her pale cheeks. So intense was her distress that she was uncertain of the exact moment when she felt Rogan's cheek move under her palm, when she heard his first, hoarse whisper.

Her heart pounding as his head slowly turned toward her, as his eyes opened to narrow slits of gold, Gabrielle saw his lips move feebly once more.

"Rogan!" She saw the effort he expended to speak, and her anxiety soared. "Don't press yourself. You must rest."

"No . . ."

"Don't try to talk, Rogan."

Gabrielle's words came to an abrupt halt as he raised his arm to cup the back of her head with his palm. Then, his strength waning, his gaze flickered as he rasped, "I love you, Gabrielle."

A soft sob his only reply, Rogan managed, "Lie beside me . . . close."

Slipping up onto the bed, Gabrielle did as he asked. Placing her arm around him, she pressed herself tight against him, even as his hand suddenly dropped back to the bed and his eyes closed.

Gabrielle abruptly went still. Her heart pounding, she waited for the brush of Rogan's breath against her lips, the rise and fall of his chest against her arm that would mean—

He breathed in sharply and she gave a short sob of relief as his steady breathing resumed. She closed her eyes, prayers of gratitude racing through her mind as she drew him closer. She was where she belonged, where she wanted to stay. Beside the man she loved, the man who loved her in return.

She would never again leave him.

* * *

The night deepened. The lamp flickered low. In the shadows of semidarkness, Gerard Pointreau sat silent and motionless in a corner of his sitting room.

He could not sleep.

He *would* not sleep.

Until Gabrielle was returned to him.

The night deepened. The lamp flickered low. His shoulder pierced by a sudden stab of pain, Rogan stirred sharply from the gray, nether world in which he had been drifting.

Struggling to raise his heavy eyelids, he recalled the soft voice whispering in his ear that had briefly dispelled the darkness.

. . . forgive me . . . I love you . . .

And he remembered.

Forcing his eyes open, Rogan turned his head to the pillow beside his. Gabrielle. It hadn't been a dream. She had said she loved him. He had told her he loved her. Had she heard him? Did she know?

The pain stabbed once more, and Rogan clenched his eyes closed. He remembered other things as well—a debt yet unpaid and a vengeance that would allow him no respite. Opening his eyes with his last ounce of strength, Rogan indulged himself in the sight of Gabrielle lying beside him.

But would she still love him when she discovered what he now must do . . . ?

Chapter 12

Otis Benchley shivered as he approached the governor's office. His eyes darted nervously around the corridor. He was in trouble. He knew it. A night and another day had passed since the prison escape, but there had been no sign of Captain Whitney. He recalled, as he had countless times in the hours since, the sight of his cohorts lying bloodied and dead on the prison floor.

He was still uncertain about how it had all happened!

The sudden, unexpected confrontation as they had made their way toward Whitney's cell—gunshots in the shadows—the thud of falling bodies!

He had been incoherent when questioned, though the governor had personally pressed him for more details. It was obvious that Claiborne was not satisfied with the answers he'd provided because he had been summoned for another interview.

Benchley paused outside the door to the governor's office, intensely aware that Claiborne was not his greatest threat. Captain Whitney had escaped. Pointreau would never forgive him for that. He knew without a doubt that he would soon be as dead as his cohorts. It was just a matter of time.

Wiping the perspiration from his brow, Benchley took a shaky breath. There was only one way to save himself.

Steadying his hand, he pushed open the office door.

* * *

Gabrielle raised a weary hand to her forehead as another evening dawned. She glanced at the bed beside which she sat, her spirits lagging. She had been so encouraged the previous night when Rogan had spoken those few words. She had spent the night lying beside him, certain all would be well.

Awakening at dawn with a start, she had found Clarice standing beside the bed.

That moment too painful to recall due to the torment in Clarice's eyes, Gabrielle scrutinized Rogan's pale, motionless face. Dr. Thoreau had returned later that morning, but his comments had been noncommittal. All depended upon Rogan's powers of recuperation, powers that seemed to be lagging dangerously.

For Rogan had slept the night and the day away, awakening for only brief moments. She had gently bathed his face and had checked his bandages as the doctor had instructed, but he had shown almost no reaction, drinking and eating little.

Rogan, so strong and now so powerless . . .

That thought stirring more pain than she could allow, Gabrielle stood up and resumed a silent pacing. Rumors were flying that the escape at the prison had infuriated the governor, that his men were scouring the city for a sign of the prisoner, and that he had sworn not to relent until the man was behind bars once more.

It appeared, however, that her father was conspicuously absent from the public scene and that her disappearance had not been reported. Those facts adding to her anguish, Gabrielle realized that her father knew she had left him of her own accord. Refusing to speculate any further, knowing she could not afford to indulge in thoughts of the torment he must have suffered when reaching that conclusion, she had spent the day in attempts to occupy her mind. She had washed Rogan's bloody shirt, and it now lay clean and darned, due to skills she'd learned in the convent, and neatly folded on the dresser nearby with the rest of his clothing . . . awaiting his recovery.

Gabrielle frowned at the pistol lying beside the neatly folded garments. Pierre had visited that afternoon and had left it for her protection in the event of an emergency. Polite, generous Pierre, who was so much in love with Clarice, had been unsparing in his support, as had Madame, Dr. Thoreau, and Clarice. She knew she could never repay them for their kindnesses.

She turned resolutely toward the pitcher nearby. The hour was late, and the long, anxious day had left her exhausted. Filling a glass, she moved to Rogan's bedside. She slipped her arm under Rogan's pillow, raising his head as she whispered to him.

"Open your eyes, just for a few moments. The doctor said you must drink. Rogan . . ."

Rogan's eyelids moved. They raised slowly, the glowing gold revealed meeting her gaze with an intensity that was both unexpected and startling as he parted his lips to drink. She was about to speak when his eyes dropped closed again. Placing the glass back on the nightstand, Gabrielle sighed. She then lowered the lamp before climbing onto the bed beside Rogan. She slipped her arm around him and closed her eyes.

She would wait another night, or two, or three—as many as it took before Rogan was restored to her. And she would not leave him . . . ever again.

The room was silent. Opening his eyes as Gabrielle's breathing became slow and rhythmic, as her slenderness grew lax against him, Rogan shifted his weight. He raised his arm and curved it around her. The effort was less difficult. His strength was returning. It would not be long now.

The dawn was gray and without sound.
The city still slept.

Silence reigned within Madame's house of pleasure in the wake of the vigorous activity of the night past.

No one saw the tall, broad figure that emerged from the room in the rear quarter of the house to walk unsteadily toward the exit. No one saw him stop to glance back one last time before he pushed open the door to the alleyway beyond and slipped into the shadows.

Gabrielle awoke slowly. Disoriented, she closed her eyes against the sliver of silver light that slanted through the window, announcing the dawn.

She shifted uneasily. The bed on which she lay was unfamiliar.

No, it was not. Yet, . . . something was wrong.

Her eyes snapping open with a start, she glanced to her side. Unwilling to believe her eyes, she smoothed the ruffled bedclothes with a trembling hand.

Was she dreaming, or was Rogan truly gone?

Jumping from the bed, Gabrielle searched the shadows of the room, shuddering. She covered the distance to the dresser with uncertain steps, to stare down at the spot where Rogan's clothing had lain.

Oh, God, it was gone.

Her heart lurched at the realization that the pistol was gone, too.

No . . . no . . .

Gabrielle pushed a tangled lock back from her face, swaying dizzily at the sudden realization. Rogan could have summoned the strength to overcome his injuries for only one purpose.

A vise of fear closing her throat, she took a wobbly step toward the door, then another, and another. In a moment she was running down the darkened hallway.

* * *

Rogan paused to steady himself against his recurring weakness, drawing back into the remaining shadows of the cobbled street as dawn began its full assault. He glanced around him, realizing that early morning traffic would soon begin, focusing his attention on the long line of mansions, their oak doors gleaming. He surveyed the street again, aware that his strength was waning.

Fragmented memories of the two nights most recently past flashed vividly across his mind, bringing with them the whispers that had penetrated his semiconsciousness.

Pierre Delise's voice.

They were coming for him . . . Pointreau's men . . . We managed to escape . . .

The doctor's low tones.

A chest wound . . . Captain Whitney has lost much blood . . . the rest is up to him . . .

Gabrielle.

. . . I love you . . . forgive me . . . forgive me . . .

Rogan's throat constricted painfully. A love that had been born in conflict—a love that suffered because of what had gone before . . .

But he heard other voices as well, haunting voices that had filled the void between.

His first mate's cries of pain echoing up the dark corridors of his mind. Then the sudden silence . . .

The calls of his slaughtered crew resounding against the dark sea . . .

The gunshots . . . the smoke . . . the water claiming him . . .

Pointreau.

It was time to put an end to it.

Moving through the shadows of Pointreau's yard moments later, Rogan approached the back door. A simple thrust against a windowpane, a twist of the lock, and he was inside.

The house was silent, asleep.

Rogan walked silently down the hallway toward the foyer. He turned toward the staircase, looking up to the floor above.

Reaching for the pistol in his pocket, he started forward, only to freeze in his step as a familiar voice shattered the silence with a rasping hiss.

"So . . . you've arrived at last."

Rogan turned sharply toward the sitting room behind him, stiffening as a figure materialized out of the shadows.

Pointreau.

But it was a far different man than Rogan had ever seen before. His clothing wrinkled, his person unkempt, his bearded face ravaged, Pointreau emerged into the light to stare at Rogan through eyes that were darkly ringed and bright with hatred.

His sudden laughter was shrill. "I knew you would come! I knew it! And so I waited—here—unmoving since the hour when I returned home to find Gabrielle gone."

Pointreau's eyes grew wild. "You turned her against me! You took from me the only true thing of worth in my life! You sought to achieve vengeance for the past by destroying the future—the future Gabrielle and I would share! You should not have done that! She is my daughter—Chantelle's and mine! She is flesh of my flesh as surely as if it were my seed with which she was conceived! But I tell you now that you will not live to enjoy your victory! You have made a fatal mistake, you see! You underestimated the blow you struck against me! You believed only through my death would you achieve true vengeance! But I will tell you now—when it is too late— you were wrong! You see, there is no life for me without Gabrielle! No future! All is negated without her—my fortune, my possessions, everything I have achieved or hoped to achieve! Had you realized that, you might have walked away unscathed, knowing you had emerged victorious!"

Pointreau's piercing laughter sounded again. He walked closer, spittle spraying from his lips in his vehemence as he spat out, "Fool! You have erred, and in erring have delivered me my victory! In a few moments my servants will awaken to the sound of shots. They will run into this room to see you lying dead on the floor—killed as you broke into the house to murder *me!* Your presence here will prove to the governor, to New Orleans, and, most importantly, to Gabrielle that all I claimed about you is true! I will be hailed as a hero!"

Pointreau's ravaged face sobered. "She will return to me then. I know she will. I will convince her that you attacked me and left me no recourse but to fire my weapon. She will believe me—because she will *want* to believe me. I will forgive her transgressions and things will resume as they were before."

"No, Gabrielle knows the truth." Straining against an ever-encroaching weakness, Rogan grated out. "She won't believe your lies any longer. She knows you're not the man she believed you to be, and she will never return to you."

"Bastard! She will!"

"No."

"She will!"

"No, Father, I won't."

Rogan's gaze snapped toward the doorway in which Gabrielle appeared suddenly, framed by the growing light from the street beyond.

Rogan halted her step toward him with a sharp hiss.

"Stay back!"

"I will not."

"Stay away from him, Gabrielle!" Pointreau's voice held an edge of madness. "He is a pirate and a murderer! He came here to kill me!"

"Father, please . . ." Gabrielle's light eyes filled with pity. "Put down your gun. I'll take Rogan away."

"No! You don't know what you're saying! Would you leave with the man who attempted to kill your father?"

"I know everything. It's no use pretending anymore."

Pointreau's dark eyes grew wilder. "You don't believe the things he's told you about me, Gabrielle! You *can't* believe them!"

"Father, please put down the gun. Rogan and I—"

"There *is* no Rogan and you!"

"I love him, Father."

"No! You don't!"

"I do."

Pointreau turned toward Rogan. "You did this! You stole my daughter's love!"

"No, Father! I love you still. I will always love you."

"You've taken Gabrielle away from me!"

"The truth drove her away!"

"Rogan, please . . ."

Rogan swayed and Gabrielle started toward him. She halted as he said again, "Stand clear of me, Gabrielle."

"Tell her the truth, Whitney!" The gun in Pointreau's hand shook visibly. "I'm warning you. This is your last chance. Tell her you lied to her! Tell her everything you told her about me was untrue! Tell her now!"

"Gabrielle already knows the truth."

"You must speak to her."

"No."

Pointreau took another step, trembling wildly. Rogan saw the flicker in his eyes the second before he rasped, "Damn you to hell then, where you belong!"

"Father! No!"

Pointreau's finger twitched on the trigger as Rogan reached for the pistol in his pocket.

Gabrielle threw herself between the two men.

A gunshot cracked!

Gabrielle slumped against Rogan as her hands clutched him tightly.

Horror snaked through Rogan. His arm snapped around Gabrielle and he gasped, only to see her look up at him, then draw herself erect to turn toward her father as Pointreau slid slowly to the floor.

Incredulous as Pointreau's eyes fell closed, as his last breath ended in a rattling gasp, Rogan heard a voice say emotion-lessly from the doorway, "The elegant beast is dead."

Gabrielle turned toward the old woman who stood there, a smoking gun still in her hand.

"Marie!"

A sob escaping her, Gabrielle looked back to her father. Freeing herself from Rogan's arms, she walked toward Pointreau and dropped to her knees beside his motionless body. She took his hand in hers.

The old woman limped into the room. The gun hung loosely at her side as she addressed Gabrielle in a tremulous voice.

"I buried my dear Manon yesterday, you see."

Still holding Pointreau's limp hand, Gabrielle looked up sharply.

"*Ma petite beauté* did not survive the beast's cruelty, and it occurred to me in the time that followed, neither could anyone survive his love. I remembered then that Manon had begged me to help you, and this morning, as daylight dawned, I realized what I must do."

Tears trickled down Marie's lined cheeks as she placed the gun on the nearby table, then limped slowly toward the door. She turned back briefly before leaving. Her voice was a serene whisper when she spoke again.

"*Ma petite* Manon rests in peace now."

The old woman slipped out of sight as Rogan drew Gabrielle up from Pointreau and held her close against him. He whispered against her hair, simple words ... consoling words ... loving words, knowing full well that words alone could not dissolve her pain.

Justice had been served. His slaughtered crewmen rested in peace now ... with Manon ... in peace.

It was over.

Out of hatred and vengeance had come love.

An unanticipated treasure ... an unexpected love.

Rogan drew Gabrielle closer, knowing that love, now free, had only begun.

Epilogue

"Tell me what you want, and it is yours."

Rogan purred softly into Gabrielle's ear as he drew her against him, love reverberating in the sound. Their naked flesh warm and sweet against each other in the wake of passions rapturously spent, Gabrielle paused in reply as the midnight darkness of the sea rocked them gently in their loving bower.

The captain's bunk . . . the captain's cabin . . . the captain's ship.

Rogan's ship.

Gabrielle slid her palm up through the fine mat of dark hair covering Rogan's chest, unconsciously tracing the scar from a wound that had almost prophetically all but obliterated the ragged letter *P* formerly burned there. She allowed the pale silver of her gaze to linger on Rogan's face as he awaited her reply.

The bloom of health had returned to Rogan's sun-darkened skin during the months that had passed. He had grown strong and whole again.

Father was gone, but Gabrielle knew he would never be fully forgotten. Burned into her memory was Governor Claiborne's expression when the hearing into Father's death uncovered the extent of his duplicity. The guard called Benchley repeated a confession originally delivered the evening before her father's death, confirming in detail Rogan's claims of physical abuse under questioning imposed at Father's command, as well as the torture and death of Rogan's first mate and the deadly mission on which Father had sent Benchley and his two comrades the night Benchley's cohorts were killed. The governor had been horrified and dismayed to realize the full extent of his unknowing participation in the persecution of an innocent man.

Rogan's crew had been immediately released, the charges against them and Rogan formally dismissed. Governor Claiborne's honor, however, had not yet been satisfied. Using his influence to Rogan's advantage, he had delivered the loan that had enabled Rogan to start anew.

Rogan's first voyage was already behind him. With a hefty profit received, and restored to legitimacy, he again had a bright future before him.

Tears momentarily welling, Gabrielle recalled the moment she had learned that although Father's name and memory were forever tarnished, his fortune remained intact. Increased by ill-gotten gains and bloodshed that could never be washed away, it was left solely to her.

Gabrielle had known that she had no choice in what she need do with that fortune. She had immediately turned a portion of it over to the heirs and orphans of Rogan's original crew, although she knew the sum could in no way compensate for the losses they had sustained. She had then deeded the small house where Manon had spent her last hours to Marie, where the old woman, cleared of a misdeed in the shooting that had saved Rogan's life, might spend her remaining days close to the memory of her *petite chérie*. The remainder of the estate had gone to the church and to the convent, with the plea that Reverend Mother remember Father in her prayers.

For, strangely, Gabrielle loved him still—the part of him he had reserved for her alone and which had filled her childhood with love.

She had retained the Pointreau plantation, finding herself unable to sell it, remembering that her mother, too, had loved Father in her special way, and that a youthful Chantelle

Obréon and Gerard Pointreau had once roamed happily on its grounds.

She had buried Father there, beside her mother, where his heart had always lain.

"Gabrielle . . ."

The warm gold of his eyes glittering into hers, Rogan cupped her cheek with his hand, drawing her mouth to his. Kissing her long and deeply, he drew back only far enough to whisper against her lips, "Don't slip away from me again, my love . . ."

Gabrielle smiled. No, she never would.

Pressing her lips lightly to his once more, she turned her thoughts to happier contemplations.

The tribulations of the past were now over . . . for so many.

The clear gray of her eyes became a glowing match for the silver shaft of moonlight shining through the porthole as Gabrielle trailed her fingers against Rogan's lips. She whispered, "When will we return to New Orleans?"

His dark brows knit unexpectedly. "So anxious to return already? Are you growing tired of my solitary company?"

"Solitary company?" Gabrielle could not suppress a laugh. "On this ship?"

The memory of their wedding flashed in to her mind, a beautiful, simple ceremony, celebrated in the convent chapel with only a few in attendance. Bertrand had stood beside Rogan, with Clarice and Pierre hand in hand a few steps away. Madame, at the rear, had been smiling. Unintimidated, she had been welcomed by a contingent of black-clad nuns that consisted of Mother Superior and Sisters Madeleine, Marguerite, Juliana, Marisa, and Juana.

Happy tears had flowed freely, but not from Gabrielle, who had looked up to see her joy reflected in the glowing gold of Rogan's eyes when he had claimed her as his bride.

A tenderly beautiful ceremony became a tumultuous celebration when the chapel door opened to the cheers of

Rogan's crew! Oh, the revelry! The dancing, the singing, the good cheer that lasted long into the night!

The maiden voyage of Rogan's new ship had been their wedding cruise, during which his crew had seemed almost lighthearted, without exception greeting her with a smile in their daily contacts with her. Gabrielle's lips twitched with amusement as she recalled that even Dermott's one, ferocious eye had sparkled!

As for Bertrand, a warmth rose in Gabrielle. His scarred face now smiled easily. She knew the demons from his past had been expunged, and he was ready to go forward with his life. And she knew that she had found a friend.

She laughed again as Rogan continued his silent scrutiny, saying, "No, I haven't tired of your company, my dear husband. I inquired as to the date of our return because . . ."— She shrugged a smooth shoulder, chills of pleasure running down her spine as Rogan caressed it with his lips—". . . I am anxious to know if Pierre has been successful in coaxing Clarice into a more binding relationship, now that she has left Madame's employ."

"A happy matron anxious to see others join her order . . ." Rogan paused. "Tell me you *are* happy, Gabrielle."

Gabrielle's clear eyes linked with Rogan's suddenly sober gaze. "I am."

"Tell me you love me—as I love you."

"I do love you, Rogan. Very much."

"Tell me you don't miss being the wealthy, pampered heiress you once were, with the satisfaction of your slightest whim at your fingertips."

"Oh, Rogan, you underestimate yourself." Gabrielle's voice grew husky as she trailed her fingers across his chest. "Satisfaction is still at my fingertips . . ."

Rogan's gold eyes warmed. "Give me your answer, then."

"What answer?"

"Tell me what you want, so I may give it to you—so I may content myself that you are left wanting in no way."

Puzzled, Gabrielle whispered, "Why is that so important to you?"

"Because . . ." Lifting her up with a swift, breathtaking movement that stretched her full, naked length upon his, Rogan whispered with a throb of deepening passion, "Because I have discovered that the little witch who fought me so bravely when I abducted her from the convent, who angered me and tormented me, who teased me and surprised me, and who touched me as no other woman ever had, also taught me to love. That convent maid gave me a gift far more precious than any I ever thought to receive. And I want to give to her in return."

Kissing her long and deeply, warming her with the heat that hardened him against her, Rogan drew back to whisper, "So tell me, Gabrielle, or forever hold the burden of my discontent. Tell me what you want, and it is yours."

"What do I want . . . ?" Liquid silver melded with burning gold as Gabrielle held Rogan's gaze. "Let me see . . . During those days that seem so long ago when I sat in my convent schoolroom, staring out the window at ships on the horizon, I wanted so many things. I wanted to be able to sail away on one of them, to feel the deck beneath my feet, the wind in my hair, the salt spray on my face. You've given me that. I wanted to experience all the facets of life that were withheld from me in the convent, to meet the world and have the world meet me. You've given me that, too. And I wanted to experience love . . ." Gabrielle's voice dropped to a husky softer note. "You've not only given me that, *too*, Rogan, you've given me another thing that I, in my girlish daydreams, did not conceive. You've made me love in return—so completely that my heart is filled with the joy of it. You've given me all that, Rogan. So what is left for you to give me, my darling?"

A thrill chased down Gabrielle's spine as eyes of molten gold became predatory once more. She gasped as he met her passionate challenge, and Rapace, her loving raptor, proceeded to show her.